puppy love

ELLE SPRINKLE

Author's Note & Trigger Warnings

When I first sat down to write Puppy Love, I had an entirely different story in mind. A carbon-copy of one I knew to be true, one I experienced myself. But the more the words spilled out of me, the more twists and turns weaved themselves throughout. These characters turned into their own people, the story created a mind of its own. And while I liked the book I set out to write, I love this one so much more.

That being said, despite the lack of following my own intentions, this story is still based on truth. And I hope it finds the people who see their story within it. To those people in particular, I do want to preface this with a content warning. If any of the topics below are triggering for you, please read carefully, or find another story to consume yourself in.

Trigger Warnings: *Mental illness, anxiety attacks, parental death, substance abuse, mentions of child neglect, mentions of sexual assault, and emotional abuse.*

Please take care of yourself and if you don't have the mental space to consume those topics safely, I urge you to find a story different than this one.

Before signing off, I want to acknowledge two people I couldn't have done this without. Firstly, to my wife Hailey, thank you for making this possible. Your patience, love, and support means everything to me, and I know that Puppy Love wouldn't exist without you. You're the wife everyone wishes they had. You're my Violet. And to my baby boy Dawson, thank you for coming into my life at the time you did. Maybe it was divine intervention, or maybe you really were just a street dog forced to live with two overly-affectionate lesbians. Either way, I love you more than life.

Lastly, to my readers. The amount of support I have received from complete strangers surrounding this novel has made me realize that humanity isn't all bad. In fact, I think because of you, I've grown to love people. I hope this book is everything you dreamed of, and more. I hope all the emotions rush through your body, making you blush and tingle and tear up. I hope the characters become your friends, and your family, and know that to me, you fall into those categories too.

xoxo,

Elle

P.S. if you know me in real life, do us both a favor and sit this one out

To Hailey, for making this possible. To Dawson, for having more personality than every other organism on the planet combined. To Roxie and Snickers, for taking care of my wife while you were on this Earth. And to everyone else who found family in our four-legged friends.

P.S. also for the sapphic girlies who never see themselves in books. I'm working on it, babes.

Playlist

Tip: Keep an eye out while reading for these *little numbers, followed by an asterisk*, which marks the end of the section. These are quotes or sections where the songs fit into the story! For the best listening experience, press play when you spot the number. If you reach the asterisk before the song is over, stop reading until it ends.*

1. Daddy – Coldplay

2. notice me-acoustic – ROLE MODEL

3. scared of everything – zeph

4. In My Mind – Lyn Lapid

5. Thirst – Nyline

6. anatomy – kenzie

7. Pillowtalk – Sofia Karlberg

8. Jealous – Nick Jonas

9. she calls me daddy – KiNG MALA

10. I Wanna Be Yours – Arctic Monkeys

11. Daddy Issues – The Neighbourhood

12. Family Line – Conan Gray

13. Too Sweet – Hozier

Bonus: Too Sweet Rewritten – Katie Lynne Sharbaugh

14. July – Noah Cyrus

15. Scared to Be Lonely – Martin Garrix, Dua Lipa

16. bad idea! – girl in red

17. Gorgeous – mansionz

18. Shh...Don't Say It – FLETCHER

19. i am not who i was – Chance Peña

20. Let's Fall in Love for the Night – FINNEAS

21. girls girls girls – FLETCHER

22. Graceland Too – Phoebe Bridgers

23. Tears in Heaven – Eric Clapton

24. comethru – Jeremy Zucker

25. My Kind of Woman – Mac DeMarco

26. Drunk In My Mind – Benson Boone

27. Good Luck, Babe! – Chappell Roan

28. What Do You Want – Benson Boone

29. Cry – Benson Boone

30. Loving & Losing – Delaney Bailey

31. Means Something – Lizzy McAlpnie

32. I'd Rather Overdose – honestav, Z

33. Landslide – The Chicks

34. Scared To Start – Michael Marcagi

35. Matilda – Harry Styles

36. Through the Dark – One Direction

*not on spotify

ONE
Black Coffee

CAM

COMMODE. *LOO. TOILET.* WHICHEVER term suits your vocabulary, my head is two inches past the rim as coconut-infused bile rises up my throat. *Ugh. Malibu.*

A gentle hand rubs circles across my shoulder blades, while another holds my tangled, dirty blonde hair behind my head, away from the acidic geyser currently possessing my body.

"I don't want to say I told you so, but—"

Blegh.

"I told you so," Adrian finishes, still rubbing my back as they hand me a cup of water.

I wrap my fingers around the blue plastic cup and tilt my head back to let the smooth, cool water glide down my throat. Disguised as relief, the anticipation in my nauseated body eases. But the water quickly returns, like a letter sent to an address that doesn't exist, and once again, I find myself up close and personal with *The Porcelain Throne.*

A loud knock erupts from the bathroom door, ricocheting off the insides of my hungover skull, and an angry voice booms through the barricade.

"Can you hurry up already? I have to take a shit!"

"Sorry, out of order!" Adrian sings back, their tone much kinder than that of the voice outside the bathroom. The hinges of the door slowly chip with each knock against the wood, and my brain practically rattles. *I think I'm going to throw up again.*

"Can you open the door?!"

I take another sip of water, this time locking my throat closed as I gargle the liquid and allow it to soothe my burning tonsils. I don't think there has ever been a relief as sweet as this. Adrian lets out a subtle sigh, and I lift my head to watch as their dark, dainty hands twist the gold in the center of the doorknob. *Click.*

The door opens, and Adrian's roommate Avery stands bitterly in the frame. Short brown locks shoot out in every direction possible, and his thick brows furrow over his squinting, hooded eyes.

"I really gotta—"

Blugch.

The last contents of my stomach now forever swims in the pool of Adrian and Avery's latrine. I slide my bare forearm across my face, wiping the sour residue off my mouth. Another exhale slips from Adrian's lips, and they hang their head.

"Okay, let's get you some Gatorade," they say in defeat.

If anyone should feel defeated, it should be the person who just threw up twenty-three dollars' worth of Zabinski's Takeout. Adrian's hand extends to me, and I weakly place my palm against theirs.

"Dude. You're fu—" Avery starts to speak, but I hear a slight waver in his voice. He swallows instead. "How are you still—" *Gulp.*

He *wants* to make some snarky remark about me heaving like a momma bird, but it seems he's having trouble getting his words out without an astringent taste in his own throat. I look at him, perplexed, then turn to face Adrian for answers. I've never seen anything quite like this before.

"Avery is emetophobic," Adrian explains, their shiny, jet-black coils bouncing. "He's *terrified* of vomit."

The corners of my lips tug at the sides, forming a cocky smirk I have no remorse for. Avery Clark is many things, but above all, he is annoying. So, the thought of him being so sensitive to something like *puke* amuses me.

Avery is less amused. His brows dig further into his eyes, a red tone rising to his squared cheeks.

"Fuck off," he sneers, before turning into his bedroom and furiously slamming the door closed behind him.

I lock eyes with Adrian, and after a brief moment of silence, we erupt into uncontrollable, gasping-for-air laughter. My ribs start to ache, and my vision goes blurry as tears create a glossy coat over my eyes. Adrian's arms flex, tightly gripping my pale, shaky hands in theirs as they pull me to my feet.

"Remind me to *never* drink Malibu again," I say as I follow them to the living room.

Empty bottles litter the counters and coffee table, and the entire apartment *reeks* of booze. The smell is so nauseating that I'm grateful there's nothing left inside of me to projectile vomit. I reach down and move a pair of unconscious legs to the side so I can sit down on the tawny, pilled sectional.

"Mmfffgmm."

"That's not a real word, Hayden," I say, grabbing the blanket trapped underneath him and pulling it over myself. Hayden huffs as he rolls over, though not enough to make the blanket-pulling any easier.

"Bright," he finally manages to croak. His arm drapes over his eyes dramatically to shield him from the sun peeking through the blinds. At least I know I'm not the only one who got a *little* too drunk last night.

Adrian, Hayden, Avery, and I held a cocktail party. "Party" meaning us and the dogs. Pumpkin, Avery's prehistoric Chihuahua, sat most of it out, and Eloise, Hayden's retired service dog, spent most of the night passed out under the table. Dawson and Major, however, partied just as hard as we did. If not harder.

"Cam, I love you," he mutters, still not opening his eyes. "But I am *never* celebrating anything with you again."

Look, I'm not usually the party type. On my birthdays, I like to binge True Crime and spend an absurd amount of money on books that will probably take me years to read. But last night marked the end of something huge. Bigger than a birthday. Better, even.

Yesterday was my last day working at The Dog Shop.

The Dog Shop is any dog groomer's biggest nightmare. It's worse than chipped blades and matted coats, angry parents and labor violations. It's worse, because it's all of those things *combined*. I mean, if the gays have a place in hell, so does corporate America, given that it fucks pretty much *everyone*. Everyone except the founders of corporations like The Dog Shop.

Honestly, I'm surprised they don't have more lawsuits on their hands. Maybe it's because years of overbooked schedules, micromanaging supervisors, and neglected animals make you too tired to do anything. But the days of putting up with that are finally over.

"You could throw up," I suggest. "It made me feel better. Kinda."

Hayden's hand moves to his stomach, his fingers clutching the fabric of his shirt.

"Please, *please* don't talk about throwing up right now."

Major, a white standard poodle puppy, nudges Hayden's hand with his nose, and I watch a soft smile slowly form on his face as he complies with his dog's demands.

Hayden is just about the most charming man in existence. Emotionally, mentally, *and* physically. Well, minus the congenital heart defect. His blonde hair is lighter than mine, thicker too, yet somehow always perfectly styled. Even now, after a drunken night passed out on the couch, his hair is messy in such a precise way you wouldn't know it wasn't supposed to look like that. Mine is frizzy and tangled, like a lion's mane. A lion who *desperately* needs a deep conditioning treatment. His eyes are blue, but not blue like the ocean. They're softer, gentler, with just the slightest tint of purple in the right lighting. And that *smile.* Hayden has the type of smile that can get you to do just about anything. It's bright and sweet, effortless but not perfect in a way that seems fake.

Hayden Ayers is the type of person you *should* be in complete, uncontrollable love with. But, for some inexplicable, universal revenge, it would feel like *incest* if anything were to happen between us. I can't say I hate that, though. He makes a pretty good fake brother.

"So, are you excited for your first day?" he asks, slowly pulling himself upright. I sink further under the blanket, trying not to make any sudden movements that could trigger my stomach acid's evacuation.

"Yeah," I say casually, trying to act as if my entire insides aren't vibrating with excitement and anxiety. "I'm pretty stoked."

If I'm being honest, I thought I was going to work at The Dog Shop until it was time to crawl into my *grave*. Not because I had to—my contract ended two-and-a-half years ago. Not even really because I wanted to—who would want to work somewhere so hostile?

No. I was going to work at The Dog Shop for the rest of my life because the thought of starting over somewhere new was terrifying enough to make me stay.

Key word: *was.* Thanks to my psychologist, Dr. Burton and Adrian's pleas to Avery as their supervisor, I am now officially an independent contractor at Furry Friends Pet Resort, starting Monday.

Furry Friends isn't *really* a grooming salon. According to Avery and Adrian, it's more of a five-star hotel for dogs. Customers had been requesting they add grooming services for years, and last month, the owner finally agreed.

That's what Avery says, at least. I would be lying if I said I wasn't shocked that he picked me. Even though Pumpkin is one of my most loyal clients, Avery and I aren't *exactly* one another's favorite person. So, when Adrian told me he hadn't even posted a job search, my jaw practically shattered from hitting the floor. Avery told me that he picked me because he doesn't trust anyone else with his own dog, and to not "read too much into it."

I read too much into everything, yet this was a riddle even I couldn't quite solve.

A forty-five-pound black ball of energy thrusts itself on top of me, sending my stomach swirling and goosebumps rising on my skin as the nausea builds. I clutch my churning gut and curl into the fetal position.

"Dawson! *Off*!" I command.

Completely oblivious to the immense discomfort he has just caused me, Dawson obeys, sinking into a wiggly sitting position. A long strip of hair from the top of his neck leads down the center of his back to his forever-swaying tail, forming a coarse mohawk. Peppered white paws and a patch of wispy white hair on his chest contrast against the remainder of his dark coat. He looks up at me lovingly.

"Freakin' border collies," I mutter, as if he isn't the love of my life.

Dawson isn't a border collie, at least not entirely. Honestly, I'm not exactly sure what he is. His body screams collie, but his wiry coat is that of a Brillo Pad.

My hand cups the underside of his chin, and I scratch him gently. From the kitchen, Adrian tosses two cold, red bottles of fruit-punch-flavored Gatorade at Hayden and me.

"So, I was thinking," they say cheerily, like they didn't down four Monacos last night. Adrian has this superpower that makes them physically incapable of being hungover. At least, *I've* never seen it. "Do you want to carpool on Monday?"

Everyone is scared of something. I *was* scared of starting a new job, Avery is scared of vomit, and Adrian? Well, Adrian is *terrified* of driving.

I've come to the conclusion that this fear was a *major* contributing factor to them moving in with Avery. The two mostly work the same shifts, so they carpool. I mean, that *has* to be a factor, given that Avery is bothersome most days, though I think I'm the only one who notices.

Not that I'm always pleasant company myself. Adrian always says that I'm not a "glass half-full" or a "glass half-empty" person, but more of a "drinkable water is a finite resource" type. But my relentless anxiety attacks about global warming and life changes and *that thing I didn't mean to throw away that one time*, aren't really in my control. Avery's blunt comments and egotistical stance? Yeah, that's all on him.

I narrow my eyes at them in suspicion.

"Are you just asking me because Avery opens and you don't?"

Adrian's expression shifts, and they cross their arms over their body.

"Snitch."

A loud chuckle erupts from the bathroom, and Adrian flips Avery off through the wall. They turn back to me with pleading, puppy-dog eyes, and I *swear* they are the human embodiment of sunshine. Their bouncy black curls, their smooth dark skin, that adorable gap between their two front teeth. Adrian Barlowe might be one of the sweetest people ever born. When they aren't angry, of course.

I roll my eyes. "Are you going to complain about Luigi?" I ask with a sigh. Adrian gives me a coy smile, and bats their eyelashes.

"Is he going to *break down* again?"

Luigi is my golden 1999 Lexus LS400. The car boasts fabulous leather seats and a mechanical moonroof, complete with a polished wooden interior. That being said, Luigi is a real piece of shit. He gets about twelve miles to the gallon on a good day, is always leaking some*thing* from some*where*, and has a love letter engraved on the outside of the driver's door that reads *"cunt,"* left by my *charming* ex-boyfriend Cody. Still, I love him. Luigi, that is. Cody can get hit by a train.

"Probably." I shrug. Adrian frowns. "He's on a pretty good streak right now. It's been—" I count silently on my fingers. "Three weeks with no trouble?"

Hayden clears his throat from the couch. "Cam, don't you think it's about time to let him go?" He runs his fingers through the thick white fluff posted on top of Major's head. "I told you my parents and I are more than willing t—"

I shoot Hayden a glare that I hope he can physically feel.

[1]"I'm *not* getting rid of him," I say flatly. "*Ever.*"

I don't care that Luigi's repairs cost more than his worth. I don't care that he stops working on a regular basis. To me, he's *invaluable.*

The creaky moonroof, and the worn leather of the seats brings back memories I'm scared to forget.

The wind funneling through the sunroof on hot summer days. The CD station that was once new and high-tech but is now "retro" and rarely touched. My dad getting on me for allowing Cooper, my childhood dog, to sit on the seat beside me.

"Cameron Felicity Miller, he's going to rip a hole in the leather!" he'd always say, but I could still see him smiling through the rearview mirror.

Those memories, I'm scared I'll forget. But his voice could never slip my mind.*

Hayden puts his hands up defensively, and Adrian sucks in a breath through their teeth.

"Okay, okay," he says. "The offer is always there."

"On second thought," Adrian says, smiling awkwardly. "Luigi is perfect. I *love* him actually. No complaints here!"

The pitch of Adrian's voice reaches a frequency that is a little too high for someone as hungover and non-caffeinated as I am. As if he's reading my mind, Hayden peels himself off the couch and moseys his way to the door.

"I'm making a coffee run," he squeaks, shoving his feet into a pair of Avery's slippers that are much too large for him. "Who's coming?"

Evergreen Grounds is the world's *best* drive-through coffee kiosk. Or, Greenrock Valley, Washington's, at least. You wouldn't expect the most delicious coffee to come from a green shed on the side of the road, but it's our go-to stop, no matter our destination. I think our group single-handedly keeps the business afloat, which might say more about us than them.

"One dirty chai, one hot caramel macchiato, one iced pistachio latte, and one black coffee, right?" the barista asks, her dark lashes almost long enough to touch her bangs.

"And two—" I look behind me from the passenger seat to make sure I'm counting correctly. I'm not. "*Three* pup cups please."

Pumpkin stayed home.

The barista nods, scribbling onto a blue notepad. "Anything else?"

"We love you, Aurora," Adrian says, blowing a kiss through the back window. Aurora laughs brightly and blows a kiss back before sliding the drive-through window shut.

Adrian doesn't really know Aurora all that well. None of us do. We see her frequently, sure, but it's not like you're going to make best friends with your drive-through barista. Unless you're Adrian, of course. That's exactly the kind of person they are. They love everyone until they have a reason not to. I wonder how they do it, and sometimes, I'm jealous of it. But I know that realistically, it's more of a curse than a blessing.

On the way home, after the dogs have licked their cups of whipped cream clean and everyone but me has passed their drinks around to taste test, Adrian starts to talk about their business, Rise.

The business doesn't exist yet, and to be honest, sometimes I struggle to understand what it even *is*. If someone held a gun to my head and asked me to describe it, I only ask to be buried somewhere warm.

I guess if I *had* to try, I'd say it's like if a bookstore, café, and art gallery had a threesome. And then a bar, yoga studio, and meditation retreat joined in.

In retrospect, the vision is there. It's just a matter of learning how to explain it to somebody else.

"—and on the walls, I'll line up *all* my paintings. Well, not just *my* paintings, but other local artists too. And on Saturdays, we'll drink mimosas and do yoga."

"Can you do those things at the same time?" Avery asks, cradling Dawson on his lap. Adrian shoots him a glare, and Hayden adjusts his rearview mirror like a disappointed father.

"Be nice," he says like a warning, really embodying the paternal role.

"It's going to be awesome, Ry," I say, sipping my coffee. The bitter flavor hits my taste buds, melting into my mouth before I swallow. I don't particularly like black coffee, I'm not going to lie. I don't hate it, it's just a bit plain. But I haven't tried it any other way. It's overwhelming, staring at the menu, knowing that, out of hundreds of combinations, you could pick the one you simply don't like. Or worse, one that gives you a gurgling, upset stomach. I know what black coffee tastes like. I know how it affects me. So, I order it every time. That way, I know what I'm getting. That way, nothing changes.

Two

The Cursed Margarita

VIOLET

I FLICK MY WRIST, watching as my half-empty margarita creates a whirlpool, tilting up the sides of my glass and slowly absorbing the salt-lined rim. I squint at the clock on the wall.

9:45.

Unsurprisingly, forty-five minutes have passed since Mallory was *supposed* to arrive at Monsey's to sign papers. As if on cue, finally, the bar's large oak door swings open, and her familiar slender figure steps through the frame.

"Sorry, the group session ran late," Mallory says, before dropping a thick stack of papers onto the center of the table. She's still in her dance clothes: a pair of magenta leggings and a matching cropped long-sleeve. Her warm amber hair is pulled back into a sleek ponytail. It's the only warm thing about her. "I'm going to go get a drink first, do you need another?" Her tight, nasally voice sucks all the air out of the room, and not in a flattering way.

I take a deep breath. "No, but thanks."

"Okay then."

Mallory sashays up to the bar. Her slim hips move from one side to the other, as she intentionally drags each sway out farther than it would naturally go. She pulls a sheer pink tube from her pocket and applies a thick, glossy coat over her lips. The woman *loves* putting on a show.

It was something I used to love about her, watching everyone's eyes light up when she walked in the room, like she was the star of the show they called life. And what I loved even more was watching her glow as she basked in that attention. Mallory *is* stunning. Her pale skin is chiseled perfectly around her face, and her shiny red hair causes everyone's heads to turn, no matter where she is. I knew everyone stared. I also knew everyone wished they had a chance with her. I just didn't realize then that they actually *did*.

But it's been almost a year since I found those graphic texts, and now that the divorce papers are finally being signed, I'll be able to put it all behind me.

All twelve years.

Ruthie is going to be stoked. My sister has been waiting for this day for just about as long as we've been together.

Mallory returns to the table with another margarita and a glass of merlot.

"I figured you could use it."

She slides the drink across the table to me. I want to ignore the gesture, but I just can't bring myself to be so petty.

"Thank you," I say, though I push the drink to the side. I don't like the idea of hurting someone's feelings, even though Mallory completely annihilated mine. Sometimes, I wish I could do it, give her a taste of her own medicine. But every time the thought pops into my head, I get a bitter flavor in my mouth, and my throat grows dry. So, no matter how impatient I'm getting, I'm going to be nice.

"Are you ready?" I ask. It was the first thing to pop into my head that isn't outwardly rude, and it's a really *stupid* question. There are very few people in this world who are "ready" to end a relationship with their high school sweetheart.

But my jaw practically drops when Mallory picks up the pen, scrawls her signature perfectly on the thick black line, then holds it out in my direction.

"I have plans," she says.

I'm not going to lie. I expected more... *emotion*. More crying, some reminiscing, maybe. "Remember when"s and "I'll miss you"s. I mean, Mallory is quite literally a theatre kid, now all grown up. She lives for drama and angst. She loves to make things harder than they need to be. But I guess this particular drama has been a long time coming.

I figured the bar would be closing by the time we left, after all the empty glasses and smudged mascara.

But I might actually have time to stick around now, listen to some karaoke. Maybe play the divorce card and get a couple drinks. It's been a year, sure, and though I'm completely ready for it to be over, I haven't actually *moved on.*

By moved on, I mean had sex.

Not because I haven't wanted to. It's just, when you spend your entire adulthood with the same person, you forget *how* to have a one-night stand. But tonight, I'm ready. I even wore my nicest pair of black lacy underwear which are currently climbing *into* my ass. It feels weird to be waiting for this to be over so I can get laid, but to be fair, it's been a *long* time.

I tilt my head back, letting the rest of my drink slide down my throat, before I take the pen and sign my name on the second black line. The signature doesn't look half as nice as hers.

"Is that it then?" Mallory asks, tightening her ponytail.

I nod. "I guess so."

She unscrews the lid of her insulated tumbler and pours her leftover glass of wine inside before putting the lid back on.

"I'll drop these off at the courthouse in the morning," she says, scooping the large stack of papers into her arms. "I'll see you around, Violet."

And just as she had sauntered into the bar, Mallory saunters out of it.

"Ten o'clock karaoke begins in two minutes!" a woman calls through the speakers. "Sign-ups are almost full!"

I look down resentfully at the margarita Mallory bought for me, even though it's a completely innocent bystander. Drinking it will mean absolutely *nothing,* especially now that she's gone, but for some reason, it will feel like she's won. Won at what? I have no *fucking* clue. But I am not drinking this damn margarita.

I pick it up, the thick glass cold between my fingers. But as I lift it off the wooden table, I see something small and cylindrical. Light pink and expensive.

It's Mallory's lip gloss. Her *favorite* lip gloss, actually. She doesn't go anywhere without it.

Cursed margarita in one hand, Mallory's forty-dollar tube of lip gloss in the other, I shuffle to the door, hoping to catch her attention before she pulls away. The wooden door is thick and heavy, and it takes a hefty shove to push it open.

"Mallory, wait I—"

But just as I step outside, I bump into something with just enough force to send the tube of lip gloss, and *some* of the margarita, flying. The lip gloss bounces off the concrete once, then barrels toward the storm drain. The margarita, however, just *barely* tips over the edge of the glass, splashing onto the front of a *beautiful* emerald green dress.

"Shit!" I take a step back and, just then, watch Mallory's car speed off into the distance. My eyes slowly focus on the woman in front of me. "I'm really sorry I—"

"Wasn't paying attention?" the woman asks, her eyebrows furrowed as she wipes the slush off the front of her dress. "Was running outside of a bar with a *full-to-the-brim* margarita in your hands?"

I smile sheepishly, scratching the side of my neck.

"Yup! *That's* the one. I'm *really* sorry," I say again. The woman's expression doesn't shift. In fact, I think there might just be the beginnings of a frown tugging on the corners of her mouth. *Fuck.* "I can uh—" I stumble over my words, trying to find a way to diffuse the situation. I hold out the cold cup still in my hands. "Do you want it?"

I could be imagining it, but I think the ghost of a smile flickers across her face.

"You mean the drink you just spilled all over me?" she asks, her eyebrow arched in a dissatisfied manner. "No thanks."

"*Right*," I say through a half-laugh half-please-god-help-me-wince. I clear my throat. "Well, what if I buy you a new one? Unspilled guarantee?"

Honestly, I was really hoping to be the one getting a free drink tonight. But I will do just about anything to get this woman to stop looking at me like I've just *completely* ruined her night. I hold my breath, waiting for her to answer. She sighs.

"Alright," she says. "*One* drink."

As the woman orders her Vodka Cranberry (a boring choice if you ask me), I begin to notice all of the things I hadn't had time to notice when she had been frowning at me. The slope of her nose, the rosy tint to her cheeks. A small black mascara smudge just below her eye. The frizzy blonde waves down the back of her slightly-stained sleeveless dress. But the stain isn't from the margarita. It's dry, a small dark splotch embedded permanently into the fabric. And her *shoes.*

How am I just now noticing her shoes? Fuzzy, hammerhead sharks wrap around her feet in a comical contrast to the elegance of her outfit. In the short moment of panic about what an absolute *mess* I had made, I hadn't considered that maybe this woman was already a bit of a mess all on her own.

"Is there a reason you're staring at me, or should I be worried you're having a stroke?" The woman quirks an eyebrow, leaning against the bar. She redirects her gaze to the bartender.

Actually, there is a *very* good reason I am staring at her, and it isn't just the ocean creatures attached to her feet. Call it cliché, but this woman may be one of the most beautiful people I have seen in my entire life. With her dark brown eyes and coral lips, she's pretty in a completely natural, truly messy kind of way. And despite her strange choice of footwear, this woman knows what she's doing. That dress hugs her body like she was the inspiration behind it. The cutout at her waist, the curve of her hips, every inch of her silhouette is perfectly captured in a wave of silky green. And it occurs to me, at this moment, there are so many more *fuckable* people on this planet than Mallory Freaking Sinclair.

And tonight, I am going to prove it.

I shrug, giving her a sly smirk. "Just waiting for you to say thank you," I say, letting my chin rest in the divot of my hand.

She rolls her eyes. "*Thank you?*" she scoffs.

"Yes, *thank you*. It's a phrase people use when they want to express gratitude. Might be foreign to *you*, but it's pretty custom here."

Her jaw drops, those delightful pretty lips parting in true surprise. I can't help but break into laughter.

"I'm sorry," I say, trying not to choke on air as I continue to laugh. "I'm just fucking with you."

The woman blushes, shooting me what I can only hope is a falsely irritated glare. The dark red glass clicks against the polished wood as the bartender sets her drink down and gives her a singular nod. She lifts it, letting the cup clink against the rim of the margarita I had no intention of drinking. But now, I'm starting to think maybe it wasn't cursed at all. I smile, sliding the stem of it between my fingers before lifting it to my lips.

"*Thanks*," she says, raising her eyebrows and lowering her tone to ensure I catch that her gratitude is pure sarcasm. Mine, however, is not.

Thank you, Mallory.

"Well," I say, in an equally sarcastic tone. "When you put a damsel in distress, sometimes you gotta fix it with a Vodka Cranberry."

The woman tries to stifle her laugh, but I can see her lips fighting to break into a smile.

"A damsel in distress?"

"I mean—" I gesture to the sharks attached to her feet. "If the slipper fits."

I hold my breath, waiting to see if she bites. Bites the flirting bit or bites my head off. Either one could happen. Her tongue pokes the inside of her lower lip, and I think, in my completely biased opinion, that she just might be trying to hide another smile. She doesn't say anything, so I continue.

"*Maybe*," I say, gesturing to her now. "Maybe more of an *Ice Princess* than a damsel."

Now, the woman scowls. "What's *that* supposed to mean?"

She's so cute that I don't even care.

"*Definitely* an Ice Princess. With your whole 'I clearly hate people and want to be left alone' thing."

"Do you have a name, or do you just go around giving other people fake ones?" She purses her lips, like she's proud of that comeback. I'll let her have it.

"Violet," I say, sticking out my hand. The woman looks down at it, almost like she's analyzing it before she takes it into hers. Her palm is soft and just a little bit clammy in contrast to my dry, calloused skin.

"Cam."

Cam.

I wonder what that's short for. Camille? Camilla? Probably something like that, but I can't say it matters too much. I don't need to know her full legal name to have her screaming mine.

Heat rushes to my cheeks at the thought, but I stay composed enough to investigate if she's thinking the same.

"So what brings you here, *Cam*?" I ask, gesturing to the crowded bar. "Alcohol? Friends? A man you met online whose photo features a dead animal?"

Cam bites her lip to hold back a laugh, but just a drop of her drink slips out of the corner of her mouth in the process. I reach my hand up and swipe the red liquid away with my thumb. Her eyes lock onto mine for a moment, before darting down to my chest. She swallows, her bottom lip curling back between her teeth. Heat grows between my thighs as she blushes.

"Doesn't everyone come to the bar for alcohol?" she asks. I shrug.

"Not *that* guy." I point to the man on the karaoke stage who's belting out a rather pitchy version of The Beatles' "Don't Let Me Down." "He's here to perform."

Another smile breaks across Cam's face as she takes another sip of her drink.

"Okay, *fair*," she says, her eyebrows lifting. "But my friends aren't coming, and there's no animal-murdering Tinder date. I just..."

Her eyes travel down my body, and her breath hitches as they lock onto my chest again.

"You just?"

Cam nods, her eyes flicking up to me. If I thought she was blushing before, she's sure as hell flustered now. A red tint grows over her cheeks, not unlike the color of her drink.

"I have to go to the bathroom," she says, standing up abruptly. She looks at me through her thick brown lashes, before quickly walking away.

My fingers tap against the thick margarita glass as I watch the man on stage finish his rather drunken performance. Then, my stomach drops.

Shit. Was that a move?

I haven't actually done this before, pick up a girl at a bar. Is going to the bathroom a euphemism? Was I supposed to follow her, or is it just going to lead to some really awkward silence?

The Beatles Man stumbles off the stage and approaches me.

"Heyyy pretty lady," he slurs, his eyebrows wiggling.

Fuck it.

The roof of my mouth freezes for a moment as I suck down the rest of the margarita and slam a few one-dollar bills onto the bar as I make my way to the bathroom.

When I push open the swinging door, I catch Cam staring at herself in the mirror, seemingly attempting to fix her hair and makeup. Which makes no sense if I was supposed to follow her, because she would've known I'd just mess it up again. Still, I have to at least *try* to pretend I know what I'm doing.

"Enjoying the view?" I tease. Cam's cheeks flush.

"More like cringing," she says, taking a wet wad of toilet paper to the mascara smudge. I step in front of her and cup her delicate face in my hands. Then, I swipe the smudge gently with the pad of my thumb. Cam's breath hitches, and I shake my head, clicking my tongue disappointedly.

[2]"Can't have the Ice Princess talking about herself that way now, can I?"

Damn. I've still got it. Cam's throat bobs as she swallows, those full lips parting ever so slightly, but no words come out.

"Can I?" I repeat.

Her stare darts from my eyes to my lips, her eyes darkening. Long, soft fingers snake around my waist, sending a shiver down my spine. She pulls my pelvis into hers.

"Do you *ever* shut up?" she asks, her head tilted innocently. Then, her chin lifts up, her lips tracing mine to close the space between us. Our positions shift, as she guides my back against the sink. I reach out blindly, twisting the lock on the door until I hear the satisfying *click*, then let my hands venture back to her body.

My fingers trace up her thighs, her skin soft and supple. They glide under the curve of her ass, squeezing it not too gently in appreciation.

I think Cam was the blueprint for every sculpture ever crafted of a mythical goddess.

Her hot breath melts into my neck as she sucks the skin softly, drawing a quiet but not meaningless moan out of me. She places a single finger against the skin of my stomach, then drags it upward slowly and delicately. She is barely touching me, and I *swear* she can feel how wet I am through my jeans. When her finger reaches my bra, she carefully outlines that too, teasing me with her soft fingertips.

"Fuck," I mutter, letting my hands journey to the front of her panties. I hook a finger on the fabric, waiting for a consenting nod before I slip my hand inside.

It probably shouldn't, but my ego boosts just a smidge when I feel that Cam is just as wet as I am. She's practically dripping, and my fingers find their spot just in the center of the slick mess I helped her create. Cam lets out an angelic moan, a sound I now feel I'll never be able to go without. She grips the back of my neck, pressing herself further into me.

"Just like that. *Good girl*," I mumble during the short moment in which my lips aren't attached to her neck. My fingers glide against her clit, curl my knuckles on the way back, then carefully repeat. Cam's body jolts against mine as she practically collapses into me, one hand still gripping my neck as the other tugs at my hair. It's a great thing I've never been tender-headed.

"Fuck," she whines, and I know that's my sign to keep going. My thumb dances over her clit, a hot pulse emulating in my core as she pushes her thigh between mine. I groan, picking up the pace and moving my fingers to—*

"Is anyone in there?!" a woman's sharp voice calls out, followed by incessant, eardrum-shattering knocking.

Cam's eyebrows shoot up, her face flushing a bright, hot red. She pulls back, my fingers begrudgingly slipping out of her completely soaked underwear.

The knocking continues. "Hello?!"

I let out a short, uncomfortable laugh. This is still salvageable, right? I mean, we can finish this elsewhere. I look back at Cam, ready to suggest we get out of here. Her wide eyes are still glued to the door, her lashes rapidly fluttering.

"Hey, do you—"

But before I can finish my sentence, Cam-Camille-Camilla twists the silver lock, *throws* open the door, and sprints out of the bar as fast as someone in fleece slippers has ever run before.

I didn't even get a chance to pull down my shirt. The woman on the other side of the door stares at me with wide eyes and a slack jaw. I quickly tug it down and give her a sheepish smile.

I guess the margarita *was* cursed after all.

Three

A.D.D.

Cam

I'VE KNOWN I WAS bisexual since I was nine years old.[3] Everyone makes their Barbies scissor; it doesn't mean you're gay. But naming your Barbies after yourself and your fourth-grade best friend...

Still, even with that rather young realization and my father's full support, I've never actually *been* with a woman. Well, not until last night.

When I finally put in my two weeks' notice for The Dog Shop, Dr. Burton was *ecstatic*. Adjustment Disorder makes things like that difficult, and as if that isn't bad enough on its own, I happened to get the trifecta.

"Adjustment Disorder *with* Depression and Anxiety," Dr. Burton called it. Changes can be scary for me, so he constantly encourages my friends and I to try new things together.

"Try these shrimp tacos, Cam! They're really good!"

"We should watch the extended edition of this instead."

"They were out of vanilla, so I got you caramel."

I think everyone was completely shocked when I actually accepted Avery's offer. Myself included. But even though I cried the entire therapy session afterward, I realized what a relief it was to move on from such a hostile environment. That got me thinking that maybe I was ready to move on from *other* hostile things.

Like Cody.

From the start, my friends hated him. And Hayden and Adrian don't just hate anybody. Even Avery told me he was a tool, but I always take his opinion with a microscopic grain of salt. Of course, by the time I realized they were right, I had already attached myself to Cody's hip, so it took four years and one traumatic walking-in-on-him-in-our-bed-with-another-woman for me to actually let him go. And last night, I was really ready to completely move on.

Move on *and* try something new.

Dr. Burton suggested a more casual approach to the situation. Because of the co-dependency in Cody and I's relationship (his words not mine), he thought it might be better that I look for a no-strings-attached type of situation. A one-night stand.

Obviously, that's not really an experience that you share with your friends, so Adrian and Hayden helped me devise a plan. The *A.D.D.* plan.

The A.D.D. plan consists of three *obligatory* criteria for my first one-night stand with a woman, and my first one-night stand since Cody.

Attraction: *You must be attracted to your one-night stand. Otherwise, what's the point?*

Distance*: Your one-night stand has to be a complete stranger. That way, you can't get attached to them, because you'll never see them again.*

Which brings us to the last one.

Deal breaker: *Your hookup must come with a deal breaker.*

This one is important. Maybe the *most* important. If there isn't something you dislike about your hookup, it's a one-way ticket to Relationship Town. And I'm supposed to stay far, far away from that place.

So, in my nicest, but still thrifted, emerald green dress and a pair of black kitten heels that squeezed my feet in a way that made me wish I were dead, I went to Monsey's Bar & Grill. I know the more typical route would be Tinder or Hinge, but I've seen enough Dateline to know how that ends. Plus, Monsey's is my go-to, and I was trying enough new things as it was.

I should have known the entire situation was going to be a disaster when the moment I stepped out of the car, my heel snapped. Still, I could hear Hayden's voice in my head, telling me he believed in me, and Adrian hyping me up about what a "hot piece of ass" I was. So, I improvised. I grabbed the only other pair of shoes in my car, my favorite shark-shaped slippers that I run all my quick errands in. You know, picking up takeout, grabbing snacks at the corner store, those types of things. Then, I put them on.

I guess I also put on rose-colored glasses, because the universe sent me yet *another* warning sign I completely ignored.

When the tan woman with the aquatic tattoos dumped half her margarita on me, I should have turned around right then and there. Two strikes should have been enough for me to realize this wasn't going to work out in my favor. Tonight was not my night. But I was so blinded by her dashing smile and those hazel, aphrodisiac eyes that I pushed those rose-colored glasses up the bridge of my nose and let her buy me a drink.

To be fair, she was hitting all the right criteria.

With her shiny chestnut hair, thick dark lips, and facial piercings that glistened in the low bar light, Violet looked as if Artemis and Asteria had a lesbian love child. "Beautiful" did no justice, but "ethereal" was too soft. This woman was the *physical embodiment* of Mother Earth. Everything about her, from her forest-colored eyes to her small, boulder-like hands was like she was hand-fucking-crafted by nature. Attraction? Check.

And distance was no question, given that I had never seen her a day in my life. It kind of seemed like a cruel joke, to meet someone so beautiful just to see them only once in your life. But I hadn't known her, and she hadn't known me, so distance? Check.

It wasn't until we were locked inside the bathroom with her hand inside my underwear that I realized I *massively* fucked up. There was *no* deal breaker.

I tried to think of one, scouring my brain to find anything she could have said or done that ruined any chance of me thinking about her the next day. I couldn't stay mad about the spilled margarita because I've spilled about six different substances on this dress already. I couldn't hate her for the taunting because it was actually quite charming and was *definitely* turning me on. And the fact that I'd never had a sexual encounter with a woman before couldn't be a deal breaker, because that was the *entire point*. I was trying something new. I was moving on.

Then, I was moving *out*. Out of the bathroom, out of Monsey's, out of Violet's life.

I don't know why I panicked so badly. Adrian thinks everything just became too much too fast. I only gave them a brief synopsis, because it had been humiliating enough, but I have to say I agree with them. I just kind of wish I could have explained that to her, because *damn* did I want her to fuck me in a way I hadn't been fucked before.

But I couldn't really control that.

In my twenty-three years of life, I've learned that controlling my body and my mind is nearly *impossible*. Although they share the same vessel, the two are complete enemies. My brain can never make my body do what I want, act how I want, or even *breathe* how I want. The only thing my brain *does* control is ensuring constant worry is always present. Last night, it might have kicked into overdrive, but today, I can think of many reasons why it's feasible.

I'm starting a completely new job, with new people and a new atmosphere. There will be new customers and dogs and rules and equipment. The only familiar things will be Adrian and Avery. And still, I only like *half* of them.

"It'll be fine," Adrian says in a comforting tone. We stand outside the large building, hand-in-hand. Dawson lets out an excited whine, his tail gently swatting the concrete slab. "Everyone is really nice. I mean, the owner is a little uptight, but she's pretty much always on vacation. All you have to do is what you're good at."

Usually, Adrian's consoling helps, but sometimes, it just reminds me of all the things there are to stress about. The things I hadn't thought of in the first place:

1. *What if I'm not good at my job?*

2. *What if everyone hates me?*

3. *What if I mess up and get fired?*

Half of my brain knows that, in reality, the chances of all of those things happening are slim. But the half that comes up with that shit works overtime, so I can't forget they're all still *technically* possible.*

As we step into the lobby of Furry Friends Pet Resort, the smell of bleach and wet dog baptizes me. Various retail products line the light blue walls from floor to ceiling: brushes, toys, food, leashes, anything a dog owner could ever need, anything a dog could ever want. When the door closes behind me, a bell hidden somewhere near the top of the frame chimes. I barely finish looking around before Adrian drags me through a side door near the back of the room and leads me to the inside of the facility.

The aroma immediately transforms from bleach and wet dog, to *strictly* wet dog. I analyze my surroundings while Adrian leads me to a large set of green lockers. The facility is *huge*, like a warehouse-converted-dog-hotel. Loud barks echo off the walls, bouncing around one another and ringing through the building. My head throbs at the sounds, but I try my hardest not to show it. To the left, four large garage-type doors sit up on the wall, daylight flooding in through each opening. Vinyl fencing surrounds the doorways, creating separate yards for the dogs. The same soft blue from the lobby encompasses me, fire hydrants and squirrels and paw prints painted on top. On the right side of the facility, dozens of rooms sit along the wall, each with a clipboard next to their windowed doors.

"You can put your bag in here," Adrian says, interrupting my sight-seeing. "Listen, I'll give you a tour sometime soon. But today we've got like six dogs on the schedule, and one of them is a seventy-pound doodle. So, let's get your ass into the salon."

I nod and start to follow Adrian once more, but I feel resistance from the leash gripped in my hand. After giving a short tug to get Dawson to move, I start walking again, but there's no budge. I turn to see what's causing the holdup, and my jaw drops to form an overwhelmingly horrified "o." A yellow puddle forms at the bottom of a vinyl post, Dawson's leg hiked high into the air.

"You've got to be kidding me," I mutter, as my dog continues to take what has to be the *longest* piss of his life on the epoxy floor of my new job.

Adrian's cheeks grow pink, and I can tell they're trying not to laugh from the way they bite their lip. I appreciate the effort, even if I can still see their very obvious amusement.

"I'll go put him into daycare," they chuckle softly. Their finger points to a bright yellow bucket in the corner. "There's a mop bucket over there."

I sigh loudly, shaking my head as I approach the bucket. I'm reaching for the wooden, splintering mop handle when a voice startles me, and my heart practically rams against my ribs. I clutch my chest.

"Can I help you?" the voice asks. It's smooth yet raspy, and I swear I can sense familiarity in it. Turning around slowly, as to not let whoever it is know that they almost had me pissing my pants, pure mortification floods my body.

So *that's* why she sounded familiar.

A small tan face, with perfectly plucked eyebrows, and a pierced angular nose blinks at me slowly. Those thick full lips are parted ever so slightly, her jaw just barely hanging open. Recognition floods her face, and while my cheeks are scalding, hers go ghostly pale.

"Oh, Vi!" Adrian's voice interrupts us, before either of us has the chance for a verbal reaction. "I see you've finally met Cameron."

FOUR
Sunny's Neighborhood

VIOLET

YOU KNOW THOSE DAYS when *nothing is* going well and *everything* is falling apart?

Yeah, I *love* those days. I feel like they really put me to the test. Force me to stay smiling in situations that feel impossible, some sort of twisted positivity game.

"Can you still stay happy with all this bullshit going down? Stay tuned to find out!"

Spoiler Alert: *of course I can.*

The problem is that, this time, things got a little *too* bizarre.

I had already dealt with one upset customer, one employee calling in due to COVID, and one little cut on a crazy corgi's paw pad when it came to my attention that I'd massively fucked up.

I don't need Adrian to introduce us, because the second Cam turns around, I realize exactly what had happened.

Cam. As in *Cameron.* As in *Cameron Miller,* the dog groomer that Avery hired.

I keep staring at the woman in front of me, hoping her face will distort itself into someone new. Someone different. Someone who wasn't pressed against my body in a bar bathroom last night. But that doesn't happen, of course. Cam blinks up at me with the same dark brown eyes and pretty little lips as she had last night.

I stare, tightening the muscles in my face to form the best smile I can manage under the circumstances. My hand reaches out in a professional gesture, and I thank the universe for programming that into me, because it wasn't a conscious decision.

"*Cam*," I say, nodding as I accentuate her nickname. Our eyes lock, Cam's widening into giant, terrified saucers. "I've *heard* a lot about you!"

Cam's hand slides weakly into mine, a montage of memories flooding into my brain from last night. Her smooth fingers gliding against my skin. Her warm breath heating up my neck. Soft sounds of desperation coming from the both of us. We give an awkward handshake before quickly pulling away.

Adrian shoots Cam a look, and at first, I'm terrified Cam might say something. But she stays silent.

When I ran into her, tipping that stupid margarita onto her dress, I wasn't planning on making a move. No, I didn't decide that until we sat down. Her hair was a tangled mess, her features soft and gentle. Despite her smudged mascara, her eyes were like shimmering espresso. When she looked at me the way she did, it felt like the only caffeine I'd ever need. Sweet coral lips and an adorable button nose, this woman looked like someone you'd see on the big screen.

But I didn't make a move on her because she was pretty. Even her exposed skin played no role.

The reason I decided to flirt with this woman was because of her *foul-ass* attitude.

I like to think of myself as an objectively pleasant person. Even when I don't want to be, I try my hardest to stay in a positive mood.

When I was a kid, I'd stay up and watch this cartoon that only aired at night as I waited for my parents to get home. Sometimes they'd get back at three in the morning, sometimes they wouldn't get back at all. Either way, I watched it. The show was called *Sunny's Neighborhood*, and it was about a smiley face with arms and legs that walked around his neighborhood and put smiles on everyone's faces, even when they were having a hard day.

Sometimes their dilemma would be simple, like their favorite toy breaking or their stomach hurting. Other times, it would be deeper, like family struggles or bullying. Think *Sesame Street*, only it's a slightly terrifying animated smiley face. Regardless, Sunny was my childhood mascot.

"Every day's a treat when there's smiles on your street!" he would say. It's kind of a stupid slogan, now that I'm thinking back on it, but for some reason, it stuck with me.

In hindsight, I don't think the show necessarily set the best *example*. Sunny would make kids smile even when crying or yelling would have been a more appropriate response. But I can't deny that it kind of works for me. It's easier somehow, to just keep smiling. So, because of that, because it's easier, I have the utmost respect for people who wear their emotions on their sleeves.

Respect, admiration, attraction. *Whatever.*

Yet, somewhere between feeling her tongue against mine and her barging out the bathroom door, I seemed to have made a mistake. What that mistake was, I have no idea. But now, I have to admit that it doesn't feel like a mistake at all. It feels like divine intervention.

I mean, if things had gone further...

"Well," Adrian says, locking their fingers between Cam's. "Cam has a lot to do today, so I'm gonna go get her set up in the salon."

I nod, stepping to the side and giving them both a smile. "Of course!" I say and then wince at how high-pitched my voice comes out. I clear my throat. "Let me know if you need anything."

I have a feeling that Cam will, in fact, not be letting me know.

I pinch the bridge of my nose with my fingers and take a slow deep breath to force my body to calm down. Normally, I wouldn't think this was a big deal. Even though I might be slightly humiliated about running off one of the most jaw-dropping women I have ever seen, I can easily move past the awkwardness of things.

What I can't move past is the idea that both of our jobs are at risk if Angela finds out.

I'm so busy scouring the lobby for my misplaced coffee that when a loud melody fills the air around me, for a moment, I don't even realize it's *my* phone.

I pull it out of my pocket, and my stomach sinks when I read the name across the screen. *Speak of the devil.*

"Hello?" I say, pressing the cold glass screen to my ear. Where the *fuck* is my coffee?

"Hi, Violet. It's Angela."

Angela always makes phone calls and sends text messages like the option to program the contact into your phone hasn't been invented yet. She also tends to speak so loudly that it sounds like she's always on speakerphone. I tighten my vocal cords to force an excited and surprised tone, even though I am neither excited nor surprised about this phone call.

"Hi Angela! How's Thailand?"

The great thing about owning a highly profitable business instead of managing it is that you can always be on a cruise somewhere instead of working.

"It's fantastic!" Angela says, her voice nasally and tight. "I'm calling about the text you sent me."

The great thing about texts is that you can just send one back.

"Yes?"

"You want to hire an assistant manager?"

Her tone remains unpleasant but is now mixed with dissatisfaction.

I expected this. Yesterday, I sent Angela a text asking if I could promote one of our supervisors to assistant manager. Between making the schedule, working fifty-hour weeks (or more), handling upset customers, sick employees, injured dogs, and rotating staff, I'm starting to be stretched too thin.

Actually, I've *always* been stretched too thin at this job. This is just the first time I've stood my ground, demanding help. And for good reason. Despite the generous profit Furry Friends Pet Resort makes (I would know, I handle the communications with her accountant), Angela does not *particularly* like to fork out extra money. Every dollar is a dollar less she can spend on her next trip around the world.

"Yes," I say. I don't yet elaborate because I know I will just get cut off. I wait for her to snap or yell.

Typically, when I mention anything that involves spending extra money, that's what happens. My eyes scan the office one last time and I finally locate the white paper cup sitting on the front desk next to Martha, our receptionist. I grab it quickly and wave at her before ducking into the back of the facility. Martha *loves* to eavesdrop.

"And *where* is that money going to come from?"

Her condescending tone is a step up from the irate screaming I received when I asked if we could purchase new cots. I clear my throat.

"Well, I was thinking... Cam—" The name gets stuck in my throat, and I take a heavy swig of my coffee to wash it down. "*The new dog groomer* starts today, and she and Avery agreed on a 1099. So, she's paying us salon rent. I figured we could use that money to increase Avery's wage."

"Avery?"

I try not to make my sigh audible. I told her all of this. *Four times.*

"Yes. I think he's right for the job. He's already a supervisor, so he knows the ins and outs of everything. It wouldn't be a drastic change for him or the team, and the customers love him."

Angela's silence forces me to hold my breath and brace myself for whatever she's going to say next. Avery is by far the best employee we have, but Angela isn't a fan. She's only met him once, and she wanted me to fire him immediately after they spoke. Avery is reserved and comes off kind of aloof if you don't know him. But his understanding and genuine love for the dogs makes customers happier than other employees' peppy personalities. I had to show her the *twenty-seven* five-star reviews we've received specifically mentioning his name to cool her down.

"You'll have to cut labor," she says flatly. "And tell him to smile more. There's no reason someone who looks like that should have such a blank face all the time."

I feel my mouth stretch into a smile, but I try not to sound overly excited.

"Okay," I say. "Okay, I will. Thank you."

"Mhm."

My phone beeps, signaling the end of the call, and I quickly down the remainder of my lukewarm coffee before tossing the cup into the garbage can. A wave of relief crashes over me. I've been asking for an assistant manager for *two years.* Avery already does everything he can to help, but I only let him do so much because it isn't fair to him to not be paid his worth. Now, he can be the same amazing Avery *and* help me juggle it all. I have a feeling that everything is about to get a whole lot easier.

Five
Criminal Dinner

CAM

I S IT TOO SOON to quit?

I mean, I think if I asked really nicely and apologized for the three-page letter I wrote about how terrible their company is, The Dog Shop might just give me a second chance.

After Adrian dropped me off in the salon so they could go about their day, I've been spending the rest of *mine* ankle-deep in dog hair and regret.

The problem is, I'm not sure if I regret the making out or taking this job. The making out was too amazing to regret, but this job is going to pay my bills.

I've never been good at first impressions. I always talk too much or too little. My body throws internal muscle raves, and it always feels like Judgement Day. I've also been told once or twice, or six times, that I come off as "uninviting." Dr. Burton was one of those times.

This first impression, however, might just have taken the cake.

Now, six hours into my shift, I am *struggling*. I'm struggling with the fact that I know what my boss's lips taste like, and I'm struggling with this giant, stubborn dog. What Adrian failed to mention about the large doodle is that he's only nine-months old and, on top of that, has *never* been groomed. The giant puppy is apprehensive and completely matted, and although I hold my patience well, not much progress has been made. He keeps throwing himself off the table as if ending his life would be a more suitable conclusion to this day than the haircut.

Maybe we have something in common.

I take a deep breath before attempting, *again*, to soothe the anxious pup.

"Hey baby, it's okay! It's okay! You're being so brave! Yes, you are! You're the bravest boy!" I encourage him as I gently run my clippers behind the back of his leg. "Good boy!"

This tactic is *not* working, but I keep trying anyway.

I might be trying to soothe the dog, but my tone is more so pleading with him at this point. Today did *not* start off well, and it isn't really showing signs of improving. It's only my first day, and this dog, due to no fault of its own or mine for that matter, is an absolute *mess*. I push the switch on my clippers backward, bringing the vibrating sensation in my hand to an end.

I rifle through my blue denim bag until I find the orange cylindrical bottle that frequently saves my life. I like to think I don't have to depend on my medication often, but my periodic Xanax refills say otherwise. Beebo the Goldendoodle definitely isn't the only thing causing my anxiety to spike.

I turn around, inhaling methodically, and my eyes travel from a dirty pair of shoes on the floor up to a recognizable, *aggravating* face. Avery is standing in the doorway, watching with a patronizing smile.

"What are you doing!?" I snap. I'm already getting frustrated, and sometimes, just *looking* at Avery puts me in a sour mood.

"I need to borrow a pair of hemostats. A dog has a splinter stuck in his paw pad. What are *you* doing?" Avery asks, cocking his eyebrow. His husky voice is filled with arrogance, and it pisses me off to no end. I know he doesn't actually want to know what I'm doing, but I'm holding in enough, and I can't stop the words flowing from my mouth.

"I can't get this dog to sit still long enough to shave him. And the parents didn't even want me to shave him, but he's totally matted, and I tried talking to him and soothing him, but—"

"Do you have the hemostats?" Avery interrupts impatiently, shaking his head to dismiss anything I may have mistaken as interest.

Probably for a combination of reasons, I snap. "Wow. You're a real charmer, you know that?!" I retaliate, the stress now boiling to anger. Avery has a special way of pissing me off.

Avery quirks a brow, no doubt finding my mental decline humorous. He watches my cheeks grow red and my eyebrows drop further down as I continue my rant.

"—because you think you know everything, but you don't! All you know how to do is—"

"Scratch his tail," Avery cuts in.

"You—what?"

"Scratch his tail. Beebo loves getting his tail scratched," he explains, his tone continually degrading.

I study Avery's face for a moment, attempting to decipher the rules to the game he's trying to play. I can't.

"You really think that is going to make a terrified, unsocialized puppy stop spinning and alligator-rolling? Scratching his *tail*?"

Listen, I've groomed a lot of dogs in my years as a groomer. I've baby-talked, scratched chins, and handed out mountains of beef-smelling treats that leave oily residue on my hands. I've tried all the holds and all the tricks, and *nothing* stops a doodle puppy from being a complete psychopath for its first haircut.

A dramatic scoff exits the back of my throat when Avery approaches me, his tall, broad body towering over me.

I will never, *ever* say this out loud, but Avery is *hot*. His shoulders are broad. So broad that I couldn't wrap my arms around them if I wanted to. His eyes resemble amber, and when he steps into the sun, they melt into honey. His facial hair is always kept short but scruffy, and then his personality ruins it all. I step aside, continuing to glare. I have to admit, I'm rather excited to see Avery get donkey-kicked by a seventy-pound puppy.

"When I start scratching his tail, you can go ahead and start. You'll need to move fast though. Is it just the back legs?" he asks, already positioning his arm under the nervous pup.

"Yeah, the back legs, and then I'll just hand-scissor his face."

Beebo relaxes into Avery's touch as he softly rubs the base of his tail. I tilt my head to find the right angle, part of my tongue peeking out the side of my mouth while the clippers do the work. Minutes later, I turn them off, and the majority of Beebo's haircut is finally done. Though it may not be as even as I would have liked, I'm grateful it's over with. Avery grabs the hemostats out of the toolbox and sneers.

"Told ya."

I roll my eyes so hard that it physically hurts.

Adrian, Hayden, *begrudgingly* Avery, and I host "theme nights" every Tuesday, where we watch *Criminal Minds* and cook cuisines from different countries. It was started as part of my therapy in an attempt to incorporate new foods into my rather repetitive diet. We call it "Criminal Dinner," partly due to the *Criminal Minds* element, but more so due to how criminally disgusting my dish always is. A few weeks ago, we did Filipino food, and I completely botched the Bagnet Kare-Kare. While the pork was like eating a bicycle tire, the show's third season finale didn't disappoint. We all enjoy these nights, but Adrian loves them the most. Plus their culinary skills blow everyone else out of the water.

This Tuesday, Adrian may have done their best. Or so Hayden and Avery say.

"This might be the best Gyro I've ever had," Hayden says through a mouthful of meat and pita bread.

Avery nods his head. "Agree."

I poke at mine with a fork, carefully peeling off the outside layer of bread that hasn't touched anything inside.

"Oh, come on Cam," Avery groans. "It's not like *your* dish. This one is actually edible."

How I managed to fuck up garlic hummus is a mystery to me. The dry, crumbling chickpeas made their way directly into the garbage can, as did my homemade mozzarella sticks from last week.

"Respectfully," Hayden says, before taking another massive bite, "I don't know why we keep letting you make the appetizers."

I shoot him a glare and toss a piece of pita bread at his face. It hits his cheek and falls onto the couch cushion, from which he picks it up and pops it into his mouth.

"Gross!" Adrian yells, little rays forming on their skin as they scrunch their nose. Hayden shrugs, and I let out a light laugh.

"It's fine," I say. "Probably just a little dog hair."

Adrian pretends to throw up, and then Avery gets mad because it makes him actually nauseous.

"For someone who's terrified of food poisoning, you're really gross."

"I'm a dog groomer. I accidentally eat dog hair all day long."

I push my gyro to the front of the coffee table, Dawson eyeing it inconspicuously as he lies on the floor nearby.

"How was your first day of work?" Hayden asks, clicking through the season seven episodes to find the specific one he's looking for.

A pit forms in my sinking stomach, and my heart palpitates. I wonder if it feels anything like Hayden's arrhythmia: loud, fast, thrumming against the inside of my ribcage. My breath hitches.

Truthfully, the day in itself was great. The rest of the dogs on my schedule were absolute angels, and it felt so relieving to be able to do what was right for the dogs instead of just trying to make the customers happy. A weight has been lifted off my shoulders in that I no longer have to worry about random corporate policies that make no apparent sense.

In fact, other than Beebo trying to DIY his own death, the only part of my day that was less than amazing was learning that I shoved my tongue down my boss's throat last night.

The most horrifying part of it all is that, with absolutely no warning, I fled the scene like I had just committed a crime. To be fair, that's kind of how it feels right now. I don't know why. We are two consenting adults who *were* having a good time. But in the pit of my stomach, it feels like I did something illegal. I think that's why I haven't told Adrian or Hayden yet.

"It was good," I say, walking over to the refrigerator. I pull out a cinnamon applesauce pouch and twist the plastic cap until it snaps off. "I like having my own space.”

I suck the sweet puree into my mouth and slide down on the floor next to Dawson. He lifts his head just for a moment, then rests his chin on my lap, a small spot of drool leaking onto my thigh. I know it's kind of gross, but I love when he does that.

“By the way,” Avery says gruffly, “Beebo's mom said thank you for the suggestions on brushes.”

My eyebrows press together so hard that I'm surprised it doesn't leave an indent. “What?”

Avery shoots me a confused glance, then looks back at the television and takes another bite of his gyro.

“She left a tip in the till for you too.”

Okay. Now I *know* Avery is fucking with me. Because never, in my five years of dog grooming, has a client *ever* been polite, or even thanked me, when I spent hours shaving their dog who was pelted to the skin. I get “I asked for a Teddy Bear cut,” or sometimes the occasional shocked laugh when their dog comes in looking like a bear, then leaves looking like a naked horse. But never, *ever*, “thank you.”

“Ha-ha,” I say sarcastically, scratching gently behind Dawson's ear. He groans in appreciation, his toes spreading out in front of him in pure bliss. Adrian quirks an eyebrow, and Avery looks back at me again with that same confused expression.

“Cam, she left fifty dollars,” Adrian says, and their tone tells me they aren't bullshitting me. I swallow, still shocked as to how this can be true.

“Huh? But I charged her $200!”

Avery chuckles, shaking his head and Hayden whistles dramatically.

“Babes,” Adrian says, placing a gentle hand on my shoulder. “People who can afford to bring their dog to a dog *hotel* don't give a *shit* about money. And Beebo's mom is awesome. She owns Mountain Scoops, so she always brings us free samples.”

Mountain Scoops Creamery has the best ice cream known to man. All of its flavors are Pacific-Northwest-themed. Puget Sound Pistachio, Huckleberry

Lilac, Rainier Rocky Road. But my favorite, and the only one I've ever tried, is the Seattle Strawberry Swirl.

"What?" I ask, my eyebrows practically touching my hairline. They both chuckle again.

"Wow. Corporate really did a number on you, huh, kid?" Avery says. He always calls me *kid* like he isn't only a year older than me. It's so condescending. Adrian bursts into laughter and smacks Avery's arm repeatedly as they struggle to get their words out.

"Remember when Carlos-wh-when he thought the Peanut Butter Dream was for humans, and he ate the entire pint because he didn't know it was a sample for the dogs?" They cackle, gripping their stomach as their eyes well with hysterical tears. Avery's cheeks pink as he recounts the event.

"Oh my god, I forgot about that."

Hayden and I giggle at the thought, even though neither of us were there.

"I don't think I met Carlos," I say, flipping through mental flashcards of the few people I was introduced to today. There was Martha, the receptionist. Brooke was young, no older than sixteen, and I was honestly kind of confused as to why she wasn't at school. Then, there was Malcolm, a twenty-something-year-old that was possibly but not definitively stoned. And of course, who could forget Violet? But nothing comes to mind at the name "Carlos." Avery shakes his head, running a hand through his thick brown hair.

"Oh, Carlos doesn't work there anymore," Adrian says, waving a hand like it's nothing to worry about. "He got fired."

Hayden's eyes widen, and I choke on my applesauce.

"What?"

People get fired anywhere. I know that. But if there are any random things I could do that would get me into trouble, I want to know what they are. You know, like telling parents how to brush their dogs.

"Calm down, calm down," Adrian says, already knowing exactly where my brain was dragging me to. "It was an unconventional situation."

I stare at them, anxiously tugging at the strands of hair tickling the back of my neck.

Vague explanations don't work for me. I need to know the exact details of a situation. The fine print. I'm the type of person who reads the terms and conditions before clicking "accept." Adrian knows this.

They sigh, leaning back into the couch. I know it gets exhausting for them, to have to hold my hand through every little thing. I feel terrible about it, and I try really, really hard not to do it all the time. But it feels impossible to just move on. My brain gets attached to the subject until my mind is at ease. I can't eat, sleep, or think about anything else until I get the answers my brain is looking for. That's another reason Adrian is so amazing. They always break things down for me, even if it has no significance at all in the end.

"So," they say, now leaning forward, their arms resting on their knees like they're about to tell a campfire story. Adrian is a wonderful storyteller. "Once upon a time, there was a manager named Carlos. Carlos was kinda cool. Then, one day, Carlos hired a girl named Annie. Annie was kind of a bitch."

Hayden clears his throat, shooting Adrian a dissatisfied glance. Adrian rolls their eyes and corrects themself.

"Annie was *unpleasant*. Annie and Carlos started dating, but secretly, she was giving another kennel tech Dale shifts on the side. If you know what I mean." They wiggle their eyebrows, and all three of us shake our heads, stifling our laughs. "Well, one day, Carlos found out, and it was pretty much World War III in the lobby."

I give them a "seriously" look, but Avery's eyes widen, and he nods his head, confirming.

"Carlos and Dale were straight up mauling each other," he adds. "It was gruesome."

"Damn," Hayden mutters. "I mean, you know how much I love women, but no woman is worth all *that.*"

His eyes flick over to me, and I nod in agreement. "*Nobody* is worth all that."

"Right? Especially bitc-*people* like Annie."

Adrian doesn't use the word "bitch" in a derogatory, woman-hating manner. They use it for any gender of person, either out of love or pure distaste. And if Adrian is calling someone a bitch, chances are, they probably are one.

"Anyway," Avery says, taking my uneaten gyro into his hands. "That's why Angela made that rule."

I tilt my head, frowning. "What rule?"

He takes a massive bite of the gyro. "You know. The 'no fucking' rule." Adrian lightly smacks his shoulder.

"He means the 'no fraternization' rule. After that, Angela decided to instate a strict no-dating, no-nothing policy, which is totally fair if you ask me."

It feels like I swallowed a rock, with how large and dry the lump in my throat is. It's difficult to funnel air into my lungs with it blocking its path. I cough, feeling as if my lungs are filling with water. Heat pours over my cheeks, my throat burning as I continue clearing it repetitively. Avery casually slides a glass of water over to me, and Adrian hops off the couch to rub circles on my back.

"Damn, babes, you good?"

I try to nod my head, which in some twisted way is supposed to communicate that I'm fine. I take a strained breath and finally feel like I can breathe for the first time in sixty seconds.

"It's okay, Cam," Hayden says, after I give them all a thumbs-up to signal I'm okay. "I don't work there, so we're totally good."

Six

The Stick

Violet

WHY ARE GOLDEN RETRIEVERS so *cute* and simultaneously complete psychopaths?

I pry a fluffy ginger puppy's jaw off the sleeve of my sweatshirt, a small puncture torn through the fabric from his razor-sharp teeth.

"*Okay* Tex, I think it's time for you to go into the Party Pen," I say, draping a leash over his head. I wave Brooke, our *genius* kennel tech, over. Literally, she's a genius. The girl is sixteen and has already graduated high school. I'm pretty sure her IQ is in the 190s. Why she's working at a pet resort instead of taking classes at Harvard is a mystery to me. But I'm not upset about it, seeing as she's one of my favorite coworkers.

"What's up boss?" she asks, brushing her pin-straight platinum hair out of her face. She boasts a cheerleader smile, the kind that is so big and bright you can't help but return it.

"Can you *please* take Tex to the Party Pen?" I ask her sweetly. "He's getting a little bit too... *extreme* for these guys." I gesture to the crowd of small puppies surrounding me.

At Furry Friends Pet Resort, we divide our dogs into four playgroups. There's the Small Dog Pen, the Large Dog Pen, the Puppy Pen, and the Party Pen. As I'm sure you can guess, only the absolute *nutjobs* go into the Party Pen. I think Tex is really starting to earn his spot.

"Absolutely!" Brooke responds cheerfully, before grabbing the leash from my hand. I always appreciate her optimism, as it reminds me of when mine starts slipping. Managing a pet resort is all fun and games, except if fun and games were also hell. Don't get me wrong. I *love* dogs. They're pretty much my entire life. But try being in charge of one hundred and fifty of them, then see how *you* feel.

I exit the Puppy Pen behind Brooke and make my way to the Big Dog Pen to receive Reese, my six-year-old boxer who may as well be my child.

"Can you guys please send Reese out of the play area?" I ask through my walkie. The message travels to the employees in the large dog play area, and I retrieve my dog from the gated cell. His broad, white body strenuously wiggles, his short nubby tail practically reaching his face as his body curls with excitement.

"You wanna…" I ask in a high-pitched voice, clapping my palms to my thighs. Reese grows even more animated, loud snorts coming from his shortened nose. He jumps up, his front paws digging into my knees. "You wanna go on a walk?"

Reese lets out an excited growl from the back of his throat, before tilting his head to the ceiling and bellowing a loud noise somewhere between a bark and a howl. I can't help but laugh. "Alright bubs, let's go!"

I get an hour lunch break every day. And every day, I spend it walking Reese to Al's Taco Truck a couple blocks down. I order my lunch, then sit on a nearby bench and feed him the scraps of chicken that inevitably fall onto my lap. Reese trots seamlessly next to me, each step matching perfectly with mine. My phone rings in my pocket, and it's no surprise to me when I read the name dancing across the screen. I click the "answer" button, then lift the phone to my ear.

"You *fucked* one of your employees?!"

Typical Ruthie. No "hi," no "how are you?" I blow an elongated sigh through my pursed lips.

"Well hello to you too," I say sarcastically, but I could never be mad at Ruthie. Like Reese, she's pretty much my child too. Or *was*. She's all grown up now.

"Yeah, yeah, whatever," she says. I can practically hear her waving her hands in the air dismissively. "Details. Now."

"It…" I pause, trying to choose which details I want to include and which would be better left out. "It was a misunderstanding."

Ruthie waits a beat before answering. "So, she wasn't your employee?"

"No, she was. I just—"

"Well, you're being confusing, Vi! Just get to it!"

I don't know how exactly Ruthie grew up to be so bossy because it sure as hell didn't come from me.

"Will you stop that?" I shoot back. "It isn't funny! I could get into serious trouble if Angela finds out."

I hear a quiet babble in the background, which is probably my niece Willow. Next, a loud, "Don't touch it Willow, you're ruining it!" which would be my older niece, Tyler. Ruthie says something inaudible to her, then comes back to the phone.

"Sorry. Willow is trying to draw on top of Tyler's cat drawing. Oh-*dog. Sorry.* Does she know that?"

I furrow my brows. "What?"

"This Cam girl. Does she know about the giant stick up your boss's asshole?"

I can't stop myself from letting out a hearty laugh, then clasping a hand over my mouth, ashamed for it. Angela might be a really strict boss, but it was still mean. Mean and funny.

"I-I don't know actually."

"Well, you better figure it out. Next thing you know she's bragging about shacking up with her manager, and you're both sleeping in my backyard. I'm out of space, Vi. *No vacancy.*"

I sigh, shaking my head. "Maybe you should kick them out then," I say. "But I don't think she's going to be bragging about us anytime soon."

Ruthie ignores my comment about our parents taking up residence in her home. "That bad huh?"

"Well..." I think about what to say. It wasn't bad. Not at all. It was amazing, actually. Up until it was suddenly not happening anymore. "It was good while it lasted."

Ruthie chuckles, clicking her tongue.

"Well, that's probably normal for someone who just went through a divorce. Don't take it too hard."

"Shut the fuck up," I say.

Then, we say our goodbyes and hang up. Ruthie never says hello, but she always says goodbye.

When we arrive at the taco truck, Al already has one chicken taco and one tostada ready to go when I approach the window.

"Whatchu smiling at?" Al asks, his thick mustache like a small nest over his upper lip.

"What, I can't smile?"

I take the food from the man's outreached hands and replace it with four wrinkled dollar bills and three quarters.

"I just haven't seen it in a while." He shrugs and tosses a piece of chicken to Reese, who snaps his jowls closed around it mid-air.

"I smile all the time!"

Al shakes his head. "No. No, not like *that*." He gestures to me, as though that explains something. "Not *that* kind of smile."

"Well," I say, pinching a piece of shredded cheese between my fingers and popping it into my mouth. "I guess I'm having a pretty good week."

"Good," he responds, as he hands me a pile of napkins. "You deserve it."

Al has such a genuine demeanor about him, which is part of the reasoning behind my daily lunch routine. He knows more about my life than my parents, and he actually seems to care, even if sometimes he gets a little *too* personal.

"Hey, how'd it go with Mal?" he asks. The sound of the metal spatula scraping against the grill makes me cringe, or maybe it was the name that came out of his mouth at the same time. I can't help but scrunch my nose at it, which feels mean even though it was a biological reaction.

"Okay, okay, nevermind," he says defensively. He quickly changes the subject. "That new girl start yet?"

The mention of "the new girl" makes my stomach do a strange twist. I don't know if it has to do with the heat of the interaction, the embarrassment at being ditched, or the shock that she now works with me. Still, it's better than talking about Mallory. I consider telling Al about what happened, but there are some things that should remain unsaid. No matter how amazing those things may be.

"On Monday," I say, tucking my food into the side of my cheek while I speak. "She's kind of a mess."

"Okay," Al says with a confused, breathy laugh. "And we're smiling about that because?"

Because I had her tongue down my throat a few days ago.

"*Because* she's going to be great!" I say instead.

"You just said she was a mess."

I swallow a mouthful of crunchy tortilla and spicy green tomatillo salsa and ponder for a moment how both things can be true at the same time. Sure, I may have said it to deter from the fact that we had an... *encounter*, but that doesn't mean I'm lying.

Cam is different. She's definitely more reserved, like Avery, and maybe even a bit unfriendly at times. Messy too, given the random stains on her dress and the cute little mascara smudge. Of course, that could all be circumstantial.

I've peeked through the salon window multiple times to check on her (not to check her out, obviously), and she just looked happy. In her element. Even when I saw her struggling with a rather snappy Shih-Tzu, she controlled her emotions and took the time to gain his trust. The dog's mom was ecstatic and said every other groomer has had to muzzle him.

It's the same reason I hired Avery. You wouldn't expect this large, masculine guy to be such a softy. Yet, he knows every dog in the facility, maybe even better than I do. Not just their names, but what they like, what they don't like. How old they are, what they're allergic to. If they were rescued, rehomed, or purchased from a breeder. He even remembers to take pictures of them wearing birthday hats on their birthdays. When I offered him the assistant manager position, his only concern was that he wanted to still be able to work with the dogs.

I get the same sense of dedication and patience from Cam.

"I just know she can take it."

Al bobs his head, understanding. "Yeah, well, I don't know how y'all do it. Dogs are assholes. I can barely handle Remi."

I chuckle, taking another bite of my tostada. Al *isn't* wrong. Dogs *are* assholes, and this job isn't just playing with puppies like everyone thinks. Your day is spent in piss, shit, vomit, shit-vomit, then vomit-shit. Dogs will jump up, bite, snap, and pummel you. You have to know which dogs get along with which and who hates who.

It's a lot, but I like it enough. Well, I like the dogs. The job itself, I could do without.

"You should've thought about getting a Basset Hound or something. I told you Rotties are a lot of work."

"Whatever."

I crumple the foil wrapper into a tight ball and toss it from the bench into the garbage can, missing horribly. After getting up to throw it away properly, my fingers dip into the fabric of my front pocket, and I pull out a smooth, round black stone. I hand it to Al, who looks confused.

"What's this one? Doesn't look very *healing*." Recently, I've been teaching Al about crystals.

After he lost his daughter to cancer, I didn't see him for a really long time. When I finally noticed the little white truck parked down the block again, I went to say hi. The man was a *wreck*. He could barely speak more than a few words at a time. Frankly, it broke my heart. I'm not religious. I don't believe in God, or Satan, or any higher power at all really. But I do believe in energy.

"I mean, Einstein stated that energy cannot be created nor destroyed, so when you die, where does it go? It has to manifest somewhere," I said to Al one day, after staying up all night researching. A lot of the things I read sounded like bullshit, but when I came across the idea that energies manifest again, it made sense to me in some weird way. "Life came from the Earth, so who's to say it doesn't get recycled when it's over?"

He laughed at me when I brought it up, but I didn't mind. It was the first laugh I had heard from him in months. He took the first stone, an amethyst for healing, while still making fun of me. It only took him two weeks to ask for another. That's when I brought him a clear quartz, for clarity. Four weeks later, I gave him a Topaz for good fortune, and coincidentally (or not), his truck started to get really popular. Though he hasn't yet asked for another, I know he needs it.

"It's obsidian," I say, placing it in his palm. "It helps get rid of negative energy and releases any emotional blockages you're having."

"Sounds like you could use your own," he grunts, though he slides the rock into his pocket. I'm about to give him a snarky response when I'm interrupted by a loud chime from my back pocket. I wave goodbye to Al, then beckon Reese to my side as I pull out my phone and begin to walk back to work.

Hi Violet, it's Angela.

How is the new groomer?

Did you cut any labor this week?

Also, I want to raise prices in December.

I look around before allowing myself to see each crease in my brain as I roll my eyes. An aggravated sigh escapes my mouth. She raised prices only a few months ago, and customers were upset enough.

But of course, when you spend 80% of the year on cruise ships in other countries, there's never enough money.

The new groomer is great. I was able to cut 6 hours of labor this week.

I'm worried that raising prices again will drive people away.

6 hours isn't enough.

It won't. We're the only resort in a 45-minute radius, they'll pay whatever we ask for.

Raise it by 2% and cut more hours next week please.

Yes ma'am.

I slide my phone back into my pocket, letting out an exasperated sigh. Angela has always been this way. Greedy. Demanding. Immoral. But that's what it takes to run a business, right?

I settle my annoyance by forcing a smile, even though nobody is around to see it. The walk back to Furry Friends Pet Resort brightens my mood. Martha greets me eagerly upon my arrival.

"Hey Vi! How was your break?"

I know it's just a formality, but that's what makes Martha's customer service so great. She knows exactly how to make people feel like she's *actually* interested.

You mean how was the pushy phone call from my sister or the greedy texts from our insufferable boss?

"It was good! I'm going to take Reese back, then I'll swap you."

Martha couldn't really handle the stress of being a kennel tech, but the customers loved her, so now, she mostly just answers phone calls and schedules appointments. I didn't mind keeping her on because, even though I'm the manager, I *hate* customer service.

I would rather spend my day in the grossness of the dogs, watching their body language and scooping poop than answer a single phone call. It's what I miss most about dog training. Ruthie's friend runs a training business in Clarkston. When I lived there, I would train dogs while they boarded at my house. I don't miss being tied to my house all the time, but I do miss the rest of it. I miss understanding every aspect of my job. I miss teaching dogs how to sit and settle and heel. I miss building a connection with them.

I understand dogs. I do *not* understand people. They always seem to get upset over the most mundane things, and their words and body language rarely match. I'm never sure which thing to trust. Dogs, on the other hand, wear everything on their sleeves. If they're stressed, or happy, or nervous, or angry, you *will* know. Even though some people have trouble reading them, to me, they're straightforward.

"Sure thing, Vi," Martha says, shuffling a stack of papers around on the desk.

I beckon Reese to my side and lean down to pet him as we walk through the swinging door to the back. I look down at the dirty residue left on my palms.

"Ew, Reese. You're disgusting," I say, wiping my hands on my jeans. That is the one and only thing Mallory ever did for Reese. I always took care of all the vet appointments, nail trims, and ear cleanings, but Mallory took him to get a bath every three weeks. With everything going on, it's the one thing I've let slide. I wonder if Cam has any extra time.

I peek through the salon window at the frizzy-haired woman, who's brushing out a small white poodle. Despite her overall abrasiveness, she really is gentle with the dogs.

I knock on the frame twice before stepping into the fur-filled room. Cam's head snaps up, her eyes wide and her chest tight, like she's trapping the air inside her lungs. I think she's scared I'm going to bring it up, but I think we both know the best way to navigate the situation is to pretend it never happened at all. Still, it isn't easy. Every time I see her, I just wonder what it would have been like if she'd let me finish the job.

"How's it going in here?" I ask, trying to find a good segway for "do you have time to bathe my dog?"

Before answering, Cam smiles. Like, *really* smiles, and it catches me completely off guard. She had given me a few upturned twitches before, but this is a *smile*. Straight, white teeth shine through her pink lips, and the smallest dimple on her right cheek reminds me that dimples *exist*.

Her attractiveness isn't news to me. How do you think we ended up in the bathroom together? But this dimple? This dimple *is* news. It's small and deep and placed at just the right spot to have me recounting the events that led to her disappearance, wondering what exactly I did to make her leave.

Of course, now we know it was for the best. But trying to look at someone you've kissed like you haven't kissed them feels impossible.

"It's great," she says. Her gentle voice doesn't stutter. For the first time, I think, her tone matches her warm appearance. I wonder if the Ice Princess is still somewhere inside. "I really love it here, and Eddie's being a pretty good boy."

That dimple consumes me. I can't help but smile back. Not a forced Sunny smile, but a *real* one. The kind that makes my cheeks burn.

"Great! I'm glad you're liking it. Everyone's being nice to you?"

I try to think of the questions I've asked other employees, making it a point to prove to myself that this one is no different. I think part of me is buying it, but most of me isn't.

"Everyone is great," she responds. Tufts of fur stick to her messy, dirty-blonde ponytail, and her eyes are a deep, dark gradient, like a brown agate. I'll have to research later on what brown agate is supposed to do. I nod, looking down at Reese, then remember my reason for coming in here in the first place.

"Are you super busy?" I ask. Cam lets out a short laugh, gesturing to the dog on her table. I smile. "I mean your schedule. Is it super full?"

"Not really," she shrugs, gliding a metal comb through the poodle's thick hair. I gesture toward Reese, grinning sheepishly.

"Want one more?"

Cam nods, and that stupid contagious dimple returns. "Sure."

I lean down and unclip Reese's collar to let him loose into the salon. He stays attached to my ankle.

"He's not a fan of people, especially people he doesn't know. But he won't bite or anything. He'll just stand all stiff and uncomfortable."

"Same," Cam mutters. She looks embarrassed when she realizes I heard her say it, but it entices a hearty laugh out of me.

The Ice Princess is *definitely* still there.

SEVEN

Citrus Soap

CAM

"**H**AS THERE BEEN ANY movement on this... *Violet* scenario?"[4]

Dr. Burton's cheery face fills the screen of my laptop. In my not-so-humble opinion, it's *too* cheery for this particular topic of conversation.

"No," I shrug, an uneasy tension settling in the pit of my stomach, "I think there's a mutual understanding that we'll just pretend it never happened."

Dr. Burton nods, scratching his chin. "Have you given more thought to quitting then?"

The most subtle smile creeps across his face, and it irritates me knowing that, when he said I should wait a bit longer before resigning during our last session, he was completely right. I *hate* it when he's right. My teeth sink into my lower lip irately as I suck in a steady stream of air.

"I'm not going to quit," I say, watching as that subtle smile turns broad.

"And you're content with that decision?"

I don't even have to think about my response. I am completely and utterly in love with the salon.

"*Very.*"

"Good, good. And what about operation... What was it? *ADHD*? Is that still going?"

My cheeks grow pink as I stifle my laugh, holding up a finger to correct him.

"*A.D.D.*, and *no*. I don't think we're going back to that for a very long time."

Dr. Burton scribbles something on the little blue notepad in front of him, and it takes everything in me not to ask what it is.

"That's understandable," he says, clicking his pen once. "Is this because of Violet? Or are there other outliers influencing your decision?"

I know what Dr. Burton is trying to get at when he mentions *"other outliers."* But this has *nothing* to do with that. This isn't fear of change or of having an unattached hookup anymore. It's just about the fact that everything that could have gone wrong in that situation, *did*.

"Just Violet," I answer definitively. Dr. Burton raises a bushy eyebrow but doesn't press any further. Thankfully, he changes the subject. "If you're willing, I would like to check in about the nightmares. Does the Prozac seem to be mitigating that?"

I hate this subject so much that I almost wish he would go back to talking about my failed bar bathroom boss hookup. *Almost.*

I don't think I've had a good night's sleep in the last five years. The issue doesn't lie with going to sleep. I can fall into a comatose-like state only moments after lying down. My issue lies in the fact that, while my body is unable to move and my eyes are unable to open, my brain decides to trap me with flashing montages of every terrible thing that could ever happen. Food poisoning, public speaking, cars crushed into tiny, unrecognizable pieces of metal.

The Prozac is supposed to help with that.

Unfortunately, I wouldn't know if it's working or not because I accidentally forgot it exists. My lips roll inward, which I know is all too telling.

"Cam, we've talked about this. You need to actually *use* these tools to see if they'll help. Doing nothing will *do nothing*."

I wave him off, even though he has a *very* valid point. "I know, I know. I'll try and start it tonight. I just…what if I'm allergic to it or something?"

A soft sigh slips through his lips, and he looks at the camera, which is the virtual therapy version of eye contact.

"Well, you haven't been allergic to any other medication you've taken, and most have a similar compound. So, I don't think that's something that needs to be considered."

My brows knit together. "But it's in The Realm."

The Realm of Likely Possibilities, or just *The Realm*, is a term Dr. Burton uses to separate *likely* scenarios from *unlikely* scenarios. While unlikely scenarios are still possible, they aren't probable. I don't really understand it. To me, if anything is possible, it is likely to happen. Dr. Burton shakes his head.

"Fortunately," he says, fidgeting with the pen in his hand. "It is not." I personally fail to see that, but okay, *Doctor*. "I'll see you next week?"

I nod, as if that ever changes. "See you then."*

I THINK THIS PLACE was made for me. Or maybe I was made for it. Since the Furry Friends salon is a one-woman operation, I'm allowed to do things *my* way. The freedom feels good.

When The Dog Shop first hired me as a trainee, I couldn't have been more ecstatic. The thought of helping dogs as a career was everything I could ever want.

Although I've never excelled at painting or drawing like Adrian, I love art, and this is a niche form. Like humans, I believe each dog has a specific look. I'd spend hours carving different hairstyles into different dogs to match their personalities. Some were meant to look like teddy bears, others like elderly men who smoke cigars and read newspapers. I even made a Pomeranian look like a member of the band *KISS*.

But it wasn't just the art that I fell in love with, it was the neglected dogs too. Some pups would come in with fur pelted to their skin. I can't even count how many flea baths I gave in the summer. Dogs' nails would curl into the pads of their paws, breaking the flesh. I had the opportunity to help those dogs, and to show them love.

But after months of learning, practicing, and experimenting, management began to crack down. Once I had the necessary knowledge for the position, I was indebted to the company, forced to work long hours with short breaks. Each day consisted of various Catch-22s: Take a lunch break, or finish the dog on time? Upset the customer by going too short, or potentially nick the pup trying to cut through the mats? Get unapproved overtime, or give a choppy haircut?

Even as a strict-rule follower, there was no way I could follow every rule at once.

At first, I thought I was beginning to hate it. But it didn't take long to realize that I didn't hate my *job*. I hated my employer. I actually loved my job.

Pine Paws Animal Sanctuary partnered with the location to provide full grooms for the animals in their care. Knowing I was helping them made me feel like I was doing some good for the world. I couldn't get that same sense of accomplishment from answering phone calls or serving food. Not to mention, working with dogs meant my hours were spent with canines instead of people, which obviously is a win on its own.

Although I don't own it, the salon at Furry Friends feels like mine. I get to make my own rules, using the equipment I like and the techniques I find safe.

My knees bend, squatting behind a large Bernese Mountain Dog as I place my hands under his hips and lift his back end into the stainless-steel tub.

"You should learn to ask for help, or you're going to break your back."

I jump back, startled by the familiar voice. Something about the coarseness of it melting with an angelic tone manages to seep into every wrinkle in my brain. I turn around to see Violet standing against the wall behind me, her bottom lip tucked between her teeth and her arms crossed. Her eyes dart from the floor to my face. For a moment, I think she may have been checking me out. But the thought quickly leaves when I remind myself where we are, and who she is.

In truth, I've been trying to avoid her these past two weeks. If she were going to bring up Monsey's she would have by now; I know that. But that doesn't eliminate the embarrassment of the situation. It doesn't fix the twist in my stomach every time I see her walking through the facility, or the annoying pulse between my thighs every time those tattooed arms flex. I didn't just hook up with my boss. I had a *failed* hookup with my boss. And somehow, that is so much worse.

"You should learn not to sneak up on people," I reply. Violet lets out a quiet chuckle as she approaches the tub. Her hand presses to the dog's head.

"Are you being a good boy, Leo?" She ruffles the feathers behind the dog's ears, his humorously long tongue hanging out the side of his mouth. I turn the water on and tediously adjust the handles to ensure it's the proper temperature. Violet continues loving on Leo as she leans against the metal bath.

"What are you doing?" I ask suspiciously. Violet has been, at least I thought, avoiding me too. I've noticed it: the quick glances through the window and the awkward hesitation before she checks in on the dogs in the salon. I don't know whether to be grateful for it or to simply let the humiliation consume me.

"I'm the manager." Violet's head tilts ever so slightly. "Am I not allowed to check in on my employees?" Her tone is so serious, but there's a hint of a smirk tugging at the corners of her mouth.

"*Technically,*" I say, moving the hose up and down Leo's body. Water flows over his thick black coat. "I'm an independent contractor."

Violet arches one of her perfect, pierced eyebrows, and her subtle smirk grows.

"But *no,*" I add quickly, remembering that, regardless of the title, she has every authority to fire me. "No, you're definitely allowed to."

"Oh, well." She bends down, stretching out her arms, and I realize she is displaying an invisible curtsey, "If you say so."

Trying not to roll my eyes, I use my hands to glide through the layers, making sure each section of the fur is soaked. After briefly scanning my options, I grab a white bottle of shed-control shampoo. Winter coats are making their appearance, leaving the forgotten summer coats behind. Violet stands at the edge of the tub and watches, making me nervous this is some kind of test. I pump a generous amount of the clear, gelatinous substance into my hand, the aroma of citrus radiating from my palm, and do my very best to ignore her presence.

My fingers run through the dog's coat, fingertips softly brushing against his skin as I scrub him. Violet clears her throat.

"So, Lana's dad called and wants to know if you have room for another bath today. His wife is coming home from the hospital, and he wants to surprise her. I said I'd call him to let him know."

How do you say no to that?

"Lana...?" My mind shuffles through mental flashcards, failing to find one referencing the name "Lana."

"Yellow lab, about fifty-ish pounds, really sweet, light's-on-but-no-body's-home. I think she jumped on you in the lobby yesterday morning."

Why does she remember that?

"*Oh!* Lana! Uh..."

A loud clinking sound bellows from the tub, metal against metal. Our eyes dart to Leo, who has decided to vigorously shake his entire body. We try to shield ourselves from the wave, but it's too late. Warm soapy water washes over us in a wet surge.

"Leo!" Violet whines, using her sleeve to wipe suds off her face. She shakes her hands out, droplets flying in every direction, then looks up at me with an amused grin. "Well, I guess we're even then."

I think she's just as shocked about her comment as I am, because the second it leaves her mouth, the whites of her eyes go round and face grows red, her jaw snapping shut. Heat rushes to my cheeks, and I swear I could start to liquefy. I open my mouth, but I have no idea why. I have nothing to say.

If I acknowledge the comment, then we both recognize the situation. And if we both recognize the situation, that means it's real. And I'd like to keep pretending that it didn't happen. My lips press together in a flat, dissatisfied line. Violet's lips part again as she clicks her tongue awkwardly. I swear to God she is scared of silence.

"So...Lana?" she asks, scratching the back of her head.

"Right! Uh..." I continue to scrub Leo, my face itching from the suds still soaking into my cheeks. I scrunch my nose repeatedly, attempting to soothe the irritating sensation, but to no avail. My cheek lifts as I squint my left eye. I probably look ridiculous, but it doesn't matter. "Yeah, I should be able to swing that. ETA?"

Scrunch.

"He said he'd be back just before closing."

"Sounds good."

Scrunch.

"Are you okay?"

"Yeah, no I'm good, I just—"

Scrunch.

"I just have an itch and my hands are covered with soap."

A light laugh slips through her lips, and her eyes draw to mine. "Where?"

I close my left eye, bringing the joining cheek up as I squint. "This cheek," I reply desperately, as the itch intensifies.

Violet's hand reaches out toward my face. I remember how her fingers felt against my skin, dry and calloused, but also gentle and skilled. It's obvious that she puts them to work each day, the proof in the wear. I find that charming.

Violet's fingertip curls gently over my cheek, and her eyes move up to share a gaze with me.

"Did I get it?" She smiles, her eyes still locked on mine as her fingertip rests gently on my cheek. My stomach feels hot and fluttery, and I really need her to stop touching me. I swallow.

"Yup."

Her hand pulls away quickly, and air slowly seeps back into my lungs.

"Alright, well I'm going to go call Lana's dad," she says. "Thanks!"

With that, Violet promptly turns and walks out of the salon.

EIGHT

Monetized Friendship

VIOLET

"**Y**OU WANT TO CORRECT that." I take the leash from Hayden's hands, tugging upward slightly so that the perfectly white dog attached to the other end looks me in the eye. "Sniffing things will get you an *immediate* failure on the public access test."

He gives me a charming grin.

"I know," he says, holding his hand out. I place the leash back into his palm, and his long, thick fingers tighten around it. "Major's just *really* curious. Do you think he's going to make it?"

Hayden's voice heightens as the question slips out, his brows sewn together in worry.

When Adrian overheard that I used to be a dog trainer, they asked if I'd be willing to take on their friend Hayden as a client. Even though I already had enough to deal with at the time—my impending divorce, and fifty-hour weeks running a pet resort while Angela vacations in Thailand (and Hawaii, and Costa Rica)—I figured it would be good for me to do something I love, especially if I'm getting paid for it.

I've thought about it, starting my own training business. But I can't imagine the demand in Greenrock is high enough, and besides, I don't want to end up like Angela. If you have to turn into a total monster to live off your business, I don't want anything to do with it.

Still, working with Hayden makes the idea seem possible, sometimes. He's the perfect client. He only wants private sessions, and everything I say to him sticks in his brain. He works with Major for hours between appointments and tracks his improvement in some goal app. Even though I've volunteered to train the world's most stubborn poodle to be a medical alert service dog, every moment is enjoyable because of him. I'm not sure if it's his dedication, his personality, or a mix of both, but Hayden is just a pleasant guy to be around. And next to Al, he's the closest thing I have to a friend. Even though it's through hourly payment.

It's not like I'm bad at making friends. I'm great at it, actually. I'm great at being other people's friends that is. The part where you actually let others know things about you? That part I suck at. But to give credit where it's due, Hayden sure does try.

I look down at Major, who is still staring at me with laser-like focus. His pupils dilate, his eyes fixated on the meaty treat in my hand. The white top knot on his head has grown out some since I saw him last, and it's beginning to hang over his eyes.

"He's kind of a dick," I say, giving him his well-earned reward. "But he's going to make it. Maybe he's not listening because he can't *see*."

"Yeah, I know. He's got an appointment scheduled with Cam soon. How's she doing by the way?"

The concern in Hayden's voice seems to have eased, his fingers gliding through the mound of white fluff on Major's head. Hearing Cam's name come from his mouth catches me off-guard. I don't know why, but every time I think about her, I start to feel... overheated.

Well, maybe I *do* know why.

Maybe, it's because of the fact that I know what her tongue feels like inside my mouth. I know all about the curve of her waist beneath my fingertips. Maybe it's because I've had to pretend it never happened while simultaneously not being able to get it off my mind. It's been a long time since I've touched anyone in that way, or even looked at them, and though Cam is completely off the table, there's no rule saying I can't reminisce on the interaction. So long as I don't let another stupid sentence slip out of my mouth.

"She's good." I shrug.

Hayden looks up at me, the cool beam from the fluorescent store lights making his indigo eyes shimmer. That charming smile returns to his face.

"Look, I know you're a pretty *private* person. But with the whole Mallory thing—" I cringe at her name. "Sorry, with the whole... you know... *divorce* and stuff... it's just really important to have friends to support you."

I furrow my brows. "What makes you think I have no friends?"

"Listen, Vi, I'm just worried about you. I'm pretty sure I'm like the *only* person you talk to, and I know I'm amazing—"

A prickly heat flushes in my cheeks, defensiveness taking over me.

"I talk to other people!" I attest, like by "other people" I don't mean the occasional conversation with Ruthie or Al.

"You need other people too. And I think you and Cam could really hit it off. You two, like, need each other. You know, she also got chea—"

I don't need to hear any more of this. I don't *want* to hear any more of this. Cam is an employee, and it's better we don't even consider crossing that line. *Again*. I'm doing just fine on my own, and besides, I don't need anyone else thinking there's more to it.

"Thanks, but no thanks."

I keep walking forward, pretending to look at the different tubes of deodorant lining the aisle, so I don't have to look at Hayden. He follows next to me, and Major trots seamlessly beside us, focusing his attention on his handler. Hayden shrugs.

"Okay. Not going to force it. But, think about it," he says, continuing to the end of the aisle.

Truthfully, these bi-weekly training sessions have been my motive lately, the thing I look forward to.

Getting to hang out with Hayden and develop a dog that can save his life always makes me feel better about my own. I've considered asking him to hangout outside of the sessions, but I'm not sure how to go about it. Plus, I can't help but be wary of how things will end.

I didn't realize I was friendless until Mallory and I split. Everyone I called a "friend" happened to be Mallory's friend first, so there wasn't anyone to run to when I found a string of texts describing the seemingly *mind-blowing* sex she had with one of her clients.

Apparently a six-session hip-hop package included a *Free Fuck* coupon. They didn't just take Mallory's side; they chastised me for telling her to leave the house. The house that *I* pay for.

Discovering all of my friends weren't really mine was a big blow, until I realized it actually wasn't. It occurred to me, after the initial shock of their two-faced cruelty, that I had never actually opened up to them anyway. I spoke about my job, and Mallory, and the trails I wanted to hike that month, and I called them my "friends," but I never actually *talked* to them. Not about things that mattered. And that wasn't a choice *they* made. It was mine.

I watch Major intently as the white poodle parades around the bakery section. He's *brilliant*, and his only weakness so far seems to be food. I've gotten him to ignore cats, birds, children, and even sirens. At nine months, he has already learned to alert when his handler's heart rate increases too rapidly. But when Major smells anything that could be even a little bit edible, his nose goes *wild*.

Today, however, he seems to be doing well. The leash is loose, and his front feet are parallel with Hayden's, his eyes fixated on the man. Hayden grins from across the table of baked goods between them and gives me a cheesy thumbs up. I return the gesture and walk further away from the duo to give them space. I'm not *training* Major. I'm training *Hayden* to train Major.

Consequently, hovering will only stunt their growth as a team. I step in when and where I need to and let Hayden take the reins. It's *his* service dog, after all.

Major's nose twitches, different scents of flour and almond and sugar wafting into his nose, but he never breaks his gaze from Hayden. They loop around the section three more times before approaching the corner I've been lingering in, pretending not to stare.

"Did you see that?!" Hayden asks excitedly. If he were any happier, he might bounce off the walls. I can't help but let a smile take control of my face. I've really missed this. The adrenaline people get when their dogs accomplish things they didn't think they could.

"Yes. It was pretty dang good."

"Do you think he'll be ready for his PA test in December?"

I ruffle my hands through Major's top knot. "I do."

Nine

No Calm, Just Storm

Cam

"YOU'VE GOT TO BE fucking kidding me!"

My palm slams against the wooden steering wheel of my absolutely *ancient* car. Heavy drops of rain pound against the moonroof like someone is pouring a thousand marbles on the glass. Each one makes a loud *thunk* as it lands and then dissolves into small puddles on the window above me. You would think its midnight, given the dark, dull sky. Black clouds surround me, the late October wind whistling like a forgotten teapot.

"Come on Luigi," I plead. "Don't give up on me now!"

I press the brake pedal down harder, turning the keys one last time, as if the pressure of my foot will magically revive the ignition. But my desperation has no enticing factor to it, and he remains still and silent.

While being stranded in your work's parking lot in a Pacific Northwest storm sucks, I have to be at least a little grateful that it's rain and not snow.

I pop the hood, droplets pelting my cheeks relentlessly as I try to connect the cables of the portable jump starter I found in my trunk to the car's battery.

How does it go again? Red to Neg?

The rain soaks into my clothes as I stare blankly at the cables in my hand. I've never actually had to use these before. Not by myself, at least.

It's definitely Red to Neg... right?

I hook them up, looking at them for a moment before nodding to myself as if to say *"Yes, Cam. Looks great."* My fingers hover over the little black button, ready to turn on the battery.

"I wouldn't do that if I were you, Sparky!"

I look up, squinting through the heavy rainfall, and my eyes adjust onto

Violet. Her arm shields her eyes from the thick falling droplets as she approaches me.

"You've got it backwards," she says. I stare down at the wires.

I could have sworn it was Red to Neg.

"Oh," I mumble, embarrassed that my boss was seconds away from watching me possibly cause an explosion in the middle of the parking lot. Or whatever happens when you do it wrong. "Thanks."

I unclip the clamps, swapping their positions, and look back at her for approval. She nods, and I hold down the black button on the battery, waiting for the light on the side to shine a luminescent cherry red. Nothing happens. I press it again.

"Do you want some help?"

"No," I say. I've already humiliated myself enough. I press the button again.

"Are you *sure*?"

I press it again.

"Yeah. I just think maybe—" I press it again. "I think it's dead. But I'm fine."

I try to say this in a tone that comes off grateful for her assistance, but simultaneously tells her to please leave me alone. I think I'd rather be stranded in the rain with a dead battery than ask Violet Wolfe for help.

"I can call Hayden."

Violet frowns, standing directly in front of me now with an unconvinced expression on her face. "Doesn't he live like, thirty minutes away?"

Shit. I forgot she knows exactly who Hayden is.

"Twenty-eight," I mumble, but she's already walking toward her obnoxiously large Jeep. The flooded rain sloshes underneath her off-road tires, and I have to step back to avoid getting splashed when she pulls up in front of me. She hops out, grabs a pair of jumper cables from her back seat, and attaches them *properly* between her car and Luigi.

"I'm going to start my car, but wait a minute to start yours, okay?" she says. I have no choice but to comply.

I grab a towel from the floorboard and drape it over the driver's seat before climbing inside. My father would roll over in his *grave* if I sat on the leather soaking wet. Dawson whines in the back seat, scratching against the barricading seat cover. After a minute, Violet flashes her headlights, and I turn the key in the ignition, completely blind.

Violet might be a little cocksure, but I didn't take her for the obnoxiously-bright LED headlights type of person.

Nothing happens, so I twist the key again. Still, nothing from Luigi. Violet hops out of the Jeep, mud splashing up the legs of her jeans as she steps into a puddle. She doesn't seem to care. Reluctantly, I climb out of the dry safety of my own car.

"We can try letting it charge up for a few more minutes," she says, leaning forward to peek under the popped hood. Her eyebrows shoot up, and her gaze flicks over to me, her jaw slack.

My brows drop over my narrowing eyes.

"What?" I ask. Violet shakes her head.

"Dude. Your battery is like, *completely* corroded." She tilts her head, examining it closer. "How did you even make it to work this morning?"

I know I should probably feel embarrassed, but the only emotion running through my veins right now is defensiveness. It isn't Luigi's fault that his battery is older than me.

I cross my arms over my chest. "I *drove* just fine."

"Just *barely*." She points at a spot on the battery, and then another, and then another. "That's a hazard, Sparks."

I scowl at the repetitive nickname, and Violet turns around, climbing into her driver's seat.

"Wait, what are you doing?" I ask, stomping over to follow her.

"I'm turning off my car. We *cannot* jump start that thing."

A stream of air huffs out of my nostrils.

"What? But I can't just—"

Violet's eyes lock onto mine, her gaze holding me hostage. I squirm uncomfortably, but for some reason, it works.

"Cam, this car is currently undrivable. I'm sorry, but you need someone who knows what they're doing to come replace the battery." She pats the passenger seat, and I swear a puff of dust flies out of it. Not that I'm really in the place to judge the condition of a car. "Hop in. I'll give you a ride home."

I step back from the door, my wet hair rubbing against the back of my neck in a way that drives me crazy. I shake my head.

"I can't. I have Dawson in the car and—"

"Awesome! Reese will have a buddy." She tosses her head to the side. "Get in."

This feels like an absolutely terrible idea. "It's okay. I'll just text Avery. He can—"

"What is this? Stranger danger or something?" Violet hops down, back out of the warm comfort of her car, into the pouring rain. "Look. I'm not going to force you, but I'm also not going to go anywhere until I know you have a safe ride home." She eyes Luigi for a second, then adjusts her gaze back onto me. "I wouldn't put it past someone as stubborn as you to try fixing something you shouldn't."

I want to ask her what exactly she means by "someone as stubborn as" me. But I can't seem to get my vocal cords to tighten in the way they need to get a single sound out. Besides, I'm starting to think that Violet Wolfe is not the type of person you just "say no" to.

I still scowl at her, because how dare she, before I stomp over to my car and practically rip off the handle of the back door. Dawson hops out wearily, crouching as he walks like it will aid him in avoiding the rain. Violet doesn't even try to hide her smirk, and it only makes me more irritated.

"You might look into getting a new car soon," she says, just as I close the Jeep's heavy door behind me. I shoot her a glare and toss my phone, mapped to my address, onto her lap.

"You might look into minding your business for once."

Violet laughs quietly to herself, and I immediately feel bad for snapping, even if she kind of deserved it. Maybe "deserved" is the wrong word, but *nobody* gets to shit-talk Luigi. She pulls onto the road, and I'm just about to apologize when she starts to speak.

"I'm sorry, I just, I have to ask. Are you this *nice* to everyone, or just people you make out with in bar bathrooms?"

I swear every blood cell in my body has rushed to the tops of my cheeks. I don't need to look into a mirror to know they are bright red. I suck in a breath.

"Do you make out with everyone in bar bathrooms, or just people whose dresses you spill margaritas on?"

I expect something from Violet. A blush or a frown. Maybe a dissatisfied glance. What I don't expect is the corner of her lip to twitch upwards, as she adjusts her rearview mirror that I know needs no adjusting.

She waits a beat before replying. "No," she says finally. "Just you."

I slump back into my seat silently. Not by choice. I just can't find the words to express to this woman how badly she's getting on my nerves. Especially because I *planned* to apologize.

"Look," I say, sucking in a shaky breath. If there is any time to address this thing, it may as well be now. "I know about the policy, the no-fraternization or whatever. So, I'm cool with pretending nothing happened. I'd prefer it, actually."

Violet doesn't look at me, but she nods in acknowledgement, tapping the steering wheel with her fingertips like she's listening to an imaginary song.

"Okay," she says after a moment. "Me too."

"Great."

"Great."

It's almost the same type of relief I felt when I quit The Dog Shop. Like I just put in my two weeks' notice of never talking about that night at Monsey's again. Except this one is more immediate, which makes it even better.

Rain drops pelt the windows as Violet steers down the winding roads. I love the way it sounds, now that I'm not trapped inside my own car pleading for it to start. The sound is soothing and rhythmic, a song created by the clouds. As we make the final turn onto Jadewood Lane, Violet clears her throat, and all the little blonde hairs on my body stand straight up.

"Can I ask you something?" she asks, her voice soft. "I promise it'll be the last time I bring it up."

I feel my stomach twist, forming a pretzel inside of my body. Whatever it is,

I don't want to know. I don't want to have to answer it. But the promise of her never bringing it up again afterwards is tempting, and I have a feeling that, if I don't say yes, this question will come knocking at my door in a few weeks.

I may as well get it over with.

I nod, and Violet looks over at me before redirecting her focus onto the road.

"Why did you bail that night? Did I—" She scratches her neck. "Did I *do* something?"

Oh.

The question hits me like a bus. I was expecting her to ask why. I was bracing myself for it, actually. On the road to creating an actual, *valid* excuse. But I wasn't expecting her to think she played any role in it. If anything, I was simply expecting her to make fun of me.

I swallow, hard. My throat is so dry that I'm tempted to stick my tongue out the window to catch droplets of rain in my mouth. Violet pulls into the apartment complex, sliding the shifter into "Park." Both of our bodies rock forward, then backwards gently from the change of gear. She turns to me, tucking a strand of dark, wet hair behind her ear. My lower lip is raw between my teeth, and I take another shuddering breath.

"I—" My voice is squeaky and high, and I clear my throat, embarrassed. "*No.* Not at all," I say earnestly. "You—" I let my eyes travel up slowly, until they finally land onto hers. Those gentle, yet powerful, kinetic hazel eyes. "I had a good time with you, a *great* time actually. And you didn't do anything wrong. It was the opposite, actually. I—" My words get caught in my throat again, not ready to be spoken aloud. I try again, but still nothing. I'm an honest person. I think the truth is more important than just about anything. But for some reason, it simply won't come out. "I got startled by the woman knocking on the door. It just, it kind of freaked me out, and I panicked. I'm sorry."

It's not the most flattering excuse, but it's half-true, and still better than "I've never had sex with a woman and was scared I'd get attached to you." I wait to see that taunting smirk return to her face. Even just a flicker of amusement dancing across those eyes. But it never comes. Violet just smiles at me through those thick pierced lips, and I swear my heart is vibrating in my chest.

"You don't need to apologize," she says softly, her fingers gently brushing across the top of my hand. My breath hitches, and I feel as if I'm frozen in time. My eyes flick up, looking back into hers. We aren't saying anything, but somehow, I can't hear the rain anymore. I can't hear anything but the quiet breaths coming from Violet's lips.

Those soft, thick, round lips that I hate to admit make me ache when I think about them. When I think about that night and how it could have ended. I know it's outside The Realm of Likely Possibilities. Hell, it should be outside of the realm of *desired* possibilities. But no matter how hard I try, staring down at them now, remembering the sharp pressure of her lip piercing against my jaw, I can't force myself to wish it never happened. In fact, I wish it was happening again right now.

"I should go," I say softly, my gaze darting from her lips to the door handle suddenly gripped in my hand. "Thank you, for the ride."

This is the opposite of what I want to say. The opposite of what I want to do. A massive contradiction to the words dancing on the tip of my tongue, the gravitational pull I feel from her body to mine. But that's what I do best, I think: turn into a helpless deer that sprints away at the slightest scent of danger.

Violet nods, pulling her hand away.

"Okay well, let me know if you need a ride tomorrow?"

I hop out of the car, the thundering sound of pattering rain flooding back into my senses. Wet droplets run down my face, my damp hair sticking to my cheeks in a way that makes me itch.

"Sure," I say. "Okay."

Dawson jumps through the passenger door behind me, and I close it, turning away without another look back.

Ten

Novemberween

Violet

I OPEN THE LAST suite in the aisle and poke my head inside to see Murphy, a dark brown Newfoundland, fast asleep on his sofa-shaped bed. Then, I step back and twist the latch to secure it shut.

Furry Friends feels kind of eerie after closing, but not in a haunted type of way. It's just so distinctly opposite to how it feels during the day, or even in the mornings as we prepare to open. Usually, it's loud and lively. Barks echo throughout the building in a way that can become overwhelming at times, dogs voicing their excitement to eat breakfast and be let out of their rooms. Even when they're all in their playgroups, there's light and sound and motion. But in the evening, when everyone has eaten and they're all exhausted from the hours of stimulation, all you can hear are slight snores from some of the brachycephalic pups.

I stay after hours rather frequently these days. It's a lot easier to get some of the smaller, more tedious things done then, like cleaning the air vents, scrubbing out the shop vac, or restocking supplies, which is what I'm doing now. Another upside is that I don't have to be stuck in my house alone. I'd rather be alone here than be reminded of why I'm alone there. With either option, after six-thirty PM, I will always be given the silence needed to let my brain go haywire. I really try not to give in to that silence.

Usually, I'm good at it. I just keep myself busy, keep talking to people and letting my brain fill with useless information so it runs out of space to think about anything important. It's how I can stay calm, no matter how bad the situation is. I just distract myself, or I let others distract me for me. Even when I found out Mallory had been cheating, I didn't yell or scream or cry. I simply turned on the TV and asked her to leave. After a little pushback, she did.

But Cameron Miller doesn't believe in "a little" pushback. In fact, the only "little" thing about her is her height.

She has a big attitude, a bigger ass, and a giant map to my fucking buttons. She has to, because she managed to press just the right ones to get me to open my mouth and say something I shouldn't have.

And now, she won't even look at me.

That was normal, in the beginning. It was easier to pretend nothing happened if we silently agreed to avoid one another. But I couldn't avoid her forever, I knew that. So, I started coming around, and Cam started letting me.

But then she pushed me to open my mouth, and now, we're starting over. That's how it seems, at least. And I guess, really, I can't blame it entirely on her. She may have pushed me to make a snarky comment about that night at Monsey's, but I asked why she left all on my own. It was a question begging to be answered. I considered going back to the bar and trying again. But I couldn't do that without knowing what I did wrong the first time.

Or I guess now, what I didn't.

Still, I can't help but feel gross. Like Cam's avoiding me because I made her uncomfortable. She'd have every reason to feel that way. It doesn't matter what buttons she was pressing. I shouldn't have said it. Any of it.

After peeling plastic grocery bags off the gallons of KennelSol I asked Avery to pick up earlier in the day, I place them tidily on the rickety wire shelves in the storage room. The metal clangs as the heavy bottles drag against the wires, and I form neat rows of chemicals.

Usually, I would just toss them onto the shelf and be done with it. But it's hard once it starts, silencing your thoughts. The ones that make you wonder why you ever thought you could have a one-night stand in the first place. My gaze darts over to the door when a loud chime pierces the silence. Then another. Then another.

I know that sound. That's the sound of the supply closet being unlocked from the outside.

I'm not usually one to get scared of things like this, but that's *too* fucking creepy. Nobody else should be here right now, and—

Beep.

That's the last tone in the sequence. The lock clicks, and the door handle slowly turns downward. My heart pounds inside of my chest so hard I can hear it, but my hands stay steady. Instinctively, I grab the first weapon I can find.

A broken mop handle.

The door creaks open, and I'm ready to pounce when the woman in front of me lets out the loudest, most ear-piercing scream I have ever heard in my entire life.

Oh. Wait. That was me.

Cam jumps back, completely startled as she clutches her chest. She breathes out slowly when she recognizes me. Then, she bursts into side-aching laughter.

"Fuck!"

My head collapses into my hands, my chest heaving as I squeeze my temples, eyes clamped shut. Cam continues laughing and even though I've been curious as to what her laughter sounds like, I can't find any humor in the situation at this moment in time.

"It isn't funny," I bark, letting out a controlled breath. My eyes dart up to Cam, and now, she's biting her lip hard, which I think is her best attempt to hold in her laughter.

She looks so cute, her cheeks all red and her eyes teary. That stupid fucking dimple makes its way to the corner of her mouth, and I swear it exists just to taunt me. The laughter bursts back out of her like a flame, but this time, the tension in my body eases, and I start shaking my head, laughing along with her.

"You scared the shit out of me," I say, letting my body ease into the final stages of relaxation. Cam's eyebrows shoot up.

"*You* were scared? You were about to stab me with a mop handle!"

I grimace, clicking my tongue to the roof of my mouth. "Well, *yeah*! I mean—" I gesture to the room around us. "I thought I was the only one here! We closed like, an hour ago."

Cam leans against the wall, tilting her head as she listens to my excuses as to why I was fully planning to fight Michael Myers in the Furry Friends storage closet.

"I had a lot of cleaning to do," she explains. "I haven't done a deep clean this week, and *you guys*," she points a finger to the center of my chest, "don't have any vent circulation in there. So all the hair just *sticks to the walls.*"

"Oh *well*." I put my hands up like a sarcastic surrender. "Let me just hop right on that."

The words come out satirical, but I actually *do* want to "hop right on that," if it's causing an issue for her. I want Cam to be happy here. She does an amazing job, and even though she never interacts with the customers, they all rave about how much they love her. The goal is to keep her from going anywhere. That way, the customers stay happy, and I have the money to pay Avery to keep me sane.

Cam lets out a soft chuckle but doesn't say anything in response. Her laughter hangs in the air for a moment, then slowly dissolves into the space around us. The silence grows steadily, thickening with every moment.

"I'm—" I start to speak before I realize that, if I say what's sitting on the tip of my tongue, I'll be breaking the promise I made the night before. When I said I'd never bring it up again. When I said I'd leave her alone.

But I'm not bringing it up for answers. There's no ulterior motive to get back at her or beg for the truth. I just want to apologize for yesterday, for that day in the salon. For all of it.

"I'm sorry, if I made you uncomfortable," I say, stepping closer to look her in the eye. "I never should have said any of that yesterday, and I know I'm not supposed to bring it up now. But it was really unprofessional of me, and I just—" Cam's gaze flicks up to me, looking intently through those soft brown eyelashes. I swallow. "I would hate to put someone in a situation they aren't comfortable in."

Cam's head bobs as she nods slowly, the corners of her lips subtly turning upwards. She lets a stream of air flow out of her mouth, and it brushes against my lips, causing goosebumps to rise on my skin. I take a quiet step back.

"You didn't make me uncomfortable," she says quickly. Her throat tightens as she swallows, her chest sinking down as all the air squeezes out of her lungs.

"I didn't?"

Cam shakes her head, and relief washes over me like a rainstorm, doubt dripping off my body and flowing into the gutter. I don't like believing people, especially people I barely know. But I can't force the doubt to return to my body. Cam always says what she's thinking. She had no trouble voicing her disapproval when I spilled that drink on her dress, nor when I mentioned her car situation yesterday. So really, I have every reason to believe her now.

"Oh good. Because I really thought... Well, I had been kind of working in silence for a while, trying to tidy up around here and I started to think that maybe I did."

Cam blinks slowly, that shallow dimple deepening with each word that comes from my mouth. She doesn't say anything, but I know she has something to say. Cameron Miller doesn't just smile for anyone. It's hard work, to earn that dimpled dream. I don't know what I did to deserve it.

"What?" I ask. Cam's head tilts slightly, her smile fading but not quite entirely.

"What do you mean 'what'?"

My gaze narrows, like if I squint hard enough, I'll be able to see through her eyes and into her brain.

"There's something you're not saying."

Cam shakes her head, a smiling scoff slipping through her lips. "I don't know what you're talking about. If I have something to say, I say it."

"That's how I know."

Cam's eyes scan mine, in an almost intimidating way. But I don't give in. I stare right back, forcing the muscles in my face to harden.

"We can stay here all night, Sparky. I'm not busy."

And with that comment, Cam breaks. She huffs out a laugh, her gaze dropping mine as she bites the insides of her blushing cheeks.

"You didn't make me uncomfortable. That's all."

After a quiet beat, she glances up at me. I stay stagnant, still not breaking my stare.

"And?"

Another uncomfortable laugh slips through her lips, her tongue pressing against the inside of her lower lip.

"And nothing. That's it."

I don't believe her, not one bit. But I'm also not going to force a confession out of her. If she doesn't want to tell me what's on her mind, that's her decision, and I have to respect it.

"Okay," I nod, turning back to the shelves. I adjust the bottles in front of me, even though they're already lined up. "I liked that about you, but if you don't want to tell me, that's just fine."

Out of the corner of my eye, Cam's brows furrow, her arms crossing over her chest. I fight back a smile as I keep pretending to straighten out gallons of chemicals.

"Liked what?"

I shrug, still staring forward.

"What, Violet?" she repeats, this time more desperate. My lips twitch up, and I'm forced to look at her.

"That you always say what's on your mind," I say casually. "But I guess there's times you can't. I mean, if I said everything I thought, there'd definitely be a problem."

I chuckle, shaking my head at the thought, but Cam's brows raise. She steps closer to me.

"Like what?" she asks, her lips parted just slightly. My quiet laughter stops abruptly when my eyes land onto hers. A tightening forms in my chest as I fall into those dark brown eyes. I suck in a breath.

"Nothing. I just meant—"

"*No*," Cam says firmly. "You can't try to persuade me to tell you what's on my mind when you won't tell me what's on yours."

"I didn't say there was something on my mind."

"Maybe not, but you said that, when there is, it's something you can't say out loud."

I let out an uncomfortable laugh as Cam takes another step closer to me. Her arm brushes against mine, and goosebumps wash over my skin.

"Sure, but that goes for everyone. I mean, you're essentially saying the same thing right now."

Cam's lips tug at the corners, though I don't think she means for them to. Her eyes drop to the floor, the warmth from her skin still radiating against mine.

"That's because what I'm thinking isn't something you say. It's something you do."

She looks up, and her lashes pin to her brow bone as her eyes lock onto mine. A pink tint rushes to her cheeks, and her breath becomes shaky. I tilt my head, confused.

"But you can still say it. Like, I can say 'I am thinking about walking to the store.' but it doesn't mean I have to actually walk to th—"

My words stop as I'm cut off by a warm, delicate pair of familiar lips. They lock between mine gently, pressing into me with just the right amount of pressure to make my mouth part.

Oh. I get it now.

I sigh softly, melting into the tender touch. But after not nearly long enough, Cam pulls back, her eyes wide and her cheeks flushed.

"Fuck, I—" she mutters, stepping backwards into the wall. "I—"

I don't care what she's about to say, mostly because it's probably something along the lines of "I'm sorry." And nobody with lips like that should ever apologize for pressing them to mine.

My hand snakes around her waist and pulls her body into me. Then, my mouth crashes back into hers. Cam shudders, her fingers gripping the front of my shirt desperately as our lips intertwine again. She pulls back softly, and I can feel the vibrations of her whisper against my skin.

"What about policy?" she asks, her breath soft. I look down at her lips, before flicking my gaze back to her anxious eyes desperately.

[5]"*Fuck* policy."

ELEVEN

Manners

CAM

I THINK THIS PLACE might be haunted. Or maybe it's Violet herself. Something happens when I'm around her that forces me to do things I didn't know I had the capability or even desire to do.

Like kissing her.

I knew I liked to kiss her, but I didn't think I'd ever find myself doing it again. Yet here I am, pressed against a wire rack in a dingy storage closet.

What the *actual* fuck is happening?

Sweet vanilla lips melt into mine. Violet's fingers slide gently underneath my shirt, her rough fingertips tracing circles on my skin.

"Is this okay?" she whispers, her warm breath brushing against my lips. I try to answer, but my throat tightens, so I nod instead. Violet smiles, pressing her body against mine as her fingers slowly venture downward. Her tongue traces the vein in my neck, the cold metal piercing in her nose tickling the trail behind it. The hair on my arms stands up, my skin tingling from the delicate touch.

"Can I?" Violet asks, her voice raspy, but controlled. She tugs at the drawstrings on my scrub pants. I nod again, and the band around my waist loosens, before two fingers dip gently inside.

A shaky breath escapes my mouth, my grip around Violet's waist tightening.

"You're going to have to let go of me if you want more, Sparky," she mumbles, and my thighs clench together unintentionally, heat rising to my core. For a moment, I think about arguing back. Challenging her for trying to boss me around. But I don't think I could get a word out if I tried.

I nod, forcing my grip to soften as Violet's fingers dip lower into my pants, tracing the line where my thigh and hips meet. My chest brushes against her cheek as I inhale, then quickly retreats as I let the air back out. She tugs at the collar of my shirt, pressing her lips against the skin on my collar bone, sucking gently. I groan, and she smiles against my skin.

"You like that?" she whispers, before taking my earlobe between her teeth. I nod, and she sucks it into her mouth, her tongue tracing around it, warm and wet. I swallow.

"If you're going to fuck me..." I manage to get out in a ragged breath. "Get on with it."

Violet freezes, then pulls back slowly, the cold air hitting my ear as it slides out of her mouth. Her eyes lock onto mine, and she tilts her head slightly, raising a curious brow.

"You're talking a lot of shit for someone who's shaking," she says, a confident smirk stretching across her face. My eyes widen, my gaze dropping down to my arms.

Violet's right. I *am* shaking. Why am I shaking?

I cross my arms tightly to alleviate the twitching muscles, my back still pressed against the wire shelving.

"It's cold," I lie with forced confidence, as if my knees aren't currently buckling. Violet leans back into my ear, her lips grazing so faintly I almost wonder if I felt it at all.

"Don't worry," she whispers. "You'll be sweating before you know it."

I don't even have time to react before she drops to her knees, her fingers hooking into my waistband and pulling my pants down along with her. She slides them off, over my rainboots. The cool air hits my body, sending a shiver down my spine. Now, I really am cold. Violet's gaze flicks up to me, her tongue tracing the inside of my thigh.

Goosebumps spread across my skin, my toes curling inside my shoes.

"Still cold?" she teases.

I frown. "Yes, actually. I—*Fuck*."

Violet presses two rough fingers against my heat and parts them slowly to spread me open. I try to finish my sentence, but her warm mouth presses into me, her tongue dragging up from my dripping entrance to my clit.

My back arches at the sudden contact, my knuckles scraping against the wire shelves behind me as I reach for something, *anything* to hold onto. Violet's fingers curl around the back of my left thigh, lifting it over her shoulder to get a better angle. My hips buck as her tongue traces circles just around my clit, but not actually on it.

"*God,*" I mutter, gripping the shelving tighter.

I look down. Violet's eyes are closed now as her head moves methodically from side-to-side, her tongue gently brushing against my clit with each movement. My clit pulses, a steady thrum between my thighs quickening as my body tenses and one hand moves from the shelves to the top of her head. Coarse, ridged fingertips drag slowly up the inside of my thigh, then graze against the delicate skin on my pussy before sinking back down. I don't mean to, but I let out a desperate whimper, aching for more.

Violet doesn't hesitate to give it to me.

Her hands grip my hips, pulling me down into her as her tongue presses against my entrance, my clit rubbing against the little ball of plastic in her mouth. I groan, my fingers curling around strands of her hair.

"God, you taste good," she mumbles, the vibrations of her voice echoing off my delicate skin. "You want me to fuck you, Princess? You want my tongue inside of that tight little pussy of yours?"

Holy fuck. Violet's words, just her voice even, is like quicksand, pulling me in, suffocating me in all the best ways possible. I nod quickly, desperately, my fingers gripping her hair tighter. The heel of my boot digs into her back, and I roll my hips forward, feeling the warm wet pressure of her tongue sliding between me.

"Use your words," she says, pulling back.

I let out an exasperated, pleading breath, but I comply.

"Yes."

"Yes *what?*"

My gaze lowers down to her, and those dangerous hazel eyes lock onto mine, challenging me. Pushing me.

"What?" I ask, my chest heaving as the cold air washes over my exposed pussy, wet and slick against the inside of my trembling thighs.

"Say *please*," she orders.

I let out a breathy, unintentional scoff.

"What?" I mean to ask it with some force, but it comes out as more of a desperate moan. Violet's head cocks, the corner of her mouth revealing a taunting smile.

"It might be foreign to *you*, but it's pretty custom here."

God, this woman. It's no fucking wonder she ended up as the boss of this place. She has a way of getting you to do things and making it feel like you wanted to all along.

My clit begins to ache, pleading for the contact Violet has broken. It pulses steadily, the pressure inside of me building like a dammed river. I swallow, letting out a loud huff and making sure she hears it.

"Please," I mumble, tilting my head back to look at the ceiling. I can't bear to look at her while she wins.

Violet's tongue clicks repeatedly. "Please *what*?"

I let out another scoff, but I know she isn't going to budge until I give in.

"*Please*, Violet." My eyes shut, and I can't believe I am giving her the satisfaction. "Please *fuck me*."

Violet's lips graze against my inner thigh, and the cold metal of her piercing drags closer and closer toward my heat.

"Good girl."

She tugs me downward, all my weight collapsing onto her face as her hot tongue enters me, rolling against the walls.

"Fuck Violet, I'm going to crush you!" I squeal, but I can't stop rocking myself further into her face. Violet just tightens her grip, pulling me down even harder.

Holy shit.

My stomach tightens, my hips rolling rhythmically as Violet's tongue dances around the inside of me. She pulls it out and drags it against my slick center, circling my clit with more pressure this time. My knuckles turn white, tightening around fistfuls of her hair.

"F-fuck Violet. I'm-I'm gonna—"

I try to get the words out, but my voice is shaky and tight. I would think she hadn't heard me, if her fingers weren't curling into my skin as she rolls her head from side-to-side. Her tongue traces parts of me I swear have never been touched before, and I wonder how I'm supposed to ever want anything that isn't this. My stomach tightens, my thighs trembling on either side of her as I buck my hips, the pressure building, trying to fight its way out.

"God, shit!" My brows press together, my head rolling back and my eyes along with it, as my thighs squeeze together, tight around Violet's face. "Fuck, Violet!"

My teeth sink into my lower lip so hard I know it will bruise, as I completely unravel on top of her, a string of curses I'm not sure are real words crawling from the back of my throat. I let out one last shaky moan and thrust forward, feeling her tongue graze my pussy before I completely collapse back against the shelves and then sink to the floor.

My chest heaves heavily, the room around me blurry, and for a moment, I think I might need my medication. But then, a rough hand brushes the hair out of my face, her thumb gently sliding across my bottom lip. My heartbeat slowly steadies, my chest rising and falling softer and softer.*

"Are you okay?" she asks gently, and my eyes slowly start to focus on the woman in front of me. A final, shuddering breath escapes my mouth, followed by a shaky, quiet chuckle. I nod, but Violet's eyes lock onto mine with concern. "Cam, are you sure?"

There's a shallow valley between Violet's brows as she presses them together, and I can't believe she would think I wouldn't be okay after... whatever the *fuck* that was. I am *very* much okay. I am *more* than okay. I am...

Exposed. And wet. *Very* wet. I scramble around the dark room, searching frantically for my pants.

"Looking for these?"

My head whips around to face Violet once more. She's standing confidently, one hand propped on her hip, while the other dangles my black scrub pants, a pair of completely soaked, bright pink boy shorts hanging out.

Oh my god.

"*Yes*, actually," I grumble, reaching out to grab them. Violet pulls them back quickly.

"Ah-ah, not so fast," she tuts. "Tell me you're okay."

I scowl. Not because I'm not okay, but because I just spent the last ten minutes following her every command, and I think I've just about had enough of it. Violet keeps staring at me, a small smirk on her face. I want to wipe it off right here right now.

But she's not the one with her vagina out, so...

"I'm fine," I say, snatching the pants out of her hand. My underwear slips out, landing onto the floor. I pretend I don't care, even if my cheeks are probably the same color as they are right now.

"Sheesh." Violet brushes her bangs out of her eyes. "Was it really that bad?"

"No," I say promptly. "It was many things, but bad was not one of them." Violet gives me a cocky grin, leaning against the wire rack she had me pressed against only minutes prior.

"So, same time next week then?"

I shoot her a glare, which loses its meaning when I break into a smile I hadn't meant to show. I slide on my underwear, rolling my eyes.

"Ha-ha," I say with sarcasm, like the thought of it doesn't make me weak all over again. I slide my scrub pants on and somehow, the center of them is wet too. I groan, checking the time on my phone.

"I have Criminal Dinner in an hour," I huff. "Now I have to go home and change."

Something washes over Violet's face, accomplishment maybe, and her tongue pokes the inside of her lower lip.

"You didn't seem too upset about it a minute ago." I shoot her another dirty look which I know has no meaning at all. "And what *exactly* is a Criminal Dinner?"

I finish adjusting my outfit and pull my hair back into a sweaty, tangled ponytail.

"It's a thing we do," I say, like that means anything. "Avery, Hayden, Adrian, and I."

A laugh escapes Violet's lips. "Well, you're quite the storyteller."

"God, you're nosy," I mutter. "We watch Criminal Minds and eat food. Good enough?"

Violet nods at my vague explanation, then clicks her tongue once.

"Ohh. *Criminal*! I get it now." She points at me, flashing a crooked smile. "That's funny."

I shove her playfully, my cheeks sore from fighting back a grin.

"Okay, *you're* ridiculous," I say, reaching for the door handle. "And I have to go."

Violet crosses her arms, her fingertips tapping against the whale shark tattoo on her bicep. My fingers draw downward, admiring it for a moment. I've always liked tattoos. There's a sea turtle on her left forearm, and a dozen small fish spread throughout. But near her wrist on her other arm, surrounded by an array of jellyfish and water, is a vacant spot. Everything around it is filled and finished, with shading and highlights, clearly healed. The space is so abrupt, so random, a bare piece of skin. I frown, looking back up at her.

"Why is it bare?" I ask, pointing at it. Violet looks confused for a moment, before her eyes follow the trail of my finger to her exposed arm. She looks back up at me.

"I'm saving it."

"For what?"

She shoots me a cocky smile. "Who's nosy now?"

My brows furrow, and I roll my eyes.

She sighs. "I don't know. I haven't decided yet. But it's the last part of the piece so—" She shrugs. "I wasn't ready to fill it yet."

I nod, then turn back to the door, reaching for the handle again.

"Aren't you forgetting something?" she asks behind me.

My hand drops, and I spin around, letting out a loud sigh.

"What?"

Her head tilts in a way that tells me I should know what. But I don't. This is how these things go. You fuck, you leave, you pretend it never happened. That was the whole point, right?

"If you say please—" Her weight shifts from one leg to the other. "You're supposed to say, 'thank you.'"

I prop a hand on my hip. "Do you try to be this annoying? Or is it a natural thing?"

Violet's lips part into a cheesy grin.

"You like it," she says confidently. I purse my lips, sucking in my cheeks.

"*No*," I respond, my pitch heightening to prove the lie.

"If you didn't, you'd have left by now."

Heat rushes to my cheeks as I reach for the door handle. Violet points accusingly at me.

"Ha!" she exclaims, her smile widening. I twist the handle, pushing the door open.

"Shut up," I say, blushing. Then, I step through the frame and walk out.

Twelve
Haircut Stickup
Violet

"**I**N THE STORAGE CLOSET?!"

I wince, snapping my phone away from my ear. Has Ruthie always been this *extra*? I pinch the inner corners of my eyes and rub them for a second, like that somehow makes all of this better.

"Ruth, can you please shut the *hell* up?"

Ruthie gasps dramatically, and I can only imagine the invisible pearls she's clutching.

"Don't use my legal name, Violet *Jean* Wolfe. I'm not the one who fucked my employee, in a storage closet!"

"Technically she's an independent contractor," I mutter, like that changes anything.

Not that I want anything to change. Well, maybe Angela's stupid, twat-blocking policy. But the rest of it, I'm pretty pleased with.

Pleased, and completely *shocked*. I knew Cam had an attitude, but given her constant stuttering and dislike toward the majority of humanity, I have to admit, I'm impressed. I didn't expect her to do something so ballsy, like kiss me.

I definitely didn't expect her to let me do *that*.

"Same difference. Are you coming down for Christmas? Tyler won't stop talking about how much she misses Reese." She pauses. "And *you*, of course."

I let out a soft chuckle, knowing she added that last bit just to make me feel better. Rough fingertips trace my scalp as I run my fingers through my hair.

Do I miss Ruthie and the girls? More than anything. But I don't know if I can stand being within a thirty-mile radius of my parents for more than a few hours. And the fact that they're leeching off Ruthie, living in the house she and

Jeramiah worked so hard for?

"Vi, *please* come. I can't do another holiday without you. Plus, it's going to be their first Christmas without Mal."

"Are you really going to play that card on me?"

Truthfully, she has a point. Even though Ruthie was never really a fan, the girls *loved* their Aunt Mal. Willow is too young to really miss her, but Tyler's old enough to know things are different. Mallory used to teach her different dance routines during the holidays, and at the end of the night, Tyler would make everyone huddle on the couch to watch her perform. It was the only thing that could force me into the same room as my parents.

Sometimes, I wonder how Ruthie is able to cut them so much slack. They dragged us away from Oregon when we were too young to remember. So instead of growing up surrounded by culture and family and jaw-dropping views of the Pacific Ocean, I got to live in Happy Trails Trailer Park in Clarkston freakin' Washington. I don't know if that name was intentional, but I like to think it was, seeing as it's the only interesting thing about the place.

But that isn't even a *portion* of my issue with Elon and Gemma Wolfe. My feud is fueled by the fact that they spent their twenties becoming addicted to whatever they could get their hands on, rather than raising the two kids they chose to put on this planet. So, as the only one home with the motor skills to function, I single-handedly kept Ruthie alive.

She turned out alright, considering.*

"Fine," I grunt, checking the time. *Shit.* "I'll be there. But I gotta go. Love you."

"Love you!" Ruthie calls out. I hang up and slide my phone into my pocket.

Remember when I said looking at someone that you've kissed like you haven't kissed them is impossible? Yeah. Trying not to look at someone whose pussy you ate like it was angel food cake in a storage closet is *so* much harder.

"Are you having another stroke?" Cam asks in a tone I'd like to fuck out of her. My eyes dart up to meet hers. *Shit.* Was I staring again? "I told you he'll be ready in ten."

A pair of curved shears glide over the top of a golden retriever's grinch-like feet. The loose feathers fall as she slices through them seamlessly, golden threads floating through the air.

"Right!" I smile but still don't move. It feels like my feet have been cemented to the floor. Like my eyes have been super glued to Cameron. She lifts an eyebrow, jutting her chin out with attitude.

"Aren't you going to go let his mom know?"

I forgot about that part.

"*Right.*"

I nod, this time literally pulling my feet off of the concrete and forcing my way over to the lobby. Normally, I'd be happy to run this quick little errand, stoked to do anything to help anyone. But since Tuesday, anything that isn't looking at Cameron Miller feels like a chore.

I need to snap out of it, but I'm not exactly sure how to. This hasn't ever happened to me before. Being around someone never made me so... *needy.*

Not that Mallory wasn't gorgeous herself. But even in the beginning stages of our relationship, I was much more focused on building us a life than I was on getting her into bed. Don't get me wrong; we had sex. A lot of it, actually. But for the most part, I hadn't been the one to initiate it. I had other things to think about. The only reason I even wanted to take someone home that night at Monsey's was because I could finally do it without feeling dirty. The relationship was over, and it had been for a long time. But the legality of it hung over my head like a constant reminder of what Mallory did to me.

It scared me that I could ever do anything that could be perceived as similar.

But I guess that's the point of hookups like these.

One-night stands, no-strings attached. The sole purpose of your interaction is sex, so you aren't busy thinking about anything else.

Unfortunately, I hadn't considered that when Cam's pretty little pussy was sitting on my face. I kind of forgot about the fact I'd have to see her on a daily basis, in a professional setting.

"She's got about ten minutes left," I say to Jessa's mom, flashing her a smile. I hope it's the normal kind, and not the I'm-totally-thinking-about-sex-at-work kind.

"Can you ask her to not trim the feet this time? My husband wants to grow them out."

Oh. I keep smiling, now hoping it's not the you-are-way-too-fuckin-late kind.

"Oh! Umh," I stall, unsure of why because the brief time I'm gaining is not nearly enough to build a time machine. "Did you let Martha know at drop off?"

Martha's head shoots up from behind the desk at the sound of her name, her eyes darting over to me in panic.

"Yes," the woman says confidently. I swallow, then let the I'm-so-fucking-sorry kind of smile creep across my face. When you work in customer service, you learn lots of kinds of smiles.

"I *think*," I say, even though I actually *know*, "she *may* have already cut them." The woman frowns, irritated, and I know I have about three seconds until she erupts into a flaming ball of fire. "*But* I can give you a free day of daycare if you'd like!"

Normally, I don't offer free services to someone until they're in the screaming "I'm leaving a one-star review" stage. But it isn't Cam's fault that Martha forgot to put the note in. She shouldn't have to suffer. Jessa's mom crosses her arms, tapping a long acrylic nail against her bicep.

"Okay," she says after a moment. "Alright. Don't worry about it. Can you bring her out to the car when she's done?"

I try to hold in my relief rather than sighing it out.

"Absolutely!" I say with a smile. The woman walks out and climbs into her shiny black Mercedes. I turn to Martha.

"Shit, Vi! I'm *so* sorry. It was really busy this morning and—"

I put my hand up, not dismissively but rather in comfort.

"Oh it's fine." I wave. "Just put one in there for next time, will you?"

Martha nods and immediately begins to type furiously on the keyboard.

"You *owe me*," I say when I get back to the salon.

Cam loops a slip lead over Jessa's head and guides her down from the table. She looks at me, confused.

"*Why*?"

"Because Jessa's mom was on the verge of throwing an absolute bitch fit about her feet getting trimmed. I offered her a free day of daycare though, so we're all cool now."

Both of Cam's eyebrows shoot up, and she rifles through her toolbox, pulling out the day's schedule that Martha had kindly color-coded.

"Was that in the notes? I—"

"Oh! No, no." I shake my head, watching as the tensed muscles in her face slowly relax. "No, Martha forgot to put it in."

Cam holds out her hand like she's gripping an invisible purse. "Then why should I owe *you*?"

"What?"

"If it wasn't my fuck-up, and I did what I was told I was supposed to do, why do *I* owe *you*?"

Cam is confusing because, when she's not completely unsure of herself and the entire world around her, she is extremely fucking direct.

"Well, I...um—"

"Mhm?"

"You know, because she could have—"

"Could have?"

Cam's eyebrow arches, waiting patiently for an answer she knows is never coming. I, however, am not yet ready to accept defeat.

"Well, she could have refused to pay," I finally get out. Not the strongest argument, but at least it's something. Cam shakes her head.

"I can't really see you letting that happen," she says, walking over to me with the leash stretched toward my hands.

"I would," I lie. "In the right circumstances. Like, if she had a gun or something."

That dimple returns to Cam's cheek as she smiles and *holy fuck*. How does something so innocent drive me so wild? Her shimmering dark eyes give my own eyes no choice but to look.

"A robbery," she says, her hand grazing mine as she hands the leash to me. "For a haircut?"

My cheeks flush but I pretend it's from the heat of the room, rather than the heat of the moment. Cam's right. Without ventilation in this room, the water hangs in the air like dew on a humid morning.

"Wow, we really need to put those vents in here, huh?" I shake the front of my shirt, as if I'm trying to ventilate it just to seal the deal.

"Get on it, boss," she says, turning around. Her hips sway in a completely natural and totally sexy manner. Not forced, like Mallory. Cam isn't putting on a show. She's just naturally the star of the film. "I've been waiting."

My throat bobs as I swallow, hard. I was wrong the other night, when I said we were starting from the beginning. We're past it, I think. The uncomfortable avoidance.

Who knew all it would take was finishing the job I started?

"I'll call the electrician now."

WHEN CLOSING TIME ROLLS around, I do my regular walk-through, then go to the lobby to turn off the "open" sign.

"Bye Vi!" Adrian waves, and Avery nods, stepping out the door behind them.

"Night guys!" I say back. "Careful out there, it's supposed to freeze."

Avery shoots me a thumbs up, the door closing behind him. I turn the lock and watch them walk through the dimly lit parking lot. A gold shimmer catches my eye, my gaze drawing over to Cam's car. I think about that night in the rain, how her car wouldn't start, and secretly wish it'd happen again so I have an excuse to drive her home.

But I don't have an excuse, and unfortunately, I'm above popping hoods and cutting wires to force the idea. I *am* above that, right?

"Staying late again?"

I turn around, and my eyes land on that pretty round face of Cam's as she leans against the desk. Dawson sits next to her, his tail swatting the laminate flooring. I shake my head.

"No," I answer, walking up to her. Then, I lean down and scratch behind Dawson's lopsided ears. His head tilts into the touch, his mouth stretching wide to show his satisfaction. "I was actually getting ready to leave. You?"

Cam shakes her head, gesturing toward her dog. "I think he might kill me if I make him wait for dinner a minute longer."

I let out a soft laugh, knowing all too well that nothing on the planet is more demanding than a hungry dog.

"How pissed was he last week?" I ask. For a second, I regret asking it. Things had just become normal between us, and I feel like I just unraveled all that progress in six words. But Cam just laughs, that dimple plunging deep into her cheek.

"Pretty pissed," she admits. "But it was worth it."

Her words shock me, only because I know she means them. I bite back a smirk, bowing sarcastically.

"My pleasure," I say, now letting the smile on my face grow. "And yours, apparently."

Cam laughs, her eyes rolling to the ceiling.

"As far as I know."

My cocky smile drops, my brows pressing together.

"What?"

"Nothing," Cam says, her jaw snapping shut as her face grows red.

I shake my head, stepping closer to her.

"Nope." I cross my arms. "You didn't let me get away with that, so I'm not letting you. Was that—" I suck in a breath, then swallow. "Was that your first time?"

If I am the asshole that took this woman's virginity in a dirty storage closet, I think I'll hate myself forever. Cam's eyes widen, and she waves both her hands frantically in front of her.

"What? No! That's not—"

"You said as far as you know."

"I know, but not like *that*. Like—"

"Like what?"

Cam stares at me blankly, her face growing redder by the second. Her mouth keeps opening, as if she's going to speak, but it simply closes each time she tries.

"Cam, if that was your first time, I am so sor—"

"I lied."

Cam blurts it out like it's been dancing on the tip of her tongue forever, and her eyes drop to the floor.

"I didn't just get startled by the woman knocking on the door. I—" She swallows, and I feel the muscles between my brows tense. *What? She what?* "I've never been with a woman before. And it wasn't some *radical* realization I just came to; I always knew I was bisexual. My cards were just all male up until that night. And I got out of a relationship last year, and the whole thing—well, *yeah*. So, I was supposed to be finding a one-night stand, and it was supposed to be with a woman. And I was scared. But it didn't scare me because I was unsure, it scared me because I *wasn't*. I knew I wanted it, and I never wanted something that I didn't already have. That...*sounded stupid*. Okay, um..."

She fumbles over her words, her eyes scanning the floor like she's reading a script she formed in her head.

"It doesn't," I cut in before she can reduce the meaning of it all. "Sound stupid, I mean. I get what you mean, I think. Like—"

I stop. Do I really get what she means, or is that just something I'm saying to make her feel better?

Usually, I wouldn't care. In the past, the goal *has* always been to make people feel better, no matter what the cost was. But Cam isn't like that. She doesn't want someone to make her feel better. She wants someone to tell her the truth.

I like that about her.

"I could be wrong," I say honestly, taking another step closer. "But, at least for me, it's like...*craving a food* you've never had before. You know you want it. You know you'll like it. But it's strange to feel so confident about that when you've never tried it."

Cam's gaze flicks back up to me, the tension in her face slowly easing. I don't normally open up to people. Not about things like this. But Cam just trusted me with a piece of herself so easily, and I can't help but feel like I owe it to her to do the same.

"I just went through a divorce," I explain, my voice slightly shaking when the word comes out. Not shaking in an emotional way. Shaking in a foreign way. I think I made it through the entire thing without ever actually saying the word out loud. "We were high school sweethearts, so she was the only person I had been with in…" I let out a short laugh. "Almost ever, really. And that night, with you, that was the first time I ever tried to…" I sigh. "Well that was the first time I tried to have a one-night stand. I knew I wanted it. I knew I'd like it. But I had never done it before. Was it anything like that?"

My pulse quickens, the beat of my heart rapping against the inside of my ribcage. I take a slow breath in through my nose, trying hard to remain subtle. I haven't told anyone that before, and even though it really doesn't matter, in this fleeting moment, I suddenly feel like it does. My mouth begins to dry as I look down at Cam, scanning her face for a reaction. My eyes find her soft, pink lips, the corners of them tugging up so sweetly I feel like I'm in a candy store.

"Yes, actually," she says, a hint of surprise in her tone. "That's exactly what it's like."

Thirteen

Frozen Egg Rolls

Cam

I WAS THREE MINUTES late to last week's Criminal Dinner, thanks to Violet. I haven't been late in over a year. So here I am, forty minutes before seven, gripping a bag of frozen egg rolls.

"You're *early*," Adrian says, throwing their arms around me. Irritated by the snow's existence, I brush it off my shoes before stepping inside. "Hayden's here too."

If I were a therapist, I think I'd diagnose the Pacific Northwest with whatever the *opposite* is of Adjustment Disorder. One day, the seats of your car are scalding your bare thighs as you sit down. The next, you're practically in Antarctica.

"How was work?" Hayden asks. Images of Violet flash through my mind, those pierced lips, her luminescent eyes. That bare spot on her forearm. The past week has been a blur of internal screaming, as I try to look at Violet like she's my boss, and not the person who made me uncontrollably scream her name in a closet. It's hard enough to do that on its own, but on top of it, I have to act like I never want it to happen again. And I have nobody to talk to about it.

Except Dr. Burton, of course.

"What did Violet say?" Adrian asks, their eyes widening. My body tenses at her name.

"What?"

"About Kira's tooth?"

"Oh! Right." I swallow. Kira is a corgi who decided out of nowhere to attack the high-speed Dremel in my hands, consequently chipping a tooth. "Her mom was cool about it."

I don't want to be talking to Adrian about Kira's tooth. More than anything,

I want to tell my best friend about Violet. About Monsey's, about the storage closet. About how good it was and how bad I want it again. But Adrian has a track record of losing things. And by that, I mean not keeping things they're supposed to, like secrets.

They don't mean to blab, they really don't.

Adrian would never hurt someone on purpose, especially not someone they care so deeply for. But, as I discussed with Dr. Burton, the entire world finding out about that night falls directly into The Realm if I were to tell Adrian.

I hold up the plastic grocery bag.

"I cheated this time. Store-bought egg rolls."

"Thank god," Avery mutters. Hayden nods, but then quickly stops when he sees that I'm looking at him.

"I'm sure they would've been great," he lies. "If you made them."

I roll my eyes and walk into the kitchen to preheat the oven.

"So I've been thinking," Adrian says, opening the box of egg rolls. They start lining the rolls up on the pan in neat rows. "It's been a few weeks since you tried the A.D.D. plan. I know it didn't end how you wanted it to last time, but I figured maybe, if we went with you, you could have some moral support until you don't need us."

"No."

The word leaves my mouth so quickly, it takes me a moment to realize I'm the one that said it. The truth is, I *have* thought about the A.D.D. plan. I have thought about trying again. I just hadn't decided I was going to go through with it until last week, when Violet joked about seeing me again. She laughed it off, and I did too. But as the words repeated in my head throughout the week, I realized that maybe it wasn't a bad idea.

I'm not usually one to break rules. I might be the only person in existence who actually sees speed signs as a limit and not a minimum. And hooking up with Violet? Well that broke all sorts of rules. Not just Angela's "no fucking" rule, but it broke the A.D.D. criteria.

The attraction is still there, no matter how insufferable Violet can be. But the difference now is that while I have a deal breaker, her being my boss, I no longer have distance. In fact, Violet and I see one another every day.

And still, I can't get the idea off my mind. We both want something, something we can give each other, so I learned the other day. I don't want to have to go back to Monsey's. I don't want to go through the stress and anxiety of finding someone who meets all of Adrian and Hayden's criteria every time I'm ready to try something new.

Violet is already there. She knows what I need, and though she's almost as annoying as Avery, she does know what she's doing. So, I made a list.

Cons:

1. She is my boss.

2. Fucking her is strictly against policy.

3. Breaking policy could get me fired.

4. She's kind of annoying.

5. Definitely not an A.D.D. hookup.

Pros:

1. Sex.

2. I already went through the initial dumpster fire of meeting her.

3. Sex.

When weighing out pros and cons, it isn't about numbers. It's about need. And while I *need* this job, I also need whatever happened that night to happen again.

"Okay." Adrian nods, giving me a soft smile. "That's okay." Their hand presses against mine, and I look up at them. "No pressure."

I should tell them. I should tell them right now what is running through my brain. *Who* is running through my brain. What kind of person keeps something like this from their best friend?

"Thanks," I say instead, pressing my lips to their temple.

"Gay!" Avery yells out, and Hayden tosses a couch pillow at him, giggling.

Adrian and I shoot him a synchronous glare, then look at each other and start laughing.

"These aren't new," I say disappointedly, pointing to the frozen egg rolls as Adrian slides the pan into the oven. "I know I'm supposed to be trying new things but—"

"But nothing," Hayden cuts in from behind me. I turn around and see his body towering over me, his lips offering a sweet smile.

"You've had a lot of changes recently, Cam. Work, trying to move on from Cody. It's okay if some things stay the same."

I lean into him, practically hugging him with my face. The familiar scent of cedarwood and honey fills my nose, and I melt into him. I think, strangely, I feel more guilty about keeping it from Hayden than I do from Adrian. Adrian was my friend first; I only know Hayden because of them. But I have a reason to keep it from Adrian. And right now, leaning into Hayden's soft warm arms, I realize there is absolutely no real reason I should be keeping it from him.

Hayden will take your secrets to the grave. I love that about him. Adrian is my best friend, but Hayden I could trust with anything. My stomach twists, a dry lump forming in my throat as guilt buries inside of me.

"I love you guys." I sigh, wrapping my arms around Hayden.

Adrian throws their arms around us both. "Me too."

"Yeah." Hayden chuckles. We all look over at Avery, who rolls his eyes.

"Don't drag me into this," he groans. "I'm just here for Derek Morgan."

I THINK DR. BURTON is mad at me. Is that a thing?

Can your therapist be mad at you?

I mean I know, logically, therapists are humans, and therefore, he has the emotional capability to be mad at me. But like, can he be mad at me from a medical standpoint?

"So." He pushes his glasses up the bridge of his nose. "Let me get this straight. You want to have a sexual arrangement... with your *boss*?"

I don't think his tone is intentionally judgy, but it makes my entire body feel like I'm standing before the fucking court.

Let the record show: *yes,* that's *exactly* what I'm proposing.

"Well, that sounds... *wrong*," I say. "When you put it that way."

Dr. Burton's eyebrows furrow. "How would *you* like to put it?"

"Well..." I suck in a breath, mulling things over for a minute. "It's a mutual, beneficial agreement between two consenting parties. If she agrees."

Dr. Burton nods, and I swear he's trying not to laugh at me.

"And what happened in the storage closet last week, that was initiated by..."

"Me." I say it confidently, like if you had told me that a month ago, I wouldn't have committed you to an institution. Dr. Burton stays silent for a moment, and I swallow.

"My concern, here, Cam, is that—"

"She isn't really my boss," I cut him off. Dr. Burton raises his eyebrows, but motions for me to continue. "If that's what you're thinking. I mean, she *is,* but she isn't. And it isn't like *that.* She didn't take advantage of me or anything."

I have to say it because I know how the words coming out of my mouth sound. But nothing would have ever happened between us if I hadn't started it. If I hadn't kissed her.

"Okay." Dr. Burton nods. "I believe you. But that wasn't my concern."

My brows press together, and I frown. "What was then?"

He takes a deep breath.

"Cam, when you have Adjustment Disorder, especially with depression and anxiety, your body and brain don't react to stress and changes like a normal person's does. They start to panic, as you know, and that can lead to finding comfort in filling space, patching holes to keep things as they are. I'm not saying that this is that." He clears his throat, and I shift uncomfortably in my seat. "But I *am* saying that I want you to be mindful of the reason you wanted to do this in the first place. You wanted to move on from your relationship, and you wanted to explore your sexuality. And you did, and that's great. But the purpose behind it being casual was to ensure there was distance. To promote individuality rather than dependency. Of course, comfortability is a priority... But I am concerned that, with the constant proximity, things will get confusing for you."

I listen to Dr. Burton and don't interrupt him, even though I really, really want to. He's talking about Cody, I know it. But this isn't *like* that. I actually liked Cody when I met him. We were in a book club together at the local library, and I turned him down the first few times. I liked seeing him every week, but I wasn't really looking for a relationship.

And then, the avalanche fell. It was only a week after my dad passed that Cody asked me again, knowing full well what had just happened. Hayden says he took advantage of the fact that I was in a vulnerable state. I don't know if that's true. All I do know is that I was tired of saying no and scared of being alone. So, I accepted.

The first year was great, although we moved quickly. Cody was sweet and caring, at least I always thought so. But then, things started to go south. He stopped letting me wear what I wanted, and I couldn't go out unless he came with me. He said he was keeping me safe, and I believed him. I believed him until he stopped letting me come to Criminal Dinner. I made up excuses about not feeling well or being stuck at work, but none of them bought it. They tried to help me, but I was so blinded by Cody, by the idea of staying safe, that I ignored them.

But this thing with Violet isn't going to be anything like that. I'm not going through a traumatic event. The lines aren't going to blur. I have control over it now, my life. I've spent every waking moment since Cody making sure of it.

"Well, what if I come up with something?" I ask. "Like a terms and conditions?"

Dr. Burton quirks a thick brow. "Terms and conditions?"

I nod. "I'm good at following rules," I say. "*Mostly.* The ones I set for myself, at least. So, what if I make a Terms and Conditions? A contract stating the rules of the agreement, that prohibits the ability for things to escalate?"

Dr. Burton twirls the pen in his hand.

"Cam, I think you are a very smart person," he says, letting out a soft sigh. "If this is something you're comfortable with and something you want to do, then I have no choice but to believe you have thought it through. I know you. I know how carefully you consider things." He pauses. "But with this rule set by the owner and not being able to talk to your friends about it, I'm worried about the toll it's going to take. The stress of burying it."

I hold my breath, letting the words sink into my veins. I thought about that too. It's all I've been thinking about, actually, but it's only something I really need to consider if Violet accepts. And the likelihood of that? I don't think it falls into The Realm.

"I have you." I point out. Dr. Burton chuckles, his head shaking as his dark cheeks turn red.

"That, you do."

FOURTEEN
Terms & Conditions

VIOLET

"A contract?"

A loud cackle erupts from the back of my throat, and I turn the smooth cream paper over in my hand. "And it has a *backside*?"

Cam frowns, leaning against the door of the storage closet.

"You're the one that said it," she says, crossing her arms over her body. "'See you next week,' remember?"

I *do* remember because I had to play it off as a joke the second I looked at Cam's glaring scowl. I didn't think she'd take it seriously. I didn't want her to, in fear she'd eat me alive. Yet, here I am, holding a *literal* sex contract.

"So you wrote a..." I read the black letters inked across the top of the page. "*Terms and Conditions*?"

"Well, there has to be rules." She waves a hand in the air. "Otherwise, it's just mayhem."

I quirk an eyebrow at her. "You mean like the rule we *broke*?"

I don't know why I ask it because, if anything, it's just going to make her change her mind. And no matter how bizarre this is, I definitely do *not* want her to change her mind. She shoots me a glare that I have to admit makes me a little nervous.

"Look," she says, standing up and taking the paper from my hand. "We both have something to gain here. I need someone to help me try..." She swallows. "*New* things, and you need to—" She gestures to me. "What was it again? Move on from your ex?"

Now, *I* frown.

"I've moved on," I say defensively. "I'm just not used to casual sex."

She eyes me up and down, almost like she doesn't believe me.

"*Right.*"

"What?"

She shrugs, looking away. "Nothing."

I grab her sleeve, tugging on it until she looks at me. "Not *nothing*," I say, pointing to her face. "You have *something* written all over your face."

"Well, considering... *that night*, I wouldn't have assumed you aren't used to casual sex."

Heat rises to my cheeks, but I play it off. "Are you saying it was good, Miller?" I tease.

Cam rolls her eyes, which I now take as a sign I've won.

"If it wasn't..." She shoves the contract into my chest. "I wouldn't have typed up a contract."

I take it from her hands, looking it over again. "There's a... *schedule?*" My brows raise skeptically.

"I have a busy life. Is there a problem with that?"

I shake my head.

"No, no. No problem, just..." I shrug. "Seems a bit *predictable*, don't you think? Isn't that the fun part about booty calls, you never know when they're gonna happen? You never know when you're gonna need it?"

Cam frowns.

"Predictability is the key to survival," she snaps. "And this is not a *booty call*. It's a mutually beneficial arrangement."

"Oh, so like, friends with benefits?" I ask. Blood rushes to Cam's cheeks, and she shoots me an annoyed glance.

"*No.* You have to be *friends* to be friends with benefits."

"You sure know how to make a girl feel special, you know that, Sparky?"

"Will you stop calling me that?" Cam groans, but that dimple gives her amusement away.

"You were about to jump start your car *backwards*. I saved your life." I tap the underside of her chin playfully. "So I think I can call you whatever I want."

Cam shoots me a glare I think she only partially means. "You know what?

Forget it."

She tries to snatch the contract from my hand, but my grip tightens around it. The corner of the page rips slightly when she grabs it.

"Wait, wait," I say in surrender. "Hold on."

I hold the contract out in front of me and actually read the full thing this time.

Mutually Beneficial Sexual Arrangement Terms & Conditions

I, Cameron Miller, agree to engage in a mutually beneficial sexual relationship with Violet Wolfe on this day 11/06/2024. This contract discloses and enforces the boundaries of the interdependent arrangement between the parties.

By signing this contract, we hereby agree to the following:

1. To engage in a mutually beneficial sexual arrangement.
2. To remain strictly platonic.
3. To adhere to regularly scheduled meetups (Thursdays) unless otherwise agreed upon.
4. That communication during work hours should remain strictly work-related and not refer to this agreement.
5. To not disclose this agreement with anyone who may have a connection to Furry Friend Pet Resort or those employed at the facility.

Cameron Miller

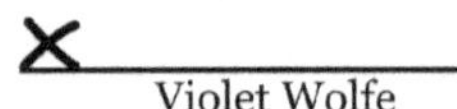

Violet Wolfe

I quirk an eyebrow at her. "You're... serious?"

Cam shifts her weight uncomfortably but tilts her chin up. "If you agree."

I chuckle, shaking my head. Is this really happening?

"Do you have control issues with everyone, or am I special?" I ask, flashing her a smirk. Cam shoots me a glare that she fully means this time, which makes it obvious she won't be answering me. So, I shift gears. "Why Thursdays?"

It isn't really an important question, not nearly the most important, but I feel like it's one of the only ones she'll actually answer. Cam crosses her arms.

"I have Criminal Dinner on Tuesdays and therapy on Wednesdays," she says firmly. "Fridays are no good because sometimes Adrian likes to go out, and weekends are personal time. So, it was between Thursdays and Mondays."

I try. I try to hold it in, but I can't. My entire body shakes like an earthquake as the laughter that had been building up in my chest bursts out of me. I clutch the paper tighter, shaking my head as Cam angrily reaches for it again.

Tears fill my eyes and I wipe them away, trying to force my body to calm down. I look up; those round brown eyes would be doe-like if Cam weren't more of a wolf. My posture straightens, my shoulder pulling back as I look down at her with a smile.

"Do you have a pen?"

Fifteen

Bet

Cam

I'VE NEVER BEEN A confident person.

Decisive? Yeah. Straightforward? Sure. But confident may as well be a foreign word.

Not concerning my appearance, I've truly never cared too much about that. I can't change how I look, not without surgery, and besides, I have my father's nose.

My insecurities appear more on the social side of things. My dad never liked the term "introvert." He always said that people used it like it was a dirty word, like it meant you were cold or miserable. He also said it completely defeated the purpose of my middle name, "felicity," which means happiness. *Sorry, Dad.*

So, he called me his Wallflower. I've come to learn in recent years that the term isn't much better. But that's beside the point. The point is: I've always had trouble saying the right things. But Violet? Words flow out of her mouth like she's a poet. During sex, at least. Otherwise, she's more of a parrot.

[7]"Your pussy is so fucking wet for me, isn't it?" Violet mumbles, her fingers pumping inside of me.

They glide in and out effortlessly. I roll my hips, my clit brushing against the top of her thigh as I ride her small, calloused fingers. I groan. "Don't stop."

Violet's eyes shoot open, pure purpose written across her face in the form of a taunting smirk.

"When are you going to stop telling me what to do?" she asks. Her legs hook around the backside of mine, and she rolls her body over until my back lands on my worn jersey sheets.

"What was that?" I huff, blowing a strand of hair off my forehead. "Krav

Maga?"

"Jiu jitsu," Violet answers, dropping the information so casually. Her fingers wrap around my waist and slowly pull until I have turned onto my side. Then, she grabs my thigh, tugging on it gently until it forms into an arch. A hesitant feeling grows in my gut, my stomach twisting nervously, but I comply. Violet stays at the foot of the bed, slowly pulling her legs out from under her.

"Um, I don't—" I swallow, worried I might say all the right things to ruin this situation. Violet's gaze focuses onto me, her head tilting slightly to the left.

"Are you okay? Do you want me to stop?"

There is no question as to what my answer is. *No.* I might not have any idea what she's planning to do, but still. Positively and definitively "*no.*"

I shake my head, and a sly smirk creeps across Violet's lips.

"Use your words, Princess," she mocks but still doesn't place her hands back on me. I roll my eyes.

"No," I say, making sure my voice comes off more confident than I actually feel. Violet nods, settling herself between my legs.

"Okay, well if you want me to stop, let me know, okay? Should we set a safe word?"

"I think '*stop*' is a good one," I say snarkily.

Violet's brows raise for just a beat before falling again. "You'd be surprised," she murmurs, her cheeks flushing. "Alright. Just tell me to stop, and I will."

I nod and watch as Violet slips her leg underneath my left one, the skin on her thigh softer than the sheets we're laying on. Then, her other leg begins to move, gliding over the top of that very same leg. Her hips move forward, heat radiating between us as she presses herself against me. Even though she hasn't done anything yet, a needy pulse thrums from my clit, begging for friction. I swear I could come just from the contact of her wet pussy on mine.

"*Fuck,*" I mutter.

Violet quirks an eyebrow. "That *is* the idea, yes."

I ignore her because her hand grips my arm, and she slowly begins to roll her hips, her slick pussy grinding against my clit. *Holy shit.*

Why did I think this was a myth? Maybe it is because this feels *too fucking good* to be true. A soft suction forms between us as Violet continues rotating her hips. My breath hitches, my fingers gripping the sheets desperately as Violet's head rolls ba—

"Stop!"

I don't even realize that the word came out of my mouth until Violet's head snaps forward. Her eyes grow wide. My chest heaves, my head shaking, as I try to figure out where the *fuck* that word even came from.

"Wait no-*don't* stop," I say, completely tripping over every word in the sentence. Violet's grip on my arm loosens but doesn't quite let go. I swallow. "I just, I haven't done *this* before. I don't know what I'm supposed to do."

The concern on Violet's face is quickly washed over with relief, then a hint of amusement.

"You're on the bottom, sweetheart." She smirks. "You just lay there and look pretty. Cheer me on, maybe."

My brows furrow, and I look up at her. God, she's fucking gorgeous. The tattoos on her arms aren't nearly her only ones. Earthy artwork is painted across her entire body, waves outlining the curves of her perfect, luscious tits, and forests climbing each muscular tanned leg. Vines wrap around her torso like a jungle, and fuck, just call me George. Her facial piercings aren't the only ones she has either. No, not *there*. But silver bars pierce through each brown nipple, and a little green gem rests at the gap of her navel. I don't know how I hadn't noticed them before. And now that I know they're there, I don't think I'll ever be able to think about anything else.

But none of those things are what makes Violet beautiful. All of that is sexy, sure. But there's more to her than the artwork painted on her body and the silver embedded in her skin.

It's her dark lashes, those mossy hazel eyes. The freckle sitting on the bridge of her nose that I'm just now noticing. The curve of her waist, the prominent bulge of her muscles underneath her skin. But the thing that makes Violet the most beautiful is the fact that she cares if I'm okay. If I'm enjoying myself. If I'm comfortable.

Cody sure as hell never did that.

"So, what? I'm just a Pillow Princess?" I ask, eyeing her suspiciously.

"Isn't that your royal duty, as the Ice Princess?" she teases. Her hips budge subtly, just once, as if to ask for permission. I can't think of anything I want more than for her to keep going. I nod, and Violet presses herself back against me, the warm wet friction gliding between us.

Moans fill the air, Violet's grip on my bicep tightening, my fingers around a fistful of sheets doing the same. Though *some* might say this is a ticket to hell, something about it feels so heavenly. Like white-hot energy. Sweat beads on the crown of Violet's forehead, as she rolls her hips in heated desperation. I swear she's glowing, her head tilted back as a string of curses leave her pretty little mouth.

"Fuck, Cam," she moans, and the sound of my name coming out of her mouth in such a hungry plea is almost enough to tip me over the edge.

"God, Violet, *please*," I whine, though I can't say for sure that it's audible. That's fine. She doesn't need the ego boost. Her hips buck, her fingers sinking into my arm so hard I'm sure it will leave bruises, but I don't care. I don't care about anything that isn't the wet pressure between us. I start to roll my hips too, thrusting upward as the friction between us tightens. Violet's head tosses back, her eyes rolling and her lip quivering as she lets out a loud moan.

"Fuck, I'm—" I stutter, my face hot, my pulse thready. I close my eyes. "I—"

I can't get my vocal cords to work in the way I want them to, but Violet knows exactly what I'm trying to communicate.

"Look at me," she commands, somehow gaining enough composure to hold her head upright. My stomach shakes, and I don't know how my body can be so malleable and so tense at the same time. Through my furrowed brows and flickering lashes, my eyes dart up to hers. I close them again.

"I can't—" She pushes, this time the top of her thigh rubbing against my swollen clit.

"You either look me in the eye, or you watch me fuck this tight, wet pussy of yours. But you aren't going to stare at the back of your eyelids while you beg for me. You aren't going to miss a single moment of this."

Jesus fucking Christ.

At this point, I'm so desperate I can't argue with her. My eyes flutter open, landing back on hers as she grinds against me, her supple breasts bouncing against her ribcage.

Pressure builds inside of me, a tight coil forming in my stomach as the heavy thrum between my thighs heats up even further, Violet's eyes holding mine hostage. She sucks her lower lip between her teeth, watching me like she's on a mission. To be fair, she is.

I can hear my own heartbeat, pounding in my head as an unbridled moan forces its way out of me. Who knew trying new things could feel so fucking good?

"Fuck, Violet!"

The corner of her lip turns upward, and she leans over, maintaining eye contact as her teeth sink into the skin of my knee.

My legs shake uncontrollably, my knuckles turning white as a wave of heat washes over me. My toes curl against the sheets. Violet's voice, begging me to come.

"Come on baby," she whispers. "Just like that."

My back arches like the curve of a crescent moon, moonlight crashing over me in a sweaty, panting heap.

The tension in my body releases, and my muscles slowly ease. The unsteady flow of air in my lungs finds its natural rhythm, and I exhale slowly, *controlled.* *

Violet slides off me and rests against the bed, pulling the thin white sheet over only half of her body. I pull myself up, so my back rests against the creaky headboard.

"Good new or bad new?" she asks breathily, like her lungs still haven't caught up with her. My face flushes as I glance at her, then to the ceiling.

"Good."

I'm not looking at Violet, but I just know she's smirking. She takes a steadying breath, tracing up my calf with her finger.

"So, are you going bowling on Monday?"

I laugh, shaking my head. "You waste no time making conversation."

She shrugs. "Life is short."

There's an unofficial, optional "team meetup" next week at Pacific Pins Bowling Alley. Optional for everyone, except me. Adrian is lucky they have a *very* cute pouty face.

"Unfortunately," I mumble, peeling a piece of lint off the damp bedsheet. Violet's finger pokes my leg, making my thigh jiggle.

"Well, at least you'll have me." She wiggles her eyebrows, a goofy grin spread across her face. I roll my eyes.

"*Double* unfortunate."

Violet lets out a bright laugh, and if that is the only sound I ever get to hear again, I won't be mad. She might be annoying, with her constant talking and permanent smile. But that laugh is something I couldn't hate if I tried. I know, because I *have* tried.

"Shut up." She shoves my knee gently. "You like me."

My brows drop, my eyes snapping over to her.

"Do not," I bark, pulling my leg away so it no longer makes contact with hers. Violet props herself up on her forearm, her nipples peeking out from under the thin white sheet.

"I've never hate-fucked someone before," she says, shooting me an unconvinced glance. "But I'm pretty sure *that* wasn't it."

I shake my head, like the words will fly out of my ears if I try hard enough.

"No," I say convincingly, but I'm starting to wonder who it is I'm trying to persuade. I don't like Violet in any way, shape, or form. Other than physically, of course. She pushes my buttons and pisses me off. She never stops talking and always has that stupid smirk glued to her face. "I *don't* like you. You bother me, actually. Like, *a lot.*"

Violet's tongue clicks against the roof of her mouth once. "And here I was, thinking we were in the makes of a beautiful friendship."

I know she's joking. The slight curve of her lips and the jade-toned sparkle in her eye gives it away. Still, a strange feeling forces its way into my stomach, settling uncomfortably between my ribcage.

She's testing me. Seeing if she can push me to the point of admitting something that simply isn't true. Seeing if she can get me to break my own rules.

While I may follow her commands during sex, I won't have her push me around in the real world.

"Violet, I like *two* people." I put a finger up. "Adrian." And then another. "And Hayden. You..." I poke her with a little more force than she had poked me with, and her head falls to the side in a curious stare. "You have not yet made your way onto that list."

Those warm, full lips part into a smile.

"*Yet*," she repeats, dragging out the word to torture me. I huff.

"God, your ego really is huge, isn't it?"

Violet quirks an eyebrow, her head tilting slightly. "It's not ego, it's optimism."

I roll my eyes.

"You can call a horse a carrot, but it doesn't make it true."

Violet cackles, clutching her chest and kicking her feet.

"What kind of saying is that?"

"The point is, *you* need to be put into your place. God, I can't wait to go bowling."

This grabs Violet's attention, her interest piqued. I can tell by the way she looks at me, curiosity filling her eyes.

"Huh?"

"I'm going to kick your ass," I say boldly. *Very* boldly actually because I haven't been bowling a day in my life. But I had to say *something* to curb Violet's ego. "I think you need a little humility."

Violet snorts.

"Me? You should hear yourself Little Miss I'm-Gonna-Kick-Your-Ass." Just as she says it, something flickers in Violet's eyes, and I'm terrified as to what twisted thought has just entered her mind. She smiles devilishly, her pupils dilating enough to hide most of her irises. Why do I feel like I've just made a mistake?

"Hmm," she says, acting as if she is deep in thought. I'm sure whatever it is will be a rather *testy* epiphany.

"What?" I grumble, ready to get it over with. Her eyes dance around the room slowly, until they finally land on me.

"What if—" Her gaze darts to my lips, then back up to my eyes. "What if we make a bet?"

Here we fucking go.

"A bet?"

She nods. "Yes, a bet."

I roll my eyes, holding my hands out in a "why-are-you-like-this" gesture.

"For *what*?"

"For *fun?* I know it isn't *your* thing—" I scowl. "But most people actually *want* to have fun. Myself included."

"I can have fun," I snap, completely proving her point.

"Oh yeah," she says sarcastically. "You're a real *bundle of joy.*"

I cross my arms defensively. I can have *fun*. I have fun *all the time*. That night in the storage closet? *Fun. I'm* fun.

"Try me."

I know I'm falling for it. I'm stepping right into her trap. But I can't help it.

"A bet then," she declares, holding out her hand.

I scoff loudly, putting extra emphasis behind the "*umph*" as I eye her hand suspiciously.

"I'm not making a *bet* with you."

Violet nods expectantly, drawing her hand back. Something about the gesture just irritates me more. She was waiting for me to decline. Expecting it. Like I couldn't have fun even if I tried.

This isn't about fun. It's about safety. I wouldn't put it past Violet to let something stupid slip out of her mouth in front of everyone.

"That's a *terrible* idea. You can hardly keep your mouth shut as it is. Plus, that has to violate the contract in some way." I shake my head, a dryness forming in the bottom of my throat. I know it doesn't violate the contract because I wrote it. But I needed to say something to get this idea out of her head.

"Nothing in the contract prohibits a bet. What?" Violet asks sweetly. "Scared you're going to lose?"

Yes, actually. I don't know exactly how I got myself into this situation, and I have no idea how I'm going to get out of it.

If I say no, Violet wins. Her point is proven that I'm no fun. But if I say yes, I will also *probably* lose. And I don't want to have to listen to her boasting about it for the next however long. I need to find a way out of this. And I need to be strategic. My eyes scan the room, nothing really catching my attention until they land on something that would make a little lightbulb appear above my head if we were in a cartoon. This might just be my one-way ticket out of this.

"What's the prize?"

Violet looks at me, her brow raised in a weary expression. "What?"

"The prize. Aren't you supposed to win something?" I ask.

Her smile turns devilish.

"If I win, *you* have to admit you like me."

I look at her, unimpressed. I can work with that. "*Really? That's* your prize? I thought bets were supposed to be high stakes," I taunt.

Violet frowns. "You have a short list, and I want to be on it. What, do you have a better one?"

I lean forward, tapping the empty space on her forearm where the tattoos suddenly stop.

"*That,*" I say confidently. "If I win, I get to choose what goes there."

Violet tugs her arm away, faster than I'd expected.

"You want to pick my tattoo?" Her eyes are wide and round. "No way!"

"Fine," I say shrugging. "No bet."

Cam: One. Violet: Zero.

Violet's brows furrow, then turn pleading. "Can't you pick something else? Something less permanent?"

I shake my head.

"Sounds like the pleas of someone who's scared to lose," I tease. But the second I say it, I know I made a massive mistake. She clears her throat, sits up straight, then stretches out her small, calloused hand.

"Deal," she says firmly. I choke.

"What?"

"Let's do it. If you win, you get to pick my next tattoo. *But—*" She looks at me earnestly. "It can't be some stupid, random thing. It has to tie into the sleeve. I don't need a fucking transformer or some shit ruining thousands of dollars of work."

My lips part, my mouth agape. *This wasn't part of the plan.* My hand trembles as it grips hers and gives a meaningful shake.

"Deal," I say. Because I'm fucking *fun*.

Sixteen

Lucifer in Levi's

Violet

Idn't Satan used to be an angel or something?[8]

Not to compare Cam to the actual devil, but *sometimes*... I thought I was going to win this one. I even wore the only shirt I own that sits a little too low for comfort to distract her. It's red and fitted and perfectly work-appropriate, but shows more than anything else I'd ever even *consider* wearing.

I planned on making this as hard as possible for her. But when I walk into Pacific Pins Bowling Alley, my body turns to Jello.

The jeans are one thing. Dark, mid-rise beauties that hug her hips in a way I wish I could. Even the rips on her thighs exposing that soft, pale skin underneath aren't what makes Cam absolutely evil, no matter how taunting. What forms a pretzel inside of my stomach is the fact that Hayden *fucking* Ayers has his hands wrapped around her waist, her ass pressed firmly against his pelvis.

I know I said fuck already, but *fuck, fuckity-fuck.*

Obviously, Cam is her own woman, and what she does with her body is frankly none of my business. But that doesn't cool my simmering blood. I know she's doing this on purpose. I know she just wants to throw me off my game. Still, I can't help but wonder how on Earth she got him to agree to it.

I look around at the group. It seems everyone is already here getting the lanes set up. Even Malcolm is entering names into the computer, and the dude is late for *every* shift. Leave it to the boss to be the last one to arrive.

"Size seven please," I say with a strained smile when I approach the shoe booth. The teenager behind it eyes my chest with a smirk, and even though this makes my skin crawl, it boosts my confidence that this isn't going to be easy for Cam either. He hands me a pair of shoes that look like they were previously owned by a baby clown. Like a *homicidal* baby clown, given the strange orange stains all over them. I put them on in the hopes that I'm not contaminating evidence for a twenty-year-old cold case.

After tying laces that I swear are disintegrating in my hands, I look toward the lanes, blue, red, and yellow lights beaming across the room. Something about the neon-patterned floor and scent of greasy food feels so nostalgic to me.

Dave, our neighbor from the trailer park in Clarkston, worked at a bowling alley for a couple years. He was a really nice guy, and even let us tag along sometimes, so long as Ruthie agreed to stop blabbing to her friends at school that she got to bowl for free. If it weren't for Dave, the only outings we'd have were trips to the local park, which was really just an empty field. Dave got new jobs a lot, so after the bowling alley, we went to the movie theater, and then the aquarium, then the Martial Arts Academy, all for free.

Is leaving this little piece of information out considered cheating?

Maybe. But Cam is smart enough to know I wouldn't have agreed to stakes so high if I wasn't going to win. Especially since she's aware I've been saving that spot for just the right thing at just the right time.

I'm not worried about it. Middle school me has this one in the bag.

I glance around and find everyone gathered around the bar. Well, not *every-one*. Brooke and Malcolm are in the arcade playing a racing game, and from the looks of it, she is *totally* kicking his ass.

I approach them. Cam is still tangled in Hayden's thick biceps, the back of her head resting against his chest.

This *has* to be part of the bet, right?

Her eyes dart over to me, and I immediately look away. I'm not going to give her the satisfaction.

"Hey Vi!" Avery nods, flashing me a soft smile. "I was wondering when you were gonna show."

Avery doesn't need to know that the reason I'm late is because I spent two hours watching bowling tips on YouTube.

"Yeah, I had some catching up to do," I say instead. Avery nods, and Adrian's head tilts slightly.

"Is there anything I can help you with?" they ask. Adrian is a sweetheart. They're always bouncing around the facility, asking everyone what they can do to help.

Everything about them screams wholesome, but you'd be shocked as to what they're capable of.

Once, a rude customer *screamed* at Brooke because she brought out the wrong "Daisy Mae." When I got to the lobby, Adrian was already telling him not to yell at her and that, if he didn't want to get the dogs mixed up, he should be more specific or—and I quote—"*Pick a less basic name.*" I did have to have a chat with them afterward, but I couldn't deny their intentions were purely protective.

I smile.

"No, I think we're all good now. But thanks."

I feel a presence behind me, a familiar voice chiming in. "I think *someone* wants to say hi," Hayden says.

Normally, I *love* Hayden's voice. It's deep but gentle, and if I'm hearing it, it means we're together. I like being around Hayden, even though he's usually paying me to be there. But images of his arms snaked around Cam's waist flicker in my mind, and I don't realize how tense my jaw is until my teeth grate together in a painful, screeching friction.

I'm not the jealous type. I loved when everyone saw Mallory the way I did. Radiant and elegant. Beautiful. She walked around with a sort of glow to her. A glow that would irritate me when people *didn't* turn their heads to look.

I'm not the jealous type, and I'm not even jealous now. I'm just pissed that, if I let Cam distract me, I might lose this goddamn bet.

I plaster a smile on my face and turn around to look at him. Hayden's grinning down at me with the most innocent face and steps to the side to reveal a tall, lanky white poodle. Major's eyes widen, and he steps back excitedly in an attempt to control himself. His gaze flashes to Hayden, and he sits quickly, without being prompted. Hayden gives him a nod.

"Okay, Major," he says, tapping his knee. "You can go say hi."

Major trots over to me, the pom-pom on his tail swaying with enthusiasm.

I crouch down and ruffle my fingers through his top knot, sinking my knuckle into his ear and scratching vigorously.

"Hey handsome," I say, grateful that I now have something else to look at for the duration of the night. Something that isn't Cam.

Hayden slaps a hand against his chest adoringly. "Awh."

My gaze flicks up to look at him, but out of the corner of my eye, I see her. I don't mean to, and I don't want to, but my eyes latch onto Cam the moment she looks back at me.

It's a brief glance. Something nobody else around us would ever think twice about. But to me, it feels like I'm frozen in time.

Mallory's eyes are blue and glassy. Sometimes, they almost looked translucent. I always thought she had the most beautiful eyes on the planet. Blue has always been my favorite color. But the way the light reflects off of Cam's umber irises is like a strike of lightning in a midnight storm. When it hits just right, it highlights all of the things you didn't know were there. The golden undertones, the bronze flecks. Her eyes aren't brown, at least not just. Whatever color you'd classify it as, it may just be my new favorite.

I look back to Major.

After we get our drinks and Brooke beats Malcolm a *second* time at the racing game, we break off into two lanes. Just my luck, I get stuck with Cam and the human straitjacket.

Kidding. Kind of.

I mean, his hands *are* wrapped around hers, guiding her body to the perfect bowling form. I'm sure this is another attempt to distract me because, for someone who threatened to kick my ass at bowling, she's sure acting completely clueless about it. Their arms draw back together, his other hand on her hip, then they roll. The ball makes a dull thud as it lands on the polished lane, barreling down the center.

I don't believe in God, but I still pray for it to roll into the gutter. When they get a strike instead, I take a long swig of my drink. Cam turns around, flashing me a taunting smile.

"Nice *practice roll*," I say. Cam tosses her head at the lane.

"Your turn."

I shake my head.

"Some of us don't need to practice." I say it confidently and teasing, but I don't know that I actually mean it. I haven't picked up a ball in years. Hayden whistles.

"Violet's getting *spicy*."

I chuckle and sit back as I watch everyone finish their practice rounds. Avery rolls first. He chucks his ball so hard I'm shocked the wooden lane doesn't shatter. He gets a strike though, and we all clap, impressed.

"You're up," Hayden says, patting my shoulder like I'm a kid on her first day of T-Ball.

I set my drink down onto the table and grab a scuffed red ball off the rack. Cam stands to the side, arms crossed as she watches me. I position my feet, one in front of the other, and make eye contact with her as I bend down slightly, revealing a small gap between my shirt and my chest.

Her jaw goes slack, just for a moment, then she quickly snaps it shut. My tongue pokes the inside of my lower lip as I try not to look too amused. My arm sways, my fingers release, and the ball glides effortlessly down the lane, crashing into the pins. They tip, falling into one another in a domino effect. But after the ball falls into the pit behind, I realize one pin is still standing. It wobbles, for a moment, then steadies itself, still upright.

"Nice!" Avery says, and Hayden claps theatrically. I pick up another ball, this one a shimmering cerulean. I line my feet up, take a breath, then release it.

The ball slips straight into the gutter, and I try not to hang my head in embarrassment. I tack on a smile instead and turn around with forced confidence.

"Who's up?"

Hayden rolls, unattached to Cam this time, and knocks down six pins, then two more. Next, it's Cam's turn. She eyes me as if she's trying to intimidate me when she walks up to the lane, a pink ball just slightly larger than the one I used in her hand.

My stomach sinks. Either it's by complete chance, or Cam knew exactly which ball to pick up. It's just right for her, thirteen pounds and the holes placed so her fingers stretch just the right amount. I swallow.

She steps back, holding the ball up to her chest, before lowering it down to her knee. She takes one step. Then another. Her arm draws back, the ball lowers down, and—

"Shit, watch out!"

The ball slips from her fingers, flying into the lane next to us. Synchronous gasps escape Hayden's and Avery's mouths as the ball thuds against the wood and barrels down the lane until it lands in the gutter.

Cam's face grows beet red, her eyes widening and her nose twitching. Maybe when Hayden was helping her, she wasn't pretending after all.*

"Hey kid, maybe you'd hit some pins if you stayed in your lane!" Avery shouts.

My next turn isn't much better. It stays in our lane at least but goes directly into the gutter. And the next round, only two pins fall over.

"Tough streak," Avery mutters, just as he rolls his fourth strike of the game. Luckily, Cam is struggling just a bit more than me, and I manage to stay a hair ahead of her the entire time.

It's the last round. Avery just finished out at 216 points, and no matter how well the rest of us roll, there's no doubt he's the winner. But I'm not focused on the overall victory. I just care about my own.

I stare down the center of the lane, letting my brain fill with Dave's voice.

"Aim between the pins."

I exhale, tossing my arm back, then strategically letting go at just the right time. That same glittery ball spins down the wood, shimmering in the neon bowling alley lighting. It hits the pins with force, but not too much force, and seven pins crash against the wood.

I can't stop myself from doing a little dance of victory as I pick up my next ball. Cam hasn't rolled anything over a six, and though I've been struggling the majority of the game too, I'm confident now that I am going to win this bet.

My last roll is a one, bringing me to a whopping total of seventy-one points. Avery grins at my excitement, no doubt wondering why I am so damn happy, when my score is so damn low. Cam, however, is glaring at me, her arms crossed, dissatisfied.

I can't help myself. I pull out my phone and click the thread titled "Sparky"

Cam's eyes dart to me when she feels the vibration in her back pocket. She eyes me suspiciously as she pulls it out and rolls her eyes in a melodramatic manner. She begins typing, then looks up at me, waiting for me to read her response.

I pause, considering what I'm about to say, then decide that watching Cam's reaction in real time will be totally worth it.

I look up, locking my focus onto Cam's face. She leans against the table, sucking on a cherry lollipop Adrian won for her from the arcade. The white stick twirls between her fingers, then suddenly stops. Her eyes scan the screen of her phone, pink rising to her cheeks as her pouty lips part, her jaw falling open. She looks up at me, blinking slowly.

I flash her a sinful smile, letting one eyebrow raise ever-so-slightly. Cam swallows.

"Not bad," Hayden says, plopping down in the seat next to her. He stretches his arms behind his head and rests the back of his skull against his interlocked palms. "One-hundred-and-forty-two."

Our eye contact breaks as Cam looks up at the screen and scowls at her position on the board. Hayden pats her back.

"It's okay, Cam. It's just a game."

Maybe it is just a game, to him at least. And maybe it's even just a game to her. I, however, could not be happier. My score might be shit compared to the boys', but there is no way in *hell* Cam is going to score nineteen points in two turns.

She gets up, trudges over to the rack, and selects that same, pink ball. She looks at Hayden, almost as if searching for reassurance, then looks at me in defeat.

She doesn't even step backwards. She doesn't crouch down as she lets go. She just kind of tosses the ball, in an almost pouting type of way. The ball glides slowly across the lane, hitting three pins on the left side. The pins fall, and Cam huffs, crossing her arms.

"Do I have to finish?" she asks. "It's just rubbing salt in the wound."

Hayden's eyes shoot up, looking at her with concern. He smiles.

"It's something new," he says. "You should finish, just so you can say you did it."

My brows furrow, and my gaze flicks back over to Cam. She lets out a heavy sigh, and my mind flips back to that conversation we had in the storage closet. The one about trying new things.

I thought it was just about entertaining her bisexuality. But this comment makes me think there might be more to it.

She grabs another ball, this time a yellow one.

It's small, and dull, and scuffed so badly I'm not sure it's even going to roll.

"You got this Cam," I say in support. I don't know why, but I just feel like she needs it. Besides, I've won.

There's no point in gloating, at least not right now.

Cam smiles at me, the dimple in her cheek just briefly existing, then vanishing again. She stands. She crouches. She rolls.

The ball spins down the alley, a tiny yellow tornado flying toward the remaining pins. It crashes into them, the front ones tipping, then toppling over into the ones behind. The ball rolls into the pit in the back, and Cam turns around. She's not smiling, but she's not pouting either.

Really, she just looks relieved it's over.

"Hey, that's not bad," I say, feeling like, for some reason, I need to make her feel better. I have no idea why. Just minutes ago, I wanted to relentlessly rub her face in my victory. But now, I don't care about that anymore. "Nine points behind is nothing."

Avery chuckles, shaking his head.

"Nine points behind *you.*" Hayden shoots him a glare, so I don't have to. "But she's got time."

My brows drop over my eyes as I look at him in confusion.

"Game's over, dude. You won."

Avery shakes his head, pointing to the screen hanging above us.

"I won," he agrees. "But the game *isn't* over. She got a spare."

Cam's head shoots up, looking at Avery, and then at the screen with just as much confusion as I did.

"Huh?"

"She got a spare," he explains. "In the last round, if you get a strike, or a spare, you get to go a third time."

Fuck.

I forgot about that. Suddenly, all the guilt and mature feelings I had about the situation crumble to the ground. Cam has another turn. Her face lights up, and she holds up a finger before running over to the next lane. She returns with

Adrian, their hands woven tightly together.

"Moral support?" I ask. Cam nods.

"Adrian's my good luck charm."

Adrian winks at me, and Hayden and Avery nod in agreement. Why do I suddenly feel like I'm completely fucked?

Adrian hands her a ball, and Cam stands in front of the lane, her eyes closed tight. Her chest rises and falls slowly, and Adrian squeezes her arm. Then, they take a step back.

We all watch as Cam rolls a perfect, pin-shattering strike.

SEVENTEEN

Clipper Confessions

CAM

COORDINATION ISN'T REALLY MY strong suit. I'm the type of person who sucks at pretty much anything athletic. Even Wii Sports is a challenge for me. Hayden's seven-year-old sister places better than I do.

So how I managed to beat Violet in bowling had to be entirely luck. Only, my luck is typically terrible too, so maybe it was more so pure motivation.

Honestly, I didn't give a single fuck about picking out her tattoo. I just chose that in an attempt to take the idea of a bet entirely off the table. But Violet's promise to fuck me until I have to call into work? Now *that's* a prize I can get behind.

Still, I did win the tattoo decision, so I may as well take advantage of it. I've been thinking about it the past few days, trying to figure out what I can choose that would fit in with the rest of her sleeve.

I think I found just the thing.

"Good boy Major," I say, praising him for simply standing still on the table. Honestly, that's an accomplishment for a nine-month-old puppy. The fact that he's a service dog in training might have something to do with his perfect behavior, but I attribute it to my patient and loving demeanor instead. The silver teethed shears glide over his perfectly straightened white coat, smoothing out any imperfections in the cut.

I'm a mess of a person, I know that. Hell, this entire Violet situation is a fucking mess. I still can't wrap my mind around it. The fact that I'm doing something so risky. So unpredictable. Everything is a mess. But Major is going to be perfect.

"I mean, I was planning to give you shit, but I gotta say... *damn.*"

"Hayden, are you even *allowed* back here?" I ask, pressing my free hand against my hip. He brushes his blonde hair out of his eyes and shoots me a gleaming smile.

"Avery let me sneak back. Besides, people pity the disabled guy who's separated from his beloved service dog."

I give him a faux pout. "Oh, you poor, *poor* thing."

"I know, it's heartbreaking. Almost makes you just wanna hold me and take care of me until I inevitably die. Maybe pity me enough to give me a kiss."

His smile turns crafty, and he finishes it off with a wink. Hayden is probably the most flirtatious person I have ever met. He'd flirt with a telephone pole if the lighting was right. I know he doesn't really mean it, at least not to me. He just has a strong appreciation for the female gender. Maybe it's because he was born in one's body, or maybe it's just who he is.

That's why we have the agreement: we pretend to be a couple in public if we don't want to be approached. He saw his ex at the bowling alley, and I wanted the chance to make Violet jealous. So, it was a win-win scenario, even if he didn't know my motives.

"It really, *really* doesn't," I say, turning back to Major and resuming my work.

He steps through the doorway he'd been lingering in, hands in his pockets as he looks around.

"Does that have anything to do with me?" he asks, his voice lowering. He stands just beside me, the heat from his body filling the air. "Or does it have more to do with the fact that you and Violet are fucking?"

My body freezes, every muscle turning into pure, thick ice. Well, every muscle besides the ones in my neck, which turns sharply so that I am face-to-face with Hayden. My lungs are like a capsule, locked tightly so nothing can come in or out.

How the fuck did he know?

"I don't—"

"Know what I'm talking about?" he interrupts, his head tilting in an all-too-telling way. Nothing I say is going to convince him otherwise. I can pretend I don't know what he's talking about. I can try gaslighting him into thinking it's all in his head. But from the way his eyebrow is quirked and how his lip twitches, I know that there is absolutely no point.

Now, the only thing that can come from denying it is broken trust between us.

Which only reminds me...

"Don't tell Adrian," I blurt out. "Please." I look up at him desperately.

Adrian is amazing. They're the type of friend you die for because they're the type to die for you. They'll stick next to you through every bump and struggle and mistake. They're my soulmate.

But this isn't a "pissing myself at the movies" kind of secret. It's not even an "I accidentally shoplifted this $70 bag" kind of secret (yes, I returned it). This is a "could completely fuck me over" type of secret. A secret that could ruin everything.

Detoxing your life is so much harder than it sounds, especially when you have an adjustment disorder. It should be easy, getting rid of the things that you know are terrible for you. But it isn't. At least not for me. I wasn't blind to the fact that Cody was abusive. And I knew The Dog Shop wasn't any better. But those things were constants in my life. Pillars of my routine. Things I knew, things I expected.

And I'm grateful that they're over with. It took a lot of work. A lot of therapy sessions and panic attacks but I did it. I'm here, in a supportive workplace, surrounded by my friends. I can't lose this. I've worked too hard to lose it.

And Violet? Well, this could fuck her over just as badly.

Hayden offers me a warm smile, his hand resting on my shoulder.

"Cam, I'm *proud* of you," he says. "I'm proud that change is filling your life, and I'm proud you're letting it." My muscles ease slightly, feeling the solace of his voice. "But I'm also worried. I know Violet, Cam. She's amazing. She's the kind of person you don't let go. But that's the problem. You're doing new things, exploring your sexuality, and I'm here for it. I'm proud of you. But this thing with Violet, it's temporary."

My brows furrow, my body tensing up again in defense.

"I know," I say. "That's the point."

He nods. "Okay. I just want to point that out. Because it kind of—the point of you having a one-night stand was to avoid attachment. And…"

I frown.

"I'm not going to get attached, Hayden."

"I'm not saying you are, I'm just—" He clears his throat. "I just want to make sure you've thought this through. It's hard to be around someone in such an intimate way without catching feelings."

I know Hayden is just worried about me. He's trying to protect me, and I love him for that. But I'm not the same broken Cam I was when he met me. Sure, I still have work to do. But I'm different now. I'm changing.

I don't need him to protect me. I'm not going to get attached to Violet. I can hardly stand being in the same room as her when we aren't fucking. My head tilts, and I lean against his arm.

"I've thought this through," I say softly. "I promise."

His hand cups the back of my head gently. "Okay," he says. "I believe you."

We stand there in silence for a moment, until Major lets out a soft whine.

"Oh buddy," Hayden says, reaching his hand out to pet him. "You're fine. Sorry for distracting her."

I shake my head and slide Major's head through the nylon loop attached to the table.

"He's just about done. He did awesome, by the way."

"We can credit most of that to *your girl*." Hayden wiggles his eyebrows as he emphasizes the word. "She's pretty awesome at her job."

"She's *not* my girl," I say, shoving him playfully. Both my hands straddle my hips, and I lean to the side, shooting him a glare. "And it's her *side* job."

Hayden coaxes Major off the table and clips a navy collar around his neck. He smirks.

"So are you, apparently."

I point to the door, an unamused expression on my face. "Out. *Now*."

Hayden tilts his head back apologetically. "C'mon, Cam, it was just a joke." I continue pointing at the door. "Fine," he grumbles, giving me a tight side-squeeze. He walks toward the closed door and reaches for the handle.

I swallow. "Hayden, wait."

He stops and turns toward me with a smile.

"How did you know?"

His blue eyes shimmer for a moment, then glaze over.

"I know you Cam," he says. "Maybe better than myself."

A crease forms between my brows as I press them together. He shakes his head.

"I saw your texts," he says. "At the bowling alley."

"Oh." I nod.

Hayden nods back, turning toward the door again.

"Love you," he says, pushing it open. I smile, waving at him even though his back is turned.

"Love you too."

Eighteen

Permanent

Violet

"I CAN'T *BELIEVE* I agreed to this."

The familiar sting of the needle glides across my skin, the hum of the tattoo gun following its path. Stacy, my regular tattoo artist, chuckles, and I open my right eye just slightly, hoping to catch a glimpse.

"Keep them closed!" Cam snaps from the corner.

I groan.

"That wasn't part of the deal."

Cam doesn't respond, and I can only imagine she's rolling her eyes at me. She does that a lot.

"How long have you two been together?" Stacy asks, wiping a dry paper towel against the raw skin. It stings, even more than the actual needle, but I don't wince.

Cam snorts, which I find kind of rude, even if I have the same internal reaction.

"We're not," I answer.

"Oh! Really? I just assumed because—"

"Definitely not," Cam interrupts. Stacy continues the tattoo, and from the intensity of the burn, I think she's adding the final highlights.

"*Okay,*" she says, not sounding convinced. I can see why. Not many people would let someone pick out a tattoo willy-nilly. But in my defense, I didn't think it was *actually* going to happen. I didn't think Cam would *actually* win.

A relieving cold, wet towel glides across my skin.

"You're all done!" Stacy announces. My eyes shoot open, my gaze falling immediately down to the tattoo.

I analyze it, tilting my head in focus, and after a moment, I realize exactly what it is. A maniacal laugh erupts from me, and I slap the armrest, my feet kicking in the air. I knew Cam could be petty, but I didn't know she had such a sense of humor.

"So I'm guessing this means something to you?" Stacy asks, quirking an eyebrow. My eyes land on the greyscale hammerhead shark, permanently inked into my skin. Memories from that night at Monsey's flood into my brain. The spilled margarita. That shiny stained emerald dress. Those fluffy hammerhead shark slippers. I laugh all over again.

"It—*no*," I say, shaking my head. "Well, *yes*, but—"

I look up at Cam. She's trying but failing to hide a proud smirk.

"Not really," she says, looking over at Stacy. "It just means that, when I place a bet, I always come out winning."

"**Y**OU MISSED THE TURN!" Cam whines, pointing aggressively at the side street I completely intentionally drove past. My eyes stay locked onto the road in front of me, one hand gripping the wheel so hard my knuckles turn white. She insisted we drive together so that I "couldn't change my mind." Sure, I might be too nice to leave her stranded at a tattoo shop she's never been to. But now, she's going to wish she had taken the risk.

"Violet!" I glance at her, then back to the road. "Violet Wolfe, take me home *now*!"

For someone who is so unsure about things, Cam is pretty damn demanding. The corner of my mouth tugs into a smirk.

"I can't," I say innocently, pressing my foot down on the brake. We stop at the intersection, the Jeep rolling back slightly as we do. I turn to look at her, her beautiful glaring eyes locking onto mine. "The tattoo was only half of the promise."

Cam's eyes widen, pink rushing to her cheeks. She drags a hand down the side of her face, still staring at me. Her mouth opens to speak, but nothing comes out, so she closes it again.

Cam might have won that bet, but I think I just won this conversation.

She keeps staring at me, jaw slack and face red. A loud honk pierces the silence, and my eyes dart back to the road, my foot to the gas pedal.

Thank God it's Thursday.

I waste no time once we walk through my front door. It's a good thing I had to get the tattoo because I left Reese at work so he could play. I tug Cam's shirt over her head, my lips crashing into hers the second her mouth pokes out from beneath the hem. I toss it. To where, I couldn't tell you. One hand strategically unclasps the back of her bra, as the other travels downward, grabbing her ass so hard it makes her squeal.

"Damn, Violet, buy a girl a drink first!" She jumps back. I grab her ass even harder this time, pulling her into me.

"I did," I say through gritted teeth. I pride myself on my ability to stay composed. To stay positive. To stay kind. But damn, does Cameron Miller make it fucking difficult. "And I just spent three-hundred dollars on a fucking tribute to you, so shut up and let me work."

I press our lips together again and suck her lower one between my teeth. Her hands press against my chest, but not in the way I want them to. She pushes me away.

"That was not a *tribute*," she says, frowning. "It was revenge. Every time you see it, you'll remember spilling tequila all over my favorite dress."

I step close to her, my lips grazing hers delicately as her eyes flutter up to look at me in aggravation.

"That dress," I say, sliding my hand against her jaw. "Was already stained. And that description—" My thumb runs across her lower lip, and Cam's breath hitches. "Sounds a lot like a tribute."

Cam huffs, but I don't let her finish getting it out before I press back up against her, this time reaching for the button of her pants. I snap it open, dragging the zipper down before hooking my fingers in the denim belt loops.

"Wait, Violet! Don't—"

I'm getting real fucking tired of this woman telling me what to do. I yank them down, trying to pull off her pants but—

"Violet!"

I look down, my fingers still curved into hooks but not attached to anything. Two, thin strips of denim hang off of the waistband of Cam's jeans, her pale skin peeks through the small holes where they had just been attached. Blood rushes to her face, and I swear a vein starts peeking through the skin on her forehead.

"Those were my favorite jeans," she snaps.

I shrug. "I'll buy you new ones."

Then I dip my fingers into her waistband, and tug the jeans the rest of the way off. They're tight against her body, so I don't even need to try to take the underwear along with them. It just happens on its own. My hands hook on the backside of her thighs, but Cam pushes me away again. Why is she always pushing me away?

"Wait, wait—" She shakes her head. "I'm not doing this again while you're fully clothed."

I frown.

"I wasn't fully clothed last week."

She shoots me an unimpressed expression. "I'm not consenting until your clothes are off," she declares, crossing her arms over her naked body.

God, Cam is sexy. And beautiful too. She's got these light pink nipples, the same color of her lips. And the pear-shaped curve of her body makes me feral, I swear. All I want is to get my hands back on that delightful ass of hers.

But nothing turns me on like her eyes. She tells me everything with them, even things she'll never say out loud. I never thought something so pure could make me so desperate. I stare into them, plastering a wide smirk on my face as I unbutton my own pants, pull them down, and step out of them.

Cam's eyes widen and lock onto me as her lips slowly part. I continue smiling as I pull my shirt over my head, followed by my sports bra, before letting them both drop to the floor.

The cold air hits my clit and my breasts all at once, causing the hairs on my body to stand up. My nipples harden around the solid metal bars, and I watch Cam cross her legs, her muscles tensing.

"May I approach?" I ask sarcastically. "Or is the Ice Princess still not satisfied?"

Cam stares, shaking her head, but then nods instead. I chuckle as I step closer to her and allow my cold hands to glide across her bare skin.

"Better?" I ask, tilting my head to get better access to her collarbone. My lips press against the skin, sucking softly at first, then harder. Cam hisses.

"Yes," she whines, pushing her body into mine. I smile against her skin, then loop my hands under her thighs and scoop her off the ground.

She grabs at my back frantically.

"Violet! What the fuck are you doing?" she squeals. I continue walking over to the laundry room, then plop her right on top of the washing machine.

"I thought this was about trying new things," I say innocently. Then, I lock eyes with her as I reach out, and turn the knob on the washing machine, pressing "start."

Cam's brows press together, a small "v" forming between them.

"Violet, I—"

But the washing machine starts, the soft hum of it vibrating the entire appliance, and Cam's eyes grow wide, her brows shooting up. Her body sways with the rumble of the machine, her thighs shaking. God, I just want to put my face between them. Cam looks at me, bewildered.

"I can stop, if you want," I offer, even though it's the last thing on Earth I want to do. Thankfully, Cam shakes her head. My hand slides between her legs, scooting them apart slowly in the process. She swallows, gripping the edges of the washing machine nervously. That beautiful pussy reveals itself to me slowly the more I keep spreading her open.

I chuckle, shaking my head.

"God, Cam. How'd you do it?" I ask. Her brows furrow, and she looks down at me.

"What?"

My mind flicks to last week at the bowling alley, Hayden's hands wrapped around her. I couldn't ask her about it before today because, if I violate that contract, I will never hear her moan my name again.

That isn't something I'm willing to lose.

"How'd you get Hayden to practically air hump you in the bowling alley?"

I know Hayden knows about our agreement now. Cam told me. But his arms were around her before that, and I haven't stopped thinking about it since. Cam rolls her eyes, the soft vibration of the machine making her squirm.

"He wasn't *air humping* me," she says. She starts to close her legs, but I shake my head, stopping them with my hand. She sighs. "We have an agreement too. We'll pretend to be a couple sometimes, in public situations. That way we don't have to deal with people."

My lip piercing clashes with my teeth as they sink into my bottom lip, images of her ass pressed against his pelvis flashing through my memory. I lean down and look up at her as my head settles between her thighs.

"This is *my* pussy, Cam," I say, heat filling my cheeks as those thoughts fill my mind. Thoughts of Hayden or anyone else touching her make my skin hot.

I said I'm not jealous. But I never said I liked to share.

"I don't remember that being in the contract," Cam taunts, tapping her fingers on the side of the washing machine. I frown, lifting my head.

"If you want to come," I say sternly, pressing two cold fingers against her pussy. "It's 'yes, boss.'"*

Nineteen

'Till It's Gone

Cam

I STARE DOWN AT Violet, her pretty slender face positioned between my thighs, her head tilted up to look at me.[10]

"If you want to come, it's 'yes, boss'," she says.

My hips unintentionally buck forward, the vibration of the washing machine beneath me tunneling through my skin and radiating in my throbbing clit. I bite my lip, shaking my head.

"No," I manage to say, though it loses its meaning with the waver of my voice. Violet's brows raise in surprise.

"What?" Her enunciation is clearer than ever. I stand my ground.

"You might be my boss at work," I say, swallowing back a moan as the washing machine starts to shake harder. "But here, you listen to me."

How I gathered the strength to say that, I have no idea. Violet's eyes darken, her gaze narrowing onto me. I swallow nervously.

She could take me apart in an instant, I know it. But I can't let her win every round. It boosts her ego. Gives her too much confidence that I'll do whatever she wants. I have control too.

Violet doesn't respond. Or she does, just not verbally. Her tongue slips between my folds, licking hot wet stripes in the center. I groan, the rocking of the machine underneath us causing her tongue to vibrate. I don't know if I should take this as a win or not.

"Shit," I mumble, rolling my hips forward. Violet slides her thumb through my slick heat, then dragging it back and forth against the delicate skin.

"I thought this was supposed to be rough," I grumble. A gasp forces its way out of my throat as two fingers suddenly sink inside of me. I jolt forward, gripping her shoulder with a shaky moan. She smirks, and I hate the fact that she thinks she's winning.

"Maybe it isn't," I say breathily, my forehead wrinkling as Violet continues pumping into me. "An agreement."

She doesn't stop, but her head snaps up to look at me.

"What do you mean?"

A small moan forces itself out of my throat, but I push past it. Watching Violet's face is going to be so much more worth it.

"With Hayden. Maybe it's just how we are."

It isn't of course. Anyone who knows us knows we're practically siblings. But Violet doesn't know us, at least not together. I bite the inner corner of my lip as her face turns red, her jaw tightening, her fingers slowing down.

"Don't say his name while my fingers are inside you unless you want to know what regret feels like."

But I very much want to know.

"Who?" I ask, batting my eyelashes angelically. "Hayden?"

But I miss Violet's reaction because my eyes squeeze shut, my head tossing back as she presses back into me. Her fingers curl inside as her tongue dances on my vibrating clit.

"God you're such a fucking brat," she murmurs before latching her mouth back onto me. My thighs squeeze around her, the washing machine rocking my body from side to side as one of Violet's arms cradles my thigh. My stomach tightens, my hands slipping from the sides of the vibrating appliance beneath me. Her fingers dip in and out effortlessly, the wet slick mess she made of me causing electricity to run through my body. I melt against the washer.

My hips thrust forward, forcing her fingers deeper inside as her tongue glides across my throbbing clit.

"Oh fuck," I groan, using her face for my own pleasure. I should have told her off a long time ago. I feel it coming, the edge I need so desperately to tip over. I rock my hips harder, my eyes squeezing shut as Violet's name forces itself from my throat.

"Oh fuck, I can't," I whimper, my hands trembling and my legs shaking against the steady pound of the washing machine. Violet looks up, her mouth wet.

"You can," she says. "You can take it."

My chest heaves as I lock eyes with her, the words coming from her mouth so genuine and so convincing. But then, the corner of her mouth slowly creeps up. Suddenly, the friction against me ceases, the pressure inside of me stuck. I frown, looking down at her with pleading eyes and thrusting myself toward her, my legs still spread.

"You can take it, but you aren't going to until you learn to listen to me."

Oh fuck. No no no. My head tosses back as I let out an indiscernible plea. I look down at her desperately, my fingertips shaking against the edge of the coated steel.

"I told you," she taunts. "You'd regret it."

This cannot be happening.

"Fuck Violet. If you knew how badly I wanted you, you wouldn't be teasing me like this."

Violet smiles sweetly, tracing a wet finger in circles around my thigh.

"Oh, princess," she coos. "That's *precisely* why I'm teasing you."

The washing machine picks up again, rocking against the back wall as I squeeze my thighs shut, desperate for pressure.

She tuts, shaking her head and sliding them back apart.

"I thought you liked rules," she says.

I squirm under the tense vibration, the feeling traveling through my body to the most sensitive parts, the parts that need her the most. My mouth opens, but nothing comes out. The muscles in my body are tense, my clit throbbing, begging for contact.

Violet stands between my legs, her dark nipples hard. I slide forward, lifting my hips to graze my clit against the cold, metal piercing on her tits. She looks down, watching me rub my swollen desperate pussy on her pierced nipples, begging for any friction at all. Then, she looks back up at me, the ghost of a smile tugging at her lips. She steps back, just far enough that I can't reach her anymore.

"You want to come?" she asks, her raspy voice making me weak.

I nod, pleading. She looks down at my dripping pussy, my legs spread wide on display just for her.

"God you're wet," she mumbles, tracing a finger up the center. She sucks it into her mouth, her eyes locking onto mine. "Who made you so wet?"

I swallow, fingers curling around the sides of the machine.

"You did, boss."*

T RYING NEW THINGS MAY just be my new favorite hobby. With Violet, at least, because holy fuck is my mind *blown*.

It's so foreign to me, enjoying something new without the constant fear of it going wrong. I don't know how she does it, makes me feel so confident about doing things I've never done before.

"I see you've made it," Violet smirks, leaning against the silver tub. I look up from the silver lab inside. "Does that mean I get to try again?"

I shoot her a glare that says, "contract violation," like I wouldn't like to see her try.

"Do you need something, or are you just going to keep coming in here to distract me?"

"Chico's dad wanted a nail trim. I was wondering if you'd—"

A melody cuts her off, singing cheerfully from her back pocket. Of course Violet would have "Walking on Sunshine" as her ringtone. How on-brand of her. She looks at the screen and smiles to herself before answering.

"What's up, Ruthie?" she asks casually. I don't know who Ruthie is, but for some reason, my stomach sinks just a little when I hear her name. My eyes dart to Violet's face, trying to read what her expression might tell me. But the second it reaches, that smile drops. Her forehead creases, her brows pressed together.

"Woah, woah, slow down. What?"

Concern fills her face, her eyes darting back and forth in front of her, but I don't think she's really looking at anything. She shakes her head, her shoulders dropping.

"No Ruthie. I'm not-I can't. I'm sorry but no. I've put them both through it four times, and I can't afford to do it again. Especially—"

I'm assuming whoever Ruthie is interrupts her because Violet stops in the middle of her sentence. She shakes her head again.

"Ruthie, they never follow through. They are never going to follow through. I know it's a disease, I'm not saying it isn't. But—"

She stops again.

"No. If they wanted to get better, they would have by now. They have the tools, they have the support."

Violet's eyes dart up to me, then quickly lower. "I'm at work. I have to go. Love you," she says, then hangs up the phone. She slides it into her pocket, her eyes still lowered to the floor.

[11]"Sorry about that," she says, letting out a forced chuckle. "You know how sisters are."

I nod, like I have any idea how sisters can be.

Violet's eyes look glazed over, her once-loose body now tense and rigid. My head tilts, and I look at her with concern.

"Is everything okay?" I ask. I don't mean to, and really, I feel like I've completely overstepped by asking. This really is none of my business, and per our agreement, it should stay that way. But Violet's forced smile has me so unconvinced that the concern I feel only grows.

"Yeah, everything's fine," she says, scratching the back of her head. "It's..."

She stops, swallowing hard and I think she too just remembered the terms of our arrangement. But I don't care about that right now. I can tell something is bothering her, and I know I won't be able to think about anything else until I know why. I look around, the door to the salon shut tight.

"I've fucked you enough times to know when something is off," I say in a hushed tone, which may not be the best approach to a serious conversation.

But if there's one thing I know about Violet, it's that "serious" isn't in her vocabulary. Her head shakes, and her eyes meet mine.

"It's nothing, really," she says, trying to play it off. "Parents are just hard sometimes."

I let out a soft laugh, not because it's funny but because if anyone knows how hard parents can be, it sure as hell isn't me. I never even met my mom, and my dad was my best friend. He wasn't ever difficult. Protective, maybe. But never hard. So really, the only thing I know about parents is that they die.

But I guess, in some way, that is parents being hard. It was hard to lose them. Sometimes, it's hard to live without them.

"Yeah," I say, looking up at her. "I get it."

Violet's eyebrow raises, her hazel eyes looking into mine like they're trying to read me. Her tongue fiddles with her lip piercing from the inside, which causes it to twist and turn. She sighs.

"It's... they haven't always been there. *Never*, actually," she says with a sad laugh. "And they've been leeching off my sister Ruthie for the past few months now because they got evicted from their house. I guess paying their rent wasn't as important as paying for drugs." She shakes her head, her gaze falling. "I've been trying to tell Ruthie to kick them out since the moment they moved in. There are shelters in the area they can go to, resources for them if they need it. But she refuses. She thinks they're going to get better."

A loud sigh escapes her mouth, and she rubs the dog's head gently. My stomach sinks, listening to her heart break. "You'd think after twenty-five years she'd stop thinking that. But anyway, she found a little baggie of something tucked under their mattress. And she's got two little kids in the house. She called me because she wants me to help her put them through rehab." Violet's voice breaks, but she swallows it down and continues with a firm tone. "Which they've already been through *multiple* times. They never stay sober for more than a week after. So, I told her no. I can't afford to keep doing it, especially if they aren't going to actually try. They've never tried." Her voice grows angry, her brows furrowed and her face red.

"Literally, for our entire lives, they've barely even been roommates. I fed

Ruthie. I clothed her. I stole shirts out of the bins behind the thrift store, so we had something to wear to school, even if they were three sizes too big. We spent weekends in the hospital, with them taking turns on who OD'd. We'd sit there, praying they wouldn't die." She shakes her head, then her eyes dart to me. "And I know it's fucked up, but sometimes, I think it would be easier if they had."

The second those words leave her mouth, everything around me begins to spin. My eyes snap up to look at her, my heart pounding heavily against the inside of my ribcage. I can feel my nostrils flaring, my jaw clenching hard.

"You have no idea what you're talking about," I snap, without even realizing I'm saying it. "Dead parents aren't something you wish for, Violet. It fucking sucks, okay? It sucks. So don't—" My voice breaks, and oh god, why are my eyes watering? "*Don't* think it's easier." I step away from her, tears falling down my cheeks. "Actually, you clearly aren't thinking at all."

Violet's eyes widen, her expression falling. "Fuck, Cam. I didn't know." Her hand reaches out to me, but I push it away. "I'm sorry. I never would've—"

"What? Wished your parents were dead? Or just said it out loud in front of me?" Violet goes quiet, her lips pressing together. I let out a loud scoff, my hands clenching into fists so tightly that my nails dig into the palms. "Just go," I say, in a tone that lets her know it isn't up for debate. "*Please,* just go."

Violet swallows, looking at me with round, apologetic eyes. But she exhales, then complies.

My hands tremble as I dig through my denim backpack, the medication bottle vibrating in my shaking palm. It's hard to take the cap off, but it finally clicks open. Two white pills travel down my throat. A shuddering breath slides into my lungs, and I hold it there steadily, wanting, in this moment, to never breathe again. *

Twenty

Strays

Violet

Do you ever fuck up so badly that you feel like you deserve an award? [12] Like "I didn't know you could say something so stupid, but here we are?"

I think I earned a gold-star for being the world's biggest asshole on Friday. Actually, scratch that. *I know* I earned it.

I thought about texting Cam to apologize, but the way she looked at me, I don't think she ever wants to talk to me again. I had absolutely no idea Cam's parents had died. When she said that she "got it," I assumed she meant her parents were kind of like addicts too. Overbearing, maybe, or just plain harsh.

But you know what they say about assuming.

I feel like I should have expected the conversation to end poorly. I never talk about my parents, not to anyone. Even Mallory only knew what she observed herself. Vulnerability is practically a how-to betrayal guide. And that's precisely what I did to Cam.

Hayden explained it yesterday at our session. How her mom died during birth, and her dad in an avalanche. I remembered seeing it a few years ago on the news. He was the only one on the bypass that evening, and the avalanche just fell. There was no warning, no signs. Just a sudden, arbitrary drop.

I cradle my temples between my fingers, rubbing them rapidly. Cam had absolutely every right to react the way she did. I might know what it's like to have shitty parents, but I don't know what it's like to have none at all. She was right. I had no idea what I was talking about.

I look up at the parking lot, leaning against the wall of the facility and taking a large breath. I should be in my car, on my way home. Actually, if I had left when my shift was over, I'd already be at home. But it's been a long day, and I needed to decompress a bit before driving. I needed some fresh air. I take a bite of the beef jerky in my hand.

Reese stands next to me, looking up at me with the cutest, roundest eyes the world has ever seen. I know I shouldn't, but I toss him a piece of jerky anyway.

I hear the front door close, the swing of the heavy door causing just the slightest vibration through my back around the corner. Reese stands, his tail wagging excitedly as he starts to approach the edge of the wall.

"Reese, co—" A little black snout pokes into sight, then the rest of a scruffy black-and-white body. "Oh. Hi Dawson," I say, my heart thrumming in my chest. If Dawson's here, that means—

"Dawson, let's go," Cam commands, giving the leash a slight tug. But Dawson's face is already pressed into Reese's ass, his tail swaying vigorously. Reese's body grows firm, but his tail stays wagging, which I know means he wants to play, so long as he's in charge. Cam tugs the leash again, but Dawson continues to ignore her. I could help her. Give her some tips on keeping his attention and getting him to listen. But I don't think Cam wants my help. Especially not right now.

"Hey." I wave my hand awkwardly, confused as to why anything came out of my mouth when I had already decided not to talk. Surprisingly, Cam looks up at me, but she quickly looks back down at Dawson.

"Hi."

Well, it's not much, but it's a start. I straighten my posture.

"Can we talk?" I ask. I want to apologize. No, I *need* to apologize. But it won't mean anything if Cam isn't ready to hear it.

"You're talking to me now, aren't you?"

Her eyes flick up to me, and if the circumstances were different, I'd think she was almost smiling. I swallow nervously.

"Yes, I know. I just mean—"

Cam laughs, and I don't think I have ever felt more relieved in my life.

"I know. I'm fucking with you," she says, stepping closer to me. "Because I'm *fun*, remember?"

I nod because now isn't the time to tease her back. Now is the time to grovel for holding the trophy of the world's biggest dick (with no dick).

"Look, about Friday…" I scratch behind my ear nervously. "I'm really sorry. I shouldn't have said that. None of it. I got caught up in the moment, and…you were right. I really had no idea what I was talking about."

I wait, trying to look at her and trying even harder not to stare. Cam hates being stared at, which I found out by her almost ripping my head off when I had been looking at her through the groom room window.

Literally, her text said:

> **Stop fucking staring at me or I'm going to rip your head off.**

It isn't my fault she's so easy to stare at. Cam shakes her head, stepping closer to me. I can only imagine what she's about to say.

"Violet, you're an asshole."

"Violet, I don't give a fuck."

"Violet, take your apology and shove it up your—"

"No." She says it definitively. No hesitation, no uncertainty. I look up at her, puzzled, but she continues. "I'm sorry. Look—" She's standing next to me now, leaning against the wall alongside me. "I was hurt. What you said hurt me, and it makes sense that it hurt. It was a hurtful thing to say."

"I know," I look at her apologetically. "And I'm so sorry."

She holds her hand up, which is my cue to stop talking.

"It was hurtful. That doesn't mean it wasn't true. I know what it's like to not have parents. And you have no idea what it's like to have dead ones. But I never had to live with the idea that my parents chose something over me. When I had them, I was always put first. I mean, my mom died—" Her eyes well slightly, but she blinks the tears away. "She died so that I could *exist*. And my dad, he did everything he could to protect me. To love me and take care of me. So I don't have any idea either."

The tip of my nose tingles, my lip sliding between my teeth as I chew on it vigorously and listen to Cam's words. She sighs.

"What?" I ask. Cam is expressive. She doesn't try to hide how she feels or what she's thinking. It's admirable. To just walk about the world so openly. She shakes her head.

"I'm just sorry you had— *have*—to go through that, Violet. It's just as terrible as it is the way I had it. Maybe, from my perspective at least, worse." Her hand squeezes my arm just briefly, and all the hairs on my skin stand up. "What happened to me, with my parents? It was awful. It was a tragedy. But you?" She swallows hard, her eyes glossed over. "It's a betrayal to be put last by the ones who created you. I'm just so sorry."

I try to adjust my eyes, but no matter how hard I try, Cam stays blurry. Then I realize: they're watering.

I blink quickly, patting them dry and turning away from Cam so she doesn't see me. Please, God, do not let the first person to see me cry since first grade be Cameron frickin' Miller.*

Cam's hand rests on my shoulder. But it's quickly pulled away when thundering barks filling the air. Dawson's body stiffens as he lets out the warning, and Reese snaps himself back to my side in his perfect heel position. Cam tugs on Dawson's taut leash, trying to redirect his attention and calm him, while my eyes dart around to find what he's barking at.

Then, I see it. Only a few feet away from us, a large, off-leash dog is sniffing the ground behind a tree. He's unfazed by Dawson's relentless barking but immediately stiffens when he sees Cam and me. She finally tugs him to her side, getting him to relax just enough to be quiet.

"Look," she whispers, pointing at the dog. I nod. "He doesn't have a collar, and he looks *really* skinny."

My head tilts as I look at him closer. She's right. Every bone in this dog's body is peeking through the skin. Every ridge of his spine, every dip in his ribs, is completely visible. Cam hands Dawson's leash to me inconspicuously. Then, she peels the slip lead I was wearing off of me and shoots me a conspiratorial smile.

There are two types of people in this world: those who try to catch loose dogs, and those who don't. The fact that Cam is the former pleases me in a way I can't describe.

"Hey buddy," she says, crouching down near the dog. "Are you lost?"

The dog lets out a low growl, his lip lifted to reveal a set of yellow jagged teeth. Cam steps back.

"Woah."

I've seen her deal with multiple aggressive dogs in the salon. Snappy Shih Tzus and mean Malteses, rude Rottweilers and grumpy German shepherds. But those dogs are vaccinated. Those dogs are restrained. This one looks like he's lived his life outside and is completely alone. So her fear of getting bit is pretty rational.

Still, I love a challenge.

"Here," I say, motioning for her to grab Dawson's leash. She walks back over to me, her brow cocked. "Let me try."

Cam looks at me like I belong in an asylum.

"Are you crazy?" she snaps in a low tone, like the dog will hear her and get offended. "He just growled at me like he *meant* it. And, he looks like the literal definition of *disease*."

I look back at the dog. Grey, scaly skin pokes out through missing patches of fur. Half of his left ear is missing, and there's a rather large scar around his yellowed eyes. I look back at her.

"Exactly, we can't just leave him! He's not going to bite me." She continues gaping. "Oh, just take it!" I say, shoving the leash into her palm again. This time, she wraps her hand around it.

"Okay, okay," she says. I wave, motioning for her to scoot even further back. She just stares.

"Move back," I whisper. "He needs more space."

Cam mutters under her breath, crossing her arms. "Bossy."

"What was that?"

"I said you're *bossy*," she repeats, like I wasn't asking just to falsely intimidate her.

She's lucky I'm on a mission right now, or I'd throw her in my car, drive her home, and fuck that attitude right out of her.

"Do what I say, or I'll show you who's *boss*," I say in a hushed breath instead.

Cam steps back.

I crouch as low to the ground as possible and slowly move sideways. I don't walk toward the dog; I walk adjacent to him. He looks up at me with the same whale-eyed nervousness Reese gets when strangers try to touch him. This dog just tops his off with a chipped, ragged smile. I avert my eyes from his, looking down at his chest instead. If this dog *is* a stray, he's probably unsocialized and doesn't trust people.

I know a little something about that.

So I let him know I'm not a threat. I sit down at a comfortable distance, making sure my body is sideways. That way, he doesn't feel like I'm staring at him head-on, but I can still see any sudden movements he decides to make.

"Be careful," Cam whispers. I can tell she is genuinely nervous for me.

I'm not scared at all. I'm not going to do anything to push the dog out of his comfort zone. If he were going to attack us out of pure aggression, he would have already done it by now. He would have bit Cam instead of giving her a warning. I just shoot her a silent thumbs-up and continue my stakeout.

It only takes minutes for the dog to approach me.

He too is crouching, wearily following his nose to my path. I don't move. He gets closer, his nose now inches from my ear. I hear the quick sniffs he's taking through his nose, trying to figure me out. Another throaty growl leaves his mouth, and for that fleeting moment, I *am* scared. I'm scared that his nose is inches from my ear, and if he wanted to, he could rip it clean off. But like I said, the moment is fleeting.

Dogs can smell fear, y'know.

I hold as still as I can, taking shallow breaths so my lungs don't fully inflate. The slightest movement could scare him away, and he may never know the safety of a home. I close my eyes.

Then, a wet, rough tongue drags across my cheek.

Talk about spreading disease.

My eyes shoot open, but I still make sure not to move too quickly. The dog continues licking me and starts to paw at my face and chest excitedly. His stance is loose, his tail wagging, but his ears are still on guard, which is fair, given the circumstances.

I slowly reach my hand out, placing it under his chin and scratch him gently. He leans into the touch, letting out a satisfying groan.

"I've got you," I whisper, continuing to pet him. He rolls over on his back, tongue dangling out the side of his mouth. That is the *ultimate* sign of trust.

I smile, and lasso the leash loosely over his head, careful not to startle him. Then, I stand slowly. Once I am fully upright, he paws my legs, asking for more attention.

My eyes dart to Cam, putting my arm in the air with a victorious fist. Her mouth hangs halfway open, as she stares at me in disbelief.

"I told you."

TWENTY-ONE
As You Wish

CAM

"Y OU'RE A FUCKING *DOG whisperer*," I yell in a hushed tone, letting all the air I had been holding hostage out of my lungs. I've tamed some beasts in my job, but that was a fucking *dragon*. Violet looks at me all smug.

"You can say it, y'know," she says in a raspy, airy tone. I scoff at her cockiness.

"Say what, exactly?"

"That I was right," she responds.

I laugh. "Yeah. Good luck."

She shoots me a glare that isn't at all daunting.

Now that the dog has warmed up to Violet, he's starting to warm up to me as well. And even though both of our dogs are fully vaccinated, I hold them tightly to my side to avoid contact. I feel bad; from the playful stance and excited whines, I can tell the dog really wants to play. But like I said, he looks like a disease.

[13]"I guess we should take him to the shelter?" I suggest, scooting further to the left to avoid contact between the dogs.

Violet's brows furrow, and she frowns. "But look at him!" she says, pointing to the rugged canine. "He has nobody to love him!"

I immediately shake my head.

"*Nope*. Nuh-uh," I say firmly. "I do *not* have the space for another dog."

Violet squats, squishing his face between her hands.

"But look at this face." She says it in a baby-talk tone, and even the dog looks up at me with big sad eyes, like he's trying to work it with her.

I continue shaking my head. "Not happening. If you love him so much, *you* take him home."

Violet stands, crossing her arms. "I can't."

"Well then, I guess he's gonna have to go to the shelter," I respond. It isn't like I don't care about the dog. I want him to have a happy family just like the rest of them. But if I took home every stray dog I've found, I'd have like *nine* dogs. Violet sighs all dramatically, like her sadness about the situation will make me change my mind.

It won't.

"Can we at least show him what love is?" she pleads. Then, she starts to sing "I Want to Know What Love Is" by Foreigner. I look at her, now about four feet away because I absolutely *refuse* to let Dawson anywhere near him. She looks ridiculous, holding the leash of this emaciated, hyena-like dog while singing an eighties hit song. Ridiculously cute, that is.

You wouldn't think Violet is the "cute" type. She's tattooed and pierced and stands like she's taller than five foot two. People like that are usually described with words like "intimidating" and "sexy." And while she is sexy, nothing about her is scary. Maybe she can be a bit dominant during sex, but that's the furthest it goes.

I glance back up at her, listening to the absolutely terrible, off-pitched cover she's still singing. Her eyes catch mine, and I am so fucking mad because I can't help but give in.

"Fine," I grumble, making it a point to increase the distance between us. "But stop creeping over here. I don't want Dawson to catch something."

Violet breaks into a giant grin.

"But he's *not* going in my car," I say firmly. "I don't want any of *whatever* it is getting spread around."

I look down at the dog. He's actually really cute, once you look past his cracked teeth, irritated yellow eyes, and patchy body.

"Deal," Violet says. "Meet you at my place?"

I nod, gesturing to Dawson. "I'm going to drop him off at home first."

"Okay," Violet says, patting her leg to beckon Reese to her side. Reese isn't even mine, but it stresses me the fuck out that he is anywhere near that dog. "See you there."

WHEN I GET TO Violet's house, which is unsurprisingly yellow by the way, I take my time looking around. Our "appointments" are usually at my place, so the only other time I've been here was that day after the tattoo. And to be honest with you, I didn't really have the opportunity or desire to look around then.

Both Reese and the stray are loose in the living room, like Violet doesn't care what objects the stray may spread his disease to.

"Would you like some?" Violet asks from the kitchen. I look at the tap water running into her glass. I wonder what microscopic things are floating around in it.

I shake my head, patting the water bottle in my backpack side pocket. "I'm set, thanks."

I look around her house cautiously, like it's a sin to get caught doing it. Picture frames decorate the wall above her couch, at least the ones that are left. Most of the wall is bare, small nails poking out where frames used to be. I wonder what they were, and I wonder what she plans to change them to.

"We should feed him," Violet says.

After locking Reese in her bedroom, we pour the stray a bowl of kibble. We don't know how long it's been since he's eaten, so we do it in sections, placing the food in a ridged feeder so he can't eat too quickly. Unsurprisingly, he scarfs it down every time.

"Good boy," Violet says, scratching behind his oily ears. Well, his ear-and-a-half. Then, she makes a face, like she just tasted something sour.

"What?" I ask. She continues scrunching her nose.

"Don't you smell that?"

"You mean the stray dog we found that looks half-dead? Yeah, I can smell him," I say.

Violet shakes her head.

"You *have* to give him a bath."

I furrow my brows, narrowing my gaze onto her. "What?"

"Cam," she says, with a very serious look on her face. "He *reeks. Please*, you *have* to give him a bath."

I've never been one to give in to other people's demands, so I'm unsure of how I find myself next to Violet with my knees against her bathroom floor while I run hypoallergenic shampoo through this dog's half-bare coat. His skin leaves a strange, flaky, oily residue on my hands that just about makes me vomit. I squeeze assholes for a living, but this is *so* much worse.

The dog shakes, and a brown soapy wave heads our way. I shield us from the blast with a towel that was luckily laying on my lap.

"I think we should name him," Violet says as we carefully pat him dry.

I look at her earnestly. "That is literally the *worst* idea. Don't you know anything about naming a stray?" I ask.

A sly smirk slowly spreads across her face, and she gives me a matter-of-fact look. "I named you."

Heat rises to my cheeks. I don't know if it's out of irritation at the dig or the slight innuendo in her tone. Whichever it is, it's making the warmth between my thighs pulse.

"I'm thinking *Buddy*," she continues.

I scoff, unimpressed.

"Buddy is like, the number one most *basic* dog name on the planet," I respond.

"So?"

"So don't you think he deserves a little better than that, after what he's been through?"

Violet looks back at the dog, like she's thinking very deeply about this.

"Buddy is an All-American family dog name. Everyone loves a Buddy."

"That may be true, but this dog is *not* a Buddy," I testify. She's won enough today.

"Fine, then what's your suggestion?" Her arms cross over her chest impatiently.

"I don't have one. I told you naming a stray is a *bad idea*."

"But if you *had* to," she pleads. "If you *had* to, what would you name him?"

I look at her, and I know I fucked up when I accidentally lock eyes with her again. Those demanding, desperate eyes. How the fuck do you say no to those eyes?

"Parvo," I say, dead-faced. She doesn't laugh. "Fine. Um..."

I think for a moment. What is the name of someone charming, yet kind of a wreck?

"Westley," I say finally. "Like *The Princess Bride*."

Violet immediately nods in agreement, her crooked smile just as bright as her eyes.

"It's perfect!"*

As our final act of showing Westley what love is, we stopped to get him a pup cup on the way to the shelter. Of course, he licked it clean in seconds and looked at us for more.

When we pull into the Pine Paws Animal Sanctuary parking lot, I actually start to feel sad. My gut churns, thinking about leaving Westley here alone.

I knew naming him was a bad idea.

"Are you sure you can't keep him?" Violet asks as we unload him from the car. I look at her sadly.

"Just about as sure as you are," I respond.

Pine Paws Animal Sanctuary is actually the best place for him, at least until he recovers. They'll make sure he gets everything he needs, and they have so many volunteers that they don't know what to do with them all. Avery stops in every week to take the animals on walks around the neighborhood. It's good for their morale. Plus, they have a behaviorist that can help with his people skills.

"It'll be good for him," I say with assurance. I can sense Violet's guilt, because I'm feeling it just the same. "They treat animals here like royalty."

Violet nods her head, but she's still upset.

"I know," she says. "I just think everyone should have a family."

I look at her solemnly before opening the front door, then nod. "Yeah. Everyone should have a family."

A bell chimes as I push the heavy oak, a sound not so different from the one at Furry Friends. Westley steps through the frame nervously, his tail tucked and ears back which breaks my heart all over again.

[14]"Welcome to Pine Paws, how can I help you?" a man asks. The voice is low and familiar, the contents of my stomach curdling as every hair on my body stands up. My gaze snaps over to the man behind the desk, recognition pooling in his eyes as they lock onto me. While my jaw clenches, his lips pull into an arrogant smile. "I was wondering when you'd finally come to see me."

A rock forms in the base of my throat, my grip on Westley's leash tightening so hard my knuckles turn white.

"What are you doing here?" I ask through gritted teeth, my voice quieter than I intended. I'm either overheated or freezing right now, but I'm having trouble figuring out which. Cody walks around the desk, his green eyes locked onto me as he approaches. The nails of my curled fingers sink into my palms, my heart pounding heavily inside my chest.

"Didn't Avery tell you?" he asks, his smirk growing as his head cocks to the side. "I work here now."

I try to maintain eye contact, to prove I'm not the person I was, that I don't back down anymore. But the piercing intimidation of those eyes and his supercilious grin forces my gaze to the floor.

They let you around animals? I want to ask. But I can't even get my mouth to move in the way it needs to form words.

"Well!" Violet's voice breaks the silence, and she settles herself in front of me, forcing Cody to take a reluctant step back. "Is that something she needs to know?"

I don't see it, the bitter smirk on his lips, but I know it's there by the way his voice sounds when he responds.

"And you are?"

My eyes flick up to Violet, her bold, unwavering stance a blockade between Cody and me. I don't want her to be subjected to another second of Cody's existence. Actually, I don't want her to know who he is at all.

"Violet Wolfe," she answers, firmly and professionally, sticking her hand out. My gaze focuses on Cody now, hoping to catch his reaction. I don't know why Violet's being this way, so proper yet assertive. I'd enjoy it, if I weren't afraid of what Cody is capable of.

He sticks his hand in hers, and both of their hands grow white as they squeeze overly-hard. Violet doesn't even flinch, which I have to admit is impressive. I know how strong Cody can be when he wants to.

"Cody," he says, that stupid smile still stuck to his face. Violet may walk around with a smile I know she doesn't always mean, but that's the worst thing about Cody. He means it, and not in a friendly way. "Cam's ex."

I swallow, my throat growing tighter and drier.

"Yeah, I got that." Violet smiles back, her eyes squinting in a way that tells me that, like Cody's, this smile isn't a friendly gesture either. They continue shaking each other's hands, staring into one another's eyes like whoever breaks first loses. I don't quite know what it is they'd be losing, but I do know Violet has a fiery side to her. The pair of them could be explosive.

I clear my throat.

"Cody, Violet is my *boss*," I clarify, which is entirely true but feels like a complete lie. I step to the side, eyeing him intently until he releases Violet's hand. She continues staring him down until I jut an elbow into her side, silently commanding her to stop. "We found this guy outside Furry Friends. No collar or tags, and I doubt he's chipped. We just came to drop him off."

Cody nods, shooting Violet an indiscernible look before walking back behind the counter. The loud clicking of the keyboard fills the awkward silence. We follow, settling uncomfortably on the other side.

"So that's where you're at now then?" he asks, his gaze fixed to the screen as his fingers continue typing.

"What?"

"Furry Friends. I stopped by The Dog Shop not too long ago, but you weren't there. I figured you finally realized you were too good for the place."

A sarcastic laugh slips through my lips, and I glance at Violet, her brows dipping. What is so ironic about that sentence is the fact that Cody was the one who said I'd never move on from The Dog Shop. He said I'd be stuck there forever. But this is what Cody does. He makes you think he'd supported you all along, so when he says something cruel, you believe him about that too. I don't believe in fate, but somehow, he convinced me I was destined for destruction.

"Well, seeing as you're her *ex*," Violet says, propping a hand on her hip, "I don't really understand why that's any of your business."

Cody's eyes snap up from behind the computer, an irritated glare glossing over his eyes.

"You're a pretty *involved* boss," he says, before breaking his stare to retrieve papers off the printer. I shoot Violet a look, one that says, "please don't push him" but she isn't looking at me. She's still staring at him, a flame burning in her eyes.

This isn't like the jealous look she gave Hayden at the bowling alley or even the envious talk of it in the days after. What Violet is holding in her gaze is something I didn't even know she possessed at all.

It's hatred.

Or extreme distaste, at least. It isn't rare for someone to feel that way about Cody, but it's completely new to me coming from Violet.

"Happy employees…" Violet grabs the paper from Cody's outstretched hand. "Happy—"

"Violet, can I talk to you for a second?" I cut in, my cheeks flushing. Violet shoots me a confused look.

"Sure?" she says hesitantly, more of a question than an answer. I look up at Cody, forcing a painful smile.

"Can you give us a minute?" I ask. Cody cocks a brow, his expression unchanging, but I can feel the curiosity washing over his face. He nods.

"Okay, I'll be back in a few."

The second the "Staff Only" door swings shut, I spin to look at Violet.

"What are you doing?" I snap, my brows knitted together. Violet still looks puzzled.

"What do you mean?"

I sigh, shaking my head. "I mean *why* are you trying to pick a fight?" My voice wavers at the end of the sentence, but I try to stay composed.

Violet scoffs, holding her hands out argumentatively. "I'm not! He's the one who got all up in your face like—"

"I don't need you to protect me," I say, firmly but trying not to come off too harsh. Violet could write a book on having only the best of intentions. But she doesn't know what she's up against. "Cody isn't someone you mess with, okay?"

Behind her eyes, I watch pieces of a puzzle slowly slide into place, confusion turning to concern.

"Cam, did he hit you? Because—"

"What? No!" Air hisses from my nose as I shake my head, waving my hands frantically in front of me. The sad truth is, I wouldn't think that was far-fetched. But Violet doesn't need to know that. She doesn't need to know *any* of this. "No it wasn't like that. He's just a dick, okay? And I want to leave. So please, *please*, just be nice."

Violet's eyes scan mine, her pupils dilating as they dissect every part of me. I try to take steady breaths, but they're choppy and ragged.

"Well, I hope that was long enough because I've got to get this guy," Cody scrunches his nose at Westley, and though I'd done the same only hours ago, it makes me hypocritically want to punch him in the face. "In with Dr. Robinson before she leaves."

I shoot Violet one last pleading glance, not caring about the desperation behind it. She gives me a singular nod, and all the tense muscles in my body slowly ease.

"Right, sorry about that," she says through what seems like a genuine chuckle to someone who wouldn't know any better. "Work stuff. You like it here, Cody?"

I'm almost amazed at Violet's ability to flip a switch. How easy duality comes to her, like second nature. Her tone can be so curt one second, then like sweet tea the next. Cody seems intrigued too, or maybe more confused. His brows quirk, and he glances at me, my stomach twisting under his gaze.

"Yeah, I like it alright. But it's just temporary."

Violet continues scribbling on the intake form, not looking up at him but ensuring the forced sincerity remains in her tone.

"That's a shame. How come?"

I chew furiously on the inside of my cheek as his eyes burn a hole through me, his gaze still unbroken. My chest twitches from my anxious breathing, which I swear puts a shimmer in his eye.

"I'm moving in January."

Violet's head snaps up, just about at the same exact moment that my heart sinks. It makes no sense really, why that sentence filled me with dread instead of relief.

The proof I've moved on is standing right next to me. But for some reason, my vision goes blurry.

"Oh Cool! Where are yo—"

"Why are you moving?"

I don't mean to cut Violet off. I don't even mean to say anything at all. But the breaking words flow out of me with no regard for my intentions.

"I got accepted into the music program at USC," he answers. I blink, a tear trickling down my cheek. Cody moving has no effect on me. I mean, *really*, I haven't even seen him since the breakup. And it surprised me, but after the first few months went by, I didn't want to. So why, in this moment, does it feel like the end of the world?

I nod, wiping my face as I sniffle.

"*Oh*," I say, my voice cracking. "That's great."

Cody nods, but our eye contact is broken by Violet, who waves a white sheet in the air.

"Here you go," she says, and Cody turns his attention toward her. He scans the paper, nodding in approval, then walks back around the front of the desk. The familiar allspice scent filling the air around me is almost nostalgic.

"Well, I'm going to take him back, and you two should be all set," Cody says, slipping a leash over Westley's head and returning the old one to Violet. He looks over his shoulder as he stands in front of the staff door.

"Call me, Cam," he says, then disappears behind it.

Violet grabs my hand without hesitation, squeezing softly.

"Are you okay?" she asks, the familiar roughness of her palm is strangely soothing. I nod, but her grip only tightens. "Cam, you're shaking."

"Huh?" I look down. My hand is trembling in hers. I realize now that, for some reason, I'm still crying. I take a shaky breath, my heart frozen in my stomach, yet racing in my chest at the same time.

"He really *is* a dick, huh?" she asks. I swallow, my shoulder shaking as I wipe my cheek against it.

"Violet *please*," I sniff. "Just don't." I look at her briefly through my wet lashes, and she gives me an apologetic nod. "Just take me home." *

Twenty-Two
Leash Laws
Violet

FROM THE MOMENT WE left Pine Paws Animal Sanctuary, I haven't been able to get rid of the sinking feeling in my gut. I'd expected it to go away after a good night's sleep, but it was still there the next morning. And today, I woke up feeling so queasy I had to sprint to the bathroom just in case.

Luckily, I didn't throw up. But the feeling is still there, digging deeper and deeper into my body. I've been trying to distract myself with work, focusing on scrubbing all the little things that get peed on most consistently. Posts, shelves, the wall where all the leashes hang, for *some reason.*

I'm having trouble pinpointing exactly what it is that's bothering me. Westley? Cody? Cam's *reaction* to Cody?

I want to say it's Westley. Pine Paws is an amazing facility, widely funded and expertly staffed. It's probably more of a resort than Furry Friends, since everyone that works there is doing so out of love and not because there are bills to pay. But something about him has my heart in a grip. How scared he was to let us in, but how effortlessly he did when he realized that we were there to help.

I feel like I'm wading in a lake, stepping further and further until the waterline reaches my throat. Like any second now, the guilt is going to wash over me.

Drown me.

But I'd be lying if I said it was that entirely.

Something about Cody irked me in a way I've never been irked before. It's hard to pinpoint and harder to describe. He's just off in some way. And even though she seemed seriously upset when he said he was moving, it was almost like Cam was scared of him, which I hate in a way words cannot explain.

It doesn't make things easier that Ruthie called me this morning to let me know my parents will be out of rehab in time for Christmas. I tried so hard not to cave, but I can't listen to her voice break and do nothing about it. So, I sent the last chunk of my savings to her, and she got them both admitted to the facility in Seattle.

I slide my phone out of my pocket and click on my now most frequent contact. I need to be thinking about literally anything else, and I need something stronger than dog piss to distract me.

> **My place or yours tonight?**

This isn't *technically* violating the contract because it's texting. I watch three gray dots dance across the screen.

> **Can't, sorry**

> **Something came up**

I frown reading the messages.

> **Tomorrow?**

The dots reappear, waving in a line in the little gray bubble, but disappear after a moment. I wait for them to come back, but they don't.

Look, I know I shouldn't go peek in on her, but maybe she isn't responding because she needs help. I peer through the salon window inconspicuously. Cam is standing there, staring at her phone. I pull mine out and text her again.

> **I'm free Saturday too.**

I watch as Cam lets out a heavy sigh, her eyes scanning the screen before she puts her phone back down. My brows press together.

Why is she ignoring me?

"Hey." I pop my head through the door. "I'm just checking in. You good?"

"I'm busy," she says shortly, her clippers working tediously between a fur-covered paw pad.

I frown. "Do you need help?"

I don't know the first thing about dog grooming, but if Cam needs help, I'll try my damnedest.

Cam shakes her head.

I look around, making sure nobody is in hearing range before speaking again.

"Got any fun plans for the weekend?" I ask. It's a completely innocent question with absolutely no innuendos. Finally, Cam looks up at me. She sighs, then turns her clippers off. Without the soft buzz of them, the room grows quiet. Cam seems to like the silence, on account of how often I find myself sitting in it with her. I swallow.

"I'm hanging out with Hayden and Adrian," she says. Then, she adds, "And Avery."

I nod, shifting my weight onto my toes, then back down to my heels.

"Okay," I shrug. "Cool."

Cam's gaze shifts around, until she reluctantly meets my eye.

Usually, Cam says exactly what's on her mind.

And when she doesn't, I can see it, flickering in her eyes or dancing across her face. But this is different. [15]I can't tell if, when she says she's busy, she means now or forever.

And I'm not exactly in the position to ask. There's a term for that. Workplace harassment?

I clear my throat.

"So, see you tomorrow then? Here, I mean?" Cam nods.

"Yeah," she says. "Here."

THERE ARE OTHER DISTRACTIONS, other vices than sex. None, in my opinion, are quite as fun or quite as effective, but some, at least, are close.

The Morgan Trails is one of my favorite hiking spots in Greenrock, and I think Reese likes it too. Even with the fresh snow on the ground, which he isn't a fan of, he's trotting next to me with his tail wagging and head held high. My favorite part about the trail is the overlook. About halfway through the loop, there's a clearing on the cliff that reveals a view of beautiful snow-capped mountains and people's million-dollar houses shrinking below. It's gorgeous, particularly at sunset, because the mountains glow with a pinkish orange hue, making everything around look like something out of a fairytale.

The bronze rocks shimmer in the dusk, turning my intended distraction into a reminder. A reminder that shouldn't be uncomfortable, but for some reason, still is. A reminder of what was expected, yet still felt abrupt, bringing me here to this stunning view in the hopes of forgetting.

I wonder what did it. If it was the fight we had in the salon or Cody making his appearance at the shelter. Or maybe, it had been coming, the inevitable end of that stupid contract. I thought I'd know when the time was near. But I guess, you can't really *know* anything. You can't always predict when someone will change their mind, and you can't know their ex will appear right in front of them, luring them back in.

I want to know if she called him. I want to know what they said. But instead of filling my brain with "what if"s, I force myself to remember the good things.

Things that choose to stay.

The trees come and go, the clouds and snow too, but the mountains are always there. I love this view because you don't quite know what you're going to get, but you know it will be there waiting. Like its sole intention is to be there for you to admire it.

But staring into the beautiful brown rocks, watching as the sun shines over each ridge and bump, I'm reminded of brown agate. I'm reminded of Cam's stupid eyes.

Balancing energies, by the way. That's what brown agate is supposed to do. The website mentioned something about calming too, but I disregarded that because Cam is definitely not calming. Quite the opposite, actually. I didn't know someone could get on my nerves so badly. She knows what makes me tick, and she takes complete advantage of it.

Took. She *took* complete advantage of it. So if it's over the way it feels like it is, I should be relieved, for a multitude of reasons. One being that I'll no longer have someone to get under my skin, to press me to say things I never would otherwise. And another being that, now, I don't have to go through the trouble of ending it myself. It was only a matter of time before we got here.

Still, I can't stop thinking about that look she gave me. Those big, round eyes. The fact that I could tell something was off. That Cam didn't really seem like she wanted to end things at all.

But the contract has nothing to do with reading her mind. It doesn't matter if I can pick up on her mannerisms, if I can tell when something is off. It doesn't matter if I accidentally let details slip about my personal life. Because those things are strings. Strong, tiny threads that weave you together.

And this was supposed to be a no-strings situation.*

I turn forward, facing the remainder of the trail now. It's getting dark, but that's never stopped me before.

The snow crunches beneath my spiked boots, Reese's own boots strolling next to mine.

"Here."

His head tilts, and I toss him a piece of dehydrated chicken. He catches it, jowls loose and swaying.

"Coco! No!" a high-pitched voice screams, the woman's tone shrill and panicked. "She's friendly! She's—"

I whip around, just as a large brown dog rushes up to us, a pink collar loose around her neck. Before I even have the chance to react, the dog pounces, and Reese lets out a high-pitched yelp.

My stomach drops as he flails underneath her, lips raised and teeth flying. Loud growls rumble from the pair of them, and I instinctually grab the dog's hind legs just as a pair of large white canines sink into Reese's leg, another piercing shriek emitting from his throat.

I tug her backward harshly, prying her off. The dog screeches, her head whipping around to snap at me. I don't care. All I care about is Reese. All I care about is getting this damn dog off of him.

"Shit! I'm sorry! She's not—" The woman finally runs up to us, her eyes wide but her body motionless. The dog is flailing in my arms, panicking from the restraint. Reese lays almost motionless next to us, blood staining his white coat.

"This is a leash-only area," I say, snatching the leash from the woman's hand. My heart pounds so rapidly I can hear it, and I force myself to take a slow deep breath.

In. Hold. Out.

The dog snaps at me when I attach it to her collar, but I am unfazed.

"I know, I'm sorry. She's really friendly, I don't know—"

I shake my head and scoop Reese into my arms.

My knees buckle for a moment with his full weight, but I gain my footing. I feel his heartbeat against my arms, his pulse thready. The woman's face grows pale as she stares at him, her dog sitting next to her, now decidedly tranquil.

"Can I do anything? Can I—"

I push past them, my legs shaking. I don't know if it's from his motionless weight, or from the feeling that my heart has sunk into my feet. "You've done enough."

I move quickly now, as quickly as I can down the trail. Blood soaks into my jacket, but I don't know where it's all coming from. It's all over him. His neck, his ear, his ribcage, his legs. My boots shuffle through the snow as I try not to slip on the slight decline. I don't know how long it takes to get to my car, but it feels like eternity.

Reese whimpers when I set him down on the back seat, and I realize, looking at him now, it's even worse than I thought. Bruises have already started to peek through his thin white coat, and blood has drenched him almost entirely.

I barge into the Greenrock Valley Vet like a force to be reckoned with. The drive from the trail should have been ten minutes, but I made it in four.

I bang on the glass door rapidly but continue to take slow, steady breaths.

In. Hold. Out.

I knock again, my knuckles turning white as they hit the cold glass.

Please, let us in.

A short man with fluffy brown hair spots us from behind the desk. His brows raise with concern as he jogs to the door, pushing it open.

"Our lobby is actually closed. But—"

I stagger into him, Reese held tight in my arms. He whimpers as he breathes, like the movement of inhaling is painful. The man looks down, his eyes widening when they land on Reese's blood-soaked body.

"Please," I plead firmly. "Please help him."

The man nods, using his back to hold the door open. He reaches his hands out, trying to take Reese from my arms. My grip tightens at first, for some reason, but then I let him. It's the smart thing to do. It's why I'm here.

"Hey! We got an emergency!" he yells out, disappearing into a hall, Reese draped over his arms. My chest tightens, and just as I begin to follow him, he returns, empty-handed. Red stains seep into the fabric of his uniform, and he slips back behind the desk, quickly pulling out a form.

"Do you know what happened?" he asks, a crease forming on his forehead. My muscles tense, forcing my body to go still. I swallow.

"Dog attack," I say, grabbing a pen out of the glass jar next to me. I begin to scribble my information down, the ink leaking messily over the page. The man nods.

"We figured. Did you know the dog?"

I shake my head. The man stays silent for a moment, and my gaze shoots up to him, my brows pressing together.

"What?" I ask.

He takes a slow breath.

"They aren't sure yet, but they think he may have punctured a lung. If so, he'll have to have surgery, but—" He shakes his head. "It doesn't look good."

For a second, everything washes over me. Fear. Guilt. Anger. The words repeat inside of my mind.

It doesn't look good.

My throat begins to close, and just when I think I'm going to stop breathing, it all washes out. Every thought, every emotion, evaporates into the air. A sinkhole forms in my chest where my heart should be, and I blink blankly at the man.

"Can I stay here, at least?" I ask, my tone flat and void. His eyes drop down to the floor, a mournful expression sewn into his face.

"Unfortunately," he says, regret ringing in his voice. "The lobby is closed. If I could let you stay, I would but…"

I shake my head, still staring at him, yet also staring at nothing at all. I slide the form to him, a corpse-like feeling taking over me.

"Call me," I say. "When you know something."

The man nods and hands me a business card before I walk out the door.

Twenty-Three
Bonds & Burgers
Cam

Hayden hands me the grease-soaked paper bag and tosses himself backward onto my couch.

"They forgot the fry sauce," I frown, as I pull out two foil-wrapped burgers and a ridiculously large cardboard container of french fries.

"I can try to wave down the driver," Hayden offers. "But I think he left already."

I shake my head, melting into the green velvet sofa.

"It's fine," I mumble, pointing the remote at the television. "Everything is fine."

A loud sigh escapes Hayden's mouth, and he chews his lower lip.

"You know, trauma bonds aren't permanent," he says softly. "Unless you want them to be." My stomach twists as I sit there, staring blankly at the burger in my hand. "You didn't call him, right?"

I shake my head.

"No. I was able to get a same-day appointment with Dr. Burton, and he talked me out of it."

Hayden nods, growing quiet. He unwraps his squashed burger, then looks at me earnestly, those pretty blue eyes melting me.

"So, why end it then?"

He asks it almost like he's scared to, which is funny because, even though he'd never say it out loud, he's the one who told me this thing with Violet was a bad idea. And he was right.

"Because clearly, it wasn't doing what it was supposed to," I answer.

Hayden's head tilts, his brow quirking. "Which was…"

"Help me move on from Cody?" I sigh, slumping further into the couch. "Trauma bonds are stupid," I mutter.

Hayden pats my shoulder gently.

"How'd she take it?" he asks.

I toss a cold, un-sauced fry into my mouth, staring at the purple loading screen in front of me. Hayden hangs his head.

"You didn't *tell* her?"

I scrunch my nose as I pull the wrapper off my burger and see a slimy red tomato right in the center between the melted cheese and the shredded iceberg lettuce. My eyes dart over to Hayden, and the moment they land on him, I know I have to talk.

"No," I admit, swapping my burger for the one in his hand. I inspect it closely. "Not *exactly*. I mean, I didn't say 'I'm never having sex with you again.' But it was impli—this one has tomatoes too!"

I let out a disgusted huff, dropping the burger onto the coffee table in front of me. Hayden picks it up.

"Implied how?" he asks, pulling back the top bun. He peels off the tomatoes, dropping it onto his own wrapper, then carefully scrapes off any seeds and juices as well. He puts it back together and hands it to me.

"I mean," I take it slowly and inspect it once more before taking a heaping bite. "I kinda just said I would see her at work."

Hayden's blonde eyebrow quirks, his cheeks puffed out with chewed hamburger.

"Huh?"

I swallow, the burger sliding down my throat with just the tiniest hint of tomato taste on it.

It's fine. It's fine.

"I just said we weren't meeting up, that I was busy. And then I told her I'd see her at work. Like, *only* at work."

Hayden nods, and on a cot in the corner, Dawson and Major throw each other around like it's a WWE match.

"And you said that? That you'd *only* see her at work?"

I pause, reaching for another disappointing french fry. "Well... not *exactly*."

"Cam! How is she supposed to know you broke things off if—"

"It was *implied*!" I huff, furrowing my brows at him. Hayden sighs.

"*Okay*," he says. "Alright. And you're... *okay*?"

A stifled laugh pops out of me. I'm doing *just fine.* Sure, I liked what we had going. Violet helped me explore things I didn't even know existed. I didn't have to chat up a bunch of strangers, and it was on a schedule, part of my routine, which helped me anticipate the new things too. They didn't just hit me out of nowhere. But clearly, it was failing to help me move on. And it was supposed to be brief. I prepared for it to be. So of course, I'm fine.

"I'm the one who broke it off," I say, pulling a big white comforter over us. "Aren't I?"

Hayden nods.

"Yeah, sure. But..." He shakes his head. "You're going to have to see her tomorrow. And the week after that, and the week after that. Is that going to be..."

"It's no-strings, Hay," I say. "That's the point. It isn't going to be *anything* because it was just for sex."

Hayden swallows another bite of his burger. "But isn't work... *strings*?"

I groan, dramatically lifting my back off the sofa just so I can toss it backwards again for the effect.

"Not this again, *please.*"

"Sorry." He shrugs. "I just fail to see how it's no-strings-attached when there's like..." He starts counting on his fingers silently, his soft indigo eyes scanning the ceiling like he's searching for a memory. "Three strings, *at least.*"

I scoff. "How'd you jump from one to three?"

He scoots closer to me on the couch, rubbing his palms against the denim on his thighs, before holding them out in front of him.

"Okay so you've got the job, obviously." He holds one finger up. "And then there's me. She's Major's trainer, so even if you hadn't worked at Furry Friends, I would have brought her up eventually."

I look at him, unconvinced. "That isn't a very compelling argument."

He ignores me and throws up another finger.

"And lastly, she's hot." He leans back against the couch, waving a hand. "*Respectfully.*"

"How exactly is being hot a string?" I ask, cocking a brow.

"It's not," he says dismissively. "Unless she has a good personality too, which she *does*. That's why—" He lifts his hand, performing "A.D.D." in sign language. "But it's a little late for that."

I shoot him a glare, but he just returns it with a sickly-sweet smile. Then his gaze grows serious, his expression soft.

"Really though," he says, his head tilting slightly to look at me. "You're really okay? With everything that happened and letting it all go?"

I know Hayden is just trying to take care of me. He's like Adrian in that way, always trying to help other people. But I don't know how many times it's going to take to convince him I really am fine. Maybe part of it is because I haven't fully confronted it, but I think Violet got the gist. I'm more disappointed in myself than anything else. I was convinced, for a fleeting moment, that I really was moving on.

"I'm *fine*," I say again, putting extra emphasis on the "fine." Hayden chuckles, shaking his head.

"I'm proud of you, Cam," he says, his hand sliding over to squeeze mine. I smile. "Just six months ago, you wouldn't let me toss a piece of lint, and now look at you with your no-strings attached and your—" He picks up the greasy paper bag. "Sauceless french fries."

I scowl, snatching the bag from his hand.

To be fair, that piece of lint came from Dawson's first plushie. It's dead now, of course. The eyes went first. But I kept one of the little tufts of fur that fell off on the way to the garbage can.

"I thought you were here to make me feel better."

Hayden stands up, walking over to the refrigerator. He pulls out a container of mayonnaise, then reaches in again, grabbing a bottle of ketchup.

"Why would I need to make you feel better if you're fine?" He shoots me a taunting smile over his shoulder, and I flip him off.

"What are you doing?"

Hayden walks closer to me with a bowl in his hand, whisking a spoon around inside it to mix something up. His gaze flicks up to me, and he holds the bowl out in my direction.

"Making you fry sauce."

We don't talk about it after that. Not much at least. He shoots me worried glances every now and then, and I pretend I don't see them and stare at the Dahmer documentary playing on the television instead. When Hayden leaves, I practically drown in those big, lanky arms of his.

"I appreciate you," I say, squeezing him tightly.

Hayden brushes the back of my head with his hand.

"I appreciate you too, Cam." He beckons Major to his side and hooks his harness around his body. "Call me if you need me?"

I nod, and Hayden steps out the front door into the cold winter night.

MY HEAD SNAPS UP, my body bent in an unnatural position from passing out on my apartment-sized couch.

"What she didn't know," says a voice on the television, deep and pronounced. "...is that something more sinister was waiting for her inside."

I sit up, wiping a smudge of drool off the side of my cheek in the process as I scramble to find the remote. If falling asleep to serial-killer documentaries could get you on a watch list, I'd be on the FBI's Most Wanted. The screen goes black when I press the off button, the voice coming to an abrupt end. But I jump back, my heart thrumming against my ribcage, when it's replaced by a loud knock ringing through the living room.

Dawson erupts into an uncontrollable fit of barking, which seems to be a theme for him lately. I groan, peeling myself off of the couch.

Hayden must have forgotten something.

"Shh," I shush Dawson, scooting him to the side as I open the door.

But there isn't a tall, charming, blonde-haired man towering over me. Instead, I jump backwards, clutching my chest as I stare directly at a blood-soaked Violet.

"I didn't know where to go."

TWENTY-FOUR
One to Ten

VIOLET

I DON'T RECALL EXACTLY how I got to Cam's. I drove, I'm sure of it, because my car keys are still gripped in my hand. But the roads I took, the entire drive here, I can't remember any of it. I can't even remember deciding I was going to come. I just know I'm standing in her living room, Reese's blood soaked into my clothing.

"Hey, hey," Cam says softly, brushing my hair out of my face. I blink, trying to focus my gaze, but no matter how hard I try, I feel like I'm just staring through her instead of at her. Her eyes are wide, a bewildered look sewn into her face, but she maintains that smooth tone as she slides my jacket off. "What happened?"

I try to speak, but my throat closes, only a hoarse squeak coming out. She tosses my jacket into the washing machine and returns.

"Violet, talk to me." Her hand finds mine and squeezes it tightly. I take a shuddered breath.

"R-Reese," I manage to croak. "H-he got at-ttacked. They said-they said they didn't know if he was going to make it. And that their lobby was closed."

Cam looks up at me, tears pricking her eyes, but she holds them back.

"Oh, Violet," she says softly. "I'm so sorry."

I just shake my head, still staring at absolutely nothing. She wraps an arm around me, squeezing tightly.

"Let's get you into the shower, okay? I think you'll feel a lot better."

I shake my head. This isn't Cam's job. She doesn't need to take care of me. She was very clear about the boundaries of this. And she was clear in her avoidance today.

"No, I-I didn't mean to put you in this position. I'm sorry." I shake my head.

"I just need to go home."

The void in my chest expands, and I swallow. I shouldn't be here. Why am I here?

Cam's head rubs against mine as she shakes it softly.

"No," she whispers. "I'm not letting you go home. You shouldn't be alone right now."

I swallow, the dry lump in my throat rising. "I don't know how not to be."

The soft pads of her fingertips brush against the crown of my head as she pushes my hair out of my face. Then, silently, she takes me by the hand and guides me to the bathroom.

My body shakes and shivers, but I don't feel cold. I don't exactly know what's happening to me, I just know I want it to stop.

Cam's fingers slide underneath the hem of my shirt, her eyes locking onto mine in an unspoken question. I give her a shaky nod, and she carefully peels my blood-soaked shirt over my head. It leaves streaks of red down my face and neck as it grazes the skin. She tosses it onto the tile in the corner of the bathroom. Then, her hands glide around my back. She looks down at the floor as she unclasps my bra. When her eyes draw up to me, it isn't a look she's ever given me before.

I'm used to the distaste. The annoyance. And I've grown to need the lust. But this isn't any of those.

This is pity.

I feel so weak, letting her see me like this.

Defective. I'm breaking all my own rules, while breaking all of hers at the same time. I should put my clothes back on. I should leave. But my buckling knees refuse to budge, no matter how hard I try to take a step forward. My chest tightens every time I take in a breath.

Like I'm underwater, sucking in the ocean until I drown. "Is it okay if I keep going?" she asks quietly. Her words graze my skin, goosebumps washing over my half-naked body. I'm exposed, but it has nothing to do with the clothes lying on the floor. My eyes draw up hesitantly, until they land on hers.

I was wrong. Cam might be aggravating. She may push my buttons to a point

I didn't know they could be pushed, and she might have an attitude comparable to a teenage bull. But those eyes *are* calming. I know they are. Right now, they're the only thing keeping me here.

"Yes," I answer breathily, and Cam delicately tugs my jeans down my legs, taking my underwear with them. She helps me into the shower, making sure the temperature is right before I step inside. My legs tremble, and I grip the sidebar as I lower myself to the floor. Cam grabs the green shower curtain and tugs it closed. She pokes her head inside one last time.

"I'll be right here, okay?"

I know I'm pathetic. I know I'm here, sitting in the shower naked and emotionless, while Cam is standing next to me completely composed. I know, and I hate it. But I can't think of anything I need more right now than Cam's skin against mine. Than her eyes guiding me silently to solace. For once, I'm scared to be alone.

"Can you—" My voice cracks. "Can you sit with me?" I shake my head apologetically as the words tumble out. "Sorry. I don't know..."

But Cam nods, her grip on the curtain releasing. "Whatever you need."

She steps out of her clothes and climbs inside the tub.

I stare at the iron-stained floor, the water running down my body turning red before it hits the bottom of the tub and circles into the drain. My eyes close as I tilt my head back and let the warmth wash over me.

A pair of familiar legs slide on either side of me. Cam's bare body grazes against my back, and I shudder at the contact. Her hands find my hair and travel through the bloody tangled mess, scrubbing gently along the way. My eyes stay closed, absorbing every moment, every second of her touch. Images flash through my mind. That dog. Reese. His motionless, whimpering body. My head falls into my hands, my shoulders shaking as a weak sob slips out.

"You're okay," Cam says softly, continuing to stroke my hair. "You're okay."

She reaches for the soap, pumping it generously into her hand before running her fingers back through my hair, scrubbing the scalp tediously but gently.

With care.

I've never been cared for. Not to say nobody cares *about* me. I've just never been taken care *of.* I've never shattered into pieces and let someone else put me together. Not my parents, not Ruthie. Not Mallory.

"I'm going to rinse it out now, okay?" Cam asks. I nod, parting my lips to speak but nothing comes out. She helps me stand and turns my back toward the shower head. Warm water streams down my face, the suds washing backward out of my thick hair. Cam runs her fingers through it, making sure every sud, every bubble washes out. Then, she reaches for the loofah.

She lathers it up with soap that smells like sweet mint and eucalyptus, then presses it carefully to my body. I wince, for a second. I don't know why. It doesn't hurt. It just feels unnatural to have someone doing this for me. It feels unnatural for her to be seeing me like this.

The loofah glides across my skin, the rough beige sponge scrubbing gentle circles around me. Cam's sure to be careful as she glides over the hammerhead, though the healing process has moved along nicely and the peeling is almost gone.

I look down at her finally, letting her eyes meet mine. God, she's beautiful. And I'm a complete disheveled wreck.

"One to ten," I ask weakly. "How good am I being compared to your regular clients?"

I force a smile, and I can tell by her reaction that it isn't really a smile at all. It feels more like a grimace. But Cam offers me her own fake grin, her eyes dropping down to the loofah gliding across my chest.

"Eight," she says softly. Her eyes flick up. "You're a little dirtier than most."

I let out a chuckle that isn't forced but isn't genuine either. It's both, in a way. Neither, in another. My hand cups the back of her waist, gently pulling her close to me.

"I'm sorry," I say, my gaze dropping to the floor. I watch suds slide down the ribbed fiberglass and into the drain. "I know what you meant earlier. And I shouldn't have shown up—"

"Don't." Cam shakes her head. "Don't talk about that right now. Please."

I look up, her eyes giving me a subtle, silent plea.

I nod.

"Okay."

Cam sets the loofah on the side of the tub, then steps forward, closer to me. Her arms snake around my waist, and I look down at her for anything that may be a distraction. From Reese, from the contract. All of it.

Her blonde hair is dark in the shower. The true beauty of her eyes is hidden by the low lighting, but I know what really lies inside. Her thick brown lashes clump together, little drops sitting on their tips which shake as she blinks. Water pools in the curve of her lips, and her tongue peeks out to clear it.

[16]She is the most beautiful distraction ever created. My hands cradle the back of her neck, my thumb tracing her jaw. Cam's breath hitches, and I lean in to press our mouths together.

Her lips are wet and soft. Full and warm.

Everything about them is perfect. A perfect distraction. She pulls back.

"Violet, you're not—" She swallows, her hands tightening around my waist. "You're not in a good state of mind. We shouldn't—"

"If you aren't comfortable, I don't want to," I say, the shower raining down on us in warm, steaming patter. My eyes search through Cam's, scanning her face for anything. Anything that isn't pity. Anything that shows understanding for the fact that I need a distraction. She pauses, looking at me carefully. Then, she leans back in, pressing her lips to mine.

"I want to."

Cam's fingers glide delicately across my back.

There's no haste in her movement. No desperation. Her lips travel down my neck, rain drops hitting my back softly. Cam's knees bend, her lips traveling lower down my body now. She kisses the tops of my breasts, then between them. Her lips journey down my ribcage slowly, like a stroll on the beach, soaking in every inch. My body tenses when she meets my hip and sucks the skin gently between her teeth. But she doesn't try to leave a bruise. She kisses it like it's a butterfly's wing, careful not to break it. I swallow, tilting my head back into the shower.

"Are you sure you want this?" she asks. Her knees are against the stained floor of the tub, her eyes looking up at me with concern, but also with desire. I bite my bottom lip and nod my head.

"I want *you*."

Cam lifts my leg over her shoulder, just like I had done to her in the storage closet. Her face settles between my thighs, hesitating for just a moment before she licks a hot, wet stripe up the center of me. I groan, gripping the sidebar to steady myself. Cam looks up at me with a soft smile, then does it again. My veins tingle from the sensation, my fingers curling desperately. It's been a long time since I've had someone touch me like this. All tongue and hands, warmth and care.

Cam pulls back slightly and then slides two fingers through my slick center.

"God, baby," she groans and watches as her fingers unravel me. My hips rock forward, one hand still on the sidebar as the other finds the shower curtain and tightens its grip around it. Her fingers dip inside me, one at first, then both. They curl, tracing my inner walls as my eyes squeeze shut. A hot sensation, a slick one, finds its way to my clit. She licks circles around it, her fingers circling inside of me as they dip further and further in.

"Cam," I groan needily, releasing the shower curtain so I can find her hair. I run my fingers through her thick, wet locks, before I tighten my grip around them. Cam's head tilts in circles, her tongue dancing around my clit and making my stomach tighten. Despite the warm steam from the shower, goosebumps brush across my skin when she mutters against my heat.

"God, Violet. You look so gorgeous with your pussy in my mouth."

Fuck.

I groan, pulling Cam's face further into me by her hair. I release it immediately, as guilt washes over me.

"Shit, sorry. I didn't mean t—"

"Violet," she cuts in, tilting her head to the side. "Do you trust me?"

I look down at her, and drops pelt her pretty pink cheeks. Her lips glisten in the low bathroom light, and I don't know how to explain to her why I do. Why I trust her. I nod.

"Then ride my face like you don't care if I live."

My hand slides to the back of her head and pulls her face back into me. The warm familiarity of her mouth finds my throbbing clit instantly, and her fingers travel back inside me like they were crafted to fit. Heat floods my body, but I don't think it has anything to do with the water. My heart thrums against my chest, and my head rocks back with every roll of my hips against Cam's sweet, gorgeous face. Her free hand grips my hips, her nails sinking into the tender skin.

"Fuck, *yes.*"

Cam's grip around me tightens, and my own in her hair does the same. Her tongue slides back toward my entrance, where her fingers twist just right to run along the inside of me, then back up to my swollen clit. I feel it building, the pressure, the need. A high-pitched moan escapes my lips, which Cam takes as her cue to speed up.

"God, fuck!"

I hold the back of her head steady, my heel digging into her spine as I buck my hips inward, the curve of her face giving me just enough friction to come undone. She lets out a moan too, pulling me into her with so much force, that my standing leg begins to buckle. I leverage myself against the wall. I give one last thrust into her, the knot in my stomach releasing.*

My fingertips tingle as something rushes through my stomach. The void in my chest slowly closes as I look down at Cam, her face dipping out from between my thighs. Her cheeks are red, her lips swollen, and I don't know why I feel like I'm about to fall apart. My chest heaves as my muscles relax, and Cam stands, her hand immediately moving to cup the underside of my chin.

"Hey," she says softly, waiting for me to meet her eye. I swallow, hesitantly guiding them up to look at her. "You're okay. I've got you."

TWENTY-FIVE
The Dirty Shirley

CAM

GRIEF IS WEIRD.

Some people lock themselves into a room for years, completely isolating themselves for the rest of their lives. Others, like me, latch onto everything they have left and refuse to let go. Then, of course, there's Violet.

I can't judge how she reacted when she thought Reese was going to die. Nobody can. When the person you love most is jeopardized, there isn't any room for comparison on how you respond. I just can't help but feel like I failed by complying.

It was amazing, don't get me wrong. I can't find it in myself to regret it. But it wasn't supposed to happen. The contract was supposed to end.

I don't usually beat around the bush. I'm pretty forward with what I want. But it was different with this. I couldn't look Violet in the eye and tell her I didn't want to do this anymore because she would know, in an instant, that it was a lie.

And when she looked at me how she did that night, desperate for a distraction from the tragedies around her, it felt like a sin not to comply. She didn't make me feel that way. Violet would never make someone feel like they had to do something they didn't want to. But she's done a lot for me, whether she knows it or not. Guiding me through things and agreeing to a schedule. I wanted to repay her for that. I wanted to help her how I could.

Hayden had a shit-eating grin when I told him.

Dr. Burton said that he thinks I was moving on and that, just because I had been experiencing the effects of a trauma bond after seeing Cody, doesn't mean I want to go back.

"In fact," he said, a small smile tugging at his lips. "It means you don't. There wouldn't be so much internal conflict if it was something you actually wanted."

Then, he asked if I was making sure I was sticking to my original boundaries.

I lied and said yes.

The thing is, I'm not *not* sticking to the boundaries. Not exactly. I've set an alarm every Tuesday to remind me about Criminal Dinner, and the non-disclosure part still stands. But the schedule part, well... that's taken a bit of a hit.

After that night in the shower, I realized Violet was right in the beginning. Not about it being a booty call, but that you can't predict when you'll need one another. You can't schedule your need for a distraction. So, I scratched that part out, with a thick black sharpie. Violet grinned as I did it, and even gave me a high five, which I thought was her mocking me at first. Then, I realized she was being serious.

"Do you ever just lie there and smell his paws?" Violet asks.

My head snaps up to look at her, her shiny chestnut hair strewn across the pillow. Reese's head rests on the quilt covering my lap, his loose jowls squished against my bare thigh. Shaved patches cover the majority of his bruised skin, but small scabs are beginning to form over the punctures. Next to me, Dawson is cradled in Violet's arms, like he's a fifty-pound baby. His toes spread as he stretches his arms out, the pad of his paw grazing my cheek. I giggle.

"It would be a crime not to," I say, grabbing Dawson's foot and shoving it into my nose. I take a deep inhale, the earthy scent of dirt and the salty smell of corn chips wafting into my nose. Violet laughs.

"My sister thinks it's the grossest thing ever." I roll my eyes.

"People smell newborn babies fresh out of the vag. If I want to smell my dog's feet, I'm gonna."

We lay there for a moment, silently staring at one another, before breaking into laughter.

"He really likes you," Violet says after a moment. I look at her, her gaze fixated on Reese who has completely melted into me. So much love fills her eyes when she looks at him, like he's the only one in the world.

"I love him," I respond, dragging my thumb gently across his ear. "I'm really glad he's okay."

Violet nods, running her fingertips gently across his skin, avoiding any bruises and punctures. "You have no idea."

I pick my phone up off the nightstand to check the time. Have I really been here for six hours?

"It's Saturday," I remind her. Violet quirks an eyebrow at me, before realization pools in her eyes.

"Oh right, Adrian's art show," she says. I nod. "Well, I'm super excited for them."

I chew on the inside of my cheek, thinking about the words dancing around my tongue. I shouldn't say them. I know I shouldn't. But they're right there, forcing their way out.

"Are you gonna come?"

It isn't an absurd question, even though it feels like one. Adrian invited the entire staff, and even told them to bring friends and family. Greenrock only has one art show a year, hosted in the very tiny Greenrock Valley Gallery of Fine Arts. Violet scans my face, a hint of confusion behind her eyes.

"Do you want me to?" she asks.

Instinctively, I shake my head.

"No," I blurt out, though I immediately know it's a lie. "Well, no, not that I don't *want* you to, but I don't *not* want you to." I correct myself. "I just know it will mean a lot to Adrian if more people come."

Violet nods slowly but doesn't say anything.

Then, after a moment, her lips part.

"I wasn't planning on it," she says. "Because I didn't want to make you uncomfortable."

I swallow, knowing that is a completely valid reason for her not to go. Still, it doesn't stop the strange twisting inside my stomach.

"Well," I say, not really understanding why the words are coming out. "Maybe it would be better if you did. I mean." I gesture to her. "Maybe it will come off stranger if you're the only one who doesn't go, you know?"

A smile tugs at the corners of Violet's lips, her pierced brow rising.

"Are you asking me to come, Sparky?" she asks. I roll my eyes and look back down at Reese. My fingers glide gently over the shaved spots along his body. On his ear, his cheek, his neck, his ribcage. The one on his leg is the worst though. It tore, rather than punctured, most likely from the other dog not letting go. Black stitches poke through the raw skin, holding him together.

"I'm asking you to come for Adrian," I say firmly, still not meeting Violet's eye. I slide out from under Reese and gently lower his head onto the mattress. "I couldn't care less, personally."

A DRIAN LOOKS STUNNING. Of course, they always do.

With their glowing skin and shiny black curls, Adrian couldn't look bad even if they tried. But they look especially dapper tonight, in a dark blue tux and masculine bun. I lean forward to tighten their patterned tie.

"*You*," I say, my eyes meeting theirs. Adrian has brown eyes in the way I wish I did. "Are going to be *great*."

Adrian taps their feet side to side like a penguin.

They aren't usually nervous about these things. They aren't usually nervous at all, unless it's about me. But tonight is huge. Anassia Walker, the owner of the biggest art gallery in the Pacific Northwest, will be there, looking to add to the Pacific Mountain Gallery of Fine Arts.

These opportunities don't come by frequently to Adrian, not unless they travel to Seattle. And the past few years, they've been saving that money for Rise. So this, well, this could change everything for them.

"I know," they say, exhaling a stream of air through their pursed lips. "It's going to be great. *I* am great."

"You sure are," Hayden says, pressing a quick kiss to their temple. He's wearing a gray suit, the handkerchief in his pocket almost the same captivating color as his eyes. Major boasts a matching gray harness, all the patches accented with the same blue. Hayden Ayers is a man of style. Avery nods in agreement, his hands fidgeting in the pockets of his own boxy tux. I stick my thumb in my mouth to wet it and scrub at the stain on my infamous emerald dress, knowing it isn't going to come out.

I got that stain on my way home from a date with Cody. Luigi had broken down, of course, and I was messing with the engine, at least *attempting* to do something, while Cody pouted in the passenger seat, muttering about what a piece of shit my car was. He had no car of his own, which was another topic in itself. I sat back down, wiping my greased hands on my dress as I asked him to not say that. It was thrifted but new to me. It was my favorite dress then and still is. I refuse to let Cody ruin that.

"I can't wait to finally see it," Hayden says excitedly, bouncing on the tips of his toes. I nod, looking around at all the easels spread throughout the gallery. A large white sheet covers Adrian's canvas.

"Yeah, Ry! I've been dying to know what it is."

Adrian's been working on this piece for months now, but they refuse to let any of us see it. Avery wiggles his brows, letting a sly smile creep across his face.

"I know what it is," he taunts. Adrian smacks him lightly with the back of their hand, and Hayden and I shoot him a jealous glare.

"What?!"

Adrian smiles sheepishly.

"Sorry," they say, now taking their turn to shoot Avery a glare. He shrugs, like he has no idea what he did wrong. "He saw it when I was loading it into the car."

I wrinkle my nose, staring at Avery. But out of the corner of my eye, I catch a glimpse of something.

[17]No—sorry. Not *something*. *Someone*. A group, actually, of Furry Friends employees. Brooke looks beautiful, in a light blue, cowl-necked dress. Martha boasts a red skirt, a white button-up tucked inside. Malcolm must have missed the memo, as he trudges next to them in ripped jeans and a tattered "I Heart MILFS" T-shirt, which entices a chuckle out of me.

And at the center of the group, in a pair of black high-waisted slacks and a matching, asymmetrical cropped blazer, is Violet. The top is just long enough to cover the strip of skin on her stomach, but it's classy, and chic. If she were to lift her arms, that skin would peek through. Her piercings are still there, shimmering in the overhead lights, but looking at her now, you would never guess she was covered in tattoos. For a moment, I forget there is anyone else in the room.

No. I forget there is anyone else on the planet.

A sharp elbow pokes my ribs, and my head snaps up, shooting its owner a scowl. But it's Hayden, his brows raised slightly in a cautionary glance. My cheeks flush, knowing exactly what he's saying without saying it: I am standing here, jaw-dropped, eyes fixated on Violet Wolfe.

"Thanks," I mutter, and Hayden gives my arm a brief squeeze.

"You made it!" Adrian squeals, running toward the group with their arms stretched wide. They practically throw themselves into everyone, and the team all wraps together in a big group huddle. Violet's eyes flick up to me, and she shoots me a sparkling grin.

"Wouldn't miss it for the world."

"One Vodka Cranberry," I say to the bartender. She nods, reaching for the unopened bottle of Grey Goose. After filling a short plastic cup with ice, she pours in the thick clear liquid, mixes in a dark red juice, and garnishes it with a lemon wedge, which hangs off the rim of the cup. She sets the drink in front of me.

"Eleven dollars please."

I nod, reaching down into my purse to retrieve my wallet.

"I've got it," a voice behind me says, and I don't have to turn around to recognize the angelic rasp. My cheeks flush, and I wait a moment for it to go away before looking up at Violet.

"I can buy my own drink, *boss,*" I say, reaching back into my bag. Violet slaps her card against the bar, nodding to the bartender.

"And one Dirty Shirley please," she asks sweetly. The bartender takes her card and swipes it on the machine before making her drink. I look at Violet, unimpressed.

"A Dirty Shirley?" I ask, my eyebrow cocked in a taunting way. Violet crosses her arms.

"What, not sophisticated enough for the woman in the oil-stained dress?" she asks, gesturing to me. "It's pretty much the fun version of a Vodka Cranberry."

I shake my head.

"It's really not," I say, fighting a smile. I take a long sip of the drink in my hand. My eye twitches when the vodka hits my tongue.

Damn that's strong.

I must not be hiding my disgust as well as I thought I was because Violet's lips tug into a smirk.

"Here's that drink, miss," the bartender says, interrupting our eye contact. Violet smiles at her, then swoops her drink off the bar, and walks away without another word.*

I take an even longer sip of my drink this time, staring at her as she saunters away. The bartender shoots me an amused look. I give her an awkward laugh.

"Bosses, am I right?"

She nods, like I'm completely insane, and I shuffle away quickly to find Adrian.

"Can I have that?" they ask, pointing to the cup in my hand. If I'm going to get through this night without sneaking Violet into the bathroom, I'm gonna need help. But Adrian's eyes are desperate, their brows pressed together in a stressed plea. I nod and hand them the cup. They suck half of it down without even blinking.

"Alright, ladies and gentlemen," a woman announces, standing on a make-shift stage in the front of the gallery. Adrian clears their throat, stretching their arms out, and gestures to their body from the tops of their head down to their toes. The woman glances over, her head tilting as she looks at the silent spectacle they are making. Her face flushes. "And *others*. We are so excited to begin our night here at the Annual Greenrock Valley Art Walk!"

Everyone in the room claps, Malcolm letting out a loud cheer. His cheeks turn red when he realizes this isn't quite that type of event. Violet chuckles, and Hayden sneaks him a fist-bump.

"Love the enthusiasm."

"As I'm sure you are aware, Anassia Walker, the founder of the Pacific Mountain Gallery of Fine Arts will be joining us tonight, searching for a new addition for her institution."

Anassia Walker is a tall woman, and by that, I mean she is probably five-foot-ten, but the black strappy heels she wears boost her to be closer to six feet. A coral top beneath her gray suit jacket makes her skin glow, the matching gray pants below tailored to her height perfectly. She steps forward, waves, then steps back.

"She's hot," Avery whispers, and we all shoot him a glare. His face turns red, and he adjusts his posture to sit up straighter.

The speaker continues.

"Other than that, there is a bar in the corner." She points in the direction of the bar, and Malcolm gives another whoop. This time, everyone laughs. "And have fun!"

Everyone claps again, a bit louder this time, and Anassia turns, walking toward the easels on the other side of the gym.

We all turn to Adrian and watch their hand grip the white sheet draped over their piece. They take a deep breath, then pull it down to reveal a huge, colorful, textured canvas. I step back to see it in its entirety, my eyes adjusting to the popping colors, and variating textures.

"Is that... us?" Hayden asks quietly. Thick oil paint sculpts out recognizable faces on a recognizable tawny couch, in a recognizable living room. I can see it now, so clearly, Adrian's soft brown skin and Avery's thick hair. A tuft of white fur clinging to my scrub pants. Shining blue eyes looking down at me. The uneaten gyro sitting on a painted plate on the coffee table in front of us.

Adrian beams.

"It wasn't what the original painting was supposed to be," they admit. "But I started this one, and I liked it so much more."

Tears prick my eyes as I stare at the piece in front of me. Every detail, every curve, perfectly painted in colors so bright my eyes have to adjust. I blink, a singular tear trickling down my cheek. My eyes dart to Violet, and her brows press together in a concerned gaze. The sleeve of a gray suit jacket presses to my cheek, Hayden patting the tear dry.

"Cam," he whispers. I shake my head and clear my throat.

"I'm fine," I say, sniffling. I square my shoulders and look at Adrian in a loving gaze.

"You know how much I love you?" I ask. They pull me in, squeezing me tightly.

"About as much as I love you."

After the rest of the group gets a chance to "ooh" and "ahh" at Adrian's painting, they wave their hands in the air dismissively.

"You don't have to stay here," Adrian says, turning to our group. "Go look around!"

Avery and I share a concerned glance, and Adrian rolls their eyes, pushing us away.

"*Space*," they say firmly, but giggling. "Give me some space for when Anassia comes." Then, their hand grips the sleeve of Avery's suit jacket, their eyes darting up to him. "But come back."

We nod and start to spread out, taking different routes to different pieces that caught our eyes earlier in the night. I approach a sculpture, sitting on top of a sleek black display table. The sculpture isn't of anything, at least nothing discernible to the naked eye. Still, something about it has me tilting my head, intrigued.

"You gonna make it?" Violet says behind me. My eyes roll as I turn to face her.

"Are you going to creep up on me all night, or can you find a different hobby?"

Violet sticks her hands up defensively, her almost empty Dirty Shirley waving in the air.

"Cool it, Sparks," she says. "I was just checking on you. You seemed kind of upset back there."

My cheeks turn pink, heat rushing to them at the thought of Violet watching me cry.

Crying isn't embarrassing. At least I tell myself that, since I seem to do it frequently. I never think to myself when someone else is crying that they should be embarrassed. But knowing Violet watched me tear up at something so simple as a painting makes my stomach crawl.

It wasn't simple though. That's the thing. That painting is my family. Even the parts of it I'm not so fond of. I shake my head.

"I'm fine," I say, looking back at the twisting yellow sculpture. Violet steps beside me, either analyzing it or pretending to. I glance at her briefly. I don't know why I do. I don't mean to, and I don't want to. I don't want anyone who might be watching us to think anything is going on. But she looks so beautiful in this suit, her hair slicked back, her hazel eyes beaming. I look back in front of me.

"I like your outfit," I whisper, continuing to stare forward. Violet looks forward too, but out of the corner of my eye, I can see a smile.

"Thank you," she says, tilting her head at the art in front of us. "I like yours too. Although…" She takes a sip of her drink. "I do feel like it's missing something."

My head turns to look at her, my brows furrowing. "What?"

She taps her index finger to the spot on her arm, the one that used to be empty. The hammerhead shark. Then, she bites back a smile as she turns and walks away.

Later in the night, after Anassia told Adrian their painting had "truly captured the modern-day family" and Avery left because he got overwhelmed by the constant flow of people, I see Violet, leaning against the bar, a full glass in her hand. But this drink is different, something blue that looks like it would for sure make me throw up. My eye is drawn to the person in front of her, the person she's talking to, who's holding the same blue drink in her delicate hands.

Anassia Walker.

I chew on the inside of my cheek as I walk over to them. Not to *them*. To the bar, of course, that's all. If they happen to be there, that's none of my business. I clear my throat, stepping between them to order.

"Can I have another Vodka Cranberry please?"

I watch the bartender as she makes my drink, but a hand tugs on my bare bicep.

"Cam!" Violet says my name louder than I would like in a public setting, but quieter than I would like in a private one. "This is Anassia. Anassia," She gestures to me. "This is one of my employees, Cam."

Heat fills my cheeks as I look up at the woman towering over me, her tall slender build not unlike a feminine version of Hayden's. I know it shouldn't, because that's exactly what I am, but the word "employee" sticks to the sides of my brain, like a degradation. I frown.

"It's nice to meet you," Anassia says, reaching out a thin pale hand. She has coral acrylics, ones that match her button-up. They're ugly, to be quite frank. I stick my hand out, shaking hers firmly. As firmly as I can, actually. I don't know why; the intention wasn't to hurt her. But I don't like being looked down at like I'm just an "employee."

"Your boss is really something, isn't she? She's not too hard on you I hope."

"Here's that Vodka Cranberry," the bartender says, looking at me with al-most-pity behind her eyes. "On the house."

I grab it, taking a dramatically long sip and assure all the muscles in my face stay tight and unmoving. I set it back down, a tiny splash landing on the counter.

"Nope."

I cut the word in half, turning it into two syllables instead of one, popping my lips on the "p." A valley forms between Violet's eyebrows as she presses them together. Anassia looks back up at her with a perfectly straight smile.

Are those veneers? I bet they're veneers.

"So, Violet, what brings you to the show? Are you an artist yourself?"

Violet chuckles, shaking her head, and I let out an abrupt, loud laugh. Anassia eyes me, dissatisfied, then looks back up at Violet over my head. I mean, I'm literally standing right here?

"No," Violet says. "I'm actually here for an employee of mine. You may have met them. Adrian Barlowe?"

Anassia nods her head, a smile forming on her face.

"Oh yes," she says, and I swear to God she bats her eyelashes. "What was their painting called? Handmade?"

"*Homemade*," I cut in, because I just can't help myself. "Like a Homemade

Family."

My eyes dart to Violet, something washing over her face. Understanding or realization, her eyes focusing onto me with a sort of shine.

"That's right," Anassia says. "*Homemade.* It's quite lovely, isn't it, Violet?"

Violet nods, and I can't listen to this woman's sophisticated accent anymore.

"Yup! They're the best," I say, pointing to Adrian who is starting to pack up their things. "You should talk to them, *over there.*"

Anassia quirks a brow at me, and I have a sneaking suspicion she is looking down at me, not just due to her height. Violet chuckles, shaking her head but not saying anything.

"I think I might," she says, matter-of-factly. "It was very nice to meet you, Violet." She reaches her hand out again, and Violet shakes it firmly with a smile. When she releases it, Anassia's hand points down toward me. "And you too..." Her dark blue eyes click with mine. "*Pam.*"

Violet waits for Anassia to walk away before bursting into a fit of laughter. I don't hesitate, however, to let steam pour through my ears.

"*Pam?*" I scoff, propping my hand on my waist. I throw the rest of my Vodka Cranberry down the back of my throat. "I mean, that was *clearly* a dig. What a rude woman."

Violet scoffs, a wide smile sewn into her glowing cheeks.

"*She's* rude?" she asks, twirling the red straw inside of her disgustingly blue drink. "Says the one who quite literally interrupted our conversation by standing *between* us."

I frown, glaring up at her. "Well, what were you doing anyway?"

Violet smirks, taking a sip of that taunting drink. "You told me to find a new hobby," she shrugs. "Was I not supposed to do that?"

Heat fills my cheeks, and I shoot her a menacing scowl.

"I don't care *what* you do, Violet." My eyes dart to the drink, then back up at her. "This is just a mutually beneficial sexual arrangement, remember?"

The bartender chokes behind the counter, like she's getting front row tickets to some weird American soap opera.

"It kinda seems like you *do* care, Cameron," Violet says, my name coming from her lips like sweet, thick honey. She leans against the bar, looking at me through her lashes.

"I don't," I say. "But if that's the case then—" I cross my arms. "We have to start using protection."

Violet chuckles, shaking her head.

"It's not the case," she says. "You think I want to go around hooking up with people I meet at art shows?"

I shrug.

"I don't know. Isn't that what divorcees do?"

"Maybe," she says. "But not me. Don't worry, Cam. You're my only hobby."

She tucks the red straw between her lips, the blue line of the drink sinking downward.

"What is that?" I ask, eyeing it suspiciously.

Violet shrugs.

"I don't remember what it's called. Anassia bought it for me." A little crescent forms on the corner of her mouth as she gives me another sly smirk. "Wanna taste?"

I frown, crossing my arms.

"No, actually." I look across the room at Adrian and Hayden. Adrian is chatting with, ugh, Anassia, but Hayden's eyes are glued to me, a blonde brow raised. "I have to go." I wave a hand in the air dismissively. "Bye."

Violet chuckles, muttering under her breath, "Night, Sparky."

Twenty-Six

Cunt

VIOLET

IT'S FUNNY HOW, WHEN you spend enough time with someone, little things start to remind you of them. Like how, every time I see a service dog, I think of Hayden. Little shiny tubes of lip gloss make me think of Mallory, no matter how hard I try to fight it. But it seems, after that night I showed up on her doorstep, *everything* reminds me of Cam.

The little shark-shaped gummies at the gas station when I go inside to pay. Anything brown: the mountains, bare branches, my morning cup of coffee. I see people walking their dogs through my neighborhood, and I wonder if she is the one who cut their hair.

I even find Cam in things that have nothing to do with her at all. Veering through the winding, snow-clad city streets, I'm reminded of her bright, dimpled smile. It's breathtaking and rare, and even though it's something you have to earn, I never feel like I deserve it. Everything in pairs reminds me that she's a Gemini, which is funny because it makes so much sense yet none at all. Every time I watch a movie, I wonder if she's read the book. I think about what differences there might be, and if maybe I should read them too, so I can experience the story the same way she does.

I've never really been a reader. It's hard to focus when it's quiet, but it's difficult to comprehend the words in front of me when I'm surrounded by noise. Cam loves reading though, and she makes me want to love it too.

Even now, standing here next to a bright yellow mop bucket, I'm reminded of her. Of the day after we met, that wide-eyed look of panic on her face. The silent nervous nods, and her refusal to meet my eye. I think about how we ended up in that shower two weeks ago, and how the two days almost seem like different worlds entirely, different dimensions merged into one.

I guess that's what life is like with her around. Multidimensional.

Water trickles down the wringer into the murky mop bucket. Sounds of movement permeate the air around me, dogs barking and tussling, imperceptible staff conversations. It's nice not to have to create my own noise like I do at home, blasting music or turning on the television. It's one of the few things I *do* like about this job. The dogs, of course. And my coworkers, they're amazing. But what I'm most grateful for is the lack of silence.

That's why I'm still here, thirty minutes after my shift ended. I can't afford silence right now.

"Still here?" Cam's head turns, her eyes traveling to meet me. I pull the salon door shut behind me, the splintering wooden mop handle gripped in my calloused hands.

"Figured I could do a little cleaning up," I shrug, then flash her a teasing grin. "Kinda *grimy* in here, don't you think?"

Cam cocks a brow, then readjusts her gaze onto the dog in the tub.

"It wouldn't be so *grimy* if you installed those vents I've been talking about for the last two months."

A coy smirk plays on her lips, knowing that she's won. It's a win-lose scenario when Cam wins. She starts to act invincible, like she can get me to do anything. Whether or not she's correct isn't the point. But she also gets this glow about her, a confidence she doesn't typically own. Her lips tug up, her eyebrow quirks, and the slight tilt of her head makes me want to lose just so that I can see it.

"The electrician never called me back," I say as an excuse, my cheeks flushing. "But, touché."

Cam's hands glide through the thick white suds soaked into the dog's coat. It's comical to be jealous, but if you knew the way Cam's hands feel in your hair, you'd understand. Nothing compares to the soft tug, the gentle massage of those smooth fingertips against your scalp. It's cosmic, the way all the hair on your body stands as you melt into her touch. Cam is stubborn and morose, but the worst crime she could commit would be to never let me feel those hands again.

I don't have a good reason to still be here, I know that. But if I could, I would spend every free second of my life here anyway, watching her. My eyes drop to the floor as the mop glides across a spot of dried soap.

"So did Anassia ever call Adrian?" I ask. I don't bring up Anassia's name to watch Cam's eye twitch, but it's a perk I can't say that I loathe. Just like I hadn't accepted the drink Anassia bought just to make Cam jealous, but I hadn't hated her reaction then either.

Truthfully, I had accepted it for the opposite reason. I thought Cam would feel relieved, knowing the staff would see me publicly flirt with the person that was intended to be the main attraction of the event. After that, nobody would think twice about seeing us next to one another at the exhibits.

But after she power-walked over, her brows pressed together, that angry glare in her eye, I realized it had the opposite effect. At least it would have if mostly everyone hadn't already left. I knew then, watching her stand between us, that Cameron Miller was jealous.

I haven't had anyone act jealous over me before. Mallory was the showpiece, the person everyone's eyes locked onto when she entered the room. She never had a reason to be jealous. Nobody ever felt like a threat.

I'm ashamed to say it, embarrassed really, but it's a gratifying feeling to have someone fight to keep you to themselves. I know it means nothing; maybe just like me, Cam doesn't like to share. But something still flutters in my chest when I think about it.

"She said it didn't click with her studio," Cam answers grimly. "But the Greenrock Gallery actually asked to display it, so it was a bittersweet outcome for them."

Cam's voice is like a saccharine symphony playing in my ear. It's feathery, even when harsh words are slipping out, and the slightest lisp makes me never want to hear another song again. I don't want her to stop talking, so I scour my brain for anything Cam might find worth her time.

"So, what's with the, uh, *word* carved into your car door?"

It's been a question on my mind since I saw it that night her car broke down. At the time, it hadn't seemed like a good idea to ask. It's a particular word, one even most sailors won't use. And with the depth of the carving, there was definitely intent behind it.

A choked laugh slips through Cam's lips, but she doesn't look at me. "You noticed that?"

I nod, even though her eyes are fixated on the dog in the tub.

"So." She chuckles again, shaking her head. "Cody, you know, my *ex*—"

I do, because I have never wanted to hit someone so hard in my entire life. Something about him is so unsettling, so unnerving. I force my disgusted expression to go blank and continue listening.

"We broke up because I walked in on him with another woman. Obviously, I freaked out and told him to leave because it was *my* bed—"

I don't even mean to gasp, it just forces its way out of me. I swear, when men were created, the universe replaced their brain cells with audacity. Sure, Mallory cheated on me. But at least she had the *decency* to do it somewhere else. "He didn't!"

"Oh, but he did."

Cam's smiling, but I know how painful it is to go through that. I couldn't imagine having to actually witness it.

"Anyway, he flips it over on *me* and says I *made* him cheat, that he didn't have a choice because I had just started a new medication and, well, those things can affect that, y'know?"

The story's coming off like some big comedy skit. Like Cam isn't talking about the tragic end of a long-term relationship through backstabbing betrayal. Like the sight of him a few weeks ago didn't send her into a spiral. I'm the queen of pretending everything is fine, but when Mallory slept with someone else, it took me weeks to even tell Ruthie because every time I thought about it, I felt like I was going to throw up.

"So he carved '*cunt*' into your car?"

"No." Cam turns on the hose, wriggling the nozzle, and the suds begin to wash down the dog's body. "The woman leaves, but Cody *refuses*, so I call Adrian."

Cam's eyes dart to me, and I look back down at the floor, reminding myself to stay busy.

"Adrian calls Cody's *mom* and tells her what happened. He's always been a huge momma's boy. His mom calls him while he's still lying *naked* in the bed, and she screams at him over the phone. I couldn't make out everything, but the word 'castrate' was definitely in there."

Nothing in the story is funny to me, but I force a laugh for Cam's sake.

"The next day, that etching showed up on Luigi."

My throat tightens as my own saliva gets caught in my airway. "Luigi?"

"My car."

"Right." I swallow, uncertainty filling my mind. Part of me wants to change the topic completely, but the other part wants to tell Cam that I know exactly how it feels, that kind of disloyalty.

"Mallory cheated on me." The words come out hesitantly, almost like I don't know it for a fact. Really, I just don't know why I'm telling her. Maybe it's an attempt to make her feel better, or maybe, it's just because Cam has a way of understanding. "That's why we got a divorce. Well, that was the nail in the coffin, I guess."

I try to swallow down the dry lump forming in the base of my throat.

Where was I going with this?

Cam's gaze flicks up to me, that similar, pitying look she had given me the night I showed up on her doorstep.

"I'm sorry," she says quietly.

[18]I shake my head. "No, *I'm* sorry. Cody is a dick. Cam, you deserve someone who sees how amazing you are. You're a fucking terror sometimes, I'll give you that. But you're a privilege to be around, and anyone who knows you can see that. So don't forget it. When you—" The words get stuck at the bottom of my throat, as if I'm holding onto them. A sigh slips through my lips, and my eyes lock onto hers. "When you're ready for something more than—"

The salon door flings open. My heart sinks in my chest as I spin around.

"Hey Vi, is it cool if I dip?" Malcolm stands in the doorway, his body slumped against the wooden frame. My eyes flick to Cam, just for a brief second, her eyes wide and her cheeks pale. "Everything is done, and honestly, I want to go home."

I let out a small laugh at Malcolm's candidness. I never really wanted to be the manager of Furry Friends. I didn't like the idea of being on my coworker's asses all the time. I didn't want to become the reason they dreaded coming in. But at the time it was offered to me, I couldn't afford to pass it up. Mallory had just quit her accounting job to open the dance studio, and I wanted to do whatever I could to support her. It took some adjusting, a learning curve to balance productivity and humanity, but I think I've done a decent job at making sure the staff thinks of me as their coworker, not their boss.

"Sure. Just make sure to double check meds, okay?"

He flashes me a weak smile, and a satirical salute.

"Aye aye, captain," he says, before twirling around and closing the door behind him. I turn to Cam quickly, my chest twisting into a tight mass.

"Fuck, Cam, I'm sorry."

"It's fine," she cuts in, short but not flat. Her eyes flick up to meet mine, and that divine dimple dips into her cheek as she smiles. My teeth sink into the inside of my cheek, and my eyes lower.

"I should go," I say, my grip tightening around the mop handle in my hand. "Reese is probably tired of being stuck in a suite all day, and if I leave the cone of shame on him any longer, he might take a revenge piss on my bed."

Cam chuckles, the corner of her mouth curling inward as she nods.

"Okay," she says softly. "Drive safe."*

TWENTY-SEVEN

New Isn't Always Better

CAM

"**Y**OU SEEM CHEERY," ADRIAN says, sliding into Luigi's passenger seat. "What? Did you get laid or something?"

I demanded to drive Adrian to work this morning. They're still pretty beaten up about the whole Anassia Walker thing, and I've been brainstorming ways to lessen the blow a little bit. Apparently, though, I'm still on a sex-high from last night. I adjust my face, subtly messing with the rearview mirror to deflect.

"*Funny,* Ry," I say sarcastically, my stomach twisting. [19]I've been thinking about it more, about telling Adrian. Every single time I'm with Violet, the guilt eats away at me. I've been setting aside time for Adrian; I've been making sure of it. I don't miss a single minute of Criminal Dinner, and we still make our frequent stops at Evergreen Grounds. But that doesn't feel like enough anymore. I feel like I'm keeping a secret from them.

I don't just mean Violet. I feel like I'm keeping myself from them. I'm not letting them fully see the changes and the growth. I've tried a few times to bring it up, but every time I do, I just can't get the words out. It's hard to understand how I can trust someone with my life, but not with my secrets. It isn't their fault. To Adrian, secrets are stress. They focus so hard on trying to hold them in that the pressure builds up and explodes. Telling them and asking them to keep it bottled up seems worse somehow than keeping it to myself. But that doesn't make me feel less guilty.

Dr. Burton says I have a right to feel the way I do, and Hayden says that, while he knows it will hurt them if they ever find out, he understands why I'm hesitant.

"Hey guys!" Aurora smiles, poking her head through the window of the little green shed. She grips an iPad in a thick blue case. "I'll get that black coffee right out for you, Cam. And what are you feeling today, Adrian?"

"Actually," I cut in, looking over at Adrian and swallowing. I look back to Aurora. "Can I have something different?"

Aurora's brows raise, but she smiles and lifts the iPad up, tapping on the screen.

"Absolutely! What would you like?"

"You can just..." I swallow back the anxiety in my tone. "Surprise me."

She taps on the screen for a second and then looks back up with beaming eyes.

"Sure thing. And for you, Adrian?"

I turn, looking at Adrian in the passenger seat, who is staring at me with wide eyes and parted lips. They blink slowly.

"Did you just—"

I nod, and they keep blinking, like if they do it enough times, my answer will change.

"But—"

I bite back a smile. "What are you feeling, Ry?"

Adrian keeps staring at me in disbelief.

"Same," they say, not breaking their gaze. Aurora nods and begins working on our drinks.

"Can you stop staring at me?" I laugh, shoving Adrian's arm gently. Their brows press together.

"Cam, you just ordered a *surprise* coffee."

I nod. "Yeah?"

They shake their head.

"And that isn't a big deal to you?"

I suck in a breath and shrug. "I mean, *yeah*," I say honestly. "But also *no*."

Adrian's lips tug into a wide smile, their face beaming proudly. "Wow," they chuckle, shaking their head again.

"What?"

They look up at me, sliding their hand into mine.

"I'm going to be honest," they say, squeezing my hand. "And don't get pissed, okay?"

"Okay?" I say. I couldn't be pissed at Adrian if I tried. They sigh.

"When you started at Furry Friends, I thought, well, I thought it was going to be a disaster. I didn't want it to be, and I had every faith in your ability to do your job. It wasn't anything like that, it was just..." They swallow, their eyes meeting mine.

"Ry, I'm not going to get mad."

They nod.

"I just thought it was going to be too much change for you. And I thought, maybe, at least for a while, it would hold you back from making other changes. But I was wrong." They gesture to the little green kiosk beside us. "I mean, you're making strides compared to this time last year. And I'm just..." They sigh. "I'm just so proud of you."

Warmth radiates in my chest, my body melting into the sweet words. At least it would if I didn't feel like such a piece of shit. I have to tell them. They need to know.

"Adrian, I—"*

"One honey lavender oat milk latte," Aurora interrupts, passing the paper cup through the drive-through window. My head snaps over to her, and I grab it, forcing a smile. "And this one is a caramel toffee macchiato."

I take the second cup and place them both in the cup holders before handing Aurora my debit card. She swipes it, lets me select the tip percentage, then hands it back to me.

"Well, you guys have a wonderful day!" she smiles. "Stay warm out there!"

Adrian waves at her excitedly as I roll up the window and pull out of the parking lot. They grab both cups from the cupholder and take a sip from each.

"They're both good," they say decisively. Their hand extends out to me, trying to hand me a cup. "You can choose which one you want. I'll be happy with either."

The repetitive click on the turn signal blares behind me as I wait for a clearing in the traffic. I look over at Adrian, their sweet sunshiny face and their bright smile. I can't tell them this now. Not when they're in such a good mood. Not when I'm about to surprise them with something. I can't ruin this.

I tack on a smile, hoping they don't see through it. Then, I accept the cup and take a slow, long sip.

"Uck!" My nose wrinkles as the floral flavor bursts through my mouth. My head jolts back in disgust. Adrian takes the cup from my hand, giggling.

"Okay, okay, not a hit." They hand me the other one. "Try this one."

I look at them skeptically, but I try it.

They're both fucking awful. I hand it back to them, and they frown, disappointed.

"That's okay," they say comfortingly. "You tried. Want to turn back and get your normal one?"

I shake my head.

"I can't. We don't have time."

Adrian frowns, looking at the digital clock on the dashboard. "Cam, we have plenty of time."

I shake my head.

"No," I say, shooting them a grin. "We have a pit stop to make."

ADRIAN STARES AT THE empty spot on the wall of the Greenrock Gallery of Fine Arts, tracing their fingers along it. Their lips mouth the words written on the sign hanging below it, and they pause, chewing on their lip before looking up at me.

"I don't get it," they frown. "Where's my painting?"

I smile and point to the sign they just read.

"Read it again."

Adrian makes a face, but they comply.

"Homemade, Adrian Barlowe, 2024, Oil, has found a temporary home in—" Their brows furrow, but their eyes widen when the next part comes out in a gasp. "In the Pacific Mountain Gallery of Fine Arts!"

Their head snaps up to me, tears filling their eyes.

"What? But how?" They look back at the bare wall in disbelief, then back up at me. "How?"

I smile, giving them a shrug. "Anassia changed her mind, I guess."

Adrian throws their arms around me, squeezing tighter than ever.

"I don't know *what* you did," they say, their voice strained from the tight hug. "But *thank you*. Thank you, thank you, thank you!"

I hug them back, my face sinking into their soft curly hair.

"It's all you," I say. "She just needed a little shove."

Adrian pulls back, now eyeing me suspiciously.

"Should I be... *concerned* about Anassia? Is she, like, tied up in your trunk or something? Cause I swear I heard a noise."

I roll my eyes, pushing them away playfully.

"Anassia is *fine*," I say, her name tasting bitter in my mouth. I'm sure she's actually a wonderful person. But... "Like I said, it was just a little shove."

Adrian smiles, placing a warm wet kiss on my forehead.

"You are my favorite person in existence," they say, their eyes locking onto mine. "You know that, right?"

My heart sinks into my stomach, but I smile.

"You're mine, Ry." I swallow. "And yeah. I know that."

Adrian walked into Furry Friends like they just won the lottery. It was so cute, the way they ran about the place, telling any person and dog who would listen about their piece being shown at Anassia Walker's studio.

Avery banished them to the Party Pen, so they had somewhere to channel their energy, which was probably the safest choice.

"So, it went well, from the sounds of it," Violet says, closing the salon door behind her as she steps into the room. I look up, my overly-priced and over-ly-bent Chris Christensen brush stuck halfway through a Great Pyrenees' butt fluff. I chuckle.

"I think you made their *life*," I say, tugging the brush back through. I lock eyes with her. "Thank you."

Violet shrugs, all nonchalant. "Yeah, well, if the owner of an art gallery is going to give you her phone number, you may as well put it to good use."

I raise my eyebrows, fighting a jealous smile. Saying what I want to say is a complete violation of the contract. Well, the parts we haven't crossed out yet. Still, I can't get it off my mind, like the thought is a little worm, digging deeper and deeper into my brain.

"So what'd you have to do?" I break, turning back to the dog on my table. I pretend to be focused on the thin wire bristles brushing through the coat. "Agree to a date?"

Violet grows quiet for just a moment too long, and my gaze darts up to her, my brows furrowed. She breaks into laughter.

"Sorry." She laughs, slapping her knee. "I just had to see your face."

I frown, turning away from her again. "I made no face," I say firmly.

"You totally did."

I shake my head. "Like I said, do what you want. Just let me know if we need to start using protection."

I say it casually, like I don't know it's a flat-out lie. Like the thought of Violet with anyone but me doesn't set my cheeks on fire, doesn't twist my stomach into a tight, charred pretzel. But even just feeling that way pushes the boundaries of our rules, and saying it out loud? Well, we need to cling to the ones we have left.

"Cameron."

By the time my brain is telling my eyes not to look up at her, they've already latched on. I sigh, as if hearing my full name come out of her mouth doesn't cause moths to flutter in my stomach.

"Yes?"

"I only want you."

TWENTY-EIGHT
Barnyard Revelations

VIOLET

CAM'S BODY RELAXES UNDERNEATH me, the sweat beaded at the crown of her head drying and her breaths slowing as she lets out a soft chuckle.[20] I slide the strap-on out of her, green for her favorite color, of course. Then, I unclip the harness, and toss it to the side.

"Damn," she murmurs, her eyes drifting shut as she focuses on her breathing. A smile creeps across my face, and I poke her soft, delicious thigh with my index finger.

"You're shaking again."

Cam's eyes shoot open, and she looks at her vibrating legs briefly before shooting me a scowl. I like that scowl. Even when Cam is irritated, which is often, she looks so damn cute. Her feathered brows press together, along with the soft downward tug of those pretty pink lips. And that little crease that forms on the bridge of her nose which I can't help but trace with my finger.

"If you didn't want them to shake, you shouldn't have fucked me the way that you did," she groans, pulling herself upward in the process. Her back presses against my headboard, and I can think of a few other things I'd like to see pressed against my headboard. A curious smirk tugs at the corners of my lips.

"Better than the real thing?" I tease. Cam's brows raise, and she tugs at the blanket, trying to pull it over her naked body. I frown, letting my weight sink further into it.

"Is that a concern of yours?" she asks, shooting me a cocky grin. I shoot her one right back.

"No." I shrug. "Because even if it isn't, nobody else's name sounds quite as pretty coming from that foul mouth of yours."

Cam's cheeks redden, and she rips the blanket out from under me, covering herself with it. I pout.

"Have you watched *Shutter Island yet*?" she asks.

Sometimes, when there's enough time in the *appointment*, Cam and I will watch a movie. Sometimes it leads to more sex, sometimes it leads to her teasing me about my preference.

I *love* rom-coms. You know. *The Proposal. Clueless. No Hard Feelings.* Cam on the other hand... she likes them grim. And by that, I mean really, *truly* fucked up.

"I *haven't...*" I say, dragging out the word. "Cam, respectfully, all of the movies you pick turn out to be so *dark*."

More accurately, I find the films harrowing, some of them gruesome, and overall, just depressing. But I don't want to hurt her feelings.

"*Yeah...* well..."

"I like them though!" I lie, like I haven't been traumatized watching her recommendations on my own. "Let's watch it."

"Are you sure? It's pretty, like you said, *dark*. It's not gory or anything, but..."

"Is it darker than *The Human Centipede*?"

The whites of Cam's eyes grow around her irises, her brows shooting up.

"Oh my *god*!" she gasps, pure horror illuminating her face. "Did you *actually* watch that? I said that as a joke!"

After her initial shock, she dissolves into a ball of laughter, clutching her ribs. I feel betrayed.

"A *JOKE*?!?" I yell, the palm of my hand pressing to my sweating forehead. "I thought you were serious! I made myself watch, like, *half* of it the other night until I wondered why the *fuck* you would recommend it or even watch it in the first place!"

Cam's able to manage a few words between her giggles. "I-I thought you would know that was a joke. Who the hell watches *The Human Centipede* on purpose?"

"Well, apparently *I* do!"

My arms cross over my body, and I shoot her a traumatized glower.

"I'll tell you what," she says. "Because of that, we can watch a happy movie. Sound like a deal?"

Cam still has tears in her eyes from the laughter. They make her brown irises swirl like melting caramel and chocolate. I want to drown in them.

"Deal."

I am a sucker for unrealistic love stories, and a slut for cheesy happily-ever-afters. But with Cam's grim taste in media, I don't even want to suggest *Ten Things I Hate About You*, my favorite, or *Never Been Kissed*, ranking number two. I skim through the titles on the TV, looking for something different. Something funny and cheesy, but also cinematic and classic. Something that *isn't* Hallmark or in the Chick-Flick section on Netflix. I'm not ashamed of my preferences. I just want to find something Cam will enjoy too.

I see just the thing.

"In honor of Mr. Westley," I say, pretending the name doesn't tug at my heartstrings, "I choose *The Princess Bride*."

Cam smiles, pulling the blanket backwards so I can crawl underneath it with her. I slide between the sheets, her soft thighs rubbing against mine as I press play. I love the way her body feels against mine, maybe even more so like this than when we're having sex. She's warm and soft, and I could fall asleep with the weight of her body sinking into the mattress next to me.

"I would love to have a sword," she says, watching the fight play out between Inigo and Westley. I look at her with suspicion, sliding ever so slightly away from her in jest.

"*You* with a sword?" My eyes widen briefly. "No thanks."

Cam flips me off, then grabs my waist and pulls me back into her tightly.

A strange feeling settles in my stomach. Like nausea, but pleasant. Yet also not. It isn't twisting, and it isn't sinking. It's different, like a thousand feathers floating around inside, tickling the edges of my stomach, making my pulse quicken. I suck in a breath, forcing my muscles to relax into the touch.

Cam touches me all the time. I don't know why, but since that night in the shower, it feels different than before. I thought, at first, I was getting used to it. But the more I thought about it, the less sense that made. If I was getting used to it, wouldn't it have been the opposite? I would have felt this in the beginning, and it would slowly fade. But this feeling wasn't there in the beginning. It's new. It's feeling more and more unfamiliar each time her fingertips rest against my skin. It's a distinction I can't pinpoint, but never want to lose.

We both quote lines throughout the rest of the movie, and when Westley screams in pain, Cam grips my leg like she's anticipating whatever happens next, even though she already knows.

"I know Westley should've let Buttercup know he was alive sooner, but you can't deny the man has game," she says when the movie ends. "If I had that type of game, I'd be *unstoppable*."

I want to tell her she does have game, and I know because it worked on me. But I fight the urge.

"Yeah, you're kind of a quirky one, aren't you?" I tease. Cam gives me a falsely offended look.

"Fuck you." She laughs, shoving me.

I check the time on my phone. Usually, Cam is gone by now. That's how the schedule had been planned, at least. But we don't stick to that anymore. Cam decided we should do things based on how we feel and what we want, so long as it doesn't interfere with Criminal Dinner. And right now, I'm not ready for her to go.

I look up from the screen, thinking of an excuse, any excuse for her to stay.

"Do you like ice cream?" I ask. Cam looks at me, unimpressed.

"What the fuck kind of question is that?" she answers. I roll my eyes, and we walk down the street to Mountain Scoops Creamery.*

Beebo's mom owns the ice cream shop, and I have to say, she completely outdid herself. It's kind of retro, almost like a '50s diner, with a touch of Pacific Northwest in the mix.

The floor is tiled in a black-and-white checkered pattern, red vinyl booths lining the sides of the interior. Desaturated photos of nearby mountains and lakes are mounted on the teal walls, the names of the locations scrawled in pencil on the bottom. About a dozen flavors of ice cream sit in the freezer behind the counter, different colors and names popping out at me all at once.

"I don't know what to get," I whine, overwhelmed by all the different choices. The girl behind the counter smiles, holding tiny plastic spoons.

"You can try any flavor you'd like!" she says.

I smile and turn to Cam. "Which ones do you want to try?"

Cam shakes her head. "I don't need to try anything, I already know what I'm getting." She points to the Seattle Strawberry Swirl. "*That one.*"

I laugh. "Don't you want to try the others just in case?"

But Cam's definitive answer doesn't shock me. She doesn't like trying new things, I've noticed. Maybe during sex, but even then, sometimes she can panic. I bought a different brand of shampoo for the salon because the kind she likes was out of stock, and she let me hear about the "terrible consistency" and "revolting scent" for two weeks.

"Nope."

It took me seven samples, but I finally decided on Cascade Crunch, an espresso-based ice cream with granola chunks.

We walk back home, the blanket from the couch wrapped around us, keeping us warm. Keeping *me* warm, at least, because Cam is still shivering.

"Too cold for the Ice Princess?" I joke, pushing my front door open. A wave of heat hits us, melting all the flakes stuck to our hair and lashes almost instantly.

"Is it Princess or Sparky?" she asks, cocking an eyebrow. "I never know with you."

[21]I set my empty ice cream up on the counter and turn to face her. I love when she's cocky like this, because it gives me an excuse to boss her around. And nothing compares to those flushed cheeks and desperate, dilated pupils she gets when I'm telling her what to do.

"That depends on how good you are."

I'm about to grab her and throw her over my shoulder, but before I can, she sinks to her knees, licking the crumbs of waffle cone off her thumbs.

"You want me to be good?" she asks, batting her eyes up at me innocently. Her fingers dance over the band of my sweatpants, a single finger tucking in between the cold skin and the elastic.

Oh fuck.

I nod.

"Yes," I say, my teeth sinking into my bottom lip. Maybe I won't need to boss her around after all. A devious smile spreads across her face, and she tucks a second finger in my waistband, on the other side.

"Okay, *boss*," she says, her voice low and her eyes shining. "I'll be a good girl for you."

Cam pulls my sweatpants down slowly, following the trail with the tip of her tongue down the center of my leg until she reaches my ankle. She looks back up at me for approval, and my hands find the top of her head, running through her hair.

"Such a good fucking girl."

She stands slowly, still making eye contact with me. Then, she reaches for the hem of my sweatshirt, before pulling it over my head and taking my shirt with her. Her fingers, still cold from the ice cream and the outside air, trace my nipples, enticing a moan out of me.

"Fuck, baby," I groan quietly. Cam tilts her head to the side with a smile.

"Am I making you wet, boss?" she asks.

I nod. "So fucking wet."

Cam takes two fingers and curls them as she swipes between my slick center. Her eyes lock onto mine as she sucks them into her mouth, letting out a moan.

"You really are wet, aren't you?"

I swallow, nodding. God, I've never needed someone so badly in my life. But a smile creeps across Cam's face, and she lets out a loud giggle as she steps back, crossing her arms over her still-clothed body.

"That's too bad," she says, that taunting smirk on her face.

This fucking woman. I furrow my brows, stepping toward her.

"Cam," I say, firmly but pleadingly. "Come here."

Cam giggles, shaking her head. "Nope."

My jaw clenches tight as I swallow, my clit now pulsing with a needy ache.

"*Cameron*," I say again. "Don't underestimate me."

Cam bites her lower lip, eyeing me up and down. Then, she offers me a completely innocent shrug.

"Okay," I huff. "That's fine."

I march toward my bedroom door, Cam staring at my ass as I approach it. Her lips tug downward as she tilts her head.

"What are you doing?"

Now it's my turn to offer a completely "innocent" shrug.

"You changed your mind," I say. "But *I* didn't."

I step into my bedroom and close the door behind me, not locking it. Cam stands outside of the room, tapping on the door.

"Violet!" she calls out. "What does that mean?"

I slide into bed, reaching for the purple vibrator in my bedside table. My legs prop up, my back arching as the toy rubs against my clit, and I don't even try to hold back a moan.

"Violet!"

I rub it softly around my wet pussy. It isn't Cam, but it'll do.

"Violet, I'm coming in, and you better not—"

The door bursts open, Cam's eyes widening as her jaw goes slack. She stares at me, my legs spread wide, the purple vibrator gliding around my pussy with purpose. She frowns.

"That's not fair!"

She scrambles into the bed next to me, reaching for it.

"You can't just do that without me. You can't—" I pull my hand away, locking my eyes onto hers as I keep touching myself. She huffs.

"Okay, fine! I was fucking with you. But I changed my mind. Please—" She looks down between my dripping thighs, then back up at me desperately. "Please, let me do it?"

A smile tugs at the corner of my lips, but I fight it down.

"You want to touch me?" I ask. "Make me come?"

Cam nods, then tugs her shirt over her head, her pink nipples hardening from the cold air. I look back into her eyes. "Then you should have thought about that before trying to tease me."

I push the vibrator inside of me, my back arching as I let out a loud moan. Cam's eyes pool with needy panic. She chews on her bottom lip as she watches the toy glide in and out of me, her fingers curling into a tight fist. Her chest begins to heave, and I smile as my head rolls back into the bedframe.

"*Oh Cam...*" I groan, shooting her an evil smile. Cam squirms on her knees next to me, her throat bobbing as she swallows. She lets out a groan.

"Violet." Her hand grabs my wrist gently, and my eyes flick up to hers. Her hair is a tangled mess, her cheeks flushed, her brows pressed together, pleading.

"God, you are such a desperate fucking mess, aren't you?" I mutter.

She nods. I look next to me at the fluffy white pillow near my head.

"How desperate are you, princess?"

She squirms. "So desperate."

I chuckle, pulling out the pillow, and setting it between us. Cam looks at me confused.

"Ride it," I say firmly.

Cam's jaw drops open.

"Violet, I said I was sorry. Please—"

I shake my head.

"If you want to watch me come, you have to give me a show."

Cam swallows, reluctantly sliding the pillow between her legs.

"Good girl," I mumble, watching as her eyes light up just a little. "But you need to take off the rest first."

Cam slides her sweatpants and underwear off slowly, the already soaked panties leaving a wet trail down her thighs. Then, she folds the pillow before placing it back between them. I click the vibrator, intensifying the speed as I rub it around my swollen clit, my eyes locked onto Cam. She sucks her lower lip between her teeth, watching me, then slowly begins to roll her hips. I nod.

"Just like that," I rasp, watching her through my lashes. Cam's fingers sink into the pillow, her perfect pussy gliding across it needily. "Does that feel good, baby?"

She nods.

"But you wish it was me?"

She nods again.

"Now you know what happens when you test me like that, don't you?"

She bucks her hips, letting out a moan while her head tips back. Those pretty pink nipples are on display, and no matter how badly I want to suck them into my mouth, I want Cam to learn her lesson much more. I press the vibrator against my entrance, letting out a low moan as it sits there, hardly an inch inside. My gaze flicks to Cam, her chest heaving as she watches me with wide eyes. I cock an eyebrow at her, before sliding it all the way in.

"God, Cameron. Do you see what you make me do?" I groan, the vibration inside me traveling through my skin to my clit. My stomach tightens. "You could have been the one licking this pussy, or even better—"

I begin to thrust it in and out of me slowly, and Cam moans again.

"Fuck," she whimpers, humping the pillow faster.

"—I could have had my fingers inside of that perfect little pussy of yours."

"Fuck, Violet," she moans, speeding up. A crease forms on her brow, sweat slowly beading at the crown of her head as her lip shakes. I watch her intently, a wet streak forming along the mound of the pillow as Cam fucks it desperately. I pull the vibrator out of me and run it along my clit.

"Look at the wall," I command. Cam's chin tilts up, looking directly into the full-length mirror mounted next to my closet door. She whimpers. "Do you see what a mess you are, fucking that pillow like that?"

She nods, a tiny moan leaving her mouth that I don't think she meant to let escape. A heavy sigh slips through my lips, my stomach tightening as the pressure inside me builds.

"I'm getting close," I warn. Cam thrusts against the pillow harder, lustful tears filling her eyes. "Are you going to do it, or do I have to do it myself?"

Her eyes widen, but she doesn't stop riding the wet white pillow.

"Can I?" she asks with a pleading gaze. My hand slides over to her, the vibrator gripped in my palm rubbing roughly against her swollen clit. She gasps.

"Come here."

She obeys, sliding her body between my legs before lowering her face. I shake my head.

"Turn around. I want to see that perfect ass of yours."

Cam hesitates, but turns around slowly, her supple round ass on display just for me.

Fuck, she's perfect.

I buck my hips, dragging my swollen clit along it just once. Then, I grip her waist and pull her on top of me, so her pussy is lined up with my mouth.

"God, baby. The pillow was that good?" I ask, sliding a finger up her center. My finger returns, slick and shiny from her mess.

Cam whines.

"You have to earn this one," I say.

She doesn't hesitate any longer. Her mouth presses against my aching clit, her tongue dancing circles around it. My body jolts from the contact, my back arching as I let out a moan. She scoots back, pushing that perfect pink pussy into my mouth. My arms wrap around her thighs, pulling her in tight while I press my own tongue into her.

"Oh fuck," she whimpers, and I take it as my cue to keep going. Cam takes me apart quickly, her fingers moving fast but her tongue moving faster. My fingers dig into her soft luscious thighs as she rocks her heat into me, my tongue pushing in and out of her firmly. My thumb dances over her clit in tight wet circles.

"Shit," I mumble, bucking my hips. The pressure inside of me builds, Cam's thighs shaking within my grasp. God, she feels heavenly.

"Violet, I have to—"

"I know, baby. Me too."

She lets out a high-pitched moan, when my thumb hits her clit for one last time. Her hips rock, my tongue curling inside of her, and my own hips thrust into her. Moans force their way out of me, some of her name, some of curse words, some of nothing but pure bliss and pleasure. My body tenses against the friction, and just as I'm about to unravel, my mouth fills with sweet, warm liquid, and Cam lets out a moan that is closer to a squeal.

Holy fuck.

She collapses onto me, my own orgasm forcing its way out just from the sheer arousal of Cam coming inside of my mouth. I swallow, letting my tongue travel along my lower lip and she rolls onto the bed on her back.

Her cheeks are dark red, and her hands are covering her face, embarrassed. I sit up, wiping the sides of my mouth with a smile.

"Fuck, Cam," I groan. "Has that ever happened before?"

She shakes her head, still hiding her face. I grab her wrist, pulling her hand down to look at her earnestly.

"Cam, you are fucking perfect."*

"WILL HE EVER STOP growing?" I lean against the paint-chipped barn door, muddy snow caked on my brand-new boots. Major's sprawled out on his back in front of Hayden and I, wriggling in the cold sludge. Our regular meetup was moved to Ayers' Acres, the farm Hayden's parents own because, and I quote, "farming never stops and the cows don't give a flying fuck how cold it is."

"I think he might have been mixed with giraffe," Hayden answers with a gleaming grin. He shovels a mound of dirty snow-covered hay onto the pitchfork gripped in his hands and tosses it into the pile beside me. "How's Reese doing?"

My stomach tenses for a second, flashbacks from that night racing through my mind. Reese is totally fine. He's great, actually, almost healed entirely. I, on the other hand, can't bear the thought of him ever interacting with another dog again. Sure, he sees Dawson pretty often, but like his mother, Dawson's predictable. I don't have to worry about what damage he might cause.

"He's good. He got his stitches out on Friday."

"That's great!" Hayden smiles, leaning the pitchfork against the barn. "I'm sure it's a bit easier, seeing as Cam went through the same thing."

"What?" My head snaps up, a valley forming between my knitted brows. Hayden furrows his own brows, his eyes pooling with bewilderment.

"Yeah. Cody's dog went after Dawson once. It wasn't as bad as Reese's attack, though. All his injuries were superficial. She didn't tell you?"

I shake my head, still stunned. Why wouldn't Cam tell me this? Why is she *always* protecting Cody?

"Well," I say, buying time to make up an excuse that sounds valid but feels inaccurate. "It was kind of an unforeseen circumstance, so maybe she forgot."

Hayden shoots me an unconvinced glance, a hint of amusement tugging at his lips.

"What?" I frown. He shakes his head.

"Well, you know Cam," he says, crossing his arms. "She doesn't 'forget' anything."

I look down, gently kicking at the snow underneath me. "*Yeah*, but I don't *know her*, know her. Not like you. It's all contract for us. With you, it was natural."

A short, loud laugh bursts out of Hayden, and he immediately slaps a hand over his mouth.

"Sorry," he murmurs, shaking with mirth. I roll my eyes.

"Now what, cowboy?" I ask, trying my hardest to shoot him a Cam-like scowl. He shakes his head.

"Nothing."

I glower, my newfound power thanks to the Ice Princess herself. Hayden breaks.

"Well firstly," he says, adjusting the cowboy hat on his head, which is pointless given the twenty-three-degree overcast weather. "Nobody knows Cam like I do. Secondly, that contract bullshit might work on Cam, but it doesn't on me."

My stomach twists, the pure coldness of the air around me suddenly flooding my body.

22"What do you mean?"

Hayden cocks a brow, until he realizes I'm genuinely serious. I have no idea what he's talking about.

"Violet," he says, patting my shoulder almost condescendingly, "You do realize that you and Cam are essentially dating, right?"

My stomach flips, an unbridled laugh slipping through my lips.

"What? No we aren't. That's like—"

Hayden promptly puts his hand up.

"Sorry," he says, lifting up the brim of his hat so he can look me in the eye. "But whatever you're about to say is bullshit. You spend seventy percent of your time together, and when you're apart, you talk about each other non-stop. You can say it's 'just sex' all you want, but people who are just hooking up for fun don't memorize each other's favorite colors or show up on each other's doorsteps in the middle of crises."

I open my mouth to speak, but he just continues.

"You're like, totally in love with Cam."

Heat rushes to my cheeks, stinging against the cold sensation of the crisp winter air. I scoff, shaking my head.

"I'm *not* in love with Cam," I say defensively, crossing my arms over my chest like that will make it true. It's not like I haven't thought about it. I like being around Cam, even though she makes me want to pull my hair out sometimes. I like the way she laughs and how candid she always is. How that dimple stays hidden until I've truly earned it, and how, sometimes, it's as if she can read my mind. Whether or not that has anything to do with "love" doesn't matter, because all of it violates one of the only rules left in that stupid contract.

Hayden doesn't pay my declaration any attention.

"And I think," he continues, staring out into the vast fields in front of us. "I think she likes you too."

"What?!" I don't mean to shout, it just kind of forces its way out of me. Hayden is completely delusional if he thinks Cam has any sort of feelings for me past lustful annoyance, which is a lot better than where we were in the beginning. It would be out of character for him to be playing some strange joke on me to get me to admit to my feelings for her, but that's the only reason I can think of that he'd say something so preposterous. "Do you even *hear* yourself?"

His shimmering blue eyes meet mine, not even the slightest hint of deception mixed in his expression.

"Do *you*?" he shoots back with a soft smile. I scoff loudly.

"Did she say that? That she has feelings for me?"

I analyze Hayden's expression, waiting for defeat to take over, but it never does. In fact, he only grows more assertive.

"She doesn't have to," he says confidently. "I just know."

"You just... *know*?" I ask, unconvinced. Hayden looks back to fields in front of us, the rolling hills shaded by the thick clouds above. A steady stream of air hisses through his lips, like a long, controlled sigh. He stares out for a minute, his throat bobbing as he swallows. I can see his cheeks sucking in as he chews on them, and my stomach twists in discomfort.

"I'm going to say something," he says finally. His voice is quiet but strong, and he keeps looking into the distance. "And you're not going to freak out."

I furrow my brows, but he doesn't glance in my direction. Hayden's been there for me through my divorce, through the contract, all of it. The least I can do is give him this.

"Okay," I say. "I won't."

I look up at him, his body towering over me, his aura sinking beneath the earth. He sighs.

"Violet, I've loved Cam for like, *forever*. I know her. So when I say she has feelings for you, I mean it. She didn't say anything to me, and she won't. Not for a while, but it's obvious. And I know you don't want me to, but I know you too." He pauses, then glances at me, shooting me a convincing, genuine smile. "And you two? Well, you might as well get down on one knee right now."

My heart pounds rapidly against the inside of my chest, my stomach tightening and sinking in one swift motion.

"She doesn't know it yet, how she feels," he says, trying to steer away from the giant-ass elephant he just put in the space between us. "But I think you do."

I shake my head, unsatisfied. If I've been standing in the way of these two this entire time, I'm going to be sick.

"Hayden, I didn't know you two—"

"We're not," he interjects, his chin jolting up quickly. "We never were. I asked her out once, but Cam has never felt that way about me. And that's okay. It isn't a thing. But *you*?" A soft laugh slips through his lips, his perfect white smile glimmering. "She's head over heels for you. She just hasn't figured it out."

My stomach crawls into my throat.

"Have you..." I swallow, a dry lump forming. "I mean... does she *know*?"

Hayden shakes his head.

"No," he says plainly. Not sadly, not painfully. Just a regular old "no."

"Then how do you know?" I ask, knowing that I'm more so asking this question for myself than for him. "I mean, if you haven't told her then—"

"Violet," he says, grabbing my hand. His eyes lock onto mine, and I have never seen Hayden more serious in my life. "I *know*. Trust me, okay?"

I nod, recognizing the desperation in his plea. I see it now, all of it. The way he talks about her, how he glowed at the bowling alley when their fingers were intertwined. I don't know how something so obvious could also be so hidden.

"I just know too then," I say with completely fake confidence. Hayden cocks a brow.

"You just know what?"

"That Cam doesn't feel that way about me either."

Hayden chuckles, shaking his head. "False."

A frown creeps over my face. "*True.*"

He grabs my hand again and squeezes it, a gesture that gives me no choice but to look into his eyes.

"Violet, crystals," he says flatly. A crease forms on my brow as I stare at him.

"Well, *yeah*. So?"

"You believe in divine intervention, and that everything happens for a reason."

I cross my arms, tapping my finger on my bicep, feeling slightly attacked by this whole interaction.

"And?"

He sighs, louder than he needs to for dramatic effect. As if, like his feelings, the answer is hidden in plain sight.

"You believe in *everything* except your ability to be loved."

My stomach sinks, a dry lump forming in my throat. The inside of my cheek grows raw as I chew it furiously, my nose tingling, but I don't think it's from the cold air. His large hand presses against my shoulder, squeezing softly.

"She doesn't love me, not like that," he says. "But you, she's fond of."

The tingling sensation begins to spread over my cheeks now, a glossy coat forming over my eyes. I stare briefly, forcing them to dry before clearing my throat.

"Hayden, I *had no idea* you felt that way about her," I say, pinching the corners of my eyes. "I feel like such an asshole."

I really, *really* don't feel good. Hayden squeezes my shoulder again, and I glance up at him, a wide smile sewn into his face.

"I knew it!" he sings happily. My brows weave together in confusion.

"What?"

"I knew you loved her!" he says excitedly. "Otherwise, you wouldn't feel like an asshole."

"I don't—"

Hayden clicks his tongue, shaking his head.

"Uh-uh. I did *not* confess my love for her to you just to have you deny your feelings. I want to know *everything*."

I shake my head.

"If you're *so* in love with her, why would you want to hear me talk about it?" I ask. Maybe Hayden doesn't actually know what he's asking for.

"Violet," he says, leaning in closely. His eyes are meaningful, locked onto mine like we're both holding the same secret. "You think *that* is the hardest pill I've had to swallow?" He chuckles, a soft parenthesis forming on the sides of his lips. "My heart is *physically* broken. I was born into the wrong body and lived in it for *years*. So, seeing my best friend receive the love she deserves wouldn't exactly be a hardship for me."

Heat fills my cheeks every time he says the word "love," and I want to correct him, to say that I don't *love* Cam, I only just learned I liked her. But Hayden isn't finished, and I can tell by the look in his eye that he needs me to hear this.

"The only hardship comes when you decide not to love her anymore. When her anxiety becomes a chore, and her depression consumes her, and she refuses to breathe fucking *air* if it isn't purified first. And if that happens, if you go through with it and then later decide she is too much for you, I'll be there to pick up every single piece. I will help put her back together, knowing she'll find someone new. But please, Violet, I'm begging you." His eyes lock onto mine. "*Please* don't make me."

Hayden's eyes glow under the dull barn lights, a glossy coat formed over them from unfallen tears. My head tilts, leaning against his bicep, and I squeeze his hand just as he had squeezed mine.

"I won't, Hayden," I say softly, feeling every word of it in my chest. "I promise."*

TWENTY-NINE

Just Breathe

CAM

I NEVER LIKED THE snow, even before it killed my dad.[23] It soaks through your clothes, it takes hours to shovel, and besides, I don't like to be cold. I can't deny, though, how versatile it is.

In the same minutes, the same seconds the avalanche buried my dad's car on the bypass, I had been in the front yard, building an igloo for the both of us. Unlike me, he loved the snow. He always said it reminded him of my mom, who he met while skiing. I wanted to surprise him. But when the police rolled up to tell me what had happened, the snow packed into my gloves turned red. The blood was on my hands. At least it felt that way. Here I was, playing in the thing that had just killed the person I loved most.

There hadn't even been an avalanche warning. Nobody could have known, even the people who were supposed to predict those kinds of things. Still, I had been the one to suggest he take the scenic route on his way home instead of the city. I told him to admire the mountains, soak in the snowfall. Really, I was just trying to buy more time to finish the igloo. It was taking a lot longer than I thought it would, and I needed a little bit more time.

But I got more time than I ever wanted. More than I ever asked for.

I never liked the snow, but now, I hate it.*

I peek through the salon window, the one pointing to the parking lot. Giant flakes drift down, covering everything in a thick coat of white. It blankets the branches of the pine trees, like a perfect winter painting. I shake my head.

"I hope you have a jacket," I say to the shaved Bichon on the table. His tongue hangs out the side of his mouth in a steady pant. "'Because you are going to be *cold.*"

The silver comb glides through his tail, which is the only part of his coat I managed to save during the dematting process. I tug softly, releasing the tangled hair to create a smooth tuft. The dog turns, licking me gently, and I smile.

"Alright, let's get you home."

I scoop him into my arms and carefully carry him to an empty suite before placing him inside. But just as I reach into my pocket, darkness washes over me.

I blink, thinking at first that maybe, somehow, I accidentally closed my eyes. But when they open again, I'm still staring into a dark, endless abyss. Quiet falls over the facility, the playful barking of the dogs in daycare ceasing abruptly.

"Woah." I hear a low voice say from one of the pens. It sounds like Avery. I reach for my phone in my pocket, so I can turn on the flashlight, but a sudden loud beep emitting from it causes me to jump backward. I clutch my chest as I pull it out of my pocket.

> **Weather Alert: Greenrock Valley, WA   Civil Authorities Issued an Avalanche Warning Until 21:00**

My phone slides out of my hand and crashes onto the floor. A pit forms in my stomach, sinking lower and lower, and I kneel on the ground, scrambling around to find it. When I feel the familiar, rectangular shape in my hand, my grip tightens.

"Fuck," I whisper, to nobody but myself. I try to take a deep breath, but it's ragged and weak. "It's okay. You're okay."

My heart thrums against the inside of my ribcage, a tight pinching sensation filling my chest. I take a staggered breath.

"You're okay," I repeat again. I feel like one of the dogs on my own table, trying to soothe myself with words I don't know I truly believe.

Furry Friends Pet Resort is miles from the mountains. I know that being completely drowned in snow is out of the Realm of Likely Possibilities. But that doesn't stop me from panicking. Not now.

My feet move fast, and I don't know where they're taking me, but I'm in no position to fight back. My rubber boots thud against the floor, my chest rising and falling rapidly with each step. When the supply closet door slams behind me, I let my back lean against the wall and slide down to the floor as I bury my head in my knees.

The quick thrum of my heart vibrates in my ears as I close my eyes, trying to focus on slowing it down. But it doesn't. My hands shake as they squeeze my knees to my chest, my heartbeat growing louder, the sound pounding against the inside of my skull. Staggered breaths slide through my lips, small whistles coming from the back of my throat as I fight to breathe.

It's all my fault.

It's all my fault.

My back hits the wall as my body begins to rock, the pressure against my chest growing as I squeeze my knees tighter. I shake my head at the words repeating in my own brain. It isn't true. It isn't.

But it is.

It's all my fault.

Tears pool in my closed eyes, trickling down my cheeks in a rapid river. My lungs expand, grasping at air I don't know exists in this moment. The muscles in my throat constrict, and I choke, coughing loudly, as my entire body continues to shake.

I need Adrian. I need Hayden. Or maybe...

"Cam?" a voice calls out, piercing the noise in my mind. It's brief though, and the air around me still seems to dissipate as I try to take a breath.

It's all my fault.

"Cam, where are you?" it repeats. I know it's Violet. The familiar rasp, the strained worry.

"Check the closet," another, more grizzly voice says. I recognize this one too. It's Avery. "Violet, we *have* to find her."

My nails dig into my curled biceps, and if I were more aware of myself right now, I'm sure it would hurt. But I can barely hear the voices right outside the door. They sound a lifetime away. So the nerves in my body, the ones that are shaking? The ones that should feel a sharp, stinging sensation? They're numb.

A beam of white light flashes across my closed eyes, and I squeeze them shut tighter, continuing to rock.

It's all my fault.

It's all my fault.

Rough fingertips glide across my forearms, a warm body positioning itself behind me. A pair of arms wrap tightly around my own, compressing my chest harder. Tears pool in the corners of my lips, the salt hitting my tongue as my mouth opens to let out a choked sob.

Voices surround me, I'm sure of it. I just can't decipher what they're saying. A soft sound rings through the air, like a zipper sliding against metal teeth. Then, the sound of a shaking pill bottle. The rhythm in my chest is starting to steady from the pressure of the arms wrapped around me, but the sharp pain in my lungs persists.

It's all my fault.

"Here," Avery says, his voice low. I feel something hard and small pressed against my lips, but I still don't open my eyes. I part them, letting two pills slide inside. Then, the spout of a water bottle follows, wedging itself between my teeth.

"Take a sip."

I suck in, my chest shaking as the water fills my mouth, then slides down my throat as I swallow, the pills drifting with it.

It's all my fault.

"Take a breath with me," Violet says. "Like this."

I hear her unwavering breath as she inhales methodically.

"In. Hold. Out."

She breathes again, following her own instruction. Violet's breath sounds like the ocean, steady waves crashing on the shore to a predictable flow. I try to follow, but the air shatters inside of me.

It's all my fault.

"What's she saying?" Violet asks. I hadn't realized the words were coming out of my mouth. My eyes squeeze tighter, light specks floating around in the darkness of my eyelids.

"It's all her fault," Avery answers softly.

Yes. It's all my fault.

A heavy hand brushes the hair out of my face, one arm still pressed against my chest. I don't know for sure, but I think I can feel a head shake.

"It's not," Avery whispers, and I realize now I can feel his breath against the back of my neck. "It's not your fault."

My head shakes involuntarily, the words spinning around in my brain, yearning to rest. My cheeks are cold from the wet streaks sliding down them, and I suck in a trembling breath.

It is.

It's not.

It is.

It's not.

"It's not," Violet repeats, and a flash of light washes over me, the back of my eyelids growing red.

The lights must have kicked back on.

My eyes flutter open, but all I see is a blur. I blink, tears streaming down my face, as I take staggered breaths and sip the water. Everything around me is moving slowly and quickly all at once. Violet is kneeled in front of me, her movements lagging, but the room around her spins like a time-lapse.

Another shaky breath slides into my lungs, the pressure on my chest slowly easing as Avery's arms relax. I try to breathe through my nose, but it's stuck. I part my lips again.

"Good," Violet says, nodding. "In. Hold. Out. Keep breathing."

I blink, the tears in my eyes drying up.

"Adrian's on their way," Avery says, his voice still behind me.

I sniffle, nodding my head as I take another slow breath.

In.

Hold.

Out.

"A—"

"And Hayden." He nods.

I swallow, a strong, stinging sensation tunneling through my arms, and I realize I still haven't let go. My fingers relax, the skin beneath them raw and bruised. I look up at Violet, her eyes wide. Her gaze shifts to Avery, and I feel his head shake against my body.

"They'll go away," he says, pulling himself to his feet. He reaches a hand down to me, his fingers curling around my wrist as he helps me stand. My legs wobble underneath my weight, and I steady myself against the wall. "They always go away."

Violet nods, and Avery looks down at me, his brows furrowing slightly before looking back to Violet.

"You got this? I have to get back to the pack."

Violet nods, and my lips tremble as I stare at the wall.

Avery shoots me one last pitying expression before walking out of the storage closet. The door swings closed behind him. Immediately, Violet's arms engulf me, the familiar form of her body pressing against mine. I grow weak in her arms, my knees buckling, but her grip keeps me grounded. We stand there for a moment, just melting silently together. Then, she pulls away. She brushes off the strands of hair sticking to my wet cheeks, and her hands cup my jaw gently.

"Are you okay?" she asks, her eyes moving to find mine.

I sniffle, nodding, but I don't try to speak. I know I won't be able to. The pads of Violet's thumbs trace underneath my eyes, just like she had done at Monsey's. But it isn't like that at all, actually. It feels different. And I realize that this, I think, *her*, is what I need right now.

She pulls me back into her body, her nose nestled into the crook of my neck.

"You're safe," she whispers, her breath dancing across my skin. "And it is *not* your fault."

THIRTY

Yellow Jasper

VIOLET

IF YOU ASKED ME a month ago if I had ever felt like I couldn't breathe, I would have asked you how that could be. How your lungs could be so obviously filled with air, though your body screamed they were vacant. I would say it's impossible. [24]

But the night Reese was attacked, just before my body stopped feeling, for a second, I felt it. For a blip in time, my lungs constricted, and my throat tightened, and I couldn't breathe. That night, I realized how fucking terrible it must be to live with anxiety.

Cam is stronger than me, though I don't think she knows it. Something about that, about letting your body feel, no matter how badly it hurts, is admirable. It isn't an easy thing to say after watching her completely crumble into Avery's arms. I hated every moment of it, every second of her gasping for air, trembling and teary. And still, strangely, I was envious that she was strong enough to let it happen.*

"Have you met Wilson yet?"

My head snaps to Avery, who's lifting a Tibetan Mastiff's front legs off the ground from behind, hugging him like a teddy bear. He looks like an *actual* bear. Even compared to Avery, he's massive, his fur thick and his jowls loose. I can't fight the urge to smile at him.

"I have *not!*" I say excitedly, letting memories from days prior wash out as I walk over to introduce myself. I let Wilson sniff me, but he's more interested in getting attention from Avery.

"Yesterday was his first day," he explains. "He's *perfect.*"

In the pet care industry, the word "perfect" means one of two things: said dog either does nothing all day or is a complete terror but is so cute you can't be mad. My guess is the former, but sometimes, dogs surprise you.

"Well, hi Wilson!" I say, attempting to run my hands through his thick coat. Wilson stays stagnant, his body half-melted into Avery's arms. Avery looks down at him, a loving smile spreading across his stubbled cheeks.

Though I try hard to know my coworkers well, Avery, for the most part, tends to keep to himself. He'll make casual conversation at times, but never about anything outside of work. Everything I know about Avery, I know because of Adrian. Everything, except the long-standing tension between him and Cam.

That, she told me about.

Frankly, I struggle to understand what exactly their issues with one another are, given that they're almost the same person. Avery might just be a little less confrontational.

It surprised me, on Monday, when he swooped in to help her without hesitation. But I wonder if that's how things work between them. The rules of the "Homemade Family," putting differences aside to be there when needed. I think that's how families are supposed to work, at least.

"I just want you to know," I say, smiling up at him, "that you stepping in to the assistant manager role has completely changed things for me. You're beyond helpful, so *thank you.*"

Avery blushes, and his gaze lowers.

"Thanks, boss," he says, his eyes avoiding me as they travel up the wall. "It's twelve."

My gaze flicks up to the mounted clock.

"Oh! Thanks!"

He nods with assurance, and I grab my water bottle off the shelf before leaving the play area.

"Are you ready to go on a walk?" I ask as I open the door to a suite. I'm still not comfortable putting Reese in daycare. I know what happened that night was a fluke, and I have full confidence in all of my employees to prevent it from happening here. But I can't stomach the risk of it. Reese wriggles his way through the opening, letting out an aggravated huff as he paws at the cone around his neck. I open the snaps, releasing him, and we begin to walk toward the lobby.

As we pass the salon, I peer through the window. Cam is bent over, attempting to lift a rather fat golden retriever onto the table. The golden sprawls his legs out uncomfortably, flattening himself like a pancake onto the floor.

That ass points in my direction, like it's calling my name. I know I shouldn't look, but I know how it feels in my hands, and that's something you just can't ignore.

But when Cam turns around, she's frowning. Her brows are dipped down, and she wipes a bead of sweat from her forehead. That isn't anything different from her normal resting face, but after Monday, I don't think I can ignore it. I look down at Reese, then back up at her. She looks stressed, and if she keeps trying to lift that dog the way she is, she's going to break her back. I push the door open, poking my head inside.

"Do you need help?" I ask. Cam looks up at me with an irritated expression.

"Do you think I'm incapable?" she huffs. Small rays form around her nose as she wrinkles it at me, and I can't think anything of her but the fact that she's adorable.

I put my hands up defensively. "Woah, Sparks. Just trying to make sure my one and only dog groomer doesn't snap her spine."

I step further into the room, not intimidated by her coarseness. All it does is remind me of the day we met.

"I was about to walk to Al's for lunch. Wanna come?"

I know inviting Cam to get lunch with me isn't exactly the smartest move. It's not like I'm always bringing other employees to Al's with me, and after that conversation with Hayden, I'm scared he might not be the only person who's noticed my feelings. But I can't see how someone could think anything more of it, when nobody knows anything at all.

Besides, she looks exhausted, and frustrated, and overwhelmed, and I'm not the type of person to just ignore it. I can't ignore it, no matter who it is. It is my Sunny-appointed duty to spread the cheer, and Al's is just the place.

Cam looks up at me skeptically. "Al's?"

An exaggerated, shocked expression spreads across my face, and I give her a dramatic gasp.

"Have you *never* been to Al's Taco Truck?" I ask. Cam shakes her head, and I cross my arms over my chest, leaning against the wall.

"If you want to taste heaven, you've gotta try it."

"I don't believe in heaven," she retorts.

"Oh, you *will*."

When we approach Al's truck, I immediately pull a gold, jagged stone out of my pocket.

"What's that?" Cam asks, her head tilted as she eyes the stone.

I knock on the truck's window to let Al know I'm here. "You'll see."

Al doesn't even look up when he slides the window open. He just continues preparing my lunch.

"How's it going, mija?" he asks, topping off my tostada with a generous layer of cheese. I flash Cam a grin, then set my palms against the windowsill and rest my chin on top.

"It's good," I say. Al finally looks up, his eyes growing wide when he sees Cam.

"Vi, you didn't tell me you were bringing company. I would've prepped it ahead of time!" he exclaims, like a mom who didn't vacuum before her teenager brought over a friend. I laugh.

"It's okay, I wanted her to see the menu. Al, Cam. Cam, Al." I introduce them quickly, then gesture to the menu painted on the side of his truck. "Get whatever you want. On me."

Cam stares at the menu, her eyes widened.

"What's it gonna be, kid?" Al chuckles.

I already know what Cam is going to order. She finds one thing she likes and sticks to it. Vodka Cranberries. Seattle Strawberry Swirl. Me.

We Postmated Tex-Mex after last week's rendezvous. I offered her a bite of my enchiladas, to which she promptly scrunched her nose, and turned back to her quesadilla.

"I only want this," she said, taking a large bite into her mouth. "I only *ever* get this."

Cam continues to stare at the menu, almost like she's frozen.

"She'll take a qu—" I start to say, but Cam cuts me off.

"Make me whatever your favorite is," she says to Al. "But *no tomatoes*."

My brows press together, and I look at her in shock. A huge smile spreads across Al's face, and he points at her with a sideways thumb.

"I like her," he says, picking up his metal spatula. I shrug, shooting her a teasing grin.

"Eh, she's alright."

I look at her, still shocked at the words that came out of her mouth. Cam isn't a "you choose" type of person. She isn't someone you guess for because she only likes certain things, and she only likes those certain things a certain way.

"Are you sure you don't just want a quesadilla?" I whisper. "It's not too late."

Cam looks at me, a hint of panic in her eyes, but I can tell she's trying to hide it.

"I trust you," she says softly. Warmth fills my stomach when those words leave her lips. It's just Mexican food; I know it isn't that deep. But it is with Cam, at least partially. She's so skeptical of everything. So unsure of new things, so stuck in her ways. I think about what Hayden said, how he knew she liked me too. In this moment, I'd almost believe him. A smile spreads over my face as I turn the stone over in my hand.

I lean forward, tapping the crystal on the windowsill to draw Al's attention to it. Al tilts his head, immediately accepting it from my hand.

"*This* one," he says, holding it up to the light. "This one looks *nice*."

I grin and look over at Cam, but she just looks confused. I don't want to explain the full story to her. Not in front of Al, at least. But her head drops to the side, and I know if I leave her in the dark for a second longer, she's going to force the entire story out of me right here right now.

"I bring Al crystals sometimes," I explain. "Trying to promote good energies."

She nods, approving of my short, vague explanation. "What's that one?" She points to the yellow stone.

"That's Yellow Jasper," I say, making sure to look at both her and Al. "For happiness."

A loud scoff exits her throat. "Seems on brand for you."

"Don't knock it till you try it, mija," Al says defensively, shooting her a disapproving look. "I thought it was bullshit too but..." He looks at me and smiles. "Violet has helped me in more ways than I can count."

The warmth in my chest grows with those words. Al has helped me more than he knows too.

"It's okay," I say nonchalantly. "She doesn't have to believe in it."

"I didn't say I don't believe in it," Cam shoots back. Her eyes lock onto mine.

"Okay," I respond, not breaking the contact.

She continues, "I just don't know enough about it."

I tilt my head and smile. "Let me teach you."

Al's eyes dart back and forth between us, a subtle smile peeking from beneath his mustache. His brow raises slightly, and our eye contact breaks when he speaks.

"Here," he says, handing me a white paper bag.

We sit on the bench next to his truck while we eat. Al made her his famous carne asada burrito with spicy verde salsa, and Cam's eyes practically roll back in her head when she takes her first bite. I don't like that I'm not the only reason her eyes roll back, but I'll accept it.

"Okay," she says, chewing. "I *might* believe in heaven."

"I told you."

A small drop of green salsa pools in the side of her mouth, and it takes everything in me not to wipe it away.

After we finish, we wave goodbye to Al. He stares at us closely as we walk away, his eyes narrow and his lips turned upwards.

As we walk, I explain the full story about the crystals. About Al's daughter, and Einstein, and energy. When I had brought it up to Mallory, she'd immediately shut me down.

"It's a rock, babe," she said, in a condescending tone. "You'd have better luck wishing on stars."

But Cam actually listens. She asks questions and pulls out her phone to look up sources for my answers. She thinks about every response I give her and lets it sink in until it makes sense. And if it doesn't, she just asks more questions. She still doesn't believe in it, at least that's what the slight raise of her brow tells me, but she doesn't make fun of it either.

[25]"Now you know something about me," I say. "It's my turn to know something about you."

Cam furrows her brows.

"Why?" she asks, all suspiciously.

I shoot her a look.

"Cam, I let you sit on my face. Don't you think I deserve to be able to ask a couple questions here or there?"

After Hayden pointed it out last week, I realized he was right. I actually do know a lot about Cam. I know about her parents and her disorder. I know she likes pickles but hates tomatoes. I know her favorite color is green, and her favorite show is Criminal Minds. I know what makes her tick and what makes her moan. But when it comes to Cam, I can never know too much. Every time a blank gets filled, a new one forms, begging for its turn. I would throw away every memory if it meant I could make room to know more about her.

"Fine. Ask away."

I had expected to fight harder than that, so whatever question I had lined up in my mind completely disappears. But almost instantaneously, a new one surfaces.

"So, tell me about The Dog Shop," I say more than ask.

Air hisses out of Cam's nose as she holds in a short laugh. "Really?" she asks. "Why do you want to know about that?"

I shrug.

"It's how you ended up here."

A reluctant sigh slips from her lips, and her eyes latch onto mine in an unamused stare. But after a moment, she gives in.

"The Dog Shop got me started. I know how to do what I do because of it. They hired me, trained me, and employed me for years," she says, almost void of emotion. I cock a brow.

"Why leave then?"

"It..." She trails off. "It was hard."

I look at her, waiting for her to continue, but she doesn't. I know she has to have more to say. Cameron Miller doesn't just give up if something is "hard." I know because I watch her do it all the time. So I just keep looking at her.

"What?" she asks, all defensive. I shrug.

"Just waiting for you to keep talking."

"What if I don't want to?"

I know she's just giving me a hard time. That's what Cam does.

"Then we can walk in silence, Princess," I say with a teasing smirk. "I know you have no issue with that."

Cam stares at me with annoyance, but when her gaze breaks, she continues.

"They would pile nine large dogs on your schedule, then get mad if you worked for more than eight hours a day. They'd make you brush mats out of a dog, even if it hurt them, just because the parents asked you to. I *hated* it. I hated it there. But I loved the job."

She pauses, looking at me, and I nod for her to keep going.

"I love helping dogs feel better, and I really love the creative side of it. At Furry Friends..." She lets out a deep sigh. "I feel like it holds every part of the job I love, and none of the parts I hated. I don't have the issues I had before. I'm excited to go to work every day. It feels like I'm just going somewhere I love. Like I'm going home to my apartment or to Adrian's."

When she stops talking, she looks at me, the apples of her cheeks growing rosy. I think she's embarrassed, but I'm just in awe. I haven't heard her say so many positive things in one sentence, or even one day. It makes me happy her experience at the resort is so amazing, even if mine is different.

"Sorry," she says.

I pull a beanie out of my pocket and tug it over my ears. "I like listening to you talk."

Cam looks away, the color in her cheeks growing darker.

"Well, what about you? Have you always managed... daycares?" she asks, unsure.

"No," I answer, a hint of disappointment in my tone. I don't know how deep I want to get into this. I don't really want to get into it at all. But I can't pry information out of her, then give her one-word answers. "I used to be a dog trainer, and that was fun. It was *amazing*, actually, that's why I work with Hayden. But I worked for somebody else's company and..."

"And?" she asks. I look at her, those brown eyes staring back up at me.

I give in. I always give in with Cam.

"It was just a lot. We had to do board-and-trains, from our own homes. And having eight dogs at your house *sounds* like the dream, but you can't do *anything*. I mean *really*. You can't *go* anywhere. I think the most I left my house was for like, three hours at a time. And that went on for years. They wouldn't let me do private training, only board-and-trains. It was awesome, and I loved it, but I couldn't have a life." I shake my head. "Not that I have much of one now, but at least I can leave the house."

Cam nods, mulling it over in her head for a minute. "Do you like it?" she finally asks. I look at her with confusion.

"What?"

"The resort," she explains. "Do you like it?"

Do I *like* it? I don't know how to answer that without crossing a line. A different line than the one I've already crossed. The "boss discloses information she shouldn't to an employee" line. But when I try to talk, to say that I *do* like it, I go silent instead.

"I knew it!" Cam says, pointing an accusing finger at me. I shake my head, letting out an uncomfortable laugh.

"I like it," I lie. "I miss training sometimes, but I get to do that with Hayden so—" I shrug. "I like it."

I'm pleased with my answer only for a moment, before I look up at Cam. She looks like she's going to *actually* kill me.

"Why do you do that?" she asks, her brows furrowing. My smile falters.

"What?"

"That *thing* you do. Where you plaster on that irritating smile and make your voice all tight and pretend things are better than they are?"

"*Irritating smile?*" I ask, offended. But Cam doesn't seem to care if she hurt my feelings or not.

"Yes," she says. "That *irritating* smile. You walk around with it all day like it's part of your fucking uniform."

"I do not!" I respond defensively. She raises her brows at me.

"You do. And you do it with your voice too. You don't let anyone *know* you. Or what you hate or what you're thinking. If you don't like your job, just say it."

The words strike a sharp feeling in my chest because Cam isn't wrong. I might be getting better with it, but I don't like to let people know me. Except, Cam didn't ask for my permission to know me. She just did it.

"I do like my job!"

Cam huffs loudly, turning away from me, and marching forward.

"Oh what, so you're not going to talk to me until I say what you want? Is that it?" I ask, following closely behind. She doesn't look at me. "Real mature, Cam. Real mature."

Cam continues staring ahead. God, she is so fucking stubborn sometimes. I know nothing I say is going to please her but the truth. She knows she can get me to do what she wants, and it's dangerous. Addictive.

But this isn't an addiction you can just quit. Even if I ended the contract, which I can't find in myself to even pretend I want, it wouldn't stop me from thinking about her all the time. I could never see Cam again in my life, and I would still find a piece of her in every day. No, this isn't an addiction you can quit cold turkey.

I don't think I can quit it at all.

I sigh loudly, matching my pace with her quick one.

"Fine. I hate my job, okay? I hate Angela, and I hate customer service, and I hate having to pretend that everything is fine and dandy, but that's what works for me. You've got your whole stone-cold 'I don't give a fuck' attitude, and I have my fake smile. Everyone has their thing. Okay?"

Cam freezes, and I hold my breath. Her body turns slowly, facing me, and I realize how closely I've been following her. I'm nervous, for some reason. Maybe I took it too far. Maybe I shouldn't have said all of that.

Actually, I know I shouldn't have. But I see a smile growing on her face, that heavenly dimple sinking into her cheek. How can someone who looks so wholesome be such a fucking terror? Her eyes travel up to meet mine, and she tilts her head ever so slightly.

"Okay."*

Thirty-One

Headache

Cam

Whenever possible, I like to save the best for last. Especially on days like this, when my brain just won't stop spinning. I always eat my dessert after dinner, my books are read in order from least intriguing to most, and I always like to choose the easiest dog to groom to end my day. After you've groomed six or seven dogs, you don't want to wrestle an aggressive Maltese or a 150-pound Pyrenees who hasn't had a bath in three years.

My schedule stated that Banksy was a dalmatian. Everything else had long hair or needed something trimmed. Reuben has a tendency to nip, and Jonah pees from excitement every time you touch him. Banksy, however, has no behavioral notes. He was written down as a simple bath with a nail trim. For a groomer, that's as easy as it gets. What I didn't know is that Martha failed to note that the five-year-old pup had not been groomed—*ever*. He had never experienced the rush of water over his body, nor the quick pressure of the nail clippers. I'm not even sure his feet have ever been touched before, given his snarling and flailing reaction.

I was shivering when I left the apartment this morning, snow piled high on the ground and cold gusts of wind hitting my face. Now, sweat drips down the sides of my forehead, my one hand gripping the nail clippers, the other, a spotted, kicking foot.

Normally, this wouldn't be a big deal. I could handle the tugging and the snapping, the spinning and alligator rolling. But my mind is racing, even more than usual, and I feel like I can't even talk to Dr. Burton about it.

I don't know how this happened, how I suddenly found myself so close to Violet. How that day I had an attack and asked for Adrian and Hayden, really all I wanted was her. No eighties song sounds quite as good when it isn't in her voice, and nobody else could make me open to the thought that crystals possess special powers.

It's kind of like when I met Adrian in first grade and begged my dad for a Belle dress with the emblem on the front because I thought they looked so cool in theirs. Or how Hayden showed me the best order to watch Star Wars in, and now, I won't do it any other way.

I'm scared, though, because this is how it all started with Cody. This is how I became so dependent on him, how I thought, for years, I couldn't exist without him. I know now it wasn't the truth. But this thing with Violet could end just as badly.

Not in a romantic way, of course. There's nothing romantic about a sex contract, that's the entire point. But even though I'd never say it to her face, Violet is one of my best friends. And friendships can be just as problematic.

I coax Banksy into the kennel. Two black hoses lead from a large machine on top to the barred doors where they blow a small steady stream of air to help the dog's coat dry. It's my favorite invention ever because it helps dry dogs who haven't been desensitized to the loud forceful air from the velocity dryer.

Banksy, however, isn't pleased at all. His head tilts back, and from the back of his throat, he lets out a loud, gravely bark.

"I know, buddy. I'm not stoked about it either," I say, starting to clean the room around me. My shears and clippers are piled and sanitized, then placed back into the toolbox. The sound of the vacuum cleaner drowns out the air from the kennel dryer, and I walk about the room sucking up balls of loose hair draped across the ceiling and floor, curled into the corners like dust bunnies.

After rinsing all the excess fur and soap out of the tub, I open the door to the kennel. Banksy, who had fallen asleep during my deep cleaning, shoots his head up and sprints out of the cage. A blur of black and white runs circles around the room, his long pink tongue flying out the side of his mouth. I laugh, pouncing down and slapping my palms against my thighs.

"Banksy! You got the zoomies, buddy?"

Banksy's eyes fixate on me, and mid-sprint, he changes direction. His spotted legs move quickly across the slick floor as he barrels toward me, tongue flying and tail wagging violently.

"Banksy! Banksy, buddy, slow do-"

Banksy pounces his front feet onto my thighs, his skull colliding with mine. My knees buckle underneath me, and I collapse onto the floor, clutching the right side of my head.

"Fuck!"

A throbbing pain radiates from my face, my right eye clamped shut. Banksy stops only for a moment to shove his nose into my ear, then continues running circles the room, which is now spinning. My stomach shakes, and if I weren't fighting it with everything I've got, I'd be hurling onto the wet floor right now.

I grasp the bars on the kennel behind me, and I pull myself to my feet, still gripping my head with my other hand.

"Shit! Are you okay?"

I shuffle my feet to turn, watching each step to prevent myself from falling again. My fingers are turning white from the intensity with which they hold onto the kennel. When I finally see Avery standing in the doorway, I open my mouth to say that I'm *fine-thank-you-very-much*, but instead, a piercing pain shoots through my eye socket.

"Agh!"

My other eye shuts, making the world go dark, and when I open it again, Avery is gripping my shoulders, examining my head carefully. I try to open my other eye, but it burns, water filling it the second the air brushes against it. I immediately place my hand back over it to apply pressure, which seems to be the only thing that helps the sharp, pulsing pain. A large hand grips my wrist, pulling my hand off my eye.

"Ow!" I yell, trying to jerk away. But Avery's grip is strong, and he tightens his fingers around my wrist.

"I need to look at it!" he responds firmly, tilting the angle of his head as he analyzes me. I huff, but don't protest.

This shit hurts.

Avery gently brushes his finger underneath my brow, but to me, he may as well have just punched me.

"Fuck, Avery!" I wince, sucking air between my teeth. Avery finally releases my wrist when his fingertips part from my eye. He doesn't apologize for inflicting more pain.

"I'm going to have to take you to Urgent Care," he says instead. I step back, my cheek lifted to my lashes. I try to shake my head, but the throbbing intensifies.

"N-no," I stutter. My stomach churns, but I fight it back down. "I don't want to go to Urgent Care. I'm fine."

"Your eye is purple, and you can barely stand up," he replies shortly. "Is the room spinning?"

"Yes."

"You feel like you're gonna p—" *Gulp.* "—puke?"

"...yes."

"You probably have a concussion. I got them in college all the time when I played lacrosse. You *need* to go to Urgent Care."

"I—"

"—Violet isn't here. So as the manager on shift, I *contractually* have to take you to Urgent Care. It's not really an option," he cuts me off, then slides a slip leash from his head. He leans down and slides it onto Banksy, who is happily wagging his tail as if he has full coverage for the head-on collision that just occurred. Avery says something into his headset that I can't quite understand over the ringing in my ears, and only moments later, Brooke pops into the room.

"Hey Ayve! What's u-OH MY GOD!" Brooke screams when her eyes land on me, and I huff at her reaction.

"It's not *that* bad," I say, trying and failing again to open my bruised eye. "...right?"

Avery snickers, and Brooke's high-pitched voice only goes higher when she responds.

"Um... it's..." Brooke trails off. "It's... like... have you ever seen an MMA fight?"

Avery's snicker turns to full-on laughter, his face turning red. I try to furrow my brows, but even *that* stings. Instead of a painful scowl, I puff my cheeks out so the pair standing in front of me are aware of my dissatisfaction.

"You definitely need to get seen by someone," Brooke says, waving her hand in the air.

"She is," Avery starts. "That's why you—" He hands the leash to Brooke, Banksy tugging at the other end. "Are going to have Martha call his parents to tell them he's ready. And put him in a holding suite with some water."

Brooke nods, a large Barbie-like grin across her soft porcelain face. Her cheeks are pink, and her white teeth are perfectly straight. She genuinely looks like a Barbie.

"I'll get right on that boss!" she exclaims.

Look, I really like Brooke. She's sweet and ridiculously smart. But right now, she's getting on my nerves. Thankfully, Brooke is quickly dragged out of the room by the overeager dalmatian.

"Alright," Avery says, crouching down so my arm can easily drape over his shoulders. He looks ridiculous, a six-foot-something man squatting down to a mere five feet, but I'm not about to let him pick me up, even if my head rattles painfully with each step we take.

On the way to urgent care, Avery talks to someone over the phone. I can only make out the words "eye," "concussion," and "Banksy," but I tune the rest out. Listening to his voice is painful enough, but actually processing the words coming out is damn near impossible. Plus, I can only think of two things right now:

1. Ouch

2. Violet

I don't know what it means. Any of it at this point. The contract, the bet. The night she showed up, covered in blood, and that day last week when she held me in the storage closet.

My eyes drift closed. I just need it to be dark.

"Hey," Avery says, pulling in next to a bright red sign. I can't read it, but I assume it's the entrance to the Urgent Care. "We're here. Don't fall asleep."

He tells me to wait in the car, then leaves. He quickly appears with a tall woman, who is gripping the handles on the back of the wheelchair. I'm embarrassed and slightly irritated at Avery for doubting my capabilities. I look over at the nurse.

"Oh! Thank you, um," I look down at the woman's name tag, "*Natalie*, but I'm okay. I can walk."

I force a smile that hurts more than I let show.

"Just get in the chair," Avery commands, his voice low as if I'm embarrassing him. Natalie looks at him, then back at me.

"It's *Natalia*, and it's policy," she says in a thick Russian accent. "All head injuries must be brought in veelchair."

I swallow, squinting harder at her name tag. She's right. It says Natalia.

She helps me into the wheelchair, and I feel ridiculous right now, being pushed around like a simple head bump makes it impossible to walk. I'm taking resources away from people who *actually* need it, and it's embarrassing. It's embarrassing in the parking lot, embarrassing in the lobby, and even embarrassing when I'm taken back to a curtained room, with just Avery. I've asked him to leave twice, but apparently, it's "routine procedure" for the manager on shift to stay with the employee until family can come. The only "family" I have is Adrian and Hayden, and Adrian is at home sick with COVID.

Avery pulls out his phone and taps on the screen, before holding it to his ear. I can only hear his side of the conversation.

"Hey. Yeah, sorry. Cam got her face smashed in by a dog. No. Yes. We're here right now. Yup. Okay. Cool, I'll tell her." He puts his phone back into his pocket. "Hayden's on his way."

Nurse Natalia enters the room and asks me a string of questions, like "are you experiencing dizziness?" and "do you have nausea?" "Any chance of pregnancy?" and "what happened?"

I answer all of the woman's questions as she takes my vitals. I have no problem taking deep breaths as instructed, but I struggle when it's time to follow a long black pen with my eyes. Well, *eye*.

After Natalia listens to my heart, and reads my blood pressure, she types furiously on the computer, then turns to me.

"Your vitals are good," she says, her brows furrowing. "Your eyes, is... not so good. We will have to take tests."

"**A**T LEAST YOU'RE STILL cute," Hayden whispers when Natalia pushes me back into my room. I'm not at all upset about Avery being replaced by him. Major stands next to him, as he helps me back into my bed.

"Results should come back within an hour," Natalia says, turning to leave.

"Excuse me," Hayden says quietly with a shiny grin. "Would it be okay if I turned off these lights for her?"

With his charisma and charm, he hardly ever gets told no. I simultaneously hate and love it. Natalia flashes him a smile, which proves to be fake as she quickly drops it.

"No. We must wait for results first."

He tips an invisible cowboy hat at her and gives her a real smile.

"Thank you anyway."

I try to roll my eyes, but it hurts.

"You're ridiculous," I mumble. Hayden shoots me a grin.

"You love me."

His voice remains intentionally soft, so the agonizing throbbing doesn't intensify. Sometimes, I think he may be the most self-aware person on Earth.

"I do."

My eyes close as a gentle hand presses to my forehead. I feel myself slowly sinking, my brain fighting me to fall asleep.

"Keep talking, so I don't pass out," I say. All I want is to get some rest, but Natalia might rip Hayden's throat out if she came back to me unconscious.

"About what?" he asks, still speaking softly.

"Anything."

There's a long pause, and I almost open my eyes to shoot him a bossy look before he finally speaks.

[26]"So, you and Violet, huh?"

My eyes jolt open, and I immediately sit up, which is a total mistake. My head pounds, the room spins, and—

Bleugch.

Thank god Natalia put a trash can right next to my bed. I groan, wiping my mouth on the shoulder of my hospital gown.

"Ew. That bad huh?" Hayden jokes, handing me a bottle of water. "That's all yours, sport. Please do *not* return it."

The water rinses the back of my throat, providing cool, sweet relief from the acidity. When I finally feel my stomach settle, I lean back into the bed.

"What do you mean, *me and Violet*?" I ask defensively.

Hayden chuckles, scooting back as he shakes his head.

"Nothing really. I just—I have a feeling... that there might be more to you two than the contract?" he says, still maintaining his distance.

"I'm not going to throw up," I say, closing my eyes.

Hayden forces a smile. "Sure, love. Just being safe."

I don't have to look at Hayden to know he's staring into my soul. I can feel it, the intense stare of those sweet blue eyes. I sigh.

"There isn't anything more." I pause, waiting for him to speak but he doesn't. "I mean sure, we might, like, be friends, *sort of*. But that's it. It's platonic."

Hayden's hand runs up my arm. "It's *platonic*," he says. "But you have sex?"

I nod, then wince. "Yes."

Hayden stays quiet for a moment. Then he squeezes my hand.

"Do you want it to be?"

"What?"

"Well, you said it's platonic, but do you want it to be?"

An ache radiates in my brows as I furrow them, my lips pursing uncomfortably. I don't answer right away because I don't want Hayden to hear the haste in my voice when I say it. I want him to think it's something I never thought to consider. Finally, after a long stretch of silence, I answer him.

"I don't know."*

Thirty-Two
Nightmares
Violet

Hayden's call came in the middle of my walk with Reese. I've been sticking around the neighborhood lately, keeping an airhorn tucked in a holster around my waist just in case, so it only took a few minutes to rush back home and throw myself into my car.

Cam had been asleep for twenty minutes by the time I arrived at the Urgent Care. Luckily, her concussion is only grade one, but that was still enough reason for me to stay over for a few hours to keep an eye on her.

A sharp pain jolts through my ribcage, my eyes shooting open.

Shit. Did I fall asleep?

I look around Cam's room as I gain consciousness, only a small beam of moonlight trickling through the gap in the gray blackout curtains over her window. I must have passed out during the movie we had been watching. Flashes of cookie-cutter white men, Leonardo DiCaprio and Matt Damon, flip through my mind.

Another sharp jolt travels through my side, and I wince, sitting up quickly. My blurry eyes focus as they travel downwards. Cam is lying in the bed next to me, her frizzy hair strewn across half her face, her lips swollen, eyebrows furrowed. But "laying" may not be the right word. She's more flailing, rotating vigorously as small indiscernible murmurs leave her mouth.

Then, another jab. Her elbow digs its way into my thigh this time with force, and I hiss.

"Fuck," I mumble, rubbing the tender spot. Cam keeps tossing around, her voice growing louder, yet still not saying actual words. At least none I can make out. Her puffy lips part, her brows press together harder.

"Cam," I whisper, shaking her shoulder softly. Cam doesn't wake up, but her chest starts to heave faster, her head jolting around in unconscious panic. I shake her again. "Hey, Cam."

But she still doesn't wake up. She whimpers actually, sucking in a quiet gasp as her breathing intensifies, her body moving toward panic. It reminds me of that day in the storage closet during her anxiety attack. Inconsolable. Breathless. Scared.

"Cam," I say again, shaking her harder this time. "Cam wake up. It's okay. You're—"

Cam's eyes shoot open, her lips parting wide as she sucks in a loud gasp and sits. She has this bewildered look on her face, like she doesn't know where she is. I brush the hair out of her eyes, and Cam's gaze darts around the room in a frenzy, her chest heaving.

I don't hesitate any longer. I slide myself behind her, wrapping my arms around her chest, pressing firmly but gently, just like I saw Avery do. I can feel her heartbeat through her ribcage, pounding against the inside like it's trying to find a way out. I hold her there for a moment, burying my face in the crook of her neck.

"You're okay," I whisper. "It's not your fault. You're okay. It's not your fault."

Cam's chest heaves against my arms, but I hold them steady. The scent of her sweet mint shampoo wafts into my nose as I lie there. Her hands shake in small fists, and I can only imagine the holes her short nails are digging into her palms. She had help last time. A medication. I'm not sure that it's a good idea for her to take it, not after getting a concussion only a few hours ago. When I asked the nurse at the Urgent Care if Cam was allowed to, she said only if it was an emergency.

I don't know if this classifies as an emergency or not. I just know I don't want her to go through another second of it.

I scan the room for Cam's blue backpack, the one she brings with her almost everywhere. I don't see it.

"Where's your meds?" I ask. But she doesn't reply. I keep one arm pressed against her chest, then use the free one to dig through the bedside table drawer.

There are two orange pill bottles inside.

I grab the first one, the heavier one, reading the label.

Cameron Miller

Prozac - Fluoxetine

Take two (2) 10mg capsules daily before bed.

I open the bottle, teal and white pills filled to the top. It doesn't look like this has ever been touched, and it doesn't look like what Avery had given her in the storage closet. I set it down and grab the next one.

Cameron Miller

Xanax - Alprazolam

Take two (2) 2mg tablets as needed for anxiety.

I open it to find only four small white rectangular pills remaining. This is the one. I stare at it for a moment, contemplating.

What classifies as an emergency?

Frozen between my legs, Cam continues gasping for air. I stop thinking about it and pour out two pills in my hand, before reaching for the water bottle sitting on the nightstand. I slide the pills between Cam's lips, just as Avery had done, and she opens her mouth, taking them inside. Then, I lift the bottle up, positioning the straw between her teeth.

After she finishes drinking, I wrap both arms back around her chest and squeeze. Her hands grab my wrists, and I would much prefer she leave deep bruising crescents on my skin than her own.

I breathe in slowly, like I always do when I'm trying to regain control.

"In. Hold. Out," I instruct quietly. Cam's breath shakes as she tries to follow along, her eyes squeezed shut and her fingers sinking further into my skin. "In. Hold. Out."

Her heart thumps against my forearms, small whistles ring in her breaths as she breathes alongside me.

"It isn't your fault," I whisper, following the pattern. Cam's body relaxes slowly as she continues it, her grip around my wrist loosening. "Good. Good job."

Her body slowly eases into mine, the rise and fall of her chest steadily decreasing. I loosen the pressure on her chest, but I don't let go. I lie there, under her, feeling her body against mine, my face still buried into her neck, breathing in.

I press my lips to the back of her head, kissing it.

"You're okay, darling. You're okay."

M Y EYES FLUTTER OPEN sometime later, the room around me still dark and Cam's body still resting atop mine. I slide my arm off her, reaching carefully for my phone on the nightstand.

3:07 a.m.

I have about an hour and a half until I need to get to work. I still have to shower and change, and Reese still needs to eat and take his medication. But Cam's body moves like a wave on top of me, her steady breaths replacing the rapid ones hours prior. I want to stay here forever, her body relaxing into the safety of my arms. I want to stay and protect her from the things that torture her in her sleep.

I wasn't supposed to stay, I know that. And I probably should have left after she calmed down. But I couldn't stand the thought of it happening again and me not being here to help her. And to be completely honest, no part of me wanted to leave, even before I realized what was happening.

I never want to sleep again if I'm not sleeping next to Cam. Even though she woke me in a mumbling panic, I've never felt so at peace. Nothing compares to this, waking up to her body tangled in mine. Her smooth skin warm against my own, her hair pressed into my face. Everything about it is against that stupid contract, and everything about it makes me want her more. Makes me want her always.

It was an accident, all of it. Meeting her at Monsey's, telling her about my family, falling asleep next to her. None of it was supposed to happen. But I realize now, watching her dark lashes flutter against her cheeks, my fingertips resting on the skin of her stomach, that intention proves to be worthless when more powerful forces are at play.

The moon doesn't intend to shine. The snow doesn't intend to melt. And I had no intention of falling for her. Call it what you will: divine intervention or just a beautiful accident. But whatever happened to make this moment real will forever be appreciated by me.

This is only temporary—I know that to be true. But I would trade a lifetime of memories just for this moment. I slip carefully out from under her, making sure her body seamlessly slides onto the soft plush mattress. The thick white comforter is heavy in my hands as I pull it up and tuck her in.

Dawson hops onto the foot of the bed and curls into a tight ball, his nose pressed against his ribcage. Reese rests his chin on the bed too, but I motion for him to stay put so as to not wake her.

Cam looks at peace, her cheek squished against the pillow and her eyes shut softly. A small spot of drool pools next to her face, her lips parted just slightly. My stomach twists, my throat hardening.

I don't know how something as perfect as this wasn't supposed to happen.

A staggered breath slips through my lips, and I lean down. I brush her hair off her forehead and press my lips to it gently.

Thirty-Three

Secret Santa

Cam

I STARE AT THE little white piece of paper folded in my palm. I don't need to open it to see the name inside, because the overhead light shines through it, and I can make out a capital "V" marked in pen.

Apparently, Furry Friends plays Secret Santa every year around the holidays. It isn't a big thing. There's no grand reveal or huge Christmas party or anything. It's just a little ten-dollar gift, popped into the locker of the person whose name you drew.

And out of all twelve people, I drew Violet.

I know it should be easy to think of a gift, given how much time we've spent together the last few months. But most of that time was spent... *not talking*. And the things we have talked about? Well, it all just seems like too much. I slide the paper into my pocket, grabbing my coat off the hook.

"Heading out?" Violet asks, poking her head through the salon door. I nod, shooting her a crafty smile.

"I finished early, and..." I pat the pocket of my jacket where her name is hidden. "Well, let's just say I have some shopping to do."

Violet grins, nodding.

"Yeah, me too. Who'd you get?" She juts her chin out as she asks the question, and a frown takes over my face.

"It's supposed to be a secret," I say, crossing my arms.

Violet shrugs. "Sorry, sorry. I forgot what a *rule follower* you are sometimes."

I roll my eyes.

"Do you want to know who I got?" Violet wiggles her eyebrows, and I push past her, out of the salon.

"No," I say. "I do not."

I already know she got Brooke because she told Adrian, and Adrian told me. I also know Adrian got Martha, and Malcolm got Avery. But Violet doesn't need to know any of that.

"Okay, okay," she says, putting her hands up. "It's slick out there. Is Hayden picking you up?"

As much as I love Luigi, even with snow tires, winter isn't his strong suit. But that wouldn't prevent me from driving him, if only he would start. The temperatures have reached below ten degrees today, so when I tried to turn on the engine this morning, he pretty much flipped me the bird.

"Yeah," I say, looking down at my phone. A notification glows with his name, and I look back up at Violet. "He's here. See you later?"

Violet and I don't say "see you later." We just always assume we will. So I don't know why I asked it, like I was scared for some reason I wouldn't.

"Yeah, Cam." She smiles. "See you later."

"What's with your face?" Hayden asks as I slide into his heated passenger seat. I frown.

"What's wrong with my face?"

"Nothing! Absolutely nothing. You're beautiful as always, I just mean..." He gestures to me. "You're looking... upset?"

What Hayden means by "upset" is that there are purple half-moons under my eyes, my unplucked brows are growing a forest between them, and I'm dressed like Kenny from South Park. It's been hard to sleep this past week. Harder than usual, ever since Violet fell asleep next to me that night. The soft hum of her breath, the warm contact of her skin. How when I roll over, she follows, her arms glued to my waist. I don't know if I'll ever be able to sleep again without her. Actually, because of the contract, I don't know if I'll ever be able to sleep again at all.

I'm beginning to hate those rules, but I know they're there for good reason.

"I'm fine," I say without meaning. "I just..." I pull out the little white paper and plop it into Hayden's hand. "I got Violet for Secret Santa."

Hayden raises an eyebrow at me, a subtle smile tugging on his lips.

"Okay," he says, setting the slip of paper in his empty cup holder. "But why is that upsetting?"

I huff.

"*Because,*" I say, as if it's obvious. "That's like...*against* the contract."

"You really put that in there? No gift-giving?"

I swallow.

"Well, *no*. I put it in there that things have to remain platonic."

Hayden's brows furrow.

"How is gift-giving not platonic? You give me gifts, and we're not—"

"I don't have sex with you, Hayden."

He nods, staying quiet for a moment.

"Well," he says, finally shifting his car into gear and pulling out of the parking lot. "I still don't see how it isn't platonic. I mean—" He glances at me then back to the road. "Isn't freaking out about it the thing that makes it not platonic?"

"If you weren't driving right now, Hayden, I would smack you."

He chuckles, a bright smile stretching across his face. "You don't believe in violence," he says. "That's why you're so..." He gestures to me. "*You.*"

I roll my eyes and let them land on the passenger side window. The snow is coming down rather heavily, giant thick flakes floating through the air. It's beautiful, really. Colored lights illuminating the town around us as we drive carefully through.

"Why do you say that?" I ask, quieter than I mean to. "That I'm the one making it not platonic?"

Hayden adjusts his grip on the steering wheel but continues to stare forward.

"Because," he says, even softer than I, "If you weren't scared that you felt something more, you wouldn't try so hard to prove you don't."

I stare out the window, my eyes attaching to different objects, following them as we pass until they're out of view. Then, I find another. And then another. Hayden's wrong. I'm trying to prove I don't have feelings for Violet because I *actually* don't. Because friends can be as close as lovers, and I can't risk falling into another toxic dependency with someone. Another trauma-bond.

"Can you help me?" I ask finally. "With the present? I mean, you probably know more about Violet than I do, but if you don't want to you don't have to."

"I want to."

He takes one hand off the wheel to squeeze my arm for a moment, before placing it back on.

I DIDN'T KNOW THE Enchanted Emporium *existed* until Hayden pulled up to it. I frown, looking over at him.

"What is this?" I ask. He taps a small brown stone that hangs over his rearview mirror. It clicks.

"Oh, she got you too?" I tease.

I don't think Violet's belief in crystals is absurd. Everyone needs something to believe in, it's part of survival. Honestly, I find it much more believable than I find a man coming back from the dead or a sea splitting down the center at the command of some bearded guy. That isn't to say I believe in crystals, though.

But that doesn't matter. Violet believes in it, and that's quite enough for me.

"It's helpful," Hayden claims, rubbing his thumb over the top of it.

We walk through the emporium, dark green walls engulfing us, black book-shelf accents throughout. There's incense burning somewhere, I can smell it. And a fat tabby cat is stretched out on the nook in the front window, soaking in the last bits of sunlight left.

"Hi, welcome in," a blue-haired employee says. They give us a smile as they approach.

"I'm Ruby. Are you looking for anything specific today, or just browsing?"

"Just browsi—"

"She needs a crystal for her boss, who she is also in love with," Hayden cuts in. My cheeks turn red, and my gaze snaps over to him in a very intended glare. Here he goes again with this "love" shit. I am *not* in love with Violet. Not even close. I look back to Ruby sheepishly.

"That's not—"

But they've already turned around, motioning for us to follow.

"I have a couple options over here," they say, completely unfazed. I shoot Hayden another glare, my jaw clenching.

"Hayden, I am going to kill you," I mutter through gritted teeth.

He chuckles, throwing a large hand over my shoulder. "It would be a good way to go."

We approach a wooden table, various crystals of a spectrum of colors strewn throughout. Ruby turns around, gesturing with their hands as they talk.

"Have you tried a spell?" they ask, their expression telling me they are dead serious. Like I said, everyone needs to believe in something. I shake my head.

"No, that's not really—" I start. Hayden clears his throat, shooting me a look. "*My thing*. I don't really know much about any of this actually. I just pulled her name for Secret Santa and—"

They shove a bright jagged orange stone into my palm.

"This is what worked for me." They shrug, letting their hands fall to their hips. "But *I* did the spell."

Hayden smiles down at me, then back up at Ruby.

"Tell us more about this sp—"

"What is it?" I cut in, shooting him an annoyed glance. He bites back a smile but lets me win.

"It's Carnelian," they answer, like it's obvious. "It, like, creates sexual energy."

Hayden bursts into laughter, and heat rushes to my cheeks in a horrified stare. I quickly drop the stone back onto the table, wiping my hands down my shirt like that will ensure I'm not contaminated by the energy inside of it.

"Uh, I don't think that's the one," I say, sliding it further away. Ruby cocks a brow but doesn't respond. "It isn't what you think."

They scoff.

"That's what we all say."

I furrow my brows, and Hayden tightens his face, trying to look normal.

"*Right...* Well, with this, it really, *really* isn't like that. She just likes crystals, and I pulled her name for Secret Santa. That's all."

Ruby nods hesitantly, not really buying my very real story.

"Okay," they say, gesturing to the table. "How about you just go ahead and take your pick."

I walk around the table, looking at all the different colored stones. My eye is drawn to a blue one, and I pick it up, turning it over in my hand.

"That's Amazonite," they say. "It promotes mental clarity."

I nod but set it back down. It just doesn't feel quite right.

"What about this one?" they ask. "It's Kunzite. It promotes peace."

I look up, locking eyes with Hayden. He shakes his head.

"I don't know," I say. "I feel like she's pretty peaceful."

We continue circling around the table, analyzing all the different stones and crystals. There's a set of tarot cards that catch my eye, but Violet never said anything about tarot. Besides, it's well past the price limit.

"I've got it!" Hayden calls out after a few minutes. His eyes shoot up, his cheeks glowing with a beaming smile. Ruby and I both look up at him with anticipation. Hayden raises his hand, a small pink crystal in the shape of a heart pinned between his thumb and index finger. I immediately shake my head.

"You have got to be kidding me," I scowl. Hayden continues smiling.

"It's *perfect,* Cam. It's all about *love.*" He wiggles his eyebrows, and I cross my arms irately.

"That's *why* it's not happening," I say. "There is no *love* between me and Violet."

Ruby glances over at me, like even they aren't buying it. Like they know *anything* about my situation. Hayden frowns, but I don't care.

"Not. Happening."

He looks at Ruby, waving them over and whispering something into their ear. Ruby's eyes flick up to me, and a light giggle slips through their lips. My jaw clenches tightly.

"It isn't just for relationships," they say afterward. "It can be for self-love, too."

I frown. "I don't believe you."

"Look it up," Hayden says.

So I do. And right there, in an article about rose quartz, Ruby is proven to be correct. And another article. And another. I look up at them.

"That still doesn't mean—"

"—Cam," Hayden interrupts. "Don't you think Violet could use some self-love?"

It's funny because, if you asked me that two months ago, I would have said no. I would have said that Violet seems as if she loves herself enough. I would have believed it too.

But the way she talks about her parents, the way she always helps everyone but herself, I can't say I believe it anymore. I can't say Violet loves herself as much as she should. That she appreciates how remarkable she truly is. I sigh.

"Do you have one that isn't shaped like... *that?*"

Ruby shakes their head, and Hayden smiles.

"Nope!"

Hayden holds up the stone again, the light pink shimmer between his fingers not unlike the gleam in his eye. I let out a loud huff and look at him and Ruby.

"Fine," I grumble.

THIRTY-FOUR
Rose Quartz

VIOLET

"**W**AS IT YOU?"

Brooke stands in front of me, a beaming smile across her face as she holds out a Staples gift card.

Okay, I know that *sounds* like a terrible Secret Santa gift, but if you knew Brooke, you would know it's everything she could ever want. I try not to let a smile break across my face, to not give it away, but it forces itself out of me.

"*Maybe.*" I grin. Brooke throws her arms around me, squeezing tightly.

"You are the best!" she squeals, jumping up and down. I chuckle.

"Yep! Have fun with your... *sticky notes*," I tease. Brooke waves a hand in the air.

"Sticky *tabs,*" she corrects. "And I will. Merry early Christmas boss!"

I wave at her as she skips, *literally,* out the front door of the facility. I look at the clock.

7:02.

We closed a little over thirty minutes ago, but since it's two days before Christmas, everyone stuck around to hangout, eat snacks customers had brought us, and show off their Secret Santa gifts.

I think my Santa forgot because, when I checked my locker this morning, it was empty. That's okay, of course. I don't need physical gifts. And besides, Christmas isn't really my favorite holiday anyway. Ruthie and I always spent it alone because the casino held an annual Christmas tournament, which our parents always attended. We'd trade our old toys with one another as presents. Sometimes, we'd make paper snowflakes and tape them around the living room.

Through the window, I can see Cam's car still parked in the lot, a thick layer of snow draped over it. I think about that day in the rain, when I gave her a ride. And the week after, when I considered, very briefly, unhooking the battery so it could happen again. I would never do that now, knowing how much that car means to her. If I could make him last forever, I would.

[27]"I'm heading out," I say, watching as she tediously oils the straight-edged shears in her hands. Cam's eyes flick up to me, light pooling in her eyes as they lock onto mine. She sets her shears down and props a hand on her hip.

"That's it?" she asks, her brows furrowing. "You're going to be in Clarkston for a *week* and all I get is a '*I'm heading out*'?"

I know she wants me to pretend the smile tugging at her lips doesn't exist. But it would be criminal to not acknowledge the sanctity of it. That sweet, angelic smile invented divinity. I feel a smirk pulling on the sides of my mouth and lean against the door frame.

"Are you saying you're gonna miss me, Sparky?" I tease, my arms crossing over my chest. Cam, in her truest form, rolls her pretty brown eyes.

"*No*," she says, but her cheeks flush and she looks away. "I'm just tired of the wait."

Both of her eyebrows lift for a moment, proving exactly what she means by "wait."

"You know fair and well I'd fuck you right here if you hadn't got your head smashed in a week ago," I say back. Cam's cheeks redden even more, but her eyes simply challenge me.

"I told you," she says, walking toward me. "I'm *fine*."

This has been a theme for the past week. Cam, trying to convince me she's in any type of shape to be fucked, and me, against my biological wishes, turning her down out of pure concern. I shake my head.

"That black eye might be healing, but I want to fuck you so hard your brain rattles. So, *no*."

Cam lets out a scoff but says nothing else, so I know, in its rarity, that I won. A small shimmer catches my eye, drawing my gaze down to Cam's chest. Sitting in the center, on a thin, tiny chain, is a small silver hammerhead shark. I glance down at my own hammerhead, the ink sunk into my skin as a permanent reminder of her. I take the charm into my palm, admiring it.

"Secret Santa?" I ask. Cam nods, smiling.

"Yeah, Avery got a discount on it." She glances up at me, her eyes narrowing curiously. "You?"

My cheeks get hot as I shake my head. I don't know why they do. I really don't care that I didn't get a gift.

"I think mine forgot," I say, shrugging. "But it's okay."

Cam's brows furrow, her head tilting slightly.

"What do mean they *forgot*?"

A wrinkle forms between her brows as she presses them together, her lips turned downward. I chuckle.

"Really," I say. "*It's okay.* I don't care about that stuff."

But Cam shakes her head.

"Nope," she says. "Not okay. That's like, one of the only rules of the game. Bring a gift." Her eyes meet mine, something unrecognizable flickering in their depths. "Are you *sure* they forgot?"

It's cute Cam cares so much, but I don't dare point it out.

"Well, everyone's gone, and it's—" I look at the time on my phone. "7:18."

Cam's lip twitches, but she just nods.

"Well, that's shitty."

A laugh slips out of me, but my stomach twists for just a second.

"Yeah," I say.

I stare at her for a moment, soaking in every inch of her in order to tide me over for the next week. I don't know how I'm supposed to get through seven whole days without seeing her. Without feeling her skin against mine or listening to her ridiculous comebacks that tip me over the edge. I'm regretting agreeing to go to Clarkston at all now, but I know I need to do it for Ruthie. For Willow and Tyler too.

"I should get going. I've got a long drive tomorrow."

Cam nods.

"Right," she says, her gaze falling to the floor. Her thick brown lashes flutter against the apples of her cheeks, reminding me of that night at Monsey's. The first time I saw her.

I should have known, from that moment, that the word "platonic" was never an option for me. From the second I saw her, looking at anyone else felt pointless because nobody could ever be quite as beautiful as her.

"Did you check the weather?" she asks, her tone worried. I smile.

"Yes," I say. "No avalanche warnings."

Cam nods, but that nervous expression stays glued to her face. "And you'll text me when you get there?"

My stomach flutters as I answer. "Yes, Cam."

She looks at me, her eyes scanning mine anxiously. I can see all the gears turning behind them, all the potential possibilities flashing through her mind like a torture device, planted permanently inside her. I grab her hand, not caring at this moment what it might tell her.

"I'll be safe," I say. "I promise."

Cam shakes her head as she leans into me, her cheek resting against my shoulder. Her hair presses against my nose, the familiar aroma of her shampoo flooding my senses. If it were the only thing I'd ever smell again, I would feel privileged.

"You can't promise that," she says, and I can almost hear a break in her voice. My hand cups the back of her head as I pull her in tighter, my other hand finding its home against the small of her back.

"Hey," I say softly. Cam's eyes flick up, those beautiful brown irises dancing in the fluorescent lights. "I'm a better driver than *you*."

Cam tries to fight the sweet laugh that slips through her lips, and she pushes me off of her, flipping her middle finger into the air.

"Get out of here, loser," she shoots back, a glistening smile engraved into her cheeks. I fight my own smile and take a step backward through the door frame as my eyebrow quirks, the metal piercing grazing my forehead.

"That's *boss* to you," I taunt. Then, I turn around and walk out.

The metal latch is cold between my fingers as I pull it open, Reese erratically wiggling as he steps out of the suite.

"Come on," I say, scratching gently between his ears. "Let's go home."

We walk to the lockers, the metal ringing as I pry the door of mine open. My fingers grip the soft brown jacket inside, the fabric like butter and the color like brown agate.

But when I pull it out, something tumbles to the ground. Reese jumps back, startled, then leans down to press his nose against the object. My brows furrow, and I reach down, grabbing a little black box. I pick it up and examine the outside. It's plain. There's no bow or ribbon, no text. Just a black box, small enough to fit in the palm of my hand. I open it.

Glimmering on top of crinkled teal paper is a pink, heart shaped crystal. A soft gasp slips through my lips, and I pick it up, holding it to the light. Different shades of light pink swirl throughout it, and I don't need to keep staring to know exactly what it is.

It's rose quartz, the crystal for unconditional love.

Tears prick my eyes as my grip tightens around the rock. I know who it's from, that isn't a secret. Back at the farm, a conversation I can hardly get off my mind, Hayden said Cam had feelings, and he said I would see. Maybe this is what he meant.

Cam likes to be in control of every situation she's in. She needs to know what's going to happen, to prepare for it. Maybe, all this time, she was just getting ready. To prepare to tell me she violated rule #2 just as I had.

My eyelashes flutter rapidly when I step into the salon, trying to force the welling in my eyes to go away. Cam's gaze flashes to me, a wide smile sewn into her cheeks.

"I was wondering when you'd find it." She laughs, turning back to the clippers in her hand. She scrubs between the teeth with a disposable toothbrush, loose hairs floating in the air around her. I step closer, swallowing down the ache in my throat.

"This is... from you?" I ask, but I already know the answer. Cam chuckles, her back still turned to me as she cleans the tools.

"I've been waiting the entire day for you to open that stupid locker."

My lip quivers, and I can't understand why she makes me feel so weak.

This is what Hayden meant, it has to be. Cam wouldn't give this to me unless she meant it. That's the thing about her. The truth always prevails.

My hands shake, and I'm so scared to say the words coming from my mouth, but I don't care. I don't care about the contract, or my job, any of it. All I care about is this. *Her.*

The first person to really know me.

The first person I've ever cared to know back.

"Cam." My voice shakes, and I step closer to her. Cam turns around, her eyes widening as they land on me. My stomach flutters rapidly, powerful wings grazing the walls inside, trying to find their way out.

Don't think. Just say it.

"I love it. I've been trying to figure out how to tell you. And at first, I didn't believe Hayden. But this—"*

[28]Cam's brows furrow, and she takes a step back.

"Hayden?" she asks.

I nod, taking another step closer.

"I didn't believe him when he said you have feelings, but-"

"Violet, I don't—" She swallows, her brows knitting together. The corners of her lips pull down, regret pooling in her eyes. "I don't know what Hayden said but this *isn't*—" Cam's head shakes, and the fluttering in my stomach begins to harden, sinking into my feet. *This isn't right.* She takes the stone from my palm, holding it up.

"The employee at the emporium told me that this was for *self-love.* I figured, with seeing your parents in Clarkston and everything, you might need the reminder. The reminder that, no matter what they say or do, you're worth it. You're an amazing person. But—" Her voice breaks, and she looks to the floor. "That's *all.* I've been trying to stick to the contract. I don't—" The words get caught in her throat, and she swallows hard before she continues. "I don't feel that way. I'm sorry."

I blink, wet streaks trickling down my cheeks, and I step back, taking a shuddering breath. This doesn't make any sense. The way she held me in the shower, the way her body melted into mine moments ago. This is wrong, every bit of it.

I'm either so much stupider than I thought, or Cam is doing what Cam does: *run.*

I sniff, the muffled sound piercing the air around us. Then, I shake my head.

"I know it wasn't supposed to happen," I say. "I know it violates the contract, and you like to stick to the rules. But think about it, Cam. Are you really going to say, after this, after *everything*, that there isn't the slightest hint of *something*?"

Tears prick her eyes, a thick glossy coat washing over them. I know there's more to this. There *has* to be. But Cam steps back, her nose growing red, her lip shaking.

"It isn't about the contract," she says flatly. "There just isn't more. I got close to you because that's what I do. I form toxic dependencies on people. I'm sorry if I made you feel like there was more to it, but—"

"No," I shake my head, the room around me growing blurry. Tears stream down my cheeks, a foreign saltwater river pooling around my lips. Cam's just pulling away, like she did at Monsey's, like she did after seeing Cody. But she doesn't need to be scared with me. "I know you're scared but—"

Cam's face grows red, her nostrils flaring suddenly as her lip twitches.

"Scared?!" she snaps, her brows weaving tightly together. "What the *fuck* would lead you to believe I'm just '*scared*'? Have you ever thought that maybe I just don't—"

"Snow," I cut in. Caught off guard by my interruption, Cam stares at me, her eyes unblinking. I continue. "Red 40. Road trips. Wine." Her lips part, ready to speak, but I don't stop. "Airplanes. Lakes. Intersections where the light blinks yellow. Pinworms. Windows that don't slide open. Water that isn't filtered a thousand damn times. You're scared of *everything*, Cam. And you know what I think?"

Cam scoffs, but tears ripple down her cheeks.

"I think you're scared that you have feelings for me too."

Cam's head shakes, and she sniffles, her eyes dropping to the floor. I see it, the hurt traveling through her veins. I hate that I'm the one who put it there. Regret floods my body in a wave, a sharp sting piercing my chest.

God, I'm such a fucking idiot. I think I just created our demise. I *know*, actually, that with those stupid words, I just ended the contract. All I had to do was keep my mouth shut. All I had to do was pretend everything was fine.

"Cam, I'm sorry. I shouldn't have—"

"Get out," she says.

There's no waver in her tone, no uncertainty. But complying is the furthest thing from what I want to do. I want to wrap her in my arms. I want to tell her all the things I'm scared of too. Vulnerability. Intimacy. *Losing her*.

Her throat bobs as she swallows, and she finally looks up from the floor, every word of what I said circling around her pupils.

*"Leave, Violet."**

Thirty-Five
Rum & Revelations

VIOLET

IF THERE'S ONE THING I learned from my parents, it's that the easiest way to get your mind off something is to have a drink. I don't use this technique often, because the fear of addiction haunts my every move, but I do have to admit that it works.

Heat beams from the outdoor space heater, the snow on the patio furniture melted away long ago, leaving the metal barstools warm and dry. I hoist myself onto the chair, looping Reese's leash around the center leg of the table. A slow, steady beat flows from the inside of the building, surrounding me in a mellow melody. A gray-haired waitress approaches me, pen and notepad in hand, and I hope, in the deepest parts of me, that the teary puffiness of my face has gone down.

"Hey doll. What can I getcha?" she offers in a thick Boston accent.

"Can I have a Long Island?" I ask, looking down at Reese who's curled next to the heater like a baking croissant. This is the first time he's been out since the attack, other than our quick trips around the block. But I needed him. Everything stops when I look at him, all the hurt, all the regret. If I'm grateful for anything on this planet, it's Reese. "And a bowl of water for him?"

The woman nods. "Sure thing."

I watch her disappear into the crowd inside, and I wonder if anyone that's here was here the night that I met Cam. If they were a background character in this painful, unrequited story. She pushes past a tall, olive-toned man with buzzed hair, a box-dyed blonde woman with an array of quote tattoos, a—

Fuck.

A pale, slender, red-haired woman. Should I say "a" or "*the*"?

"Mallory."

The name surprises me the second it comes out of my mouth. I don't mean to say it, but the word slides out so naturally. Instinctually. Second nature. Right as I'm about to look away, right when I realize I've been staring, *not subtly*, at my ex-wife in the center of a crowd, Mallory's eyes lock onto mine. Her lips wear that familiar, expensive shine, her eyes the same, stunning shade of blue. I try to look away, hoping that if I pretend I didn't see her, she'll have the same courtesy. I can't do this, not now. But I can hear the tapping of her stilettos against the floor growling louder and louder.

I don't know what to do.

Should I grab Reese and make a run for it? Should I pretend I have amnesia? Running for it is probably the better move. But my foot doesn't so much as budge when I try. My legs refuse to cooperate. The clicking grows louder.

Just move damnit, move!

And louder.

Here we go.

"Violet!" Mallory's voice is slurred and shrill. She's clearly intoxicated, her drink swaying in her hand above her head. "It's so good to see yo—"

Mallory's more drunk than I had expected. I can see now the smudged lip-gloss and the drooped eyelids. And because of her quick, tipsy sway, the front of her red, open-toed heel catches on Reese's leash, catapulting her face first onto the concrete patio.

"Shit!"

My legs seem to have regained their strength. I hop down from the tall stool and grab Mallory by her arms, pulling her to her feet. "Are you okay?!" Mallory smiles up at me, her drunken blue eyes luminescent from the dim patio lighting. "Oh my god!"

Mallory's smile drops.

"What?!" she asks anxiously, stumbling backward. I tighten my grip on her arm to keep her from falling.

"Umm..." I trail off. Despite the divorce, I know plenty of things about Mallory Sinclair. I know she only likes red wine. She refuses to wear workout clothes that aren't Lululemon or Gymshark. She will never leave the house without a full face of makeup that costs more than my car payment. And I know, more than anything, that Mallory does not do well with blood. "You just have a little scrape," I lie. "Let's get you cleaned up."

"Oh my lanta!" The gray-haired waitress has returned with one Long Island, and one silver water bowl. Poor woman never saw it coming. In truth, Mallory's "little scrape" is more of a shallow gash, right in the center of her chin. It might not need stitches, but it is pretty gnarly. "You alright miss?"

I stare at the waitress wide-eyed, trying to tell her without verbal communication to not make a big deal of the nasty injury. Mallory just looks at me like a deer in the headlights. Like the answer to the woman's question is held in my hands. I look at the waitress.

"She's okay. I'm just going to get her cleaned up. Is it okay if I bring him with us?" I gesture to Reese, who somehow, is still passed out.

Oh, to be a dog.

"No problem sweetheart."

I unwrap the leash from the table and guide Mallory by the arm through the crowd, into the family bathroom.

"Oh my god!" Mallory squeals, staring at herself in the mirror. Her thin pale fingers hover over the swollen cut on her face. "Violet!"

The paper towels in my hand are pretty much disintegrating under the harsh tap flowing from the sink.

"These things are fucking useless," I mutter, tossing the wad into the garbage can. I push open a stall door and wrap layers of toilet paper around my hand, like a pre-teen who just started their period.

"Violet!"

A sigh escapes my lips as I run the wad of paper under the tap. "Mal, you're fine. It's just a scrape. I'll get this cleaned up and you can go—"

"Just a scrape?! My face is ruined!"

"What a tragedy," I mutter. Mallory shoots me a glare. "Will you just let me clean it please?"

Look, I'm not trying to be a bitch, but Mallory is being *insufferable*. I press the wet tissue to her chin, careful to dab it rather than swiping it so crumbs of paper don't get left behind. This might be the only time in my life that I have begged for silence. But it's taken almost as quickly as it's granted by a sound I never thought I'd hear again. Especially in these circumstances.

Mallory is laughing. And not a quiet, muffled chuckle. No. Mallory has erupted into uncontrollable, body-vibrating, witch type laughter as she kicks her feet around. She is sitting on a dirty bar bathroom floor, blood seeping from her face, and she's laughing.

"Did I... miss something?" I ask, pulling my hand away. Mallory only laughs harder. "What?!"

"Did you—" Mallory can barely speak through her intoxicated giggles. "Did you ever think we'd be here again?"

Listening to her laugh, I can't help but laugh alongside her. "Monsey's?"

I know what Mallory means, and I know she does *not* mean Monsey's. I kind of regret playing dumb, but I don't know what else to say. I expect Mal to tell me "no," to elaborate on the situation. To mention the fact that we're sitting on the floor of a bar bathroom together. Mallory just laughs, and I do too, shaking my head.

"I don't—I can't—" The skin on her chin stretches tight with her laughter, and I have to press the tissue paper against it again to stop the bleeding. Her eyes flick up to me, crashing waves shining in the blue depths of them. She blinks, once, before cupping my face, and pressing her thin glossed lips against mine.

They should feel familiar, but somehow, I feel like I've never kissed her before in my life. I pull back quickly, heat rushing to my cheeks. Mallory looks like she's scrambling to construct a sentence, but I don't even want to hear the next words coming from her mouth. This is wrong. Or at least, it feels that way. I know Cam and I are over. I know that it's entirely my fault. But still, something about this feels dirty. Boundary crossing, even. I know it isn't cheating, it quite literally can't be. Even when we had an agreement, the nature of it ensured that. So why does it feel that way?

"I'm seeing someone," I blurt out. It isn't something I planned to say, and really, it isn't even the truth. "Seeing someone" implies more than sex. It suggests that it's current, too. And as proven, in the small humid salon, neither of those things are true. But the words flow out of my mouth faster than I can even process them. "She's great. She's smart, and *really* fucking bossy, and she *loves* dogs, and—"

"That's awesome," Mallory cuts in, smiling. I study her face for a moment, deciphering if this is the type of "awesome" that Mallory would go home and rant about. The kind she didn't really think was "awesome". But there is no disingenuousness to her look. Pink rises in her cheeks, her eyes are teary but the care in them is real. Her smile is sweet. This may be, I realize, one of the only times Mallory has ever seemed authentic to me.

"It is," I say back. I look at the woman in front of me. My life, my history. And I know I should be feeling happy that I've proved I've moved on, in some way or another. There should be warmth swelling in my chest, triumph in my mind. I thought I was going to feel like I won when this happened. Like what she did wasn't enough to ruin me. Instead, guilt washes over me like a tidal wave on a fragile shore. Cam's voice echoes in my mind, but I don't think this feeling has anything to do with her. I mean, how could it? We were never together. It was never going to be something more.

"You don't let anyone know you."

That's what she had said to me. And it stung so badly because it was true. It *is* true. No, was. It *was* true. Hayden knows me now, and Cam does too, at least more than anyone else. More than Mallory ever had, that I know for sure. And even with her self-obsessed nature, I can't say that it's her fault.

"Mallory I—" I clear my throat. "I owe you an apology. Aht—" I put my hand up when Mallory's mouth opens, not allowing her to interrupt me. I need to say this, and then I need to leave. "I didn't let you in. At all. Twelve years, and you knew nothing about me. And that was on me. I didn't want anyone to know how I felt. It was scary. It *is* scary. But I recognize that it created distance between us. And I know that probably made you feel just as alone. So, I'm sorry."

Tears well in Mallory's eyes, her lip trembling with a soft but genuine smile.

I can't sit in here with her anymore. I can't spend another moment reminding myself of what we were, of what we would be if Mal never cheated. If I had just been vulnerable. What we were is in the past, and what we could be? We would have never been what everyone thought we were, as a couple, or as individual people. Everything we could be, everything that everyone saw us as, it was all fake. I know that now, because of Cam.

It's funny. You can spend your whole life with someone, and never truly know each other.

Her fingers graze against my cheek, cold and thin. "Violet—"

The bathroom door swings open, my head snapping to the opening in the frame. Standing there, between the wooden trim, is Cam.

THIRTY-SIX

Hell is a Place on Earth

CAM

THE BITTERSWEET FLAVOR OF vodka and cranberry juice settles on my tongue. The bar lighting is dim, but the atmosphere isn't. People talk loudly, about work, and their families, and the weather, not caring who around them hears it. Steady beats send vibrations through the floor, traveling up the bar into my glass. The red liquid inside of it shakes softly, little ripples like blood-soaked waves in my clear cup.

I shouldn't have listened to Hayden. I knew the second he held up that stupid pink rock, that the entire thing was a bad idea. The signals I'd been sending were mixed, lately. I feel terrible about it, how she became victim to my dependency. Even setting my own rules didn't work, every piece of that contract broken by the two of us.

What Violet doesn't know is that I wish it was true. If I had feelings for her, everything would be so much less complicated. I wouldn't have to explain that it isn't feelings, it's attachment. It's a trauma bond, like what happened with Cody. Except instead of Cody being the person I bonded with, he's the reason behind it.

I hate so much that this happened. Being around Violet was like seeing the world in 3D. Usually, I only ever see the bad. The things to worry about, the awful possibilities. But Violet showed me that The Realm is full of hope too. Sure, terrible things might happen. Terrible things *do* happen. But good things happen too, and she was one of them.

But that's gone now. Her confession, the way she talked to me, how clear her belief is that all I am is terrified, proved, I think at least, that all of it has come to an abrupt end.

[29]"Is this seat taken?"

My gaze flicks up, Cody grinning sheepishly, his large hand hovering over the stool next to me. I shake my head, and he sits down.

"Whiskey, neat," he says to the bartender. The bartender pours the thick brown liquid into a short glass and sets it in front of us.

"You know Cam," Cody starts, reaching out his hand to tuck a strand of hair behind my ear. "I'm really glad you called."

Goosebumps flood my skin from his touch, the hairs on the back of my neck standing straight. I clear my throat, taking a heavy swig of my drink.

"Thank you for coming," I say after. He picks up his glass, swirling the liquid around like a tornado inside, before pressing his lips against it, taking a long drink. His eyes lock onto mine, and usually, I'd look away, but not tonight. Not anymore.

"So what is it that you wanted to tell me?" he asks. "It sounded pretty important on the phone." His tone sounds almost condescending, a haughty smirk tugging at his lips.

This is it. This is the moment I've been waiting for, though I hadn't realized until tonight. This entire time, all I needed was to get this off my chest. I take a deep breath, not letting his gaze go. He's going to look me in the eye when he hears this.

"You know Cody," I say, reaching my hand out to him. He grabs it, his smile growing just a little bit wider as he squeezes it. I forgot how rough his hands are, almost like Violet's, except I don't find his charming. I find them repulsive. "I just wanted to say…"

He nods for me to continue, his eyes beaming in the warm lights.

In. Hold. Out.

"I just wanted to say, *fuck you.*"

Along with my hand, the arrogant grin on his face drops, his jaw going slack. All the light that had just illuminated his eyes drains out, his cheeks growing pale.

Cody's cheeks don't grow pale. They only ever get red. But here they are, right in front of me, white as the snow falling outside. I say it again:

"Fuck you. You took advantage of me. You knew I was vulnerable. You knew I had just been through unimaginable trauma, and you acted like you were there for me. And then, when you had me in your grip, when I finally trusted you, you made me believe that my life couldn't exist without you."

Cody tries to speak, but I don't even bother pretending I care. I don't let him interrupt me. I don't let him explain.

"You called the only piece I had of my dad left 'shit'. You tried to isolate me from my friends, from the only people I had left. You cheated on me, then blamed me for a *chemical reaction* to my medication. You told me that I'd never grow because I was too scared to try. Well guess what?"

I take a sip of my drink, my gaze narrowing onto him. Now, I *want* him to speak.

"Go on," I say, gesturing. "*Guess.*"

Cody blinks harshly, pure shock sewn into every inch of his stupid face. His brows weave together, and he clears his throat.

"You're not scared anymore?" he asks weakly, his voice almost mouse-like. It's so jarring to see him this way. I don't think he's felt small a day in his life until now.

"*No,*" I answer. "I'm terrified. But I grew anyway."

Cody swallows, the cartilage in his throat jerking. Then, he nods slowly.

"Cam, *sweetheart,*" he says softly, and you'd think his tone was genuine if he was capable of it. "I'm so sorry you feel that way." His hand reaches to grab mine, but I pull away. "I never wanted to hurt you, but sometimes, I felt like I had no choice. I mean, you were crazy sometimes, panicking about things that didn't even make sense. You were scared of getting hurt, so I tried to protect you. But I should have done it differently."

"No." The word slips out before I have a chance to register it, but as it hangs in the air, I know that it's the right one. "You can't guilt-trip your way out of this, Cody. I—"

"Babe, I *miss* you. I'm not guilt-tripping you, I'm giving you an explanation. If you would just hear a guy out, I think you'd realize that all I ever wanted was to make you happy."

A maniacal laugh erupts out of me, my fingers squeezing the inner corners of my eyes.

"You literally had sex with someone else in my bed," I say. "How *exactly* is that keeping me happy?"

"W—" Cody stops, no doubt from the lack of a valid response. I can see the ideas flipping through his tiny little brain, trying to settle on the best one. "I had a lot of pent up *energy,*" he divulges. "You wouldn't want to deal with that on your medication, would you?"

Another laugh slips through my lips, this one more of a laugh scoff, shocked at the audacity this man has.

"Go to hell."*

Then, I toss the rest of my drink to the back of my throat, stand up, and escape to the bathroom.

I weave through the thick crowds. I don't know why so many people have come to Monsey's the night before Christmas Eve. I guess I can't say much, though, because clearly, I'm one of them.

It's almost funny. The last time I was here, I was escaping out of the bathroom. Now, I'm retreating into it, the only place Cody won't follow me.

I push the heavy door open, the light inside brighter than the lowlights of the bar. It beams onto me, almost like a movie, and while my eyes adjust to the scene inside, my stomach drops.

There, on the floor, Violet is sitting face-to-face with a red-haired woman. The woman's pale hand cups her face, almost like the way Violet used to cup mine. But if that was the only thing causing my brain to swirl and my knees to go limp, I'd simply leave.

Blood drains from my face as recognition washes over me. And then, I watch as it washes over her. Over them both.

"Shit. Cam—" Violet shoots up, the whites of her eyes growing as she rushes to me. "This isn't what it looks like. I mean, not that it matters, but this—"

Everything Violet says next just flows in one ear and out the other. I can't focus on her words right now. All I can focus on is the woman on the floor. It's unmistakable, the red hair, the pointed chin. The glossy coat layered on her lips.

That's her. That's the woman Cody cheated on me with.

"Is this...*her*?" the woman asks. Her voice is tight and sharp, one of her perfectly sculpted thin brows pointed up. My brows furrow, but I can't stop staring at her.

I don't know why I hate her. For all I know, she could have been completely innocent. I doubt Cody would have been honest about the fact that he was dating me. But still, something deep in my chest is burning. Maybe it's because she should have seen the pictures on the wall. Or maybe, it's something else entirely.

"*Fuck*," Violet mutters, but I still can't look at her. "Mallory, just don't. Okay?"

Mallory. Like, *Mallory*, Mallory?

"What do you mean, *her*?" I ask, staring her down. I don't know why I feel threatened right now. There's nothing more this woman can take from me.

Mallory glances up at Violet, then back to me.

"The girl that Violet was talking about. The one she's seeing." My brain tries to process the words flowing from her mouth, but it's struggling to keep up as she continues. "But also, you're Cody's—"

The door swings open again, and I don't have to turn around to know who it is that's stepped inside. The scent of allspice washes over me, my stomach twisting into an even tighter mass. I should have known he wasn't above barging into the women's bathroom. I flip around, Cody standing firmly with his arms crossed over his broad chest.

"*Come on*, Cam. You can't hide in here forever; let's talk this out. I mean, you can *come with me* to LA."

I step aside, revealing Mallory on the floor behind me. I watch his face drop again, maybe even more dramatically than it had back at the bar. Violet showed me heaven at Al's, but this right here, is my personal hell.

Finally, my gaze flicks over to Violet. Every bit of color has drained from her face. I can't imagine what she must be thinking, how this must look. I scramble to explain, before she can think anything of Cody barging in here like this, saying those things. I don't know why I care what she thinks about the situation. But

I do anyway.

"Violet, he's not—" But I stop, my heart slipping into the depths of the floor below as my eyes latch onto a pink, glossy smear on her thick lower lip. My breath hitches, and my heart pounds, everything I've ever known disappearing to the back of my mind.

It doesn't matter. I made it clear to Violet what the rules were, and how she broke them. I was straightforward, back at the salon, that nothing I felt for her was beyond comfortability and safety. But for some reason, everything inside of me crumbles.

"You kissed her?"

Violet's brows drop for a second, almost like she's confused, but then they shoot up, her sleeve dragging over her lips to wipe away the evidence. I step back, my spine hitting the thick door behind me. Cody and Mallory both look up from whatever conversation they were having, their eyes falling onto me. Violet's head shakes quickly.

"No, Cam, it wasn't like that. It—"

I grab the door handle, the brass cold against my palm.

"If this wasn't over before," I say sharply, tears pooling in my eyes. "It sure as hell is now."

Thirty-Seven

Christmas

Cam

DIVINE INTERVENTION, ISN'T THAT what Violet calls it? When something so bizarre happens that leads to an outcome you didn't know was possible? I think Cody was my divine intervention the night before last. If I hadn't met up with him, if he hadn't chased me to the bathroom, I never would've known. [30]

I wouldn't have known that Mallory was the woman he'd slept with, and I wouldn't have known that her lips had been pressed to Violet's just hours after she confessed her feelings for me.

I have no right to be upset about it, but I am anyway.

"No, that one's for Cam."

My gaze snaps up at the sound of my name. Adrian, Hayden, Avery and I are circled around a small stack of mostly poorly wrapped Christmas gifts. The only ones that don't look like a second-grade art project are Adrian's, of course. Perfectly creased paper, handmade bows, invisible tape binding it all together. Avery shoves a box in my direction.

"Thanks," I say, taking it from his hands. Adrian rocks onto their knees excitedly, boasting a giant, beaming grin.

"Betcha can't guess what it is!" they tease. I can't, of course. Adrian is rather unpredictable when it comes to gift giving. For one birthday, they painted the most beautiful portrait of Cooper, my childhood dog. Cooper was my dad's favorite thing in the world, next to me. Luigi made third, which isn't bad. Cooper died just after dad. The vet said he was old, but I think my father being gone had something to do with it. He had so much life before dad left, so much energy. It was like my dad took Cooper with him. The medium was oil pastels, the texture of his coat rising above the canvas.

The year after, they created an accurate replica of a pile of dog shit, made from toilet paper rolls and Modge-Podge.

The only thing I know for a fact about what's inside the box I'm holding, is that Adrian created it with their bare, talented hands.

"Open it, kid," Avery whines. "I've been waiting, like, *ten minutes* for my turn."

I roll my eyes, carefully peeling off the hand painted wrapping paper so as to not tear it. Adrian tugs the box out of my hands, rips the paper off in one fell swoop, and hands it back to me.

"I was going to save that!"

"Sorry." They shrug. "I was getting impatient."

To avoid getting absolutely bludgeoned by Adrian and Avery, I open the cardboard box quickly. I reach inside, grabbing onto a thin square-shaped object. It's glass, I can tell, from the cold hardness of it.

I pull it out, holding it up to analyze it. Shards of glass, different shapes and colors, are welded together into a square frame. Holding it to the light, the glass glistens, reflecting a colorful blur onto my living room wall. But the shards, I realize after staring for a moment, are not randomly placed. Gold toned pieces meld together in a chunky, rectangular object, thin silver slices laid carefully over the top.

My jaw drops slightly in awe as I stare at it. Adrian is talented, this I knew. But this belongs in a fucking museum.

"Luigi?" I ask, staring at them in disbelief. Tears well in my eyes, and Avery nudges me, handing me a half-used napkin. Adrian nods.

"You know all that glass we picked up after the Fourth of July?" they ask. I nod, handing the napkin back to Avery and wiping my tears with my sleeves instead.

Every year, the day after the Fourth of July, we all go to Bear Lake to do a cleanup. It's where they shoot the fireworks, and where most people get drunk and leave all their garbage. At first, we just went to clear away the litter. Avery is very passionate about the environment and kept going on tangents about how much he wanted to "litter their faces with his fists." It wasn't until after that Adrian had the idea to recycle what they could into art projects.

"It's mostly broken beer bottles but, who cares right?"

I don't mean to get emotional, I really don't. I just don't know what I would do without them. Any of them, even Avery with his snarky remarks and half-used napkins. I would have nothing without my family.

"I—I love you," I let out in a choked sob. Avery pats my back awkwardly, and Adrian and Hayden encompass me in a warm and loving embrace.

After, we blast Christmas music while taking turns opening presents from one another. Avery loves the "Don't Fuck with Mother Earth" shirt I got him, and Hayden almost pisses himself laughing when he opens a pink crotchet cowboy hat from Adrian.

"Put it on Farm Boy," I tease, slapping it onto his head. "Show us how a real man walks 'round these parts."

Hayden's spent his whole life on Ayers' Acres. It's the town's go-to spot for picking fruit and visiting their goats. They even do festivals throughout the seasons, but my favorite is the Peach Parade in July.

Hayden isn't *exactly* country, but he's not exactly *not* country either. There's no southern twang in his voice, because he's from Washington obviously, but something about his mannerisms, and definitely the way he dresses, just gives it away.

"Well, Buttercup," he says with an exaggerated accent. He flashes me a smirk, making his way over to me. "I suppose you don't wanna dance, do ya?" He places an invisible toothpick in his mouth and reaches his hand down to me. I fight the smile creeping across my face, but it gives me away. I roll my eyes, slapping my hand into his as he waltzes me around the room, hand in hand. Loud Christmas music fills the air around us as he twirls me around.

"Are you okay?" he asks quietly, his beaming blue eyes looking at me with concern. He continues spinning me, Adrian clapping and Avery calling him a show off, while giving us a huge smile. My smile drops.

"What do you mean?"

Hayden dips me down, the back of my head nearly touching the floor before he brings me back up.

"Violet told me," he says softly. "About all of it."

I shake my head, looking down.

His soft blonde brows press together, and his large gentle hands hold me tightly. "I'm sorry Cam. I pushed you to get the quartz. I thought you had feelings for her. I thought I was helping."

"You weren't," I say.

Hayden swallows, nodding apologetically. His eyes are glossy, but I know that he won't cry. Hayden's like Violet in that way. He doesn't let it be obvious, what he's thinking. "But I know your intentions, Hay. I forgive you." I sigh, looking over at Adrian and Avery, who are now laughing about something that I failed to overhear. I focus back on Hayden.

"What were you doing, Cam? With Cody? Do you know how badly that could've ended?" Hayden's voice is strained with worry, and I know it's not unwarranted. It could've ended badly with Cody, I know that. But I also know that if I had done it sooner, maybe I wouldn't have led Violet to believe there was more. Maybe I would've stood firmer with the rules, or maybe, the contract wouldn't have existed at all. The point being, that if I had done it sooner, Violet wouldn't have gotten hurt.

But I don't know if she was really that hurt now, seeing as it only took hours for her to kiss someone else. Some call it a rebound. But I don't feel the way Violet claimed to, and even I can't think about kissing anyone but her.

"I know," I say softly, my gaze lowering to the floor. "I just had to tell him. I had to let him know what he did to me, and I had to let him know he didn't win."

Hayden's gentle fingers lift my chin, my eyes flicking up to meet his. A beaming smile shines on his face, his eyes growing teary again.

"You said that?" he asks, almost in a whisper. I nod.

"Yes. What else would I have met up with him for?"

Hayden shrugs, his hand still on my waist as he sways me side to side.

"I don't know," he answers truthfully. His lips part again, but hesitation floods his eyes, and he waits a beat, glancing over at Adrian and Avery. They're still talking about who knows what, Avery's fiddling with the noise-canceling headphones Hayden had gifted him. Hayden looks back at me, his voice softening.

"She didn't do it, you know."

My eyes meet his, my brows knitted together in a true fashion of confusion. "What?"

"Violet. She didn't kiss Mallory. Mallory kissed her." I stare at him, blinking slowly. My throat grows drier by the second, a large lump forming in the bottom of it. "Not that you care."

I lean my head into his shoulder as the song comes to a gradual end. Tears prick my eyes, Hayden's Christmas sweater absorbing them as they fall silently.

"Yeah," I say. "Not like I care."*

Thirty-Eight
Stop Wishing

Violet

Y OU KNOW THAT SAYING, "you never know how good you have it until it's gone"? [31]

I experienced it a little bit differently.

I didn't realize what a beautiful thing it was to feel, until I felt. I thought feeling was a fatal flaw. I thought showing it was the thing that would ruin me. But it's necessary, I realize now. Even the pain. It's a privilege to feel pain, because it means you've felt something beautiful to compare it to.

My hand grips the steering wheel as I make the four-hour journey to Clarkston. Reese sleeps in the back seat, his fur still patchy but his wounds healed. I look at him through the mirror and smile as a tear trickles down my cheek.

I wipe it against my shoulder, my eyes catching a glimpse of that greyscale hammerhead shark. I swallow, looking back through the windshield as I curve through an icy road through the mountains. The brown rock peeks through in some areas, and I can't pretend I wish it didn't.

Hayden was wrong about Cam, and her feelings for me. Maybe he's wrong in the fact that she doesn't have feelings for him too. Or maybe, all along, this was just a winding road, leading her back to Cody. But none of that, not even for a second, could make me hate her.

I think what scares me so much about this isn't the end of the contract. It isn't knowing I'll never feel Cam's body against mine again. That I could forget what her lips taste like.

What scares me, more than anything, is that I will never get to know who she becomes. She's changed so much from when I met her. She's still Cam, of course, and I hope that stays the same. But she's growing, and I'm scared I'm going to miss out on it.

Everything happens for a reason. I've always said that, and I've always believed it too. I just wish there had been another way for the universe to make me feel something, because this fucking sucks.*

I DON'T REALIZE I'VE missed my mother's voice until I hear it again.[32]

"You never visit us anymore," she says.

I changed my mind.

Her voice is weak, and raspy like fragile gravel that would crumble under your feet with just one step. I inhale deeply, letting each organ in my body lock so that everything stays where it should be. My heart still drops to my feet when my father speaks up.

"What, you don't love us anymore?"

"No guys, it's not that. I've just been really busy and—"

My mother interrupts. "I was in the hospital."

"I know Mom."

"I could've died."

I want to scream. I want to release every word, and every emotion I have ever held back, and throw them all out at this small, frail woman who's supposed to be my mother until my throat is raw and my lungs collapse. I want to ask her whose fault it is and bring up all the times I've sat in the hospital waiting for her self-inflicted demise. I want to remind her of every single graduation, birthday, and promotion she's missed because she was in some random person's basement shooting so many chemicals into her body she thought it was three years earlier than it actually was. But I don't. I just close my eyes and muster up the only words I can put in its place.

"I'm sorry, Mom."

"Yeah, well…"

And that's all she says. Ruthie brings two cups of warm tea from the kitchen, and places it on the table in front of our parents.

"Aunt Vi! Aunt Vi!" a little high-pitched voice squeals, and I turn my head to see Tyler running at me, full speed ahead.

"Hey bug!" I say, flashing her a smile. My arms open wide, scooping her into a hug.

"Are you excited to open presents?"

Tyler nods, pointing to the gifts stacked high under the tree.

"Mom said you probably weren't coming, but Dad made her wait."

I shoot Ruthie a look, and she shrugs sheepishly.

"What? It was a fair assumption."

I turn to Jeramiah and give him a nod.

"Thanks for waiting," I say. Jeremiah nods back silently, a babbling Willow attached to his hip.

"What time does the caretaker usually come?" I ask, in an attempt to make casual conversation. If I ask about their lives, my parents won't pretend to care about mine.

"Ugh, that bitch."

"Mom!" Ruthie yells. Then she lowers her voice to a whisper, pointing at Tyler. Jeremiah takes Willow and Tyler into the next room.

"What? I'll tell you what, she can't cook for shit, and she doesn't know her head from her ass even if you labeled them. I want to fire her."

"You can't fire her, Mom," Ruthie says, placing her hand on her shoulder. I stay silent. "That's part of the conditions. You guys can only stay here if you and dad are sticking with the program. NA three times a week, a caretaker visit a couple of hours each day, and—"

"Yeah, yeah we know sweetie. It's like jail but with a private bathroom," my dad interrupts.

Every day's a treat.

Every day's a treat.

Every day's a fucking treat.

My jaw clenches so hard I feel my teeth scrape against one another.

"Should we get started with the presents?" I ask through gritted teeth. My mom frowns.

"Why are you in such a rush?"

I suck in a breath, holding it for as long as I can. I look at Ruthie, and she gives me an understanding nod.

"I think it's a good idea. I know Tyler is on the edge of her seat and it'll keep her busy for the rest of the day while I cook."

She looks up at me, and I would mouth the words "thank you" if my parent's eyes weren't glued to me. From the other room, we hear Tyler cheer.

"Sorry!" Jeremiah calls out. "I should've covered her ears."

I chuckle, shaking my head and we all shuffle to the living room reluctantly.

It only takes minutes for wrapping paper to litter Ruthie's living room floor. Tyler has already solved half of a miniature Rubik's cube that was in her stocking. Willow seems much more interested in the colorful paper than the actual presents she received from her parents. Reese barks as she shoves a giant ball of it into her mouth.

"Let's save room in your stomach for something more nutritious, huh?" I sweep my finger inside the baby's mouth, causing her to cry.

"Ruthie! Your kid is trying to eat garbage!" I call out, scooping Willow into my lap as I bounce my leg to comfort her.

"I'm sure she's eaten worse," Jeremiah says, taking her from my arms. "Whose presents are left?"

"Just the ones I brought."

I begin placing the corresponding gifts in front of everyone. The kids and my parents each get a box, and between Jeremiah and Ruthie sits a single white envelope, their names scrawled across the front in what was *intended* to be fancy calligraphy. It looks like something Tyler could have given them.

"Alright, open!"

Tyler begins aggressively ripping the decorative paper off her box, while Ruthie gently slides her fingernail underneath the seal of the envelope, Jeremiah watching. I help Willow open her gift, talking in a high-pitched tone as I open the box with faux surprise.

"Wow! Isn't that such a cool stuffy?!" Jeremiah says, poking Willow's baby rolls. A small, white, smushy-faced plush emerges from the box. "Who does that look like?"

Willow babbles, with the cutest smile someone with only half their teeth could have. If I ever wanted kids, Willow would give me baby fever.

Every time we've visited since Willow was born, her and Reese have been inseparable. Everywhere Willow crawls to, Reese follows behind. And when it's time for him to leave, the baby scoots herself to the door where he waits. It's so cute that I tried to convince Ruthie to get the girls a dog, but she said she doesn't want to until Willow starts walking.

Two skinny arms suddenly fling themselves around me, squeezing me tightly.

"Thank you, Aunt Vi!" Tyler squeals, rocking us back and forth. When she lets go, her gap-toothed smile takes over half her face. "This is the coolest thing *ever*!"

Since Ruthie made it clear they were not going to get the girls a dog anytime soon, I took it upon myself to prepare them for the day their mother was ready. I found this toy at Target, a fluffy white electronic dog that walks, and barks, and yes—*shits*. Tyler is very much a hands-on learner, and this is the perfect thing for getting her prepared.

"Just make sure you clean up after it, okay?" I smile.

"Okay," Tyler giggles.

With Willow preoccupied, chewing on the miniature Reese, and Tyler off to pick up a fake dog's fake poop, I look at my sister and brother-in-law. This is where things get complicated.

Jeremiah is, frankly, just a pretty average guy. He's nice, but if he were a color, he'd be Modern Farmhouse Beige. I mean, the dude works as an *accountant*.

No offense to accountants.

There is nothing that signals what to give him, other than anything listed under "Dad Gifts" on Amazon. Ruthie, on the other hand, is ridiculously easy. She likes *things*. I could have easily found her a pair of color-block earrings or a sweatshirt that says, "Super Mom" and she'd be happy. But I didn't want that.

I didn't want to just give them generic objects that they'd use for a year then donate. I wanted to give them something more, something irreplaceable.

"I know it might be difficult, with work and stuff but…"

"It's perfect," Jeremiah cuts in before I can finish. He holds up four tickets for the New Year's train to Leavenworth. Leavenworth is pretty much The North Pole in real life, and it's a quick thirty-minute drive to Greenrock, so I'll be able to meet up with them. Ruthie throws her arms around me and squeezes tightly.

"I love you," she says. And for some strange reason, I start to cry. "Woah, woah," she says, pulling back. I wipe the tears off my face and look up at her, embarrassed. "What's wrong?"

I shake my head.

"Nothing," I sniffle. "I just love you too."

After my parents open their gifts, matching pajamas, because what else do you get your estranged parents, I help Ruthie cook breakfast while Jeremiah watches the girls.

"So, how are things going with that employee of yours?" she asks, wiggling her eyebrows. She drops a scoop of pancake batter onto the iron skillet. My stomach tightens, but I ignore it.

"It isn't," I sigh. Ruthie looks up at me solemnly.

"Awh, Vi."

I shake my head.

"It's okay," I say. "It's fine."

And it is. It's fine. I feel like I'm going to throw up. I feel like I lost everything in one singular night. But it's fine. Ruthie shoves her shoulder into mine.

"Well," she says. "At least now you don't have to worry about Angela finding out."

"Honestly, I forgot about that part."

I hadn't really thought about Angela finding out recently. Partially because how could she, and partially because I didn't care. I mean, I did, for Cam's sake. But when it came to me, I couldn't give a fuck if Angela lets me go or not. Ruthie shakes her head.

"So it was that bad huh?"

I look up.

"What?"

"Well, you must have liked her if you forgot about the whole Angela thing."

I look up at her and swallow.

"Yeah. I guess I did."

At breakfast, we sit mostly in silence. That's normal, any time my parents and I are in the same room together. I think everyone else feels like if they step in the wrong place, say the wrong thing, an explosion will occur.

They might be right, though usually, the explosion comes from my parents, not me. I have to wonder why Jeremiah agreed to spend Christmas like this, instead of with his family. I can't imagine Jeremiah Smith's Christmas would be half as uncomfortable or cold. My dad shovels a spoon full of scrambled eggs into his mouth, looking up at me.

"So, whatever happened to that chick Mallory?"

I don't know what infuriates me more. The fact that he's referring to a woman as "that chick" or the fact that he's using it in a context that makes it seem like Mallory and I hadn't spent twelve years of our lives together.

I might be angry with Mallory for what she did, but I can't hold onto that forever. While I know it's not my fault she made the decision to cheat, I can't pretend I played no part in what led up to it. And I can't pretend I'm okay with someone disrespecting her like that. We might not have been perfect. We may not have even really known one another. But Mallory isn't a bad person. And I'm not going to let someone paint her like she is.

"You mean my wife of twelve years?" I ask. Ruthie's eyes widen, and my dad's lips turn up, tauntingly.

"Yeah, that one. What's she up to these days? She didn't come out here to see us?"

My dad knows very well that Mallory and I got a divorce. Or, he was told at least. If he could remember it after getting high all those times? I can't attest to that.

My problem with my parents isn't that they're addicts. Addiction is a disease, I know that well. My problem is *this*. The purposeful jabs, the things they say just to see if they can get a reaction out of me. The fact that they were never there, essentially abandoned us, yet act like Ruthie and I should be grateful that they put us on this planet.

"Come on," Jeremiah whispers, scooping Willow out of the highchair and motioning for Tyler to follow.

"But I'm not done eating my—"

He shoots her a look, and she looks at my parents, Ruthie and I before grabbing a syrup-soaked pancake and running after him.

"*Dad*, I told you. Violet and Mallory got a divorce," Ruthie says gently. My mom's gaze flicks up to me, and she scoffs.

"I didn't raise you to be a quitter," she mumbles.

My hand tightens in my pocket, and that's when I feel something. Something cold and hard. Something smooth and heart shaped.

The rose quartz.

I stop thinking about it. About Sunny and how my parents might feel and what's respectful. I think about Cam, how she wouldn't take this for a minute. How she'd tell them all how she really feels, and I think about how badly I wish I could be like her.

And then I stop wishing.

"Actually, you didn't raise me at all."

My mom's expression drops for a moment, then quickly shifts. Her nostrils flare, her eye twitches, and her shaky hands curl into a fist.

"Violet Wolfe!" my father yells. His face is just as angry, if not angrier than my mother's. But I don't care.

"*No*. You guys always have something to say, something to critique about my life when you're barely a part of it!" I shake my head, but don't pause for a second, because I know they'll take the opportunity to interrupt me. "And don't you *dare* say that's my fault, because it isn't. You chose drugs and alcohol over me. You chose partying over me. The only reason Ruthie is so head over heels for you guys is because I protected her from seeing everything I *had* to see. You didn't raise me to be a quitter because you didn't raise me at all. And you didn't raise Ruthie either. You're lucky we turned out the way we did. You don't like my life choices? *Fine.* I'm not a big fan of yours either."

I expect to feel guilty, a giant wave crashing over me, suffocating me until I apologize. Instead, I feel the opposite. I just want to keep going. I want to say every tiny thing that has ever popped into my brain, everything I've held back. Ruthie's jaw drops, and she looks at me stunned.

My mom laughs rudely.

"Ruthie might have turned out great, but you sure didn't! You wonder why your father and I never came around? It's because we couldn't stand you!" She huffs. I swallow hard. But just as I open my mouth to respond, Ruthie's chair scoots back, her face beet red as she points at the door.

"*Get out,*" she demands, not a hint of hesitation in her voice. My parents look up at her, stunned.

"Ruthie, dear. You know what I—"

She shakes her head.

"You do *not* talk about my sister that way. Not when I'm alive because of her. This," she gestures to the house around her, "is all because of *her.* Those precious grandchildren you pretend you love so much?" She points to the other room where Jeremiah is no doubt, cupping his hands over Tyler's ears. "Exist because of *her.* So I don't care if you're sober. I don't care that it's Christmas. If you are going to speak to her that way, get *the hell* out of my house."

My parents stare at her in disbelief, but Ruthie's gaze doesn't waver.

"Ruthie we—"

She shakes her head.

"Frankly," she says, her eyes locking onto them. "I don't give a fuck."*

Thirty-Nine
Waterlanche

Cam

"So it's... *over?*" Dr. Burton asks. I nod, beaming at him proudly like the word "over" doesn't transform my stomach into a black hole. Dr. Burton keeps a poker face, so I don't know how to explain that without shifting his expression, he frowns. A loud clicking sound echoes through the laptop, the tip of his pen repeatedly tapping the edge of his desk. [33]

"Okay," he says with a straight face, his thick lips pressed together in a flat line. "And you came to that conclusion because..."

I sip my coffee, a teaspoon of sugar dissolved into the dark liquid. It's good, actually. Sweeter.

"I became codependent on her. Attached," I say after swallowing. My fingers tangle together as I place them onto the table in front of me. It's an attempt to make myself feel more confident about the decision, but it's not really working.

The past few days have been a whirlwind. Hayden stayed over last night because I kept throwing up, which is exactly what happened when I first left Cody. The difference is, Violet and I were never together. Not in a relationship, at least. It's amazing, and awful, how similar it can feel.

Dr. Burton raises a brow, and scoots forward in his chair.

"Okay. Can you explain why you feel that way?"

I pick at the skin on my thumb, already raw from the hours of the repeated action I had been doing prior to this appointment. I sigh, having gone over this with him already.

"Well, I had that panic attack," I explain slowly. Dr. Burton nods. "And she helped me through it. And she took care of me when I got the concussion. And then there was the nightmares... Do I really have to explain all of this again?"

A sharp sound rings through the speaker again, Dr. Burton clicking his pen and scribbling something down on the notepad in front of him. I frown.

"What?"

He looks up at me. "Sorry?"

"What did you write down?" I point down at the notepad lying on his desk.

"Would you like to see it?" he asks. I cross my arms.

"*No*, I just want you to tell me."

He clears his throat and adjusts his glasses as he holds the notepad out at a distance.

"Client equates vulnerability with codependency." He looks up at me, and my lips turn downward.

"I do not!"

He lowers the notepad onto the desk.

"Cam, can you give me other examples of how you are codependent with Violet?"

I scoff, rolling my eyes, but I think about it for a moment.

"*Yes,*" I say assertively. He raises his brows, encouraging me to go on. "I'm— I *was* dependent on her for sex."

Dr. Burton smiles, leaning forward again.

"Okay. Do you feel like that's something you could get from someone else, if you wanted to?" he asks.

"I mean, if I wanted to, sure. But I don't want to. That's what I'm trying to say."

Dr. Burton bites back a smile, and I scowl.

"*What?* What aren't you saying?"

He sighs.

"Cam, there's a difference between being codependent with somebody, and depending *on* somebody. Everyone needs to have people to depend on, whether it's friendship or work, or," he shrugs, "Consensual sex. Just because Violet helped you through an attack, just because she's there for you when you need it, that doesn't mean you are being codependent." He lets out a long sigh. "And that isn't to discourage you from ending this, not at all. If that's what you truly want, I support you. But with the information you're giving me..." He picks up his pen again, tapping it against the table. "I can't agree that it's codependency."

I frown, taking another sip of my sweet coffee.

"Then what is it?" I ask. "If it's not codependency, why do I feel like it is?"

He smiles, shaking his head.

"I think it's change, Cam. I think things were evolving, between you and Violet, and within yourself. And I think it scared you." He leans back in his chair. "I think you like to be around Violet, and that within itself is scary enough. But when you add the threat—" he takes a mini action figure off his desk, plopping it right down in the center, "of losing her, it's overwhelming. The idea that dependency is entirely unhealthy doesn't help either. So, you're trying to control the outcome of the situation, by ending it."

I listen to Dr. Burton carefully, my chest tightening when he says the word "scared". I think about the night Violet told me how she felt, and how she too said I was scared. It didn't make sense to me then. I didn't understand how I could be scared of something I didn't even want. But when Dr. Burton puts it the way he did, when he said that I'm scared because it's change, I realize that he's right. And that means Violet was right too.

No matter how irritating she can be, and no matter how hard I tried to fight it, I like being around her.

No.

I love it.

There's something so spectacular about Violet, how she's lost so much and still acts like she has everything. She's so courageous and so thoughtful. I never washed the pillow she used that night she stayed over, because it still smells like her. I got vanilla ice cream at Mountain Scoops yesterday, because I missed the taste of her lip balm. She makes me see all the amazing possibilities in The Realm. She makes me want to try new things.

I've spent the last five years running from change, sticking with even the worst people, the worst situations, because I was scared the next would just be worse. So, I don't know how it happened, really. How I fell for Violet and didn't even notice until now.

It's a silent killer, change. It has a way of creeping up on you. Not always, of course. Sometimes it's loud and sudden, like an avalanche. But then there's times like this. The snow melts slowly, trickling off the mountain almost unnoticeably. Then the trickles, the dewy drops, turn to streams. And eventually, without even realizing it, a waterfall forms, washing over the rock that was bare only months prior.

Falling for Violet was more like that. But finding out?

Finding out is an avalanche.

Tears pools in my eyes, the salt stinging as my head falls into my hands.

"So it's not like Cody?" I ask, my voice breaking. I don't need to ask it, not really. I know the truth. But I want to hear someone else say it. Someone who is less of a mess. Someone who knows what they're doing.

"Does she control you?" he asks. I shake my head. "Tell you what you can and can't do outside of a work setting?"

Well, she's bossy as fuck in bed but...

"No."

"Does she make you feel helpless, like you can't exist without her?"

"No."

"Well, then, Cam—" I look up, and he flicks the action figure over. "*No.* It's not like with Cody."

I drag a nervous hand down the side of my dampened cheek, wiping it over my mouth as I breathe slowly.

"What do I do?" I ask. Dr. Burton smiles.

"It's change. You let it happen."*

"IS THIS REAL?" I ask, turning the check over in my hand. It looks like a real check. Hell, it *feels* like a real check. But the number scrawled across the front in pen?

That can't be real.

Adrian nods their head enthusiastically, practically screaming as they barrel through their apartment with the human version of zoomies. They throw their arms around me, squeezing tightly.

"I'm going to throw up," they say.

I read the check again. It's from the Pacific Mountain Gallery of Fine Arts. From Anassia Walker.

Apparently, Adrian's piece has gained so much traction and publicity that she decided to make it a permanent feature in the museum.

For *one hundred thousand dollars.*

"It's all thanks to you!" they say, squeezing me tightly. "*Thank you.*"

My stomach twists, then drops.

I'm happy for Adrian, I really am. This is their dream come true. But this isn't thanks to me. Not at all. This is all because of Violet.

I hug them back, chewing on the inside of my lip.

"You're welcome," I swallow, a dry lump forming in my throat.

"Does this mean you're going to be able to open Rise?" Hayden asks, his brows shooting to the crown of his head. Adrian bites their lip and nods excitedly. Hayden runs up to them, scooping them up and throwing them over his shoulder. He parades them around the apartment, cheering loudly. "Whoo-hoo!"

My stomach sinks lower.

"This calls for some Zabinki's!" he declares, Adrian still draped over his shoulder. He turns to Avery and me, who are still sitting on the couch.

"You guys coming? Or do you want to text me your orders?"

I don't have a real reason not to go, other than the fact that if I get into a moving vehicle with Adrian, I might vomit. I've been lying to them this whole time, about Anassia. About Violet. And now, Rise, it's going to be built on that lie.

"I'll stay with all these guys," I say, gesturing to the pups. Dawson and Major, as usual, are tussling in the middle of the floor. Pumpkin is curled up on Avery's lap, and Eloise is planted on mine. "Plus," I gesture to her, "Ellie paralysis."

Zabinski's is just long enough of a drive that I think I could have a mental breakdown and clean myself up from it before they get back. But my head snaps over to Avery when he opens his mouth.

"Yeah. Me too. I'll Venmo you?"

Hayden shakes his head.

"On me, bro. Just text me what you want."

Adrian blows me a kiss as they walk out the door, and Hayden shoots me a wink. I swallow, staring at the television in front of me even though nothing is playing. Avery sighs.

"So, you still haven't told them?"

My head snaps over to him, my brows furrowing.

"What?"

He shakes his head.

"Don't play dumb Cam. I might not know the full story, but I know enough."

My heart twists, but I try to play it cool. There's no telling what Avery *thinks* he knows.

"I don't know what you're talking about," I say. Avery shakes his head and turns back to the black screen.

"Are you pretending you aren't fucking Violet, or are you pretending you haven't been lying to Adrian about it?"

"How did you—"

He clears his throat.

"I'm observant, Cam. More than you might think. I know you have your feelings about it, about *me*. But you're the same, you and me. We're observers. We see things others don't."

I scoff.

"We are *nothing* alike."

Avery nods his head silently, letting out a soft sigh.

"We are, in some ways. In others," he gestures to me, "not so much."

I furrow my brows at him, scowling.

"What's that supposed to mean?"

A long breath slips through his lips.

"Cam," he says, adjusting his focus onto me but not quite meeting my eye. Avery doesn't make eye contact, not really. "What *exactly* is your problem with me? Do you actually know?"

I let out a loud scoff, turning to face him, but not enough to move Ellie.

"Yes, *Avery*. I know *exactly* what my problem with you is." He crosses his arms, enticing me to continue. I roll my eyes. "You're annoying. You say things you shouldn't, and you're always staring at people. It's off putting and just *rude*."

Avery nods, a small smile creeping on his face.

"Who else did you just describe?" he asks. I furrow my brows, glaring at him.

"What are you talking about?"

He blows out a long sigh, almost sounding disappointed.

"I thought you'd get it, but..." he shrugs. I stare at him, only feeling more confused. *What is he talking about?*

"I don't get it," I admit. He looks at me, scanning my face for—well I don't exactly know what. Avery's confusing like that. His gaze adjusts back to the TV, his fingers tapping against the sofa.

"Do you really want me to spell it out for you?" he asks. But he doesn't sound arrogant when he says it. Still, I hate that I nod.

"I mean, *yeah*. If there's something so obvious that I'm missing, I'd like to know what it is."

His fingers continue to dance on the pilled couch cushion, his eyes glued to the black screen in front of us.

"Everything you just listed, everything it is that you don't like about me, are things you do too."

My brows drop further, defensiveness growing in my chest. I'm not like Avery. Right?

"That's different. I—"

"Have a disorder?" he cuts in. Now, his eyes lock onto mine. It's brief, but it happens. "Yeah. *Me too.*"

My heart sinks into my stomach, a lump forming in my throat. I shake my head. A disorder? Avery has never mentioned this before, not once. And Adrian and Hayden haven't either.

"What? But you don't—you never *said* anything."

He gives a subtle chuckle, then leans back into the couch.

"Yeah, well, not everyone wants to talk about it." He swallows, tilting his head back. "Did you never consider the fact that you aren't the only one in the world with struggles?"

I suck in a shaky breath. Not shaky because I'm angry. Shaky because he's right. He sighs.

"Cam, you don't like me, because you don't like those parts of yourself. And I get it, trust me. There are so many times I wish I was different. Times I wish my brain worked like everyone else's. I think the difference, though, is that I've never meant to be rude. You..." He sighs. "It's part of your personality."

My throat tightens, but I don't interrupt Avery. I listen instead, paralyzed by the unfortunate truth. He's right, and I can see it now. So many things hitting me all at once, like a million birds slamming into invisible glass.

"And I'm not saying that to hurt you. I'm saying that to inform you. I know it's a defense mechanism. I know you've been through a lot, and I can't pretend to know how it feels. But I also know that you tend to only act according to what *you* want. You're so observant, but still, you only see the things you want to see. The things you *try* to see."

I feel like he's hinting at something specific, but I don't know what.

"What do you mean?" I ask. He shakes his head.

"I can't just feed this stuff to you. You need to figure it out yourself." He sighs. "I know what this means, for your job and Violet's too. I wouldn't ever want to jeopardize that. But if you think you can't trust Adrian with that information, you're wrong. They might spill little pieces of information that they aren't supposed to. But they would never, ever do something drastic that could hurt you. And I think you're being too self-centered to see that. You're thinking about all the 'what ifs' that could affect *you*, and not how it's going to affect your best friend."

Tears spill down my cheeks, listening to the words pouring from Avery's mouth. He's right, about all of it. About how we're alike, about how I'm selfish. I could have told Adrian this whole time. I just let the fear of it consume me. I put my fears first.

"You guys never responded to my texts, so we just got two 'Binski Burgers, one with no toma—" Hayden looks up at me, his brows pressed together in a worried glance. Adrian steps in behind him, the same look taking over their face.

"Cam, what's wrong?" he asks, rushing over to sit by me. I look up at Adrian, tears streaming down my face. A choked sob escapes my throat.

"I lied," I cry. They look at me, confused, their arm pressed against my back.

"Hey, hey," they say. "It's okay."

I shake my head, and Hayden shoots Avery a bewildered look.

"It's *not*. I should have told you and I didn't because I was scared. But you," I sniff, "you should have known."

They press their brows together, looking me in the eye.

"Known what Cam? What are you talking about?"

I look at Avery, and he gives me a nod. I swallow.

"I didn't get you into Anassia's Gallery. Violet did."

Adrian's face relaxes, and they press their hand against my back.

"Okay," they say softly, but with confusion. "That's okay. You still helped."

I shake my head.

"She did it for *me* because..." My head falls into my hands. "She did it for me because we were hooking up."

Adrian's hand freezes on my back, and they suck in a breath.

"What?"

And then I tell them. I tell them all of it. That night at Monsey's, recognizing her the first day. The contract and the stone. Adrian nods silently as I sob, explaining everything that happened.

"I'm sorry, I'm *so* sorry. I should have told you sooner, and there's not—" I gasp. "There's not a valid excuse as to why I kept it from you. I told myself it was because you've told secrets before, but they were all little ones and," I sniff, wiping my eyes, "and I was just scared. But it wasn't fair to you. And I'm just sorry."

Adrian leans into me, squeezing tightly. Their curls press against my cheek, and they smell like lavender and linen.

"Cam," they say softly. "I'm not mad at you."

I sniff loudly and look up at them

"What?"

"I'm not mad at you. I understand why you were nervous to tell me. I understand how that could jeopardize your job. I know in the past I haven't always kept your secrets, and I'm sorry. Those were never my things to tell."

I shake my head, tears welling in my eyes.

"No, *I'm* sorry." My voice breaks, and Adrian squeezes me tightly.

After sixteen tissues and one bottle of water, we all finally settle onto the couch with our Zabinski's. Hayden turns on the television but doesn't actually press play. It's quiet, for a moment, just loud sounds of crinkling wrappers filling the air around us. But then, Adrian speaks.

"So, you gave her a rose quartz, in the shape of a heart?" they ask. I nod. "And then you told her you don't have feelings for her?"

I sigh loudly, a sad laugh slipping out.

"In my defense," I sniffle, "I thought it was true."

They shake their head.

"For someone so intelligent, you sure are blind."

Avery nods his head, and Hayden pats my shoulder gently.

"So, what are you going to do?" they ask, handing me a half-used cup of fry sauce. I dip a thin, floppy fry into it and toss it in my mouth.

"I'm going to tell her."

Forty

Superpowers

Cam

I F I COULD CHOOSE any superpower in the world, it would be to never throw up.

"Oh god, I think it's coming again," I say, leaning over the miniature garbage can next to me. Dr, Burton looks awkwardly away from the screen, and I retch loudly, gagging but nothing comes out. My eyes water, and I pant, wiping them. He sucks in a breath and clears his throat.

"Cam, if we need to call back later, we can."

I shake my head.

"No! No, sorry. I'm..." I gag, then swallow. "I'm fine. I *really* need this appointment."

Dr. Burton nods, pushing his glasses up the bridge of his nose.

"Okay," he says, adjusting his position. "Then take your time."

I nod, taking a long sip of water before continuing.

"I'm ready."

Dr. Burton clears his throat, still avoiding eye contact with the screen. He continues.

"The important thing to remember when confessing feelings for someone, no matter the circumstance, is to eliminate expectation. Even though she expressed those feelings for you in the past, after rejection, she could be hurt, or simply have changed her mind."

I raise an eyebrow at his words, not because they don't have meaning, but because he knows I hate it when he talks like a doctor and not like a regular person. He chuckles, then relaxes in his seat.

"Okay. You know those sweet proposal videos, where the guy is like, singing

Bruno Mars in front of a crowd?"

I nod, knowing exactly what part of my brain cringes when I see them.

"Yeah. And they're like, at Disney World or something, surrounded by every person she's ever loved and also a million random people?" I ask.

A smile breaks across his face.

"Exactly."

I frown.

"If you think that I'm the type of person to do that, I don't think you should be my therapist."

He chuckles again. I like when I make Dr. Burton laugh. It makes me feel like I've won at therapy. Like I'm his favorite patient.

"I am well aware that isn't your speed," he says. "But what I'm getting at is the intensity of the moment. You want Violet to feel like she isn't trapped. Like she can leave the conversation at any point, and like you aren't suffocating her with what you want to say. That you're also giving her a chance to express how *she* feels."

Ever since talking to Dr. Burton about what Avery said that day, he's been very helpful in keeping me self-aware. I think it was an easy thing for him to miss, because I was good at leaving out details that didn't concern me, or things I didn't want to talk about. But I don't want to do that anymore. I don't want to focus on all the bad things that could happen, because the truth is, anything could. I of all people know that. You could get crushed by an avalanche. You could accidentally almost hookup with your boss. You could accidentally fall for her.

And no matter how much you try to have control over it, you absolutely don't. All you can control is your reaction to what does happen.

I nod.

"That makes sense," I sigh. "So, what should I do?"

Dr. Burton chuckles, shaking his head.

"Cam, there is no *should*. Not past releasing expectation and opening communication. Other than that—" He sighs. "I can't tell you what to do. But I don't think I need to. I think we wouldn't be having this conversation if you hadn't already thought about it."

My cheeks flush, knowing that he's right. It's all I've been thinking about, actually, since the moment I confessed to Adrian. I stopped thinking about Angela and about Furry Friends. About that stupid fucking contract. I can find another job. I will knock on people's doors offering to groom their dog in their goddamn bathroom before I let some stupid rule prevent me from loving Violet Wolfe.

I nod.

"Do you get paid more for being right?"

VIOLET CAME BACK FROM her Christmas vacation a day late. I thought more about what Dr. Burton said, about making sure she doesn't feel trapped. So I decided to wait a few more days to ask her to meet me. I don't know why she was late coming back, but I know whatever happened in Clarkston, that it was hard.

So now, I'm here. Sitting in Luigi's driver's seat parked in the Furry Friends parking lot. I tried to think of the best place to do it, but it all felt like too much pressure, even in private. At her house, I would be invading space. At mine, she would be somewhere uncomfortable. In public is never a good idea, but somewhere too secluded could feel overly intense.

I don't know what Violet is thinking. I have no idea what she's feeling, and I have no idea if she's going to believe a single word coming from my mouth. All I do know is that I have to try. Life is too short not to tell someone you love them.

I could get crushed in an avalanche tomorrow.

Violet could be in a fatal car crash.

The world could catch on fire, and everything could turn to ash.

Whatever happens, it will happen with Violet knowing how I feel.

I swallow hard, tapping my fingers on the wooden steering wheel anxiously. Three minutes has never felt so long, and so fast at the same time. Violet turns the corner, looking down at her phone as she does it.

Her hair is pulled back into its usual, perfectly messy bun. Her lashes are in their usual perfect thick rows. Her piercings sit perfectly crooked on her perfect face. Everything about her is usual and perfect.

I take a staggered breath, unlocking the passenger door. Hopefully I can get through this without going into an anxiety attack.

"Hey," Violet says softly, sliding into the passenger seat. Everything is dancing on my tongue, trying not to spill out of my mouth the moment I see her, as I remember what Dr. Burton said. But it's hard, staring at this woman, knowing I don't want to go another day without her by my side. Knowing that she has no earthly idea how much I want her.

"Hey."

She pulls the door closed gently, looking at me for a brief moment, and then away.

"I hope you're not planning on driving me somewhere," she jokes softly, patting the dashboard. "Because last I heard, he wouldn't make it up Maple Hill."

My cheeks flush, and I roll my eyes, my mouth tugging into a slight smile.

"Adrian will take any chance to shit on him, won't they?"

Violet chuckles softly, then her expression drops. She swallows and looks up at me.

"Look, Cam, I just want to say—"

"I—" I start to cut her off, then shake my head. *No. Let her talk. Give her space.* "Sorry. Go ahead."

She smiles softly.

"This entire thing got completely out of hand. Monsey's, the contract, it was all extremely unprofessional of me. And I realize that now, the position I put you in and—"

[34]I don't want to interrupt her. I keep hearing Dr. Burton's voice replaying

in my head to just let her say how she feels. But I can't when none of it is true. I mean, sure, it was unprofessional. But Violet didn't put me in a bad position. *I* created the contract. *I* wanted to continue it. And I knew what the risks were. Violet was never in a position of power over me, at least it never felt that way. She isn't that kind of boss, the one who sits there and delegates while they watch. She's the one you forget is in charge at all because she treats everyone like a friend.

"You didn't." I grab her hands, and Violet's eyes flick up to me. "Violet, this wasn't a position you put me in. And it isn't just a fucking contract. *Fuck* the contract. Forget about it. I don't care about that anymore. You—" My voice breaks, and I clear my throat. "You changed me. And I know what a fucking cliché that is, believe me. But I was terrified of change. I was scared of anything being different than it was. I was scared that the slightest alter in my routine could be the one thing that ruined my life. Or ended it. And I wasn't wrong to think that. It's the truth."

Violet blinks at me, tears filling her eyes, but she nods for me to continue.

"I'm rambling, I know. I'll get to it in a second, just bear with me." I take a slow deep breath, just like she showed me, and continue. "I was scared of everything, and I still am. And it would be romantic to say that the only thing I'm not scared of is how I feel about you, but if I said it, it would be bullshit. Violet—"

She blinks, tears spilling down her face.

"I am *terrified* by how I feel about you." She swallows, and I take another shaky breath. "I am terrified by how I feel about you, but I am telling you anyway. Because you make me want to try new things."

Violet's lip quivers, and I rub the back of my neck.

"Fuck, I'm sorry. I wasn't supposed to..."

But Violet cuts me off, pressing her lips against mine. I melt into the tender kiss, warm and loving. She pulls back, looking at me.

"You are the first person that has ever made me cry."

I hold my breath for a moment before blowing it out awkwardly.

"Yeah well, sorry about that. Not my proudest moment but—"

Violet shakes her head.

"*Thank you* for making me cry."

Her lips press back into mine in a body-melting kiss.* But they part quickly. Startled separation forms between us when a loud knock rings inside of the car. We look out the window, a dissatisfied beach blonde woman standing there tapping her acrylics on her arm.

I recognize that woman from her photo in the work group chat and her Facebook Friend Request. It's Angela.

"Oh fuck."

I swallow, opening the door of the car, and we both get out. Angela lets out a maniacal laugh.

"So imagine this," she snaps, waving her hands in the air dramatically. "I end my trip early to come check on my business, to congratulate my manager for exceeding the monetary and rating goals we had set earlier in the year. And when I *pull up*—" her voice heightens now, to an unpleasant screech. "I see her making out with her newest employee!"

My breath hitches, my chest rising and falling in a panic.

Fuck. Fuck. Fuck. I mean, I was ready to give up this job, but I didn't think it would happen so soon.

In.

Hold.

Out.

"And I hope you don't have too much shit to pack because you, Cameron Miller, are fired!"

I swallow, tears filling my eyes as I nod. Angela turns to Violet, her thin eyebrows arched angrily.

"And *you*?! Well, you're lucky you reached those goals because they just *saved your ass*. If I get any word from anyone that you fail to do a single task, I swear—"

"Wait," Violet cuts her off, stepping in front of me. "You're firing *Cam,* but you aren't going to fire *me*?"

Angela's chest heaves angrily, her nostrils flared wide. "Don't make me regret it, Violet."

Violet scoffs and rolls her eyes.

"You can't fire Cam, Angela. The customers love her. Look at the reviews. Look at—"

Angela's eyes light up with fire, her finger pointing aggressively at Violet.

"Do you forget who owns this business Violet? I can fire whoever I want."

Violet props her hand on her hip and looks at Angela unfazed. "You can't fire Cam for violating policy because she isn't violating policy anymore. I *fucking* quit!"

FORTY-ONE
No Plan, Just Vibes

VIOLET

THE WORDS RING THROUGH the air for so long, that for a second, I don't even think I said them at all. But from the downward curve of Angela's lips, the valley formed between her brows, I know that she heard me.

And I know that she is about to lose her fucking mind.

"You should think about that carefully, Violet. Because if you say it again, I might just take you seriously."

The thing is, I want Angela to take me seriously. I don't have a backup plan. I have no idea what the next steps are. But I know that I'm miserable, and I know that, without doing what she loves, Cam will be too.

I think of her, of how happy she is every day in the salon. Cam, who smiles while giant balls of fluff cling to her hair and clothes. Cam, who gives free nail trims to dogs who need it because it pains her to see them neglected. Cam, who fought her way out of a terrible workplace, and ended up here, where she told me felt like "home." I might not love Furry Friends, but to Cam, it's everything. I want to give her the world.

I look Angela in the eye, squaring my shoulders this time as I say it.

"I quit." Angela opens her mouth, but I cut her off. "I quit, and if you fire Cam, I swear to God I will take every employee in this place with me." I watch her cheeks suck in and her nostrils flare as she listens to me. "Don't believe me? *Try it.* The only reason they're still here is because of me."

Angela's fists clench into a tight ball, her acrylics pressing into her palms with rage. Her tongue clicks against the inside of her mouth, and she looks over at Cam, then back at me.

"And what *exactly* do you think you're going to do, Violet? Go be a line cook in the back of Zabinski's? Or maybe a bartender at Monsey's?" She laughs. "I hope you don't think you have what it takes to run a business, Violet. Because if that's where you're headed." She shakes her head. "Well, you're in for a real disappointment."

I let a smile creep across my face as her eyes lock onto mine.

"Oh, Angela. Don't you know I already do?"

Angela swallows hard, and I lift my chin up.

"So I'll say it one more time," I say firmly. "And then I'm getting *the hell* out of this place. If you fire Cam, every employee in this facility will walk out with me. I might not have a plan, and I might not have the money to take a different cruise every week but pretty soon, neither will you."

Angela swallows hard, then looks over at Cam, who waves awkwardly. She stares at me, waiting for a sign that I'm lying. But that sign is never going to come, and after a moment, Angela realizes it.

"Fine," she says harshly. "Get your things and get out of my parking lot."

I beam, bringing a flat hand to my brow bone and giving her a salute.

WHEN I SAID TO Angela I might not have a plan, that was a very true statement. I have *no plan*. Not even an ounce of a plan. Not even a speck.

"*Well*," Hayden says as he walks into my living room. "You sure did go out with a bang, I'll give you that."

I chuckle, shaking my head.

"She told you that, did she?"

Hayden smiles widely, then pulls me into a hug.

"Thank you," he whispers. "For protecting her."

I squeeze him back tightly.

"Thank *you*," I say. "For trusting me to."

He smiles down at me, then steps to the side to let me see Major. My fingers glide through the soft white fluff on his head.

"So, what are you thinking?"

Hayden takes off the bag strapped to his side and sets it on the table with a very heavy thud.

"I think you just decided to open a training business."

We sit down at the table as Hayden spreads out various papers, flyers and lists and price sheets. I frown at them.

"Hayden, I don't think I can do this. I mean, I *hated* dealing with all of the management things at Furry Friends. I just want to train dogs, I don't want to have to deal with all the paperwork and the—"

He waves a hand in the air.

"You're just here for the initial planning. I already got you a receptionist. They'll deal with all the appointments and the communications. All you have to do is show up and train."

I frown.

"Hayden, I don't have money to pay someone right now. Maybe later down the road, but I—"

He puts his palms down on the table, looking up at me.

"Violet, it's me. I'm the receptionist."

He says it like it was such an obvious answer. I shake my head.

"No, Hay. I am not letting you just work for free," I scoff. Hayden rolls his eyes.

"First of all, it's temporary. Just until you can afford someone officially. Secondly." He presses his finger to the tip of my nose. I scrunch it. "It isn't *for free*. It will be a trade. You help me keep this asshole in line," he points to Major. "And I'll help you with getting all of this started."

I look at him earnestly.

"Hayden, that's too much. I can't ask you to—"

"Ah-ah-ah," he says, putting his hand out. "Apologies for interrupting a woman, I will repent for my sins later, but *no*. You aren't asking me. And *no*,

I'm not going to let you tell me 'no.' We're friends. This is what friends do."

I smile at him.

"Do you really mean that, or are you just saying that because you pay me to hang out with you?"

Hayden raises his brows, his lips tugging into a teasing smile.

"Because I pay you, obviously."

FORTY-TWO
Homemade Family

VIOLET

KATE MCNEIL IS EVEN more beautiful in person than she is on TV. Not more beautiful than Cam of course. But she's thin and blonde and rather tall. At 5'9", she towers over Cam and I in a totally not-intimidating way. Two men lean against the training building, one holding a clipboard and the other a large video camera.

"It's very nice to meet you," Kate says, her perfectly straight white teeth shining behind her bright red lipstick. I give her a firm handshake, making sure to not break eye contact. The good thing about forcing confidence is once you do it enough, it doesn't feel forced anymore.

"You too," I say, then release the tall woman's hand. My palm slides across the small of Cam's back. "This is my girlfriend, Cam."

Cam's face immediately turns bright red, and Kate waits with her hand out until Cam realizes she's supposed to be shaking it.

"Pleasure," Cam says. Kate smiles sweetly.

"Hayden showed me what you've done with the place. It's absolutely amazing," she says in her thick Australian accent. Kate McNeil is the lead anchor for the GRV News. By the fate of the universe, she also happens to be Hayden's cousin's wife.

"Thank you," I say. I look at Hayden's proud gleam, then adjust my gaze back onto Kate. "I couldn't have done it without him."

"He's a sweet little bugger, isn't he?" Kate ruffles the hair on Hayden's head, and blood rushes to his cheeks from embarrassment.

"That, he is." I smile.

"Alright, well, it's almost time to shoot. Are you ready?"

I nod, even though internally my brain is screaming *absolutely-fucking-not.* "Let's do this."

Kate walks toward the building, saying something that I can't quite hear to the two men standing against it. I start to follow but stop a few feet away from the door. I turn back, looking at Cam. The sun has started to peek through the trees and is casting a warm glow on her face. She smiles and blows me a dramatic kiss. I pretend to catch it and put it in my pocket. My eyes dart over to Hayden, who shoots me an enthusiastic thumbs-up, Major perched perfectly at his side. I face the door again, take a deep breath, and then step inside.

It only takes a few minutes for the camera men to get set up. Kate checks her watch, then motions for me to come stand next to her.

"Teeth check," she says, lifting her lips to expose her perfectly white teeth again. I laugh

"You're good. Me?" I feel silly replicating the look, but the realness of it actually helps calm my nerves. Kate is much more genuine than you would expect, and I feel guilty for thinking she wouldn't be in the first place.

"It's alright to be nervous but remember, there's really no need to be," Kate says, nodding in approval at my teeth. "People are going to be so excited about this, and you don't need to be perfect. You just need to be you. They only care if I mess up, which I never do."

She winks, and the tension in my body seems to release a bit. We position ourselves side-by-side, Kate gripping the large wireless microphone in her palm.

The camera man begins to count down, showing his fingers in accordance with the number leaving his mouth. "5-4-3..."

He starts to mouth the numbers silently, and then, the word "go".

Here we go.

"This is Kate McNeil with GRV News reporting live from The Dog Whisperer Training Facility. I'm here with the company's founder, Violet Wolfe, to discuss this exciting new business located on the outskirts of Greenrock Valley. Violet, how are you doing today?"

Kate says the sentences so seamlessly that for a moment, I forget she asked me a question.

"I am wonderful, Kate. How are you?" I respond into the large microphone pointed in my direction. I look at Kate, who offers me a smile. But it isn't a perfect "on air" gesture. It's a genuine, comforting smile, and it helps me shake whatever nerves I had left.

"I am doing well, Violet, thank you for asking. I was so excited to hear about the upcoming launch of The Dog Whisperer. Can you give some insight as to what it is that you do?"

And before I can think about it, the words start to flow out of my mouth, just as seamlessly as Kate's. She continues, shooting one question after another.

"How long have you been training dogs for?"

"What kind of training do you provide?"

I answer them seamlessly, not needing to pause and think about my answers. That is, until she asks the last question.

"Can I ask what exactly gave you the idea to start your own training business?"

It's a basic question. An expected one, even. So I'm not sure why it catches me so off guard. I shift my weight between my feet and start chewing on the inside of my cheek. *Why did I do this? Because of Cam? Because of Angela? Because of Hayden?*

"I—"

I look at the men behind the camera, then I look at Kate. Kate nods, and I take a steadying breath, the answer flooding me all at once.

"I started this business because I want to spend my life surrounded by things that I love. I love training, and I love dogs. And I want to do everything I can to help them."

"And I know you will. We're going to take a quick break and come back to give you an exclusive tour of the facility. This is Kate McNeil, reporting live with GRV News."

"And we're done!" shouts the man behind the camera, lowering it to his side. I release a heavy breath, and Kate wraps me into a tight hug.

"I am just so excited for this, you have no idea!"

I laugh at the sudden affection but hug Kate back.

"Thank you, so am I."

"Can I schedule an appointment?"

Kate's grip releases, and I step back to look up at the regal woman.

"What?"

"A training appointment. My two-year-old Cavapoo is a complete arse and always pulls on the leash. It makes me mad as a meat axe."

I chuckle, unsure of exactly what that means.

"Absolutely," I say, "I just need to get my phone!"

"Okay! Be back in three."

"I will!"

Cool air washes over me as I step out of the facility. I wave at Cam, Adrian, Hayden, and Avery and begin to walk over to them. But as I get close, I see that Adrian is talking to someone.

"Al?" I call out. Al's head shoots up, his eyes growing teary the second they land on me.

"Vi!" He waves, a white paper bag gripped in his hand. I jog over and throw my arms around him in a tight hug.

"What are you doing here?"

Al wipes tears off his smiling face, and he hands the paper bag to me.

"Lunch," he says, his voice breaking. "I am so, so proud of you."

Tears prick my own eyes, but I force them to dry. If we both start crying, we'll never stop.

"And this," he says, pressing something cold and hard into my palm. I look at it, the shimmering blue crystal gleaming in my hand.

"The blue topaz?" I ask, my eyes darting to meet his. "But—"

He shakes his head, mouth still stretched wide.

"I don't need it anymore, Vi." He pats my back harder than I think he means to. "Plus, this kiddo over here wants me to be a vendor at their... what was it again?"

His brows furrow, his eyes pooling with confusion. Avery chuckles, and Adrian shoots him a glare.

"It's a—" they start, but they interrupt their own words with a frown, like they too are having trouble describing it.

"It's basically art, food, and alcohol, thrown-up into a giant room," Cam says. Adrian nods approvingly even if it isn't the most glorifying answer.

"Right," Al says. "It's going to be *huge.*"

I smile, tucking the stone into my pocket.

"It is," I say. Al looks up at me, placing his hand on my shoulder.

"And this will be too."

My lip shakes for just a second, and I bite it to keep it under control. I swallow.

"Vi, we're about to go live!" Kate calls out from the training facility. I give her a thumbs up.

"Coming!"

I give Al one last hug, then turn to Cam and lean in to kiss her cheek.

"I knew it!" Al murmurs, and I roll my eyes, waving at everyone as I sprint back to finish the interview.

"I JUST WANT TO say what an honor it is," I bow dramatically, holding up a large Pyrex bowl of coconut chicken curry, "to be attending my first ever Criminal Dinner."[35]

Hayden lets out a loud whoop, and Adrian and Cam clap teasingly. Avery tries to hide a chuckle, but he isn't quite making it.

"I hope you're a better cook than your girlfriend," he mutters.

I look at him with a dead serious expression. "God, me too."

"Hey!" she scowls, tossing a couch cushion at me. I duck, and it goes right over my head, a grimacing smile taking over.

"Sorry, babe. But one of these days, I'm scared I'm going to get food poisoning."

Cam rolls her eyes.

"You won't," Avery cuts in. "She chars it so well even bacteria couldn't live in it."

"What is this? Roast Cam Night?" she huffs. Adrian chuckles.

"Why not, you roast everything else."

I bite back a laugh, and Avery gives them a high five.

"You could give me food poisoning, Cam, I wouldn't be mad," Hayden says, ever-so-sweetly. He walks over to me in the kitchen as I dish up the curry.

"Cool it, cowboy, that's my girlfriend," I whisper teasingly.

"I know," he says, tipping his head like he's wearing an invisible cowboy hat. "But, and I mean this with all due respect, I'll always look out for her like she's mine."

A comment like this should make me jealous, which I've learned is an emotion I actually do experience. And if it were coming from anyone else, it might. But knowing how innocently and deeply Hayden cares for Cam isn't something I could ever be upset about. I can't be upset about it because I completely understand. I love Cam too. It was just a matter of luck that she loves me back.

"And I will be forever grateful for that," I say meaningfully, handing him a bowl of curry. He smiles at me, his blue eyes glimmering.

"So will I."

We all nestle on the couch together. Even the dogs squeeze on top of us, all six of them. Dawson won't sit still but insists on lying on top of Cam. Reese is practically suffocating Adrian, while Ellie lays curled up on the ottoman. Major lies on the ground, though, by orders of Hayden that he's getting "too entitled." And Pumpkin, of course, sits curled on Avery's shoulder like a parrot.

I haven't ever been surrounded by so much love before. Everyone in this room, loving and caring for one another in different ways. It's so beautiful, and foreign, and I can't believe it's real.

"I haven't actually *seen* Criminal Minds before..." I say. Everyone stops to turn at me, their eyes wide and jaws on the floor. I force an awkward smile. "Is it like... *really* dark?"

Everyone looks around, eyeing each other awkwardly before Cam scoffs and rolls her eyes.

"Oh come on, it isn't *that bad* you guys," she says, reaching for the remote. My brows furrow, and I look over at the rest of them.

"I would like to hear that from someone who *doesn't* fall asleep to serial killer documentaries."

They make awkward eye contact again then look at me silently.

I laugh.

"Come on, really? All of you?" I look over at Hayden. "I mean surely you don't—"

He nods his head. "I tried not to give into it, but the will was too strong."

I sigh, hanging my head.

"Alright, press play."

Hayden presses play, and as the intro sounds, Adrian lets out a quiet "hmm." I turn and look at them.

"What?"

They smile and shake their head.

"It's just...I'm going to have to make a new one."

I furrow my brows.

"A new what?"

"A new painting of our family."*

FORTY-THREE
Four Months Later

CAM

LUIGI CROSSED THE RAINBOW Bridge last week. [36]Not by choice, of course. I was sobbing as the woman at the junkyard practically pried him from my hands.

Dr. Burton said that, just because I knew it was time for a change, doesn't mean it would come easily. He was right about that, which of course just irritated me and made me want to be fine out of spite.

I ended up okay, of course, but spite had nothing to do with it. Somehow, Violet had managed to keep the keys for me. They stay on my bookshelf next to my dad's favorite books and his photo and Cooper's painting, and sometimes, I pick them up and shake them just to hear to the sound.

Ted, my new-to-me 2017 black Toyota Camry, is practically silent as we curve through the bright green mountains. It's strange to not feel every bump and hear every rattle, but I can't say I hate it. Violet sits in the passenger seat, sipping melted iced coffee from Evergreen Grounds, even though we're now two-hundred miles from that tiny green kiosk. I didn't get anything, because caffeine and Prozac aren't the best of friends.

After I noticed a big difference in its effects, Dr. Burton and I completed a few exercises, and a few tests. Apparently, there's a link between Adjustment Disorder and OCD. I never considered that I could have OCD, because I don't walk around touching door frames and buying hand sanitizer in bulk. But then I learned about mental compulsions, and it all started to make sense. I was scared to tell Violet at first. To tell her yet another thing that was wrong with me. But she simply kissed my head, pulled the covers over my body, and told me she would always be there, no matter what. And I had to believe her, because she's proved it.*

"It's not too late to change your mind," she says calmly. "I promise I won't be upset if you decide you just want to go home. Or if you want to get a hotel. I don't want to push you into an attack."

"Violet, I want to meet your family. And Mallory is part of that, I get it. Tyler wants her at her birthday, but she wants us there too. I'm not going to be jealous over your ex-wife."

Violet raises her brows, a slight smirk creeping across her face as she takes a sip of her bean-water.

"Not even a little bit?" She bats her eyelashes, and I shoot her a fake glare, even though I'm smiling.

"Okay, maybe just a *tiny* bit. But not anything crazy. Just enough to make me want you on your knees."

Violet's face flushes, and she bites her lip. "Perfect."

Ruthie's house isn't unlike Violet's. Victorian but modest, and yellow too. Except now, Violet's is brown. I thought it was kind of a strange pick, but it's her house after all.

"Are you ready?" she asks, gripping a moving box in her hand. I take a deep breath and nod, gripping three nylon leashes in one hand, while I knock on the front door with the other. Violet chuckles.

"Cam!" she yells in a laughing whisper. She twists the doorknob and pushes it open. "You don't knock at Ruthie's."

My cheeks turn red as we step inside. "Oh."

"It looks like everyone's in the backyard," she says, lifting the lid of the box to peek inside. We walk through the house, photos of what I can assume are Ruthie, Jeremiah, Willow and Tyler. They're a cute, all-American family.

Reese walks neatly next to me, Dawson wearily behind. But Westley pulls us toward the back door excitedly, almost like he's been here before.

Violet and I had talked about it one night when we were lying in bed together, how everything felt so perfect yet so incomplete. We couldn't figure out what was missing. She set the contract on fire and I threw away her Furry Friends name tag. But still, something was wrong. Then, we turned on *The Princess*

Bride, for old times' sake, and it hit us.

He had no inquiries when we went to pick him up. Not a single person could look past his rough exterior, even though he looks so much better now than he had when we found him. It broke our hearts, but then, we knew it was divine intervention. It was meant to be.

"Hey!" Violet calls out when we step into the yard. A little brown-haired girl in French braids, who I assume is Tyler, races up and throws her arms around Violet tightly.

"Aunt Vi!" she squeals. Violet hands me the box, *very carefully*, and throws her arms back around Tyler.

"Hey bug! Happy Birthday!" Tyler beams up at Violet like she's her very own sun. I can't say that I feel differently. Violet gestures to me with a smile. "Tyler, this is my girlfriend, Cam. Cam, this is Tyler."

Tyler smiles up at me, the cutest freckle on the bridge of her nose, just like Violet.

"Hi!" She waves, not shy at all. Her head tilts as she points at the box. "Is that for me?"

I nod, giving her a soft smile.

"It sure is. But we have to wait for your mom first, okay?"

"Okay!" Tyler nods, then barrels off into the yard. A tall man approaches us next, wearing a pink polo shirt tucked into a pair of khaki shorts. He sticks his hand out at me and smiles.

"I'm Jeremiah, it's so nice to finally meet you." He gestures to the box in my hand, his brows raising. "Is that it?"

I nod, and a smile breaks across his face as he reaches out for it.

"I can take that off your hands. I have a setup in the bedroom, so I'll go put it in there."

He winks and pats Violet's back as he walks past her.

"Hey Vi! Your sister's around here somewhere, I think Mallory has her cornered in the garden."

Violet chuckles, shaking her head. "Thanks Jer, I'll track her down."

She turns to me.

"Ruthie isn't the biggest fan of Mallory," she says in a low voice. "But Mallory *loves* her."

"So if Ruthie hates me, it's not a deal breaker?" I ask teasingly, like I don't mean it. Violet shakes her head.

"She won't hate you." She guides me into the yard, into the corner by the garden. I see a woman who looks like Violet but a little bit taller and a little bit curvier, another blue-eyed baby on her hip. She's talking to Mallory, that shiny auburn hair glistening in the spring sun.

"Hey!" Ruthie calls out, grabbing Violet by the sleeve and pulling her in. Violet drags me along with her, face beaming.

"Ruthie, this is Cam. Cam, this is Ruthie."

She holds her free arm out in a gesture for a hug.

"It's nice to meet the face behind the contract!" Ruthie teases. "And this is Willow." Ruthie bumps her hip forward, Willow propped on top. "She likes to eat things she shouldn't, so she stays here most days."

Ruthie pats her hip. I smile.

"It's nice to finally meet you," I say. I crouch down, waving awkwardly at Willow. I don't have a lot of experience with babies. "Hi, Willow."

Ruthie's cheeks glow, and she gestures to Mallory. "And I guess you two have already met..." she says awkwardly.

Violet elbows her roughly, and Ruthie scowls.

"What?" she asks defensively, rubbing her side. Violet simply shoots her a look.

My eyes drift to Mallory, a nervous smile on her face. I don't know everything that happened between her and Violet, I just know it isn't my business. And her sleeping with Cody? Well, that was a blessing in disguise. For me, at least. If anything, I feel sorry for *her*.

"Hey," Mallory says shyly. She's beautiful, like, *ridiculously* beautiful. And I am just the right amount of jealous.

"Hi," I say back, offering her a smile. Mallory smiles back, her glossy lips shining in the sunlight.

"All right!" Jeremiah calls out, clapping his hands together. "I think it's time for presents."

"Yay, presents!" Tyler squeals, running to the porch.

His brows raise to Ruthie, and she nods, looking between Violet and me.

"Oh, thank you guys so much for bringing her up. I just knew when I saw that little face on the Pine Paws website that Tyler *had* to have her."

I smile, and Violet pats a hand on Ruthie's back.

"She doesn't come pre-trained so just—" She pats it twice more. "Good luck, kid."

We circle around the table as Tyler opens her presents. "Just Dance" from Mallory, and a few puzzles and books from her parents. She opens them all with the exact same gratuitous expression, saying "thank you" after even the smallest gifts.

"There's one more." Violet wiggles her eyebrows at Tyler, who tilts her head, confused. "We had to save the best for last, of course."

Tyler shakes her head. "Dad says that all presents are equal because the people who give them to us all love us."

Violet shoots Jeremiah a smirk, then looks down at Tyler.

"Oh, we'll see about that."

She runs inside and comes back with that same cardboard box.

"Sorry, I had to put you back in," she whispers into it as she sets it in front of Tyler. Tyler looks agitated, like she's both excited and scared to open it.

"Alright, go ahead, baby," Jeremiah says. Tyler lifts the top of the box, her eyes practically bulging out of her head as she looks inside. She squeals and jumps back to contain her excitement.

"You got me a puppy?" she whispers, tapping her feet excitedly back and forth like a penguin. Jeremiah scoops the fluffy black puppy into his arms and cradles her gently.

"Well, you're not getting another sibling so—"

Ruthie shoots him a glare, and Mallory chuckles.

Tyler throws her arms around Violet and I both, squeezing tightly.

"Thank you, Aunt Vi! Thank you, Aunt Cam!"

Violet grins at me, watching as a smile forces its way across my face. My cheeks turn pink.

"Yeah, you're definitely her favorite now," Ruthie whispers to me, and I bite my lip to hide a smile.

"Can I hold her?" Tyler asks. Jeremiah nods, motioning for her to sit back down.

"Be respectful, remember?"

Tyler nods, holding out her arms. "I will."

I feel a soft tug on the sleeve of my shirt, Violet tossing her head to the side in a "follow me" gesture. I slide my chair back and trail her to the corner of the yard.

I quirk an eyebrow, but as my lips part to speak, Violet begins to word-vomit.

"This is a really bad time, I know that," she says quickly. "But if I don't ask now, I'm going to chicken out." She reaches into her pocket and retrieves a singular silver key. "I know you love your apartment, and if you want to keep it, that's totally fine. This is a big thing I'm asking, a big change, and we can revisit it later down the road if we need to. But I would love it if you would—"

"Yes," I cut in with a breathy laugh. I nod repetitively, a huge grin breaking across my face. "Yes Violet, I will move in with you."

The tension in Violet's body eases, a smile tugging at her lips as she pulls me in and cradles my face in her hands.

"I love you, Cam," she says, pressing her lips to my forehead. I melt into her, my fingers gripping onto her shirt.

"I love you, Violet," I say back. The spring air feels warm against my skin, the sun beaming down brightly.

I'm not where I was a year ago. Hell, I'm not where I was yesterday. I was scared of it before, but now, I'm so grateful that everything has changed.

About The Author

Elle (left) and her wife Hailey (right) on their wedding day.

Elle Sprinkle is a contemporary romance author known for her narratives centered around marginalized communities, including the LGBT community, disabled individuals, and those living with chronic illnesses. Originally from Rockport, Texas, Elle now resides in Idaho, where she continues to cultivate heartfelt, smutty stories.

Before her official debut in 2024 with the novel "Puppy Love," Elle had been a lifelong writer. Being raised with deep evangelical roots, writing became a form of self expression that she previously had no safe channel for. From short stories to poetry, coping with internalized homophobia and mental illness slowly became easier. Today, when she's not weaving romantic tales, Elle can be found binge-watching true crime series, snuggling with her five beloved dogs, or paddle boarding with her stunning wife.